The Maizie Albright Star Detective Series

15 MINUTES (#1)

"Hollywood glitz meets backwoods grit in this fast-paced ride on D-list celeb Maizie Albright's waning star — even as it's reborn in a spectacular collision with her nightmarish stage mother, her deer-pee-scented-apparel-inventing daddy...and a murderer. Sassy, sexy, and fun, 15 Minutes is hours of enjoyment — and a wonderful start to a fun new series from the charmingly Southern-fried Reinhart." — Phoebe Fox, author of *The Breakup Doctor* series

"I was already a huge fan of Larissa Reinhart's "Cherry Tucker" series, but in her new mystery series, FIFTEEN MINUTES, she had me at the end of the first line: "Donuts." Maizie Albright is the kind of fresh, fun, and feisty "star detective" I love spending time with, a kind of Nancy Drew meets Lucy Ricardo. Move over, Janet Evanovich. Reinhart is my new "star mystery writer!" — Penny Warner, author of *Death Of a Chocolate Cheater* and *The Code Busters Club*

"Armed with humor, charm, and stubborn determination, Maizie is a breath of fresh air. I adored every second of 15 Minutes. Viva la Maizie!" — Terri L. Austin, author of the *Rose Strickland Mysteries* and the *Null for Hire* series.

"Child star and hilarious hot mess Maizie Albright trades Hollywood for the backwoods of Georgia and pure delight ensues. Maizie's my new favorite escape from reality." — Gretchen Archer, *USA Today* bestselling author of the *Davis Way Crime Caper* series

"This is a great start to a new series that boasts a quirky cast of characters, engaging dialogue and the liveliness that befits this delightfully amusing and fast-paced drama." — Dru Ann Love, *Dru's Book Musings*

"I love Larissa Reinhart's books because they are funny but they also show the big heart of the protagonist. Despite the movie star background Maize is down to earth and cares about everyone and justice. The situations that she finds herself in are humorous, but she isn't a joke. She is a feisty, perceptive young woman. I strongly recommend this book and look forward to the next in this series. Five stars out of five." —Lynn Farris, *Hot Mystery Review*

The Cherry Tucker Mystery Series

A Composition In Murder (#6)

"Anytime artist Cherry Tucker has what she calls a Matlock moment, can investigating a murder be far behind? A Composition in Murder is a rollicking good time." – Terrie Farley Moran, Agatha Award-Winning Author of *Read to Death*

"Boasting a wonderful cast of characters, witty banter blooming with southern charm, this is a fantastic read and I especially love how this book ended with exciting new opportunities, making it one of the best book in this delightfully endearing series." — Dru Ann Love, *Dru's book musings*

"This is a winning series that continues to grow stronger and never fails to entertain with laughs, a little snark, and a ton of heart." – *Kings River Life Magazine*

The Body In The Landscape (#5)

"Cherry Tucker is a strong, sassy, Southern sleuth who keeps you on the edge of your seat. She's back in action in *The Body in the Landscape* with witty banter, Southern charm, plenty of suspects, and dead bodies—you will not be disappointed!" – Tonya Kappes, *USA Today* Bestselling Author

"Anyone who likes humorous mysteries will also enjoy local author Larissa Reinhart, who captures small town Georgia in the laugh- out-loud escapades of struggling artist Cherry Tucker." – *Fayette Woman Magazine*

"Portraits of freshly dead people turn up in strange places in Larissa Reinhart's mysteries, and her The Body in the Landscape is no exception. Because of Cherry's experiences, she knows that — Super Swine notwithstanding — man has always been the most dangerous game, making her the perfect protagonist for this giggle-inducing, down-home fun." — Betty Webb, *Mystery Scene Magazine*

Death In Perspective (#4)

"One fasten-your-seatbelt, pedal-to-the-metal mystery, and Cherry Tucker is the perfect sleuth to have behind the wheel. Smart, feisty, as tough as she is tender, Cherry's got justice in her crosshairs." – Tina Whittle, Author of the *Tai Randolph Mysteries*

"The perfect blend of funny, intriguing, and sexy! Another must-read masterpiece from the hilarious Cherry Tucker Mystery Series." – Ann Charles, *USA Today* Bestselling Author of the *Deadwood* and *Jackrabbit Junction Mystery Series*.

"Artist and accidental detective Cherry Tucker goes back to high school and finds plenty of trouble and skeletons...Reinhart's charming, sweet-tea flavored series keeps getting better!" – Gretchen Archer, *USA Today* Bestselling Author of the *Davis Way Crime Caper Series*

Hijack In Abstract (#3)

"The fast-paced plot careens through small-town politics and deadly rivalries, with zany side trips through art-world shenanigans and romantic hijinx. Like front-porch lemonade, Reinhart's cast of characters offer a perfect balance of tart and sweet." – Sophie Littlefield, Bestselling Author of *A Bad Day for Sorry*

"Reinhart manages to braid a complicated plot into a tight and funny tale. The reader grows to love Cherry and her quirky worldview, her sometimes misguided judgment, and the eccentric characters that populate the country of Halo, Georgia. Cozy fans will love this latest Cherry Tucker mystery."– Mary Marks, *New York Journal of Books*

"In HIJACK IN ABSTRACT, Cherry Tucker is back—tart-tongued and full of sass. With her paint-stained fingers in every pie, she's in for a truckload of trouble."– J.J. Murphy, Author of the *Algonquin Round Table Mysteries*

Still Life In Brunswick Stew (#2)

"Reinhart's country-fried mystery is as much fun as a ride on the tilt-a-whirl at a state fair. Her sleuth wields a paintbrush and unravels clues with equal skill and flair. Readers who like a little small-town charm with their mysteries will enjoy Reinhart's series." – Denise Swanson, *New York Times* Bestselling Author of the *Scumble River Mysteries*

"The hilariously droll Larissa Reinhart cooks up a quirky and entertaining page-turner! This charming mystery is delightfully Southern, surprisingly edgy, and deliciously unpredictable." – Hank Phillippi Ryan, Agatha Award-Winning Author of *Truth Be Told*

"This mystery keeps you laughing and guessing from the first page to the last. A whole-hearted five stars."– Denise Grover Swank, *New York Times* and *USA TODAY* bestselling author

"*Portrait of a Dead Guy* is an entertaining mystery full of quirky characters and solid plotting...Highly recommended for anyone who likes their mysteries strong and their mint juleps stronger!" – Jennie Bentley, *New York Times* Bestselling Author of *Flipped Out*

"Reinhart is a truly talented author and this book was one of the best cozy mysteries we reviewed this year." – *Mystery Tribune*

"It takes a rare talent to successfully portray a beer-and-hormone-addled artist as a sympathetic and worthy heroine, but Reinhart pulls it off with tongue-in-cheek panache. Cherry is a lovable riot, whether drooling over the town's hunky males, defending her dysfunctional family's honor, or snooping around murder scenes." — *Mystery Scene Magazine*

16 MILLIMETERS

Maizie Albright Star Detective #2

LARISSA REINHART

Also by Larissa Reinhart

MAIZIE ALBRIGHT
Star Detective

To keep up with Larissa's latest releases, contests, and events, please join her newsletter. You'll receive a free short story and her gratitude! All subscribers are entered in quarterly drawings and a drawing to win an advanced copy at each new release, plus many other giveaways!

http://smarturl.it/LarissasBookNews

Larissa will not share your email address and you can unsubscribe at any time.

Thank you!

16 MILLIMETERS

16 Millimeters

Maizie Albright Star Detective #2

Published by PAST PERFECT PRESS

Copyright © 2017 by Larissa Reinhart

Library of Congress Control Number: 2017912585

ISBN: 978-0-9978853-7-8

Author Photograph by Scott Asano

Cover Design by The Killion Group, Inc.

Printed in the U.S.A.

To all the lovers of lunch.

Acknowledgments

I owe Terri L. Austin, Dru Ann Love, Ritter Ames, Pat Wade, and Kim Killion a huge debt of thanks for their support and patience with me in getting *16 Millimeters* published. I don't know which of us was more surprised (maybe me) when my June release had to be pushed to October because of my family's sudden move from Japan to Georgia. I couldn't have done it without their help.

I also need to thank my review team for their patience! Also thank you Minions for your continual cheering. Robin Coxon for being a good sport when I asked if she'd be okay with a not-so-nice role.

My donut helpers on Facebook: your flavors live on in the "No Sleep Till" coffee shop.

Thanks to Peachtree City, Fayetteville, Madison, and Senoia for their continual inspiration in "The Devil (Hollywood) Came Down to Georgia" theme for the Maizie Albright stories.

Thank you to my friends and family for all your support, especially Gina, Bill, Hailey and Lily! And as always, Trey and the girls. And Biscuit. xoxo

ONE

#LunchFail #AStarIsNotBorn

I have a serious thing for lunch. The exception: Hollywood business lunch. Considering I now lived in Black Pine, Georgia and was no longer acting, I thought industry lunch and I were done. For my new life, I'd anticipated a bad romance involving BBQ, pimento cheese, and fried chicken. Even a hot dog scarfed during a stakeout would've met my expectations.

Instead, my new life lunch menu involved a lot of PB&J eaten at the desk of Nash Security Solutions while I updated his billing software, typed reports from his notes, and took messages on the few (very few) calls we received involving security solution-ing. When Wyatt Nash of Nash Security Solutions had agreed to mentor me, I thought I'd learn the investigation ropes. Instead, the only ropes involved were the ones tying me to his computer and phone lines.

Real-life detective work was not as exciting as I imagined when I played the title role of *Julia Pinkerton: Teen Detective*. Just like real-life acting is not as intriguing as non-actors probably believed. But it was also not as boring as real-life security solution-ing. Have you ever vetted a list of potential employees social media accounts to see if they post anything stupid? (They do stupid. All the time.) Boring fo' sho.

Which was why I agreed to an industry lunch with my ex-manager and still-mother, Vicki Albright. Vicki was in the industry. Vicki was all about the industry. No BBQ. Instead, organic salad greens, vegan goat cheese, and artesian water with Tahitian lime wedges. Sans gas. For her.

In a show of defiance, I ordered a club sandwich with extra bacon, American cheese, and hold the lettuce. Also, because the lunch menu didn't offer anything fried.

"This is too big." Vicki handed the plate of greens and cheese-like substance to the waiter. "And no dressing. Just salt, pepper, and a spritz of lemon. Don't drench it in lemon. I want the scent of lemon, not the taste. And it better be Meyer lemon. I can smell the difference."

This was the problem with industry lunches. IMHO.

Vicki peered at me over her DITA Sunbirds. That was for effect. Under the table, she had already kicked me. "Maizie. Stop slouching. You inherited my spine, and it cannot support hunched shoulders."

If only I had inherited her metaphorical spine. Then I wouldn't be at an industry lunch to save myself from the boredom of a PB&J desk lunch. I'd be eating fried green tomato sandwiches or ham and cheese biscuits every day. While doing field work and security calls with Nash.

Of course, for those lunches, I'd also need Vicki's metabolism. Unfortunately, her metabolism did not come with the spine.

I pulled back my shoulders and slid to the front of my chair, then took a bite of my club sandwich and internally moaned. The Cove was not known for their food — more of a place to see and be seen in Black Pine — but they still did food well. They had to do everything well. As part of the Black Pine Golf and Yacht Club Resort (or BPGYCR, which is not pronounceable), moneyed Black Pine liked to lounge at the Cove for all their meals. They didn't actually eat. Mostly they drank. But that's another story. The Cove also served as a hotspot for industry insiders who had brought their film crews to Black Pine, where their production dollars stretched farther and taxes were cheaper.

Georgia had become a mini-Hollywood in the last five years although they'd begun homesteading more than twenty years ago. Production studios and sound stages had been built. Infrastructure created. Land purchased. The industry had learned words like "unsweet tea," "shopping buggy," and "y'all."

Which meant my legally required escape from LA to Georgia had almost been for naught.

"And stop moaning," said Vicki. "You act like you haven't eaten in twenty years."

I shot her a look to say, "I haven't."

She shot me a look from sea glass green eyes identical to mine that said, "You can't tell."

"Could you please stop kicking me?" I said. "I'm going to bruise."

"Leonard Shackleton is sitting to your left," she murmured. I glanced left as she whispered-shouted, "But don't look."

Leonard Shackleton was the producer of big budget "event" films. I now understood Vicki's anxious kicking. Vicki was the producer of medium budget reality shows and TV movies. Shows that used to star Maizie Albright (me) before I tumbled off the child-to-adult-star path and into the waiting arms of various addiction specialists. Leonard wasn't just an A-lister, he was a A++++ lister. It seemed he also had an insider lunch at the Cove.

I slid my not-so-covert gaze back to his table and realized his lunch date was an actress I knew from back in the day. "Cam-Cams," I squealed and grinned at the raven-haired actress with the (now) famously large, pouty lips.

She slid down her Oliver Peoples' to check me.

"It's Maizie Albright."

Cambria shifted her look to Leonard Shackleton. Seeing Leonard focused on his phone, taking no apparent notice of her,

Cambria returned the smile and waved her drink. "Hi, Maizie. Long time. What's going on? Are you filming here, too?"

"I'm from Black Pine. Moved back home."

"Oh, right. You got Judge Ellis." Cambria cut another glance toward Leonard, then pulled the sunglasses off. "Sorry to hear about that. Your show followed you?"

I doubled over, slamming my chin into my club sandwich. Brushing the toast crumbs off my jaw, I leaned to rub the shin where Vicki had kicked me — a surprisingly effective kick for a platform sandal, but she was tetchy about the show — then I twisted toward Cambria. "Sort of. But I didn't renew. I've got a new career."

"Forced into a new line of work." Her lips curled. "You've been at it so long. I figured you would have waited out the probation and launched into features or something."

"God, no. I couldn't wait to leave."

Cambria's eyebrow rose. "Isn't that what they all say? Until the comeback?"

"Maizie can return when she likes. After attending to the terms of her probation, of course," said Vicki. "Hello, Cambria. Nice to see you, dear. You're looking well since the last time I saw you. When was that? Wasn't it on Maizie's Emmy-nominated show, *Julia Pinkerton: Teen Detective*? You played her *little* friend?"

"Hello, Ms. Albright." Cambria's lips pulled tight. "Yes, except I wasn't so little. As you're implying?"

Vicki trickled a laugh. "I was referring to the part, dear, not your size."

I forced a laugh and swung a foot at Vicki. And struck a table leg. "Oh, you two. Who cares what we looked like or what we did as kids? As my therapist Renata says, 'live in the now,' right? And now you look hot, Cam-Cam. And you're blowing up the net with your comeback. I also heard you've done some great stage work."

"I thought it wasn't a comeback unless you were already famous," said Vicki. "I must be mistaken."

"Thank you, Maizie. It's nice to finally get noticed after twenty years of work." Cambria shot a look at Vicki. "I'm taking a break from the stage. I'm transitioning back to film."

"Awesome. Good for you." I nodded toward Leonard Shackleton and lowered my voice. "Big film, too, it looks like."

Cambria smiled graciously and gave a barely perceptible nod.

Still on the phone, Leonard Shackleton studied me. I glanced away and caught Vicki eyeballing Leonard. Probably analyzing his scrutiny of me. So awkward when your mother still tiger-moms all over your career. Your past career.

To make a point, I pulled out a Nash Security Solutions business card, scribbled on it, and handed it to Cambria. "Here's my new number. I don't have a phone. This is my *office* phone. But you can also reach me at Daddy's cabin."

"Daddy? Literally?" Cambria touched the card to her head. "Oh, right. I forgot. He makes some kind of outdoorsy clothing?"

Vicki pinched her nose.

"Hunting. Daddy is Boomer Spayberry," I said proudly. "Owner of the DeerNose Apparel brand."

"Don't say it," Vicki muttered. "Damn Boomer and his damn deer piss."

"What was that Vicki? Did you say deer piss? Wow," said Cambria. "That's interesting. He's your ex-husband, right? Who would've thought."

"The clothes just smell like deer pee." I felt my cheeks warm. "I think the deer like it?"

Cambria laughed and glanced at my business card. Tossing it on the table, she smirked at Vicki. "And Maizie's doing security work? Like a mall cop? How times have changed."

Vicki flinched, then sucked in her breath as Leonard picked up the card and examined it. His dark eyes flicked from the card to me, with an imperceptible glance at Vicki. Leonard set his phone on the table and turned his chair a few centimeters in our direction.

Stifling a deep breath, Vicki's chest strained against the crepe of her Saint Laurent halter dress. She tossed her platinum hair behind one shoulder to better deliver a coquettish smile. The air came out in small gasps between syllables. "Mr. Shackleton. How are you enjoying Black Pine?"

"Fine. It serves a purpose." He eyed her again, then focused on me. "Maizie Albright. You're looking well." His glance was appreciative. Too appreciative for my comfort.

I felt a disturbance in the air below our table. This time I'd remembered to wrap my feet behind my chair legs. Vicki half-slid down her chair before recovering.

"*Variety* did an interesting story about you working with a private detective," said Leonard. "I thought it was a stunt."

"No, sir."

"This," he tapped the card on the table, "is the same outfit? It's legitimate?"

"Yes, sir."

"Interesting." He paused. "I admired how you didn't try to starve yourself into a size zero. The old school, pin-up look is refreshing. Rita Hayworth or Betty Grable?"

Considering we'd battled my body's inclination for the pin-up look my entire career, I wasn't thrilled with the comparison. But then, Cambria had just endured a similar but less flattering barb from Vicki. Typical industry lunch.

"Just me. Enjoying post pin-up life."

"I like that. I'll call on you this afternoon. I have something for you." He grabbed his phone and tossed his napkin on the table. "Cambria."

I heard Vicki draw in air through her nose. Her lungs were going to burst. Or her breasts would break the seams of the Saint Laurent.

Cambria scurried after Leonard's quick strides over the stone patio. The look she tossed over her shoulder troubled me.

"I wonder what that was about?" I said, to no one in particular, and realized my mistake as the last syllable dropped off my tongue.

"I'll tell you what that was about," said Vicki. "You're back.

Leonard Shackleton, I'll be damned. I couldn't even get a table in the same restaurant with him in California. God, I love Georgia right now. It's like a new golden age. He didn't even have an entourage or a body guard. Did you see that?"

I shook my head. And kept shaking.

"Here's what we're going to do. Leonard wants to meet in that piece of shit investigation office. What if he wants you to read? It looks like hell in there. It'll be distracting. I can make a call. It's short notice but give them an hour and designers can do amazing work. I'm sure they can round up enough migrants to toss a coat of paint on the walls, haul out the furniture, and bring in new stuff. The building's old but maybe a retro theme. Like *The Maltese Falcon* or something?" Vicki picked up her phone and began scrolling through numbers.

"Stop," I said. "Mr. Shackleton obviously wants some security help. The office is fine."

"He has his own security people." Vicki waggled her fingers, concentrating on her phone. "Don't be stupid, Maizie. He saw you in *Variety*, not *Private Investigators Are Us*."

"I don't think that's a daily. Anyway, *Variety* only ran that story because of my past. The story had nothing to do with acting."

"And that's why he's interested. He's looking for someone fresh. An outsider. Maybe to replace Cambria? She can't possibly carry a Shackleton movie."

"Vicki, I worked from age three. I'm not an outsider. And Cam-Cam was always a serious actress. You're taking his comments the wrong way. He addressed us after looking at my business card. My *Nash Security Solutions* business card."

She ignored me, already conversing with the designer. "Not *Maltese Falcon* the yacht. The movie. Noir but obviously not too noir. Stylish noir. Vintage but not old."

"Nash will kill you if you do anything to his office," I said.

She nodded, then waved at the waiter who had returned with her salad. Placing a hand over the phone, she whispered with exaggerated lip movements. "No time to eat. Take it back. We have a meeting."

I glanced at my crumb-dusted plate, then at Vicki. The phone had settled between her shoulder and ear. She flicked through her iPad with one finger; the other hand signed the bill. I felt pity. Also, residual anger. But mostly pity.

"Vicki," I said. "You're making a mistake."

She covered the receiver. "Don't screw this one up, too." She spoke into the phone, "That also goes for you. If you don't know Humphrey Bogart, Google him. God, what would you have done before the internet? Honestly."

Renata, my ex-therapist, said to concentrate my energy on problem-solving, not on holding grudges. Especially with Vicki. I needed to address the problem, but to reduce personalization, I should address Vicki's actions with a leading empathetic sentence. Renata had been big on depersonalizing.

Also on detoxifying, which ironically had also involved residual anger and Vicki.

"It must not be easy to lose the star of the show you're producing," I began. "It also must not be easy when the star is your daughter."

Vicki glared at me, double-tapped her iPad, and spoke into the phone again. "Yes, an hour tops. What do you mean the paint won't dry? Find quick-drying. If they can make it for nail enamel, why can't they for wall paint?"

"It must not be easy to have brought the cast and crew of *All Is Albright* to Georgia, believing you could convince me to sign a contract for another season. And I didn't. And now you've halted production while incurring the cost of salaries and other fees while deciding what to do about a show you marketed and contracted without first signing the name attached to the show."

Rolling her eyes, Vicki hung up and dialed another number.

"It must not be easy to have spent the last twenty years managing one actress who now wants a new career. Especially when she's under judge's orders to find a new career. Not to mention the loss of money that went with the actress's brand."

Vicki covered her free ear, her mouth pursed to shush me.

"It must not be easy to understand my recent fame has nothing to do with show business but with a splashy investigation case, making Leonard Shackleton interested in my security services. Not in my old career."

She thrummed her Dior Incognito pink (with a speed dry top coat) nails on the table.

"So forget about Nash's office," I said. "I'm telling you, this meeting has nothing to do with you."

She set the phone on the table. Her mouth drew into a snarl. "I accept your apology for screwing up your career, but why go on and on when we're in a hurry? What are you waiting for? Get ready for that meeting."

This was the problem with depersonalizing with Vicki. After all those years in the industry, she'd already de-personed.

I slowed my exit to show Vicki I wasn't eager to learn what Leonard Shackleton wanted. But internally, my mind brewed with possibilities. As soon as I'd cleared the room, I scurried like an A-lister assistant on a Starbucks run.

*N*ash Security Solutions was housed in a for-real vintage brick building above the Dixie Kreme Donut shop. Boring as it was, I couldn't have asked for a more perfectly scented office from which to work. Plus, the Dixie Kreme Donut owner, Lamar, was generous with the day-olds.

I'll tell you who's not generous. Wyatt Nash. Not with the more interesting side of private investigations. Nor with details on his personal life. Nor with his heart.

Wait, did I say heart? I meant wallet. I'm making minimum wage for the first time in my life.

I found Nash and Lamar in the office. Lamar had kicked back in the office La-Z-Boy, listening to Nash. Nash paced between the outer and inner rooms, running down the details of our (his) most recent security analysis. His large, muscle-packed body strained against the Def Leopard concert t-shirt and worn-in-just-the-right-areas jeans. I glanced at the wooden floors, always expecting to see a worn groove from his pacing. Nash was like a caged animal. Wild and powerful, yearning for the touch of a gentle temptress with light auburn hair, green eyes, and bewitching curves. He'd unleash his hunger on his captor, ravishing her with unrestrained and enthusiastic desire...

Okay, I have a slight thing for my boss. Sort-of slight. Among other wonderful attributes like intelligence, integrity, and chivalry, Wyatt Nash has Paul Newman eyes. Ice blue, glowing with the radiance of sunlight on snow when he occasionally smiles. That smile would make angels weep.

It made me weep. Into my pillow at night.

Nash ran a hand over his shaved head, the small scar on his chin twitching with the grinding of his well-defined jaw.

Okay, I'll stop.

"It had to have been the dog, sneaking out and setting off the alarm," continued Nash. "The client wanted infrared lasers, and when you have a dog, lasers are not a good idea. If he'd just gone for a simple motion detector, no problem. Although anything over sixty pounds will set it off and that dog was no toy poodle."

"Lasers are overkill if you have a dog," Lamar spoke with his eyes closed. "But if the customer wants lasers, give them lasers. You need the money."

"We need the money. You may be a silent partner, but you're still a partner."

"I'm not a silent partner," said Lamar. "Jolene hasn't cashed out yet, remember?"

"Speaking of money," I said.

"I can't afford to give you a raise," said Nash.

"It's Leonard Shackleton. He has your card — our card — and he's coming by this afternoon."

"That's nice," said Lamar. "I told you she'd work out."

"Another security analysis? Does he live in town?" said Nash. "I could drive out and assess his home. Or is it for his business?"

"He's in town temporarily. I think. Leonard Shackleton. The producer." Nash's brows creased. I added, "*The Exterminator*. You know? *Time Warpers*. *The Lusitania Affair*?"

"I liked *The Exterminator*," said Lamar. "But *The Lusitania Affair* was overhyped."

"Movie guy? What's he want?" said Nash.

"I don't know what he wants, but I assume he's interested in hiring me. I mean, us. He heard about us in *Variety*. I mean, about me working here."

"Heard about you? Are you sure this isn't another of those tabloid deals?"

Nash had rules. Rule number one was no Hollywood Maizie references in the office. Which was fine with me as I didn't Hollywood anymore. Rule number two was no hugging. Rule two also made me weep into my pillow at night.

"Maybe he wants a bodyguard," I said. "Or a special security system. Or he wants you to investigate something. Maybe due diligence?"

I hoped it wasn't research. Research was not my fav. But we'd take what we could get.

"Sounds like good money, whatever it is," said Lamar. "Hopefully it'll be better than the laser job."

Nash glanced sideways at me, meeting my sea glass greens with his Paul Newman blues.

"Miss Albright." His head dipped in thanks with a smile that revealed a half-dimple in one cheek.

My heart bounced like it was jamming to a techno house party beat. It'd been a while since I'd seen that smile. Nash had been knocking himself out, trying to get the business back on its feet. Smiles were not in his survival daywear. Lately, he'd been wearing a furrowed brow, tight lines around his eyes, and a grimace.

My poor Nash.

"Good job, kid." His eyes met mine, then traveled down my

ATM scoop neck tank. He ran a knuckle against his whiskered jaw and drew a deep breath. I felt the sizzle and pop in the current that ran between us. Undercurrent. Deep current. Involuntarily, my toes curled, my back arched, and my stomach danced sideways. We'd been playing it cool, working our butts off, and ignoring the heat between us. This small sign of recognition felt like a crack in the "no relationship at work" wall we'd (he'd) created.

Lamar coughed.

Nash's dimple disappeared.

My cheeks heated to match my "Hotter Than You Pink" OPI pedicure.

And we simultaneously turned at the knock on the door.

TWO

#SeersuckerSaga #FraudSchmaud

$\mathcal{A}$ slight man entered. A ginger, like me, except more freckled. Older, but wore his age casually. His pale green seersucker suit and white CK loafers granted him that old Southern charm ID. Very dapper. I love a good seersucker.

"Theodore Malthus," he drawled and gave a slight bow to the room.

Nash snapped his mouth shut. "Mr. Malthus."

Theodore trotted forward and took my hand. "Truly a pleasure, Miss Albright. I'm a great fan of your work."

"That's nice." I reverted automatically back to starlet simpering, which couldn't be helped. Renata said love from fans helped to overcome the lack of affection from my manager. I mean, mother.

Theodore leaned to plant a kiss on the back of my hand.

I flashed him my famous Julia Pinkerton finger gun. "I'm always thrilled to meet a fan."

"Of course, I know you from *Julia Pinkerton*," drawled Theodore, "but it's your reality work that I enjoyed. *All is Albright* is such a hoot."

Nash cleared his throat.

I lost the simper. "What can I do for you? We do for you, I mean. Security or private investigation-wise?"

"That's not why I'm here, sweetie." Theodore trilled a laugh, placed his hands on his hips, and swiveled to take in the office. "She said *Maltese Falcon* noir. I think we're halfway there."

"Beg your pardon?" said Nash.

"Hells. You're the designer," I muttered. Catching Nash's look, I turned to Theodore. "There's been a mistake. Vicki has it all wrong. There's no reason for you to be here."

"I think there's every reason for me to be here. All the reasons are screaming at me. Screaming and crying and pleading for me to do my work."

"I'm confused." Nash held out his hand. "I'm Wyatt Nash of Nash Security Solutions. Why are you here?"

"I know who you are. I know everyone in Black Pine." Theodore held up his phone, touched the screen, and spoke to his hand. "Bring everything. Quickly."

Nash gave up on Theodore Malthus and turned back to me. The smile had been evicted. "Miss Albright."

"Remember Mr. Shackleton is coming? Remember how happy you were a minute ago when I told you that news?"

"Miss Albright."

"Well, I met Mr. Shackleton when I was with Vicki. My—"

"I know who Vicki Albright is."

"Right, so like, we were doing lunch at the Cove and Mr. Shackleton was lunching with Cambria — do you know Cambria? — and she…" The smile hadn't just been evicted. It had been eviscerated. I hurried the story along. "Anyway, Vicki thought Mr. Shackleton was interested in me for a role and not for private investigation work. Even though I explained, Mr. Shackleton looked at our business card and said he'd heard about the case in *Variety*. Case work. Not my dramatic work."

At those words, Nash's eyes flicked skyward then to Lamar. But Lamar was staring stonily at Theodore Malthus.

"This has to go," Theodore explained to Lamar. "It doesn't say *Maltese Falcon*."

"It says, my feet and back hurt and this chair is comfortable. First shift at the bakery starts at four a.m., and this chair is part of my break schedule." Lamar slammed the lever on the recliner. The headrest hit the wall and an explosion of dry wall rained on the stained corduroy material. "It's my damn chair."

Theodore raised his phone to his mouth. "We're going to need drywall patch, too."

"Miss Albright." Nash's voice rose.

"Anyhoo…Vicki thought since Shackleton is coming here, your office needed a little lift. Decorating lift. I tried to convince her not to do it. But she doesn't listen to me. You know how she is."

"This is my office." Nash folded his arms.

"And my damn chair," chimed Lamar. "I rescued it. It's a rescue chair."

"Y'all are just too precious." Theodore laughed. "Jolene warned me about you two."

Nash spun around. His scar beat white against his chin. "Jolene? Jolene Sweeney?"

"Oh, shizzles," I said and felt my skin turn white (whiter) as Nash spun back to me.

"Jolene. He said Jolene," Nash snarled. "You. Fix. This."

He shoved past Theodore and strode from the office.

Lamar walloped the chair lever, scooted the chair from the wall, and dusted the plaster debris from its back. "It's been nice knowing you, Mr. Malthus."

"Seriously, Mr. Malthus," I said. "There's been a big mistake."

"Call me Theodore, honey." He turned back to his phone. "Y'all just hang on a minute."

"Theodore. My manager, I mean Vicki, is confused. She misunderstood what Leonard Shackleton wants from me. And this isn't her office, so she has no right to do anything to it."

"Dear me." Theodore slipped his phone into his jacket pocket and laid a manicured hand on my arm. "Leonard Shackleton? *The* Leonard Shackleton? This is worse than I thought."

"That's exactly what I'm talking about. This isn't movie business. Vicki thinks he's interested in me for a part, when he's just interested in hiring us for a private investigation or security gig."

"Honey, everything with Leonard Shackleton is movie business." Theodore laughed. "But look who I'm talking to. You're Maizie Albright, and I'm just a lifestyle designer. *The* lifestyle designer for Black Pine, but still. Whatever Mr. Shackleton wants, you need to resuscitate this office. *Immédiatement.*"

"We can't afford it."

"Vicki's paying."

"Not when she finds out this isn't industry related."

Theodore pulled his lips into a purse and tapped his fingers on his chin. "I see. But what are you going to do when Shackleton takes one look at this rinky-dink pigsty and decides he's better off hiring an Atlanta firm to do whatever it is that he wants?"

I pulled in my breath. "I need his business. We need his business."

"So I've heard." Theodore cut me a look. "Jolene's been talking."

I folded my arms. "That woman is evil."

"She's an ex-wife. Goes without saying. At least from Nash's point of view. And Jolene says she still owns half the business."

I wrinkled my forehead, but he had a point when it came to Jolene Sweeney. "She's been fighting the buyout. Lamar's got the money, but she keeps claiming red tape."

"Oh honey." Theodore winced sympathetically. "It's because Jolene hates your guts. She thinks you're sleeping with Nash."

"But I'm not," I said.

"Listen, Jolene's a client, but she's not a friend. That woman would rather stab you in the back than look at you. Why don't I help you out?" Theodore rested his hand on his chest. "Let a fan do you a favor."

I grabbed his hands, my eyes teared. "You're so sweet. But there's just a little problem."

"Nash and Lamar."

Gripping his hands, I nodded, sniffing. "I love them. But this is a pigsty. I don't know what to do."

"You're used to luxury, you lost it, and now you're doing the best you can."

I fell against Theodore, sobbing into his seersucker. "It's been hard."

"Honey, I know. Let old Theodore handle this. Don't cry, sugar." He patted me, then shoved me away. "You're wrinkling your Anthony Thomas Melillo top. And mascara on my Haspel? That's the real crime. Now, here's what we're going to do. You need some theater back in your life. We're going to stage an office."

"But Nash'll come back and see you've changed things. He hates change. Like totally and for real."

"Leave it to me. There's an empty office next street over. I'll get the keys from a realtor friend, my boys will set up in there. Tack up a new sign, and voilà, you meet with Shackleton in a noir by T. Malthus, Esquire. Shackleton will be impressed and hire you. How could he not? My work is incredible."

"But how can I pay you back?

"Honey, you pay me back by coming to a party at my house. It's nothing. Seriously, building a mock PI office is a lot easier than tearing this one down and building it back up."

I slipped out to find a Noir-ish ensemble to match Theodore's staged office—Ulla Johnson in a black cap-sleeve lace dress that had a 40's vibe with Gianvito Rossi ankle-strap pumps—and returned to an old brick building two streets down from the Dixie Kreme. "Nash and Albright" had been sten-ciled on the storefront window.

I squealed and clapped my hands, glanced around the street to see if anyone noticed, and dashed inside the new office. The front room had a wooden railing separating the receptionist desk from the front door. Inside the PI's sanctum, two wooden desks sat perpendicular to each other with a battered (but not dusty) file cabinet between them. Green-shaded brass banker lamps, leather-bound ledgers, and blotters completed the vintage noir look.

Theodore Malthus stood in the center, surveying his master-piece. I grabbed his shoulders, screamed, and bounced, making my lace shimmy and slide. He took no notice, but stepped back and bowed.

"How?" I said.

"Big staff." He smiled. "And I'm a good resourcer."

"How long can we keep this?" I bit my lip. "Nash won't be too happy. He's not into theater. Or deception of any kind. Also, the Nash and Albright name — which I definitely think has a ring — will probably not go over too well. Probably not well at all. Like, he'll hate it. He already has a business name."

"Not to worry, honey. The stenciling isn't permanent. It's on a clear shade. We just roll it up, and it disappears before your boss sees it. If Shackleton hires you, you may need it again. But I've worked my magic. It might be used for another set, so we can keep it for a while."

"You're amazing. I can't wait to see Nash's face when he hears we got Shackleton as a client. I'm sure he'll be so thrilled he won't care I did it on the sly." I crossed my fingers behind my back. Of course, Nash would care.

Theodore gave me a slow blink and regal head bow. "I'm leaving you with a friend. Lana. She can act as your assistant for the meeting. I also have someone waiting at the old office to route Shackleton here."

Tears welled, and I sniffed. "Very few people would have done this for me. I can't thank you enough, Theodore. Are you sure I can't do more for you than attend your party?"

He shook his head, smiling.

A cute blonde in a gingham shirtwaist dress sashayed through the door. "I'm Lana Miles, your new assistant."

I threw myself at Theodore, happy T. Malthus didn't have a rule number two.

He hugged me back, then straightened his jacket. "Lana, when Mr. Shackleton arrives, have him wait no less than a minute thirty, but no more than two minutes thirty. He's busy, but we also need to seem busy. Bring him in to Maizie, and she'll do the rest."

Lana nodded and returned to the front room. Theodore turned to follow her.

"Wait," I said. "How do I get him to hire me without Nash here? Nash doesn't have me talk to the clients."

"You'll do great, sweetie." Theodore patted my hand. "It's just another role, right?"

I wrung my hands, knowing this would tick off Nash. They were his clients. He had the investigator license. I had to complete two years under his mentorship. "Better to ask for forgiveness than permission, right?"

"I like that." We air kissed, and Theodore strode to the door. "Break a leg, honey."

Dread mounted with each mincing step Theodore took from the office. I'd been excited to snare Shackleton with a better venue and hadn't thought beyond his first visual impression.

"Nash's going to kill me," I muttered, then the realization of what I'd committed slapped me in the face. "Oh my God, this is fraud. Is it fraud? I do work for Nash Security Solutions. OMG, I'm going to lose my probation if this is fraud. Please do not let this be fraud. How did I let Theodore talk me into this?"

A voice piped from a hidden intercom. "Mr. Shackleton to see you," said Lana.

"Shizzles. Hells. Hells to the shizzles." But I could do this. Or at least Julia Pinkerton could. Her character knew how to run a private eye office. As a high schooler in a cheer skirt, for cripes sake. If Julia Pinkerton could do this, I could do it. I was Julia Pinkerton after all.

Well, I'd acted as her fictional character.

I took a deep breath, resourced my inner Julia Pinkerton, and strode to meet Leonard Shackleton at my hopefully-not-fraudulent front door.

THREE

#ShackletonShakeup #MalteseMaizie

---

*L*eonard Shackleton shook my hand and gave me an appraising once-over, followed by a firm yet fleeting smile. We sauntered to Sam Spade's desk, where he took a seat in the vintage scuffed (but not ripped) leather chair and I took the antique-ish worn (but not worn-out) desk chair. I set aside the old-timey candlestick phone and placed my open hands on the desk.

"Mr. Shackleton, what can we do for you?"

He glanced around. "We?"

"Mr. Nash is currently out. But he was excited to hear you might drop in." I gave Leonard Shackleton my best Julia Pinkerton smile. Sassy with an eyebrow lift. "Mr. Nash can meet you later. Wherever you want. Just not here." I gave myself a mental slap and rushed to recover. "Do you need security help? Or investigative research?"

"It's not for me." Leonard leaned back in his chair. "It's actually for Cambria."

"Does she need investigative work? Or a bodyguard?"

"More like a babysitter."

I cleared my throat. "I'm sorry, I mean, can you explain?"

"Look." Shackleton smiled apologetically. "I know your past.

You've worked with Cambria. And there are similarities, right? Child actresses. And recently she's gone off the rails. Personally. Not professionally. Yet. Just like you."

"Sort of." I drew out the words. "But I've changed. That's why I'm here in Black Pine." As was Cambria. "I mean for work." As was Cambria. "I quit acting. And reality show acting. Anything to do with the industry."

Leonard waved a hand. "I heard. Judge's orders."

"My therapist recommended it too. But also because my heart lies in private investigation-ing."

Which wasn't a word.

"Private investigations."

I stopped talking.

"I just need someone to look after Cambria. We're filming in and around Black Pine as you've gathered. The movie is an epic role for her. Our director loves her work, and he wants her on this project. But Cambria's a hot mess. The world doesn't know it yet, but she's one meltdown away from shitting up my movie. The investors are leery of her. We almost couldn't get artist liability insurance on her. The production company requires a big policy for a film of this magnitude. Even with the bond, we had to work in the babysitting clause to get the underwriter to agree to the policy."

"Is it worth it?"

"I think Cambria's smart. She's got the chops. Ed Farmer, the director, thinks she's hot. Oscar hot. Ed says she's Angelina meets Jennifer."

"Lopez?"

"Lawrence."

"Wow."

"Exactly. She's also getting a cash break on the film, thanks to her agent. Net and gross points. We want to make sure her shenanigans are squared. Hence that chunky liability coverage. Ed believed in her, though."

"Cambria knows all this is riding on her? To be honest, I was surprised when I heard the stories about her current lifestyle. I didn't believe them. She wasn't like that when I knew her. As a kid, she was super serious. Always studying. No time for reindeer games, if you know what I mean."

"Kids change. Maybe she got tired of studying and the stage. She wanted to cut loose and didn't know how to stop." Leonard shrugged his shoulders. "Our insurance company wants to send someone to keep an eye on her, but you gave me a better idea."

"I see." I totally saw. "So you want Mr. Nash to act as her bodyguard, but really you want him to make sure she stays away from...things that will...shit up your movie."

"Not Mr. Nash. You. I'd like to work with you personally. Plus, Cambria would trust you. She'd sleep with him, and that'd be it. That's Cambria, you know. From what I hear, it's one of her addictions. You know how that is."

It wasn't one of my addictions, so I didn't really know. I thought about protesting the idea of Cambria seducing Nash. But I'd heard Cambria recently had a fierceness when it came to men. And Nash was totally sleepable. Actually, I personally didn't know that. But he looked like he was. Which was one of my many issues.

"Unless he's...unattainable?" continued Leonard.

I shook my head. Nash was attainable. So very attainable.

"So you just need me to keep Cambria from partying?" This wasn't strictly investigation work. Nash might not object. In fact, when it came to hanging out with a celebrity who liked to hit anything not tied down, he'd want me to do the job and not him. Brilliant. "I'll do it. But you should know, Cam-Cam and I worked together, but we were never best friends. Like I said, she was busy studying, and I was the one...partying."

"Earlier I think you said something about 'living in the now?'" He smiled. "I completely agree. Like I said, kids change. And Cambria is no longer a kid. Neither are you."

OMG, he'd been listening to Vicki's snide comments when we thought he was focused on his phone call. How embarrassing.

"I'll have my people draw up a contract."

"Great." I stood to shake his hand.

Leonard clasped my hand in his. "Maizie, this means a lot to me. Personally."

"You're welcome." I put away Julia Pinkerton, unnecessary now, and gave him my Maizie Albright smile. "I'm happy to help. I could have used someone looking out for me back in the day."

"Too bad we didn't know each other back in the day."

I nodded. Vicki would have killed somebody for that kind of in.

He gripped my hands. "But that's all behind you. Right? You have a sponsor and all that? Because the last thing Cambria needs is an enabler."

My smile tightened, and I wiggled my hand within his large palms. "I had therapy. All sorts. Just loads of therapy. It's all good. I'm a true professional. I mean, I'm professionally being mentored. In private investigations. But I'm so done with the old lifestyle. Like totally done. I don't touch anything. Except carbs. But we're allowed one vice, right?" My laughter was cut short by the confusion in Leonard's eyes. Not everyone thinks carbs are funny.

"I'm happy to hear it." Leonard shifted to draw my hand closer to him. "You look good. Healthy."

"Thank you." Healthy was LA speak for fluffy. Fluffy was Georgia speak for chubby. I preferred curvy.

"How did you know I was a Bogey fan?"

I didn't. But obviously Vicki did. Figured.

His eyes took a slow trip south. "You remind me of Bacall in *The Big Sleep*. I'm a Bacall fan, too. Nice dress. Very nice. I always admired your red carpet style. Back in the day."

"Thanks very much." Back in the day, I was a teenager. I yanked my hand from his. "I should go find Nash and let him know about the contract."

"Why don't we meet for dinner at the Cove tonight? With Cambria, of course. We can all get to know each other."

"With Nash?"

"If you think it necessary."

I thought it very necessary. Since I knew Cambria and Leonard knew Cambria, that meant Leonard and I would be getting to know each other. "Let me check my scheduler." I looked at the desk and realized besides the blotter and faux leather account books; there wasn't a single item I could pretend was a diary. Or a computer.

Theodore Malthus went a little too vintage.

I opened an empty drawer, pretended to look inside, and shut it. "Looks like I'm free, Mr. Shackleton."

"Call me Leonard. Eight o'clock?" At my nod, he continued. "Why don't you pick up Cambria and bring her to dinner? That'll give you an excuse to check up on her. She's staying at the club villas. Number six."

"Alrighty."

"What's your number? Your personal number. You just gave me the business number. I'll need to be in touch. A lot."

"I left my phone in California and haven't gotten a new one yet, Leonard." Which drove Nash and Vicki crazy, but I found the loss of a phone very useful. Like now, for instance. No need for Leonard to be a lot in touch. "You can leave messages for me with the office phone, and if I'm with Cambria, you can reach me by her phone. I'll see you at eight."

I slipped out from behind the desk to hold the door open for him.

"I'm looking forward to it." He dipped forward to kiss my cheek. "And Maizie. This movie is important. Whatever happens, I'm holding you responsible for Cambria."

Craptastic. If the rumors about Cambria were true, I'd have my work cut out for me.

Leonard had better pay well, because on this gig, I might lose my job, my probation, and my lunch.

*L*ana and I departed the office, making sure to roll up the "Nash and Albright" shade and roll down the normal one to hide the evidence. She dropped the key in her vintage handbag with a wink and sashayed down the street. I watched her for a minute, wondering why she looked familiar, but left that quasi-déjà vu for more serious pondering. As in how to convince Nash to sign the contract for this job with Leonard Shackleton. I traipsed back through the Dixie Kreme shop (with a quick stop-in hello to Lamar and a snagging of a sour cream donut) and up to the Nash Security Solutions office.

The office was empty. Likely Nash still avoided the possibility of a Jolene Sweeney invasion. I called him with the all-clear and mention of a job offer.

He strolled in ten minutes later.

"Were you nearby?" I sat behind his dusty desk, where the account books were not leather, but on a computer spreadsheet. The phone was vintage. If an eighties era IBM with an actual cord counted as vintage.

He shrugged and fell into a chair across from the desk. Crossing his ankle over his knee, he folded his hands on top of his head and raised his brows. "Nice dress. Where did you slip off to?"

I glanced at my Ulla Johnson, having forgotten I had dressed the part for our Bogey drama. "Thanks. Just the cabin to change."

"What for?"

I released the thumbnail I'd been nervously chewing. "The meeting with Leonard Shackleton."

"I see."

What did he see? Did he see our faux office? The sign declaring me a partner when I was two years away from finishing my mentorship? Assuming I made it the full two years. Had he seen Lana Miles in her cute gingham? Or Theodore's crew of burly men?

Nash watched me do more damage to my thumbnail. "Obviously, you convinced that Malthus guy to leave the office alone.

Thank you. No friend of Jolene's is a friend of mine, I can tell you that."

"Right. Although I don't think they're friends. More like Black Pine society acquaintances."

Nash wrinkled his nose and rolled his eyes.

"Anyway, the meeting with Leonard Shackleton went well." I gave him my *Cosmo Girl* smile. Charming, flirtatious, and trustworthy.

"Yeah, about that. I don't know if it's such a good idea. I'm trying to be careful about the cases I choose after what happened with the last big one."

"I totally understand. But this could be very lucrative. And lucrative is kind of necessary right now?"

"Some cases are not worth the money."

"But you wouldn't have to do anything with this one. He just wants me to keep an eye on Cambria so she doesn't...'shit up' his movie. Cambria has gotten into some trouble recently and—"

"That sounds exactly like something I don't want to get involved in. Babysitting a Hollywood hot mess?"

My face burned, but I didn't take the jab personally even though that headline had been used a time or two on me. "You don't have to get involved at all. Leonard wants me so Cambria doesn't suspect I'm babysitting. I used to know Cam-Cam."

"But how do you keep her from doing drugs or boozing or whatever she does? Move in and stick with her twenty-four-seven until the movie is finished? How can you work here if you're doing that?"

Admittedly, I hadn't thought that through. I took a moment of consideration. "I could befriend Cambria. Counsel her into staying clean through the picture. Sometimes what an actor really needs is a trusted friend to help them stay sober. Someone not interested in their career, money, or gaining status."

"A trusted friend hired by the producer as a ruse so he doesn't lose money on the picture?"

"I do care that she's become a hot mess. I really do. I know what

Cam-Cam's going through—mostly—even if I wasn't as big a star as she might become. Which kills Vicki, to be honest. I was the star when Cambria and I first worked together, but I screwed that... never mind. I know, rule number one." I took a deep breath. "But I honestly want Cam-Cam to straighten out her life. I hate knowing that she's gotten this far in her career and may blow it. She'll hate herself even more than she probably already does and then something awful really will happen."

Taking a deep breath, I pinched the skin between my thumb and index finger, willing myself not to tear up. My ability to easily cry proved useful in acting but was terrible for my new career. I wanted bad ass, not baby. I breathed deeply and focused on Nash's upraised biceps, bulging out of his t-shirt sleeves.

Studying Nash's anatomy was a better refresher than yoga.

I flicked my gaze from his arms to his face. "I'd hate to have that on my conscience. Like, I knew her when and I could have helped. It happens too much."

Nash studied me for a beat. "Fine. But you can't save everyone. You need to harden yourself for something like this."

"Right, hard." My gaze had drifted to his arms again. I zipped my focus back to his dreamy blues. And then to a safe, neutral spot just above his head. "And it'll be about quality time, not quantity. I'll explain our strategy to Leonard."

"This Leonard. He came here? To this office?"

I blinked away the spot and glanced at Nash, fearing he had seen the staged office. "Why?"

"I guess you used that dress to distract him from our hovel." Nash's left eyebrow took a dramatic trip north.

I smoothed the Ulla and pretended coy. The dress was totally fetch. "I heard Leonard's a fan of Lauren Bacall."

Nash pursed his lips. "Shame."

"Why?"

"I always liked Katherine Hepburn myself."

Dammit. Tweed and blazers were so not my thing.

*B*lack Pine, the city, edged along Black Pine, the lake, which bordered Black Pine, the mountain. This lack of creativity in the name department occurred when rich carpetbagging Georgians of the Gilded Age decided to escape the summer heat in the North Georgia Mountains and parked a golf resort at the base of Black Pine Mountain. In the 1930s, their children persuaded the federal government to spend WPA money on Black Pine. They dammed off a river, creating Black Pine Lake, thereby expanding Black Pine Resort into a yacht club. Now along with wealthy Georgians, rich Californians resort at Black Pine, playing golf and tennis, yachting, and boozing at the Cove bar and restaurant.

I'm sure that's exactly what Roosevelt had in mind for the New Deal.

Cambria and the other big stars, as well as Leonard Shackleton and the director Ed Farmer, stayed at the villas. The villas were part of the resort, built to resemble their '20s bungalow ancestors. The Craftsman-styled one and two bedroom cottages dotted the lake and one golf course. They were darling. Handcrafted wood and stone, with overhanging eaves, little porches, and hipped and gabled roofs. Besides the bedrooms, each cottage had a living room with a kitchenette. Mucho dinero to stay in a villa. And there weren't many. Twenty in all. Expensive and exclusive.

Hollywood's favorite words.

Leonard had called Cambria and arranged for our dinner — "for old time's sake," which was weird because Leonard wasn't part of our old time — and finagled me a pre-dinner invitation to her villa to "catch up." I showed early, hoping to find her before she began any evening imbibing. I parked my childhood dirt bike, Lucky, at the Cove.

Long story, but minimum wage and the cost of freedom meant I couldn't afford a real vehicle. Yet. But — as I like to tell myself while I rub Sisley-Paris restorative cream onto my inner thighs at night to relieve them from dirt bike fabric burn — at least Lucky is motorized and not an actual bicycle because I've always detested spin.

Anyway, I planned to be on Cam-Cam like Donkey Kong. Referrals were everything. If we did a good job for Leonard Shackleton, it could lead to any number of jobs related to Black Pine's film and television industry. And like Donkey Kong, I needed to lock Cambria in a tower to prevent the Marios of the world from carrying her off into a booze and drug-infested sunset.

Donkey Kong is so misunderstood.

Summer in Georgia promised the sun heating my bare shoulders at six o'clock. Yachts and speedboats bobbed next to the docks. A few sailboats drifted on the lake. With Black Pine Mountain in the backdrop, the tranquil lake and golf course made for a beautiful setting. The club's paths were for electric, low-speed use only. No gas vehicles, not even dirt bikes allowed. All the villa's guests were given golf carts. I wasn't a member or guest. My appearance would give me more street cred with Cambria, so, I swapped my sensible Golden Goose sneakers for a pair of delicious Gianvito Rossi Marquis d'Orsay sandals.

After ten minutes of walking, the charm and placidity wore off. Sweat pooled in my bra and darkened my Juan Carlos Obando blouse. My feet ached. After a half-mile hobble, I pulled off my Rossi's and minced off the smoldering rubber path. Taking a deep breath, I wiggled my toes in the cool grass. A cart sped from the cottages toward the resort. I pulled out a packet of wet tissues from my carryall. Checking for stray golfers, I wiped my pits and folded the tissues in the armpits of my cut out sleeves.

Ruining a Juan Carlos Obando with sweat stains was worse than getting caught with tissue hanging out of your armpits, IMHO.

Continuing along my route, I enjoyed the non-pinched feeling of my bare feet and the scent of fresh cut grass breezing from the golf course. The lane moved away from the lake, leading into the woods. Another cart flew past me, the driver intent on gunning the whining engine to its max. Which was totes ridic. Like 20 miles-an-hour was going to get you to the bar that much faster? These industry peeps needed to take a note from the South and slow the hells down. Stop and smell the roses. Or the golf greens, as it were. A sign pointed me toward "The Woodland Villas." My feet and I gladdened and together we set off to find number six. Most of the villas' tenants were out, golf carts gone. I could hear the drone of a lawn mower somewhere on the resort, but in this area, birds chirped, squirrels scampered, and the spindly loblolly pines swayed in the breeze, making a rushing sound reminiscent of the California beaches I missed.

The peace broke at the approach of villa six. Music pumped inside. I didn't hear it so much as felt the whomping bass. Despite the sunny day, lights glowed in the windows. Yet the golf cart was gone from its spot under the overhang. I slipped on my sandals, yanked the tissues out from under my arms, and did a quick clothing malfunction check (necessary when wearing a V-neck cami). My heels pattered on the slate stones leading to the villa's porch. A big basket lay askew on the top step. I recognized the basket as the resort's continental breakfast drop-off. Someone must have set it out recently because the resort wouldn't have dallied in picking it up. I righted the basket, noting the pretty checked cloth tucked around the edges had kept the pastries from rolling down the steps.

Feeling like the big bad wolf, I peeked inside the Red Riding Hood basket. Cam-Cam hadn't eaten her muffins. Of course. For a starring role in a big budget, carbs were more evil than controlled substances. And if Leonard Shackleton was producing, Cambria's part would require a mega-intense fitness regime. Her trainer would be worse — in a better way — than my old trainer. Jerry wouldn't even let me smell muffins, let alone eat them.

That thought had me reaching for a lemon poppy seed. Good old Jerry seemed long ago and far away. Plus, Cambria couldn't eat lemon poppy seed for fear of mucking up her drug test. I crammed a chunk of muffin in my mouth, knocked on villa number six's door, and fast-chewed. Pressed the bell twice, but still no answer.

Two picture windows framed the wood-paneled door. I shifted right. The drapes had been parted to display an empty living room. I angled for a glimpse inside, shading my eyes and squinting. Built-in bookshelves held matching bound books and a massive flat screen. Craftsman-styled furnishings and accessories completed the room, including the kitchen barely visible in the corner. Open bags and cases with camera equipment lay on the thick oriental rug covering the wooden floor.

Music continued to thump through the porch's floorboards. I rang, then hammered on the door again, tried the knob, and wondered what Cambria was doing with videographer kits. Maybe they were doing pre-release documentary footage for marketing and the final DVD extras. Or she had another job before Leonard's movie started.

I tore off another muffin hunk, popped it in my mouth, and thought about leaving. I glanced behind me to the long, long, long path back to the club. Wiggled my pained toes. Considered sitting on the porch to wait. With the basket of muffins. Noted the recent tightness of my jeans. Then traipsed to the right-side window to see what Cambria was doing.

Light gleamed between the curtains and shone on a California King with rumpled sheets and a spread that had half-slid off the bed. Satin-cased pillows had been piled in the middle. Other paraphernalia had been scattered across the sheets. My lemon poppy seed chewing slowed, and I felt heat suffuse my cheeks.

I didn't want to know what kind of filming Cambria had been doing. Or not doing. I backed away from the window, turned toward the stairs, and stopped.

The filming Cam-Cam might have been doing was the exact kind of "shitting up his movie," Leonard Shackleton had been talking about. Cambria could be blowing her chance for this epic part if she and her boyfriend were getting frisky in front of a camera. A professional camera, by the look of the kit.

Why would they make a "home movie" with what looked like the type of camera a documentary director would carry? This wasn't a GoPro box or a camcorder. My heart thudded and blood heated to shoot up the back of my neck.

Shizzles, Cambria was going to blow her shot, and my shot, and Nash's shot all in one idiotic, depraved video.

Unless I stopped her.

I spun around and pounded on the door. After waiting another beat, I tromped off the porch and circled the villa to the bedroom side window. A slope made the window too high for easy peeking, but the blinds were up, and no curtains barred the view. I tiptoed around to the back of the villa. At the far end, a screen door swung out to reveal a locked, windowed door leading to the tiny kitchenette. The bathroom window revealed nothing except Cambria had a crap ton of makeup.

I stepped away and spied a pile of logs. Found a sturdy looking piece cut evenly on both ends, hefted it against my satin blouse, and walked back to the bedroom window. Dropped the heavy log, missing my toes by an inch, positioned it below the window, and attempted to pull the splinters from my off-the-shoulder ruffles. Gave up on the splinters. Climbed on the log, rose to my toes, and peered in the window.

Saw the body on the floor.

And fell off the log.

FOUR

#PeepingTomasina #BrushwithNash

---

*L*ying in the pine straw, staring up at the loblollies, I listened to the soft whooshing of their breezy undulations. With my eyes closed, it had sounded like the far away murmur of waves crashing on the beach. I could imagine myself in Malibu, lying in my bed with the window open and listening to that hypnotic, successive crescendo.

I wished I were in that beach house. But no, I was lying on my back on the hard Georgia clay, cushioned by prickly pine straw. Beneath me, a sweetgum ball had lodged into my back.

And a few feet away, Cambria dead's body lay on the floor of her villa bedroom.

Tears welled in my eyes, and I pinched the skin between my thumb and index finger to stop the flow. Then I asked Cambria's angel for forgiveness for cursing her when I thought she was making a home porno. Then I rolled over and gagged, realizing I'd have to report this to Leonard Shackleton.

After a few seconds of wishing, crying, and gagging, I launched to my feet, righted the log, and climbed again to look in the window. I banged on the glass, screaming at Cambria to wake. Portable light stands stood by the front window, their LED blazing on the bed, casting a dark shadow across Cambria's legs. She lay face down on the spilled bedspread; her head cocked to one side. Her beautiful dark hair had fallen partially across her face and over her shoulder. Her famous lips were parted. Big brown eyes open and glazed. Cambria was also, unfortunately, naked. Unable to look at her face, my eyes riveted to a birth mark shaped like Florida on her left butt cheek.

Not the last thing I wanted to remember about Cambria, but better than seeing those cold, dead eyes.

I glanced away, then made myself examine the room again. Besides the photography lights, there was also a tripod standing near the window. No camera. My eyes did a slow tour of the room. Clothes were heaped on a chair in the corner. The dresser was clear, but then I had seen all her makeup in the bathroom.

Hopping from the log, I scrambled for the porch and unsuccessfully attempted to break in through the big windows. Pulling off the sandals, I ran for the next villa. Their golf cart had been parked in its half-covered gravel space, but no one answered the door. I had never learned the art of hot wiring a golf cart and moved on. Cottage five and seven were also empty and locked. I ran between the tiny houses, screaming and waving my shoes. No people and no other golf carts with keys on hand.

Giving up, I huffed through the woods and toward the golf cart path. A cart was parked on the links. Two men in plaids and pinks sat in the cart, sipping from thermoses.

I waved and hollered.

The cart sped away.

Tears threatened. I pinched my thumb skin. Gathering my courage and my stamina, I ran, jogged, fast-walked, and finally staggered from the golf cart path to the stone steps of the Cove's patio. I glanced at my watch. Six-thirty. My dinner date was scheduled for eight. Older couples and golfers sat at the Cove's tables, enjoying the pre-sunset cocktail hour. Their open-mouthed response to my chest-heaving stagger onto the patio caused me to pause momentarily. I hauled butt into the restaurant's reception.

"I need a phone," I gasped.

The hostess's eyes widened. "For..."

"The police. There's been an accident. Or death. Accidental death. At the villas."

Her eyes threatened to pop from their sockets. "Let me get my manager."

"Just a minute." I leaned over, grasped my things, and panted. Righting, I said, "Let me call my boss while you get the resort's manager. I don't think a restaurant manager's going to do the trick."

"Your boss?"

"He's sort of like the police. And he'll call the police." Nash would know the right cop to call. My mind had already sped toward the inevitable. Leonard Shackleton would want this hushed. As would Cambria's people. And the resort.

The hostess handed me the house phone and headed toward the bar to reach the resort manager. I crept toward the bathroom hall to call Nash.

Before I could get past hello, tears choked my voice and I could only manage a muffled sob.

"Miss Albright?" said Nash.

"She's dead. I don't know what happened. I didn't even start and she's already dead."

The pause was long enough for me to pinch my thumb and draw in a shaky breath.

"You got it together?"

"Yes."

"Start over," said Nash. "Who's dead?"

"Cambria."

The second pause threatened to start a fresh bout of tears.

"You sure?"

"Yes."

He swore. "What happened? Where are you?"

I explained my pre-dinner unexpected drop-in. And unexpected find.

Nash swore again. "Hell. Okay, I'll call my buddy on Black Pine PD. He's a detective. We'll meet you there in a few minutes. Just calm down. Nothing you could have done. Sounds like the girl was a mess and these things seem to happen to your kind— happen to these movie people. Tough luck. That director whatever, Shackleton, is going to raise holy hell, I imagine."

I let his Freudian slip slide past me. "Executive producer. Mr. Shackleton can't blame me, can he?" My lip quivered, and my thoughts began to career and spill. "He just hired me a few hours ago. I mean, hired us. But, oh God, Leonard Shackleton's very powerful. He's going to lose a lot of money, and the insurance people will lose a lot of money, and the director, Ed Farmer, too… Oh God, this is terrible. Cambria is dead. There's going to be tabloid reporters and paparazzi everywhere in a few hours. I think I'm going to be sick."

"It's going to be all right, Maizie. We'll keep this quiet. My cop friend won't want reporters messing with the scene. The resort won't want the bad publicity and neither will your producer whatever. Just don't talk to anyone. I'll be there soon."

I gulped back a fresh sob. "Hurry. Poor, poor Cambria."

"Go do that thing to your fingers. In the bathroom or something."

"Thank you."

"Don't talk to anyone. I mean it."

I hung up and walked the phone back to the hostess stand.

Her eyes threatened to swallow her face. "The resort manager is coming over right now. Who died?"

"I can't say."

"Did a golfer have a heart attack on the course?"

I shook my head.

"Aren't you Maizie Albright? What happened to you? Were you in an accident? You look like you fell into a ravine." She clapped her hand over her mouth. "Oh my God, was it a golf cart accident? Did you roll a cart?"

"No, I wasn't involved." I sniffled. "If only I had gotten there sooner."

The hostess raised her brows. "If it wasn't a golf cart accident, where are they? Shouldn't we send someone out to be with the, you know, body?"

My head continued a frenzied shake. "No, we should wait on that."

Her eyebrows climbed closer to her hairline. "Is it someone famous? Is that why you're acting weird?"

I backed from the stand, my head still shaking.

"Were you partying together and something happened? The resort manager is going to want to know."

I spun and ran to the bathrooms. Slammed into a stall and leaned over the toilet. Breathed in toilet cleaner fumes and exited the stall. Looked in the mirror and winced. My pale cheeks were bright red and eyes raccooned with mascara and eyeliner. My eyes glittered like emeralds against my crimson flush. I still clutched my sandals in one hand. My Juan Carlos Obando V-neck sagged open, exposing a piece of pine straw stuck in my cleavage. The satin was smudged with log dirt and covered in splinters. My feet were ridged in black and covered in grass stains. Running a hand up my neck, I patted my hair and pulled out a long piece of pine straw. And a feather.

I shook my body and hair free of debris, fluffed the ruffles on my top, and turned on the water. After scrubbing my face, I pulled a bag from my carryall and began the soothing process of reapplying makeup. While I re-bronzed and swiped on new mascara, I felt myself calm.

My mind wandered back to Cambria. The camera equipment, accessories on the bed, and nudity screamed sex tape. Which meant she was missing a partner. Someone had either left her for dead or just before. Who was she seeing?

Holy shizzilation, was he in one of the golf carts that flew past me? Why didn't I pay attention to the drivers or the cart numbers?

What kind of investigator would I make if I didn't pay attention to my surroundings?

I pinched my thumb skin and applied reason. I hadn't expected to find Cambria dead therefore I hadn't taken note of crazed sex tape partners on golf carts. I'll pay better attention next time.

If there was a next time.

Poor Cambria. I took a deep, shuddering death. An overdose. My experience with overdoses were secondhand stories in group therapy. Usually, the victim mixed a deadly cocktail between 'scrips and party drugs, or whatever they took had been laced with something unknown to the user.

My rehab stints had brought me into fellowship with a group of troubled souls. Performing often drew a personality type that didn't couple well with fame. The rewards can be great, but they came at a cost. A career built on public whims created instability. The emotional channeling required could be grueling. The hours were exhausting. Expectations from fans, family, agents, and managers took an emotional toll. Not to mention the public criticism that heightened all those neuroses. Plus, many of the rehabbers had a genetic disposition toward addiction.

I'd felt unworthy of my rehab spots. There were so many at a greater disadvantage and more deserving of the posh clinics where Vicki placed me. In group therapy, I had to share, "I grew out of my role's cheer costume, lost my teen star status, and began partying to purposefully miss callbacks because it annoyed my mother." That got me a lot of eyeball rolls.

My problems were inadequate. Kind of like now.

Poor, poor Cambria. I squeezed my arms across my chest and bowed my head.

My chin jerked up. But why the professional equipment for a home sex tape? If that's what she was doing. And was he partying with her? Did he give her the drugs?

The golf cart was missing. He must have taken it.

Pushing out the bathroom door, I raced to the hostess stand. "Where can I learn about the resort's golf carts?"

"Check with Carlos at the valet stand," said the hostess. "But the resort manager is headed here now. Don't you want to wait for her?"

"Not really." I paused before the door to the foyer. "I mean, tell her I'll be back. Soon. With my boss. And the police. I need to ask somebody about the golf carts."

Before she could question my logic, I zipped through the Cove's foyer and out the front door. A young man in a Black Pine Club and Resort polo stood behind the valet podium.

"Carlos?" I trotted over. "I have a question about the resort's guest golf carts. Are specific golf carts registered to the villas? Like, if my friend is staying at the villa and someone takes her golf cart, can we track it down?"

He nodded. "Which villa is she staying in?"

"Number six."

While Carlos radioed the resort, his gaze flicked over me. Placing a hand over the walkie talkie, he smiled. "They're checking on it. Aren't you Maizie Albright?" At my nod, he continued, "I watched y'all when you were filming in the restaurant. Are you really working for that detective or is that just part of the show?"

"I work at Nash Security Solutions. I'm not doing *All is Albright* anymore. They decided to continue the show without me."

"But—" He shifted his attention to his earpiece, then thanked the person at the other end. "The golf cart is parked at the resort in the correct spot. If someone borrowed your friend's cart, they left it in the right place. If your friend wants to report the incident, the desk manager said they could send security to the villa. Do you know what they want to do?"

"Not now. But we may need to check your security footage to see who was driving it. Don't let anyone touch it. I don't suppose you have police tape?" The rumble of a truck's engine caught my ear. I glanced behind me. A Silverado pickup turned off the resort's main drive and into the restaurant parking lot. Nash had arrived. A Tahoe followed and pulled in next to the Silverado.

"Thanks for your help," I said. "One more thing, can anyone use a golf cart or do you have to be a member or staying at the resort?"

"I'm sure I can wrangle you a golf cart if you need one, Miss Albright."

Being an ex-star did have its perks. Why didn't I try this when I arrived? I gave him my *Maxim* smile, a parted-lip pouty smirk accompanied with bedroom eyes. Generally appreciated by those with the XY chromosome pairing. "Thank you, Carlos."

His smile broadened. "Anytime." The smile disappeared, his shoulders jerked back, and his chin tipped up. "Can I help you, sir?"

I spun to find Nash standing behind me, glowering at Carlos.

Nash jerked his chin toward the sidewalk where the cop waited. I followed him. "Miss Albright, this is Detective Mowry."

A tall man with eyes the color of milk chocolate and wavy, dark hair flashed me a smile. "Ma'am."

The police detective was much younger than I imagined. Detective Earl King, the consultant on *Julia Pinkerton* who bought me ice cream every Friday, was older. Hard to imagine Detective King looking like Detective Mowry. Of course, Detective King had a neck the size of my thigh.

My *Maxim* smile felt inappropriate, so I tried the grin I used for that whitening strips commercial and shook his hand. "Nice to meet you. I'm sorry about the circumstances."

"Let's go," said Nash. "Where's your golf cart?"

"I walked to her villa, then ran back."

"Is that why you look like that?"

"I had a fall. I was trying to see into Cambria's room. That's when I found her. And fell."

A tear spilled down my cheek and I swallowed hard.

Nash patted my shoulder.

"The resort manager is coming to talk to us." I wiped the tear with the back of my hand and felt a second drop on my knuckle.

"Let me check on that. I'll get a cart, and you can explain what happened while we drive to the villa," said Detective Mowry. "Be back in a sec."

Nash watched Mowry walk into the restaurant, then he looked down at me. "You okay?"

I nodded.

"Tough luck, kid. Sorry about your friend." He ran his hand from my shoulder to my elbow and squeezed. "Mowry's a good guy. He'll be discreet."

I licked my lips and sniffed. "I haven't seen Cam-Cam in a long time. She did a season of *Julia Pinkerton* with me. She was a serious actress then—" I choked on a sob.

He released my arm to pat my shoulder. "Sorry, kid."

I held my hands before my face to hide the tears, making me cry harder. "She had such a great opportunity with Shackleton. Why now?"

Nash pulled me against his chest and gentled the patting.

"Rule number two, no hugs," I sobbed, but let my head fall against his Def Leopard t-shirt.

"It's okay." He rubbed soft circles on my back. "You're not like Cambria."

"I know." I tilted my head to peer at him. "I knew a lot of Cambrias, though."

"I suppose you did." The hand stopped rubbing, which disappointed me, but then Nash gazed down, meeting my eyes. The blue had lost their recent glacial coolness, warming with sympathy. His thumb brushed a tear from my cheek, then stroked my jawline.

"I feel horrible for her." My voice faltered, and I swallowed hard. I felt even worse for thinking about Nash when Cambria was so recently dead. A tremor of remorse rocked me, brushing me against Nash's body.

He hitched a breath, and his fingers inched from my jaw to cradle the nape of my neck. "I know you do, Maizie."

His hand lay lightly, but the intention felt heavy. The curled fingers stroked my neck. I watched him, studying me. And felt more aware of my body pressing against his. The firmness of his chest and thighs against my very un-firm curves.

The latent heat I'd been trying like crazy to tamp down over the past weeks broke and blossomed, rushing to my face to lick my cheeks and branded my neck. With my pale skin, I'd never been able to hold back the color, not even with Vicki's insistent coaching against blushing.

Great, I thought. Obvious much, Maizie? You might as well tattoo "I'm hot for my boss" on your neck.

Nash's eyes widened then darkened. His body shifted and fitted against me. "Don't cry, Maizie," he murmured and angled his face toward mine.

I closed my eyes, caught between excitement and guilt for seducing Nash when I should've been focused on my grief. The scent of his spicy aftershave drifted closer. His shirt dragged across my cheek. I moistened my lips and parted them. Just a little. Didn't want to seem overeager.

My face met open air.

I opened my eyes.

Nash had stepped away. The hand on my neck dropped to his side. He looked over my head.

I turned, running my thumbs under my lash line.

Detective Mowry held up a key ring. "Ready?"

I nodded, but I didn't move. My feet had fused to the sidewalk. Probably caused by my sudden core meltdown.

"You okay?" said Mowry.

Not really, I thought. I'm about the dumbest person in Black Pine. And worst friend. Although if anyone would understand wanting to make out with Nash in a parking lot after finding your friend's body, it would be Cambria. One of her many issues. Or so I'd heard.

"She's fine." Nash stepped closer and rested a hand on my shoulder. "Miss Albright is tough. She just has a big heart, is all. Seeing a victim's body is never easy. Particularly when you know them."

I gave Nash a shaky smile and walked to the waiting golf cart, feeling better than I had all day.

FIVE

#BodyTrouble #DoubleTake

---

*G*olf carts acquired, we sped toward villa six. The resort manager, Robin Coxon, followed in her official Black Pine Golf and Resort cart — complete with a flashing yellow light — while I explained my "finding Cambria" story to Detective Mowry and Nash. Three times. With questions.

"You ate one of her muffins?" repeated Mowry.

Avoiding looking at either man, I mumbled about the diets of starlets and my hatred of wasted food.

"You climbed on a log in those shoes?" asked Nash.

I glanced at my Gianvito Rossi's, now dirt and grass-grimed. The calfskin leather covering one stiletto had peeled. My life in Black Pine might be better for my soul, but it was hard on my wardrobe. "I couldn't see into her bedroom otherwise. The window was too high."

"I don't understand why you wanted to see in her bedroom," said Mowry. "Most people would leave if there was no answer. And if you thought she might be...busy with a friend...wouldn't that give you more reason to leave?"

I yanked up my sagging straps, not wanting to explain the laziness behind hiking back to the Cove nor the issue of the temptation in sitting next to a basket of muffins. "I worried that Cambria was using or drinking. Or doing something else that would ruin her career. The lights were on and music blaring. Mr. Shackleton was clear about keeping Cambria out of trouble. I wanted to make sure she was okay."

Nash turned off the golf cart path and onto the wooded trail to the villas. At villa six, the two carts pulled in front. The lights and music continued to blare from the cottage. Robin Coxon hopped from her cart but froze as Mowry called for her to halt.

"Stay in the cart," he ordered.

"You won't tell me what's going on and I have a right to know," said Robin. "I'm in charge of the resort and its guests. I know who's staying in this villa. I want to talk to Cambria before you do."

"I don't think she's available," said Detective Mowry. "I'll explain in a few minutes, but I need to check something first." He turned to Nash and me. "You stay put, too."

He approached the porch, scanning the ground and surrounds. Climbing the stairs, he knocked on the door. A moment later, he peeked inside both windows, ambled off the porch, and circled the left side of the cabin.

"What's going on?" called Robin. "Where's Cambria? Why are we here?'"

Nash's eyes were riveted to the side of the building where Mowry had disappeared.

"Should we call Mr. Shackleton?" I whispered. "He's going to arrive at the Cove in forty-five minutes."

Nash held up a hand. "Something's wrong. We'll wait."

"How do you know something's wrong?"

Mowry strode from the back of the cottage. "Miss Albright, can I speak to you?"

I scrambled from the cart with Nash following.

"Just Miss Albright. Stay in the cart, Nash."

Nash halted but folded his arms. "I'll wait here."

"Can I please have some idea of what's going on?" called Robin.

"Just a minute, Ms. Coxon." Mowry turned, beckoning me to

follow. We circled the side of the villa and stopped at the log beneath the window. "This is where you fell?"

I nodded. "Did you see her?" I asked.

"Let's talk about that," said Mowry.

"Okay?" I took a step toward the log.

Detective Mowry walked around me to stand before the log. "Stay there, please. Go through this with me again. You heard music, saw lights, banged on the door. Then looked through the front windows. You saw no one at that time."

"Yes. The bed was blocking my view of the floor. I couldn't see her body from the window."

"Then you came back here, went 'round to the back, got a piece of firewood, stood on it, and fell off."

"First I looked into the kitchen and bathroom, then got the wood. Then I saw Cambria and fell off."

"Can I check your head? For a lump? From your fall?"

I patted my hair. "I guess so. But I'm fine. It doesn't even hurt. I've had a lot of head injuries over the years."

His eyebrows arched.

"Oh my God, not because I look in windows. I had to do stunts on set. On *Kung Fu Kate*, I..." I stopped, remembering Nash's rule number one. Then realized this wasn't Nash. But it seemed like a good idea to stop anyway. Mowry probably didn't care about my TV past any more than Nash did.

"Humor me." Mowry took a step toward me and twirled a finger.

I turned around, embarrassed. He smelled like fresh soap and balsam. Clean pine. His fingers slipped into my hair and gently skimmed my scalp, tangling in my hair. His touch was light.

Until he found the bump.

I winced. "Ouch."

"You've got a small goose egg on the back of your skull. You should get that looked at."

"I'm fine." Turning, I found myself at eye level to Mowry's chin. I stepped back.

He smiled. "I found a few of these, too." He held up a blade of pine straw.

My skin ignited. I finger combed my hair, willing my cheeks to cool.

"You do have a nice lump that probably came from the fall. When you first saw Cambria's body, how did it look?"

"Dead."

"Did you see any blood? Any sign of injury? Was her body contorted?"

"She was lying face down, but with her head toward me. Her eyes were open."

"Her arms and legs weren't at a weird angle? And again, no blood?"

I shook my head, feeling confused.

"Okay, if you don't mind, I want you to climb on the log again and tell me what you see. I'll help so you don't fall this time."

I studied Mowry. The brown eyes were serious.

"Are you worried about what you'll see?" he asked.

I blew out a sigh, thinking about Cambria. It wasn't like seeing her again would do more damage. I was already pretty damaged. "I guess not."

"Good." He held out his hand. "I like to be humored."

I took his hand and stepped onto the log. Rising on my toes, I grabbed the windowsill.

Mowry tightened his grip on my hand and steadied his other hand on my waist. "What do you see?"

"Where's Cambria?" I scanned the room. Her body was gone along with the equipment. The bed was still rumpled, but the cover had been returned. "I don't understand."

I leaned forward, the log tipped, and Mowry dropped my hand to circle the arm around my waist. He swung me away from his body, and the log rolled away.

"Where's Cambria? What happened to her?"

"I was wondering that myself."

"What's going on?" said Nash.

I spun around to face Nash. "Cam-Cam's gone."

Robin slowed her trot to stop behind him. "What do you mean she's gone? She left Black Pine?"

Nash strode forward, brushing past Mowry to the window. No need for a log when you were as tall as Nash. Rising on his toes, he peered inside. "Did someone clean up?"

"Clean up? Do you mean housekeeping? They should have been here before three unless Cambria asked for something different." Robin's eyes widened. "Was something stolen? Is that what this is about?"

Mowry shook his head. "Please, Miss Coxon. I'll answer your questions in a moment. If you could wait in your cart, that'd be helpful. I also may need you to open the door."

Robin folded her arms. "Not without a warrant. I need to protect my guests. And I'm not leaving."

Mowry sighed.

Nash looked at me. "You sure about what you saw?"

I bit my lip, but nodded.

"She has a goose egg on the back of her head," said Mowry.

"Bumps cause amnesia, not hallucinations," said Nash.

"What lump?" said Robin.

"Getting a warrant is going to be near impossible," said Nash. "You know it."

"Why do you need to see Cambria's rooms anyway?" Robin pulled a phone from her pocket. "This is bullshit. If you're not going to talk to me, you're going to talk to the resort's lawyer."

"Miss Coxon, I said I'd speak to you in a moment. I'm just trying to sort something out before getting the resort involved. You'll thank me for being discreet later." Mowry looked at me. "Will you come to the station and make a statement?"

I nodded.

"Thank you," said Mowry. "I'm going to look around the area."

"Not without me, you're not," said Robin.

"Let's go. I'll explain as we walk." Mowry strode toward the carts and Robin stalked after him.

I stared at my log. "I don't understand. I wasn't gone that long."

"If she was dead, whoever was with her must have hung around and cleaned things up after you left," said Nash.

"If?" But Nash had a point. I shuddered. "Do you think he was hiding while I was here banging on the door? Her golf cart was missing. I thought her boyfriend had taken it. But it's parked in her spot at the resort. Carlos radioed to find out for me."

"Carlos?"

"The Cove's valet parking attendant."

Nash folded his arms and studied me for a long minute. "You've had a rough start to your evening. If you have to go to the police station, maybe you want to go home and clean up first? Mowry can get a ride back with Ms. Coxon. He's probably going to want to do a thorough search, interview guests. Whatever she'll let him do without a warrant."

"We should meet Shackleton. He'll be at the Cove soon."

"True." Nash glanced at his watch, then looked back at me. "You okay, kid?"

I nodded. "Except for losing Cam-Cam. And giving the news to Shackleton. I'm a little scared to tell him."

"Feels like old times."

Yep. Losing the client before the job begins was becoming my trademark.

Probably something to bring up with my next therapist.

*E*ight o'clock was the magic hour for the Cove. The sun had set, the air cooled, and Black Pine's martini and scotch drinkers had converged on the patio. Below the Cove, yacht party lights shimmered and the lake lapped against the docks. As Nash and I climbed the stone stairs leading to the patio, a swell of laughter and the scent of Chanel No. 5 drifted toward us. Instinctively, my stomach clenched and I ran my tongue over my teeth in a lipstick check.

"I hate this place," mumbled Nash.

"Do you feel on display?" I said. "Like you're the St. Bernard in a dog show, and no matter how well you've been trained, you know the poodle will win?"

"No." Nash cut his eyes toward me. "I hate it because Jolene and her type hang out here. What in the hell are you talking about?"

"Nothing," I said quickly.

"You feel like a St. Bernard?"

I yanked up my straps. "I'm just used to be publicly critiqued or whatever. Like show dogs. Never mind."

"Miss Albright, the things that come out of your mouth." Nash shook his head.

My spirit drooped, but I pulled back my shoulders, angled my chin, and plastered on my "suck it" face. My eyes darted around the patio and honed in on Vicki at the prime table in the corner farthest from the server's entrance. She had her back to the water and the breeze made a pretty swirl of her platinum waves. I averted my gaze but felt the heat of her eyes skimming my shoddy appearance. I sensed the accompanying snort.

"Let's wait for Shackleton in the foyer," said Nash, plowing past the tables.

He had no idea show dogs were supposed to circle and prance, not stomp through the center.

"My darling."

I almost stumbled in my ruined Gianvito Rossi's. A hand grasped mine and steadied me.

Still holding my hand, Giulio Belloni slid from his premium table against the lakeside wall. Once my (by audition) dating partner on *All is Albright*, Giulio had followed the show's move to Black Pine. The executive producer — Vicki — hadn't canceled the show yet despite my very public departure from LA. Rumor had it *All is Albright* hoped Giulio had enough star power to carry on in the role of "heartbroken ex."

Considering Giulio's heart was lodged somewhere between his wallet and penis, he had quite an acting challenge before him.

Leaning forward, Giulio air-kissed my cheeks and took my other hand in his. "What have you been doing? What are you wearing? I heard a certain summer collection had a retro-grunge look, but darling, I fear you chose the wrong designer."

Cocking his head, he half-circled me and leaned into my ear. "The girls are fantastic as usual, but darling, the fitting? It's not a good look for you."

"Maybe it needs a choker holding a little barrel filled with alcohol," I said, thinking of my animal spirit guide.

"That would be brilliant." Giulio pulled me closer. He bent to kiss my hand, knowing a double V-neck forced me to stay upright. Also knowing that his flashy poodle tricks would be rewarded. Nearby tables snapped pictures of his Balenciaga jeans pulled tightly across his perfect posterior.

Giulio always hoped a Calvin Klein rep would notice his Instagramed posterior and call his agent for a spread. Advertising spread. Giulio dreamed of showing off his six pack and V-cut for a tighty-whities billboard.

A loud throat clearing interrupted his low bow. Giulio jerked up, bounced against my chest, smiled, and spotted Nash. "Darling, it's your private dick. How wonderful. Are you on an assignation? Will you tango with a spy tonight?"

My private dick mumbled a remark about tangoing with a fist.

"We are meeting someone," I blurted. "I need to go inside. It was nice to see you, sweetie."

"Likewise, my darling. Let's do drinks sometime soon. Your *partner*, too, of course. Yes?" He smiled at Nash.

Nash glowered back.

Giulio glanced at me. "Is he always so...how do you say, grumpy?"

"Around you, I'm afraid so." I patted Giulio's arm. "It's been a long day. We really must go."

"I suppose you are meeting Leonard Shackleton and Cambria." Giulio's voice rang with melancholia. "They're in the inside bar.

Darling, I can't join you, can I? I've wanted to meet him, but they don't make it easy."

"How did you know we're meeting Leonard and Cam-Cam?" I froze. "Wait, what? Leonard and Cambria are in the bar? Cambria is in the bar?"

"I know." Giulio shook his head. "I was surprised, too, considering her issues."

Nash had already gathered speed toward the Cove's patio doors. I snapped my jaw shut and followed. Rushing through the doors, I followed Nash toward the front of the restaurant where a stacked stone fireplace always blazed. At the entrance to the bar, Nash stopped, and I slammed into his back.

Easing around Nash's giant body, I took in the bar and gasped.

Leonard glanced at his watch, then at me. Beside him, Cambria waved and sipped a drink.

SIX

#UndeadAndEd #Entouraging

"*You're* late," grumbled Leonard. He stood and took my hand to pull me forward for a double cheek kiss. Skimming a glance down my décolletage, his eyes took in my dirty blouse and ruined sandals. "Oh my dear, were you in an accident? Why didn't you call? We could've moved dinner. This is why you need a phone, Maizie."

I twisted to shoot a bewildered glance at Nash, then at Cambria. "Cam-Cam? You're here?"

She shrugged. "Of course? Leonard insisted."

"I just can't believe it. You were—"

"Nice to meet you," said Nash, thrusting his hand past me toward Cambria.

"I went to your villa earlier," I said. "I thought I saw you."

"Yeah?" Keeping her eyes on Nash, she grabbed his hand and held it. Running her tongue over the famous lips, she raised her brows.

Nash dropped his hand.

"Around six," I continued. "No one answered, but it looked like someone was home. Unless you were…sleeping?"

Cambria shrugged, too consumed with the art of seduction to catch my hint.

"We just came from your villa," said Nash. "Miss Albright was concerned."

"You must be the investigator Maizie works for." Leonard placed a hand on my bare shoulder, sliding it over the ruffles. "I've known Maizie a long time. Nice to finally meet you, Mr. Nash."

Leonard and I hadn't met before today. Maybe I had hit my head too hard. I twisted to glance at Leonard.

He winked. "I was telling Cambria that she should hang out with you while we're here. Reacquaint your friendship. Help her to get to know Black Pine."

My head felt like it was spinning between dead Cambria and this Cambria. I slipped out from under Leonard's hand to get a better look at the alive Cambria.

"Whatever you say, Leonard." Cambria leaned forward, exposing her cleavage for Nash's benefit.

Leonard looked at Nash. "You can spare Maizie for a few months, I'm sure. Cambria needs to lie low, and Maizie can provide her some company without the typical exposure."

"A few months? I'm not Miss Albright's keeper. I certainly hope there's no need for any exposure. We don't like unnecessary publicity." Nash folded his arms.

I couldn't focus on what was going on between Leonard and Nash. I slipped next to Cam-Cam and gently touched her arm. "Are you okay?"

"Maizie, can you stop staring at me and chill?" Cambria placed a hand on Leonard's sleeve. "Let's do dinner."

"Right." Leonard stood. "Everyone's waiting outside."

"Everyone?" said Nash.

"Cambria's people mostly," said Leonard. "Dahlia Pearson, she plays Cambria's sister in the production. And Ed Farmer, the film's director. I think he's having a meeting before our dinner."

I sucked in my breath. "Wow. Ed Farmer."

Cambria shrugged, but I could feel the tension vibrating off her at the mention of Ed Farmer's name. She blinked coyly at Nash. "Do you want to sit by me? Otherwise, it'll be shop talk all night."

Nash gave me a look speaking of his supreme unhappiness with this dinner.

The names at this table weren't making me feel too pleased either. I had to remind myself that this business dinner wasn't my old business. It didn't matter if I were surrounded by powerful Hollywood men like Leonard Shackleton and Ed Farmer. The old Maizie would have needed something to get her through a power dinner. The new Maizie would rely on business diplomacy. And lobster tails with clarified butter.

Clarified butter tends to take the edge off.

I glanced at Nash. He was going to need more than butter.

"Don't worry Cam-Cam," I said. "Nash and I have no interest in studio talk."

"Do you come as a pair? I could work with that." She raised her brows suggestively, sliding off her stool. Passing Nash, she gave him a hip bump, giggled at Nash's recoil, and sashayed through the patio doors.

Leonard sighed and followed.

Nash grabbed my arm and bent to hiss in my ear. "I do not want to sit next to her at dinner. In fact, I don't want to do this dinner."

"That's not the real Cambria. It's an act. Probably for Leonard, although I don't know why. You shouldn't mess around with Leonard Shackleton. Nor Ed Farmer. Those are big guns. Cam-Cam could be in trouble."

"Her trouble could make trouble for us."

Exulting in the word "us," I swung around to gaze up at him. "I can handle this. Now that the shock of seeing undead Cambria is wearing off—"

"She can't get much more alive than this. What do you think you saw?"

I shook my head. "I'm confused. I wouldn't have called you and especially the police if I hadn't thought she was dead. And now

I've got to make a police report about finding a dead woman who is certainly alive. It's embarrassing. Although I've done worse."

"The whole deal is hinky. Shackleton's lying to her."

"So she won't suspect I'm babysitting." I stilled as Nash's hand moved to pull a pine straw splinter from a cascading ruffle. "But the film equipment…something's off. I need to understand what I saw. I've got to do this job."

"No." Nash gripped my arm. "Miss Albright, I don't have a good feeling about this."

"Mr. Nash, you've had me doing accounts for the past month," I spoke in my sassiest Julia Pinkerton voice, hoping the sass would also build my confidence. "Do you want me to update you on Nash Security Solution's bank balance? We need this gig."

He released my arm. "Dammit."

"Does that mean you'll sign the contract?"

"That means you're not doing this alone." He eyeballed me. "Understand?"

I gave him my *Esquire* sideways glance with the half-smirk. "*Capiche.*"

"And Miss Albright?"

"Yes?"

"Don't look at me like that again." He ran a hand over his neck. "It's not good for business."

*O*n the patio, a table had been somewhat secluded by clearing the space around it. It was close to the restaurant and without the prime lake view, but Leonard Shackleton could sit with his back to the patio wall and observe the diners and drinkers without being the center of attention.

He was still the center of attention. Cambria and Ed Farmer made it triply so. The entourage intensified the meeting. Nash and I shook hands with Cambria's publicity manager, assistant, and agent. The agent, Alvin Murphy, shooed off the PR and assistant to a nearby table, then introduced us to Dahlia Pearson and Ed

Farmer. Dahlia smiled prettily and stepped aside as Ed introduced us to the production manager, the assistant directors, the location manager, and director of photography. Ed gazed longingly in their direction as they took their drinks and headed into the fireplace bar. I got the feeling Ed Farmer would rather be anywhere than at a dinner with us. And who could blame him?

I pressed my knees together, sucked in my abs, and willed myself not to say anything more stupid than, "Nice to meet you. Yes, I'm that Maizie Albright. And I do work as a private detective assistant. For reals."

Nash dealt business cards and kept his grunts civil.

It made no sense to introduce us to the major players in this upcoming film production. No sense whatsoever. Particularly when everyone was careful not to mention the film.

I had my back to the patio, but I could feel the weight of Vicki's interest boring a hole through my cascading ruffles. I sensed her scheming and plotting, almost sorry that she couldn't use my new relationship with industry bigwigs for the promotion of another daughter.

I mean, actress.

And then we got down to the business of pretending to eat.

The men ordered steaks. Dahlia and Cambria had grilled fish with wilted kelp. The Cove didn't have lobster. At my hesitation, Leonard ordered me grilled fish and wilted kelp.

Wilted without the help of hot bacon dressing. Another reason why I don't miss power dinners.

I stared at Cambria across the table, who had her eyes on Nash, sitting next to me. Alvin Murphy, her agent, sat across from Nash and took no notice of us. Alvin only had eyes for Leonard and Ed Farmer. Ed and Leonard took the table ends and pretended not to notice Alvin's excitement, Cambria's pouty sex plays, or Nash's simmering annoyance at everyone. Ed opened a small notebook and sketched in it throughout dinner. Dahlia chatted eagerly to everyone and no one. Leonard angled his chair to focus on me.

If Leonard thought he had a shot, he'd lost it with the wilted kelp move.

"Cam-Cam, what were you doing this evening?" I volleyed.

Over her glass of Intelligent Water, Cambria smiled at Nash. "Wouldn't you like to know?"

"I would," I said. "I would really like to know."

She flicked her eyes at me, then back to Nash. "What do you think I was doing?"

"Filming?" I said. "Any kind of filming?"

"I'd like to hear Mr. Nash's ideas about filming," she purred. "Any kind of filming."

I felt toes drag against my leg. Still feeling the effects of Vicki's earlier kicking, I yelped.

Cambria rolled her eyes and readjusted her posture.

"Anything you need, Maizie?" said Leonard. "You've barely touched your kelp."

I stared at the kelp, for once disappointed I wasn't eating kale.

A brush of air beneath the table had my legs seeking shelter beneath my chair. Nash scooted his chair back, until his long legs cleared the table, and bent at the waist to reach his steak.

Cambria pouted.

"Baby, leave the poor man alone," said Alvin, the agent. "Ed, you wouldn't believe this fantastic script Cambria just read. Cambria, tell Ed about the script. I'm so psyched about it."

Cambria cut her eyes to Ed.

Ed glared at Alvin, smiled indulgently at Cambria, then returned to his tiny notebook.

"I would like to know more about the part Cambria's portraying in this movie," I said. "Is it a zombie? Or someone with a big death scene? Do you have to lie dead for a long time, Cambria? Have you been practicing?"

I felt Nash's elbow dig into my side.

"Zombies." Ed snorted.

"I did a zombie movie once," said Dahlia. "Six hours in makeup for a ten-minute scene."

"We can't talk about the movie," said Leonard.

"Why are we here?" asked Nash. "What's the purpose of this dinner?"

Everyone stared at Nash.

"It's a casual dinner, Mr. Nash. A dinner between old friends."

"Who is an old friend exactly?"

My face reddened. "Cam-Cam and I."

Cambria wiggled her fingers at Nash.

"Maizie and I," said Leonard.

Nash stared stonily at Leonard.

"What about the sequel?" Alvin apparently hadn't noticed the tension. Or was too excited to care. "Is someone working on the sequel script? Even if we can't talk, just a nod or a wink will do. Am I right, Ed?"

"I don't wink," said Ed.

"Better send the sequel script over when you get them," said Alvin. "We've got a lot of good looking scripts, don't we, baby? We're going to need to tighten our scheduling to fit everything in. Unless you need us to clear time for the sequel and we could do that."

"I should've invited my agent, too," said Dahlia.

"We're not talking series right now," said Leonard. "We're not talking about the movie. At all."

Having given up on footsies with Nash, Cambria had been demonstrating improper behavior using a straw. Dropping the straw, she turned to Alvin. "What script? Sorry, I was distracted."

Alvin patted her hand. "Long day, I know."

"Why was it such a long day?" I said.

"She's got a huge cardio and strength workout for this role," said Alvin. "The ladder machine at the club spa broke down, so she went to Atlanta to indoor rock climb. That's dedication."

Ed beamed at Cambria.

"I love rock climbing almost as much as rappelling off them when I'm done," said Alvin. "There's a great spot in Mexico if you're interested, Maizie."

"I am," squealed Dahlia. "I love climbing. And rappelling."

"Have your tried any martial arts?" said Alvin. "I was into Muay Thai before I got into boxing in college. It's an awesome workout."

"Totally awesome," said Dahlia.

I focused on Cambria. "And you returned from your rock climb…"

"I was hot and sweaty," breathed Cambria. "Just drenched, Mr. Nash. Can you imagine?"

"So you went back to shower," I said. "But maybe you were so exhausted, you passed out on your floor. Do you ever do that? Pass out with your eyes open on your bedroom floor?"

"I never pass out." Cambria peered at Nash through lowered lashes. "I'm always up for a very intense workout in the bedroom."

Nash grabbed his napkin, stood, and put a hand on my chair. "Thanks for dinner. We're not interested." He jerked the chair back.

I tumbled forward and caught the table with my hands and whispered to Leonard. "We're interested. Mr. Nash is just tired."

Leonard peeled his eyes from my Juan Carlos Obando V-neck. "Cambria has that effect on men sometimes. She'll get bored when he doesn't respond. Why don't you meet her for her workout tomorrow morning?"

"Um," I said, hesitating on the word "workout."

He placed a hand over mine, pinning me to the table and turned to Cambria. "Maizie says she'll take you to her gym tomorrow. No worries about broken machines."

"Is Mr. Nash going to be there?" said Cambria.

"Absolutely not," said Nash. "Miss Albright, I believe you have a standing appointment at the office in the morning. It's called work."

"I don't have a gym right now?" I said.

"Talk to him," muttered Leonard. "Or I'll call the insurance company to send somebody."

"You can both come to my gym. You, too, Dahlia," said a honeyed voice behind me. "Cambria, sweetie, I had one especially built when I saw the offerings in Black Pine. Sorry to hear the resort hasn't upgraded after hearing my complaints."

I swung around. The scent of Chanel wrestled with the limp kelp and grilled fish in my stomach, knotting my intestines and strangling my voice. "Vicki. What are you doing?"

"I couldn't help but overhear. I'm Maizie's manag— Maizie's mother, Vicki Albright." She smiled at the dinner party, then turned to me. "Sweetheart, you didn't stop by my table. I hope you don't mind my coming over to say goodbye."

"I'm kind of busy."

"I see." Vicki glanced at my hand still trapped between the table and Leonard's heavy palm. A feline grin played at the corners of her mouth. "Of course, I don't want to interrupt your dinner. I thought I could help with Cambria's workout dilemma."

Vicki was a better actress than I ever was.

"Very nice of you," said Leonard. "I'm sure Cambria would love to use Maizie's mother's gym."

"It's Vicki. Vicki Albright." She sashayed to my side and dipped over our hands to drop her card near his plate. "A pleasure to see you again, Mr. Shackleton."

"That's great. A new gym for your conditioning," said Alvin. "Right, Cambria?"

"Cambria, does seven work for you?" said Vicki.

"But—" My protest was cut off. Cambria had nodded. Her hair fell across her face, reminding me of her hair spilling across her dead cheek. I still needed to understand what I saw. And we still needed to make some profit. I could put up with Vicki for both. "Okay, Vicki."

"Thanks, Vicki," said Cambria.

"Sounds great," chirped Dahlia.

"Leonard, however my daughter needs to help you, I'm sure she'll honor it. She's always been reliable if nothing else." Vicki leaned into my side to whisper, "Maizie, you know real satin doesn't hold up to off-roading. Remember what happened to your second season's Teen Choice award dress?"

A group of fifteen-year-olds with a crate of Maison Veuve Clic-quot champagne is what happened to that satin dress.

"Miss Albright," said Nash. "We have another appointment."

"We can do a dry sauna sweat detox after the workout." Vicki stepped in front of Nash. "That would be fun."

Dry sauna is not fun with Vicki. It's humiliating when your mother looks like Vicki and I looked like myself.

"Sure," said Cambria.

"Cool," said Dahlia.

"Where's your gym?" said Alvin. "I miss my Parkour classes."

"It's in my home," said Vicki. "I don't have Parkour equipment, but Jerry could probably build you one."

"Your home? You have a home here?" I said. "Wait a minute. Did you say Jerry? Jerry, as in my trainer, Jerry?"

Tiny white dots floated in my vision and my knees buckled. I felt an arm grasp my elbow and another slide around my waist.

"I thought I was safe from Jerry. How could you do this to me?" Blood pounded in the back of my head. "I've been eating like I'd never see Jerry again."

"We can tell," said Vicki.

"Time to go," said Nash, dragging me from the table. My hand popped from under Leonard's, trailing behind me like limp kelp. "We still need to drop by the police station."

"Police station?" gasped Vicki.

"Just business," said Nash.

"Right," I said, weakly. "My accident. The accident that ruined my Gianvito Rossi's."

"Not a pair of Rossi's? That's a real crime," said Cambria. "You should sue whoever did that."

If only, Cam-Cam, I thought. If only.

*T*he Black Pine Police front desk dispatcher knew me by sight. Not because of my former TV career. She also knew Nash. We'd done this before. She greeted our fame with a head shake. Without bothering to rise from her seat, she rolled her desk chair to the other side of her small compartment and hollered out the door for Detective Mowry.

I sat on a plastic chair bolted to the floor and watched Nash pace the lobby. "You think I'm crazy. Or you think I'm delirious. Or—"

Nash halted before me. "Not crazy or delirious. You saw something. But you jump to conclusions too easily. Conclusions that led me to cash in a favor."

"Detective Mowry's super nice. I'm sure he'll understand. Although I still can't explain what I saw."

"Do you know how much paperwork this will be for him?" Nash raised his brows. "If anyone needs to be nice, it's you to Mowry."

"How nice?" I scooted back on my chair. "What kind of nice are we talking about?"

"That's the conclusion jumping that'll get you in trouble." Nash resumed pacing.

The far door opened and Mowry beckoned us through.

"Hey Miss Albright," said Mowry. "How're you feeling? Your head still hurt?"

"I'm sorry. I don't understand what happened. I know what I saw, but Cambria is alive and well."

"Very well," said Nash.

I shot him an irritated look. "Anyway, I'm going to meet her for a morning workout. I'll be keeping an eye on her."

"I guess that's alright," said Mowry. "I'm not sure what to tell you either. I've seen some strange stuff in my career. There are some folks' windows you just don't want to go looking into."

"Particularly these TV folks," said Nash. "Exactly what I was thinking, Mowry. This Cambria seems like she's into some kinky stuff."

"What do you mean?" I asked.

"Film equipment, nude, and appearing dead." Nash paused.

"Unless that doesn't fit kinky these days? You're the Hollywood expert. I don't know what all goes on there."

"I'm not an expert on kink. I mean, I've met some freaks in my time — not judging — all lovely people. Sort of. But it's not like we swapped stories in therapy. Not those kind of stories anyway."

"Therapy?" said Mowry.

I sucked in a deep breath and focused on absorbing positive energy. Therapy in Black Pine did not have the same meaning as therapy in LA. Mowry was going to think I was crazy.

"In any case, I need you to detail what you saw, check the transcription, and sign the report," said Mowry. "I'll file it and we can forget about this."

I'd file but not forget. There were some things you can never get out of your head.

SEVEN

#BreakfastofChampions #GrilltheGirl

The next morning, I woke thinking of dead Cambria, alive Cambria, and Jerry. I felt concern for Cambria — both alive and dead — but Jerry had given me nightmares. He was going to kick my ass when he saw my muffin top, donut butt, and fried okra boobs. Literally, kick my ass with a kick boxing regime or whatever newest exercise craze was currently sweeping Tinseltown. And then he was going to make me shut off my hydrogenated oil intake and fill me up with colonics and juicing.

Probably all kelp. The new kale.

I wandered from my bedroom to the cabin's spacious kitchen and found my spot at the pine slab table. Carol Lynn — Daddy's second wife and the one he should have started with except I would not have been born otherwise — had made a simple breakfast of grits, eggs (fried), sausage patties, biscuits, and pineapple slices. Carol Lynn was the sweetest woman in the world and the secondary cause of the ill fit to my Black Pine wardrobe (the first cause being my lack of self-control). My half-sister Remi, six going on sixty-three, did not have this problem. Remi had inherited Daddy's stubbornness and someone else's metabolism. She was a spindly little thing. Daddy was built like a Mack truck with a full head of white-flecked auburn hair that fell to the base of his neck in a heavy beard. I inherited his copper highlights and unfortunate frame. Big bones looked better with a beard than boobs.

"Carol Lynn, thank you for fixing pineapple." I gazed longingly at the sausage and grits but forked a piece of fruit. "Jerry, my trainer, said fruit is good for breakfast because it's a natural detoxifier. Jerry loved detoxifying."

"You look healthy enough," said Daddy, eyeballing me from over his paper. "But if you're worried, maybe cover yourself some more."

I glanced at my Zobha tank and yoga leggings. True, the loose singlet tank had a racerback cutout, but that was the point when you wore an edgy twist-back sports bra beneath it. Plus, it was high-low cut to provide muffin top coverage. I thought about borrowing a sweatshirt, but I did not own a sweatshirt. Carol Lynn's sweatshirts were DeerNose brand, Daddy's line of hunting apparel. Cambria could forgive the camo, but wouldn't forgive me the scent. Deer pee. Great for hunting, but you don't want to sweat in it. The stench might drive Cambria to a morning vodka mixer.

"What's detoxifying?" asked Remi, reaching for the pineapple.

"It flushes out all the bad stuff in your body."

"Makes you tee-tee," said Daddy. "Remi, you're about as big as my little finger. You got no more bad stuff in you than that biscuit you're not eating. Everyone pees out water without this silliness. Eat your breakfast."

"I think Carol Lynn's biscuits are impossible not to eat," I said helpfully. "I used to dream about these biscuits back in LA. I think the fat content could be illegal there."

Remi scowled at the biscuit and took a bite of pineapple.

"No more talk about fat content, Maizie. Remi, eat your eggs," said Daddy. "Nobody worth their salt only eats pineapple for breakfast. You'll wither away by ten o'clock."

"I wish that were true," I said sadly. "But you do have a point. If I have to work out with Cambria this morning, I'm going to need the extra stamina."

Carol Lynn pushed the bowl of grits toward me.

I gave in and added sausage and a biscuit to my pineapple. Then pretended not to notice Remi shoving a hunk of biscuit under the table. At her feet one of many Jack Russell terriers waited for their second breakfast. They loved Remi even more than we did.

"Who's this Cambria now?" said Daddy from behind his newspaper. "New friend?"

"Sort of an old friend. She's going to star in an upcoming movie, and we were hired to watch her."

The paper folded and Daddy studied me. "Hired to watch her do what?"

"Hopefully not get into trouble." I gave him my winsome *Tiger-Beat* smile. "The movie production's insurance company wants an eye on her."

"That sounds like trouble for you." Daddy frowned at me, then at the bowl of pineapple Carol Lynn passed him. "Is your probation officer okay with you doing work like this?"

I hadn't forgotten about the "no celebrity work" clause of my probation, but I hadn't figured working for celebrities would be an issue.

I hoped.

"I'm sure it's fine. This is pure security work. Like a bodyguard who hides the liquor bottles and refuses calls from dealers." And made sure the star wasn't doing kinky snuff films on the side. "Easy peasy."

"Work that's worthwhile is never easy," said Daddy. "I thought you were doing some sort of accounting at Nash's."

"It's really boring and I'm not an accountant." I let his look slide over me and countered with an encouraging *Girl's Life* grin. "Daddy, I know you worry, but I didn't study criminal justice at So Cal just to do Nash's bookkeeping."

"Bookkeeping pays bills," said Daddy. "It may not be as exciting as a television shoot, but it keeps you out of the papers."

"Television shoots are not exciting either. It's a lot of waiting around for light and sound and then five minutes of frenetic energy only to find that the writers decided to change the scene." I pushed out of my chair. "Almost as boring as babysitting an actress whose lifestyle choices have become a career liability."

But that was a lie. I had a feeling Cambria's rumored escapades would keep me on my toes.

"Just remember, you were once an actress whose lifestyle choices had become a career liability. And look where that landed you. Almost in prison."

I delivered my *Teen Vogue* winky face. "Horse shoes and hand grenades, Daddy."

A phone rang, delivering a reprieve from another Boomer Spayberry lecture. Carol Lynn rose from the table, but Remi had already slid off the bench, crawled under the table, and popped out the other side. She hot-footed across the kitchen, the pack of dogs circling her feet, and grabbed the cordless.

It was so quaint how Daddy and Carol Lynn still used actual phones.

"Spayberry," she spat in the phone.

Beneath her, the dogs hopped and howled.

Remi cut a line across her throat, silencing the pack. They dropped to her feet and rolled on to their backs. Leaving the dogs to play dead, she traipsed across the kitchen, handing the phone to me. "It's for y'all."

I offered a hesitant hello, fearing Leonard Shackleton had called to tell me Cambria had actually died and we'd dined with a ghost. Or to ask me on a date.

"Honey, it's a fabulous day," drawled Theodore. "How'd it go with Mr. Shackleton? I heard y'all had dinner last night with the crew of *Pine Hollow*. I assume our trick did the trick?"

"*Pine Hollow*? That's the title?" How did Theodore know the name of the film when everyone was sworn to secrecy?

"Remi, let those dogs up and get back in your seat," growled Daddy. "I know you haven't eaten anything but a bit of that pineapple. Kindergartners need to eat breakfast. It's the law."

"No, it ain't," she muttered but slid on to the bench. She sidled close to me and cocked her ear near the phone.

"That's the big movie, right? Ancient secrets in the Appalachians or something like that?" said Theodore. "And Ed Farmer's directing. How was he? Amazing or scary? He's so aloof."

"Amazingly aloof." I climbed off the bench and took my sausage biscuit onto the back porch. "I'm working out with Cambria this morning."

"At Vicki Albright's place. Yes, I know all about that. I also heard you finished dinner at Black Pine police department. Do tell."

"How do you know all this stuff?"

"It's a small town, my dear. At least for some of us. People watch. They listen. They talk. What else are we going to do in Black Pine? There's only so many golf tournaments and yacht regattas to attend. We have to fill our time in between." Theodore paused. "Speaking of parties, I'm having one this weekend."

"I remember my promise. I'm happy to go."

"Of course, sweetie. But I wondered if you could bring a plus one."

"Nash?"

Theodore laughed. "You are such a hoot, Maizie. Wyatt Nash at one of my parties?"

"I'm not dating anyone." Unless the Black Pine grapevine had guessed Leonard Shackleton's interest in me. "I'm seriously not dating anyone. Particularly industry-related people."

"I was hoping you'd bring Cambria."

"I could ask her to come along." Another thought struck me. "Have you heard anything about Cambria? Do you know who she's dating?"

"I thought you were straight."

"Not for me. I'm going to be hanging out with her, and I want to avoid awkwardness." I chewed biscuit, thinking. "Actually, I'm just digging for gossip."

Theodore laughed. "Is it gossip when we're talking about a

celebrity? Isn't that considered news? I don't know who Cambria's dating. But according to the news, she's sown plenty of oats. She goes through men like I do shoes."

"I thought maybe she brought someone to Black Pine. Or met someone in Black Pine. Do you know who she was with yesterday, for example?"

"It sounds like she was after Wyatt Nash. But he left with you, didn't he? What's going on there? Tit for tat, girl."

"Absolutely nothing is going on there." Unfortunately. "We just work together."

"And the police station? Y'all went together."

"We just had to file a report. For work. Nothing exciting." Unfortunately. Well, more like luckily.

"I see." Theodore paused. "I don't know what Cambria was doing yesterday. She breakfasted at the Cove, of course. I think someone saw her in the gym, but she disappeared later. Probably working. Sorry, sweetie. But y'all have fun at your workout today. I heard your momma has quite the gym."

"Vicki really believes the body is a temple."

"We all know Vicki Albright has a goddess complex." Theodore giggled at my snort.

"I have no idea why Vicki invited us. I mean, she's always after me to get gym fit, but Cambria?"

"Vicki's not a Cambria fan?"

"She knew her back in the day. Back in the day, any female within ten years of my age was competition. And Vicki likes to stick to first impressions. She's not much for change."

"Oh sweetie, good luck. What are you wearing?"

I grinned. "Zobha."

"Cambria favors Lily Lotus. But you're going to out-sexy her in that Zobha. You have the curves that make the boys sigh."

"Thank you." I sniffled and pressed my fist against my heart. Unfortunately squeezing the sausage biscuit into a mangled pulp in the process. "You know just the right things to say."

"Oh honey, I only speak the truth. I heard you ruined a gorgeous pair of Gianvito Rossi sandals last night. I'm sorry."

"It's been so long since I felt someone really understood me." I choked on my words. "I promise to look fabulous for your party."

"Of course, you will. I'm counting on it."

*A*s Lucky was only a dirt bike given to me by Daddy on my fourteenth birthday and not a full fledged motorcycle (let alone a vehicle with sides and a roof), I couldn't drive Cambria to Vicki's. Instead, I parked Lucky at Black Pine resort and Dahlia, Cambria, and I rode in Vicki's Escalade, driven by Vicki's driver.

While enjoying the smooth, hair-friendly ride, I proceeded with my plan. First to warm Cambria with friendly banter, then question her ruthlessly about finding her allegedly dead on the floor of her bedroom. Ruthlessly nice. Because I did not want to get fired on the second day.

Also, in a way as to not alert Dahlia, whom I suspected was much smarter than she acted. Which was the problem with actresses.

"What kind of workout are you doing?" I asked. "Are you bulking up for an action role?"

"Ed Farmer wants me wiry," said Cambria. "Lean, like I work hard all day and don't get enough to eat. Lots of weights. Total cave man diet. But it's not a cave man role. Kind of *Winter's Bone* meets *Aliens.*"

"Me, too," said Dahlia. "So cool."

"Wow." My imagination had difficulty joining redneck noir and space scifi. "If anybody could put that together it's Leonard Shackleton. And Ed Farmer."

"I know, right?" said Dahlia.

Cambria yawned and fiddled with the straw on her shake.

I eyeballed her shake. I also had my narc job to fulfill. "Can I taste that?"

She handed me the bottle. I sniffed, tasted, grimaced, and handed it back.

"I know," she said. "I promised my trainer to drink this. It's supposed to be awesome for your workout. Guarana yerba maté matcha. You should get some."

"Totally." I shuddered. "I'm going old school with my pre-workout drink."

"Like a protein shake?"

"Water."

"Wow, so retro," said Dahlia. "What kind?"

"Tap."

"I don't know that brand. Is it new?"

I shook my head. Daddy didn't believe in "purchasing what God gives out for free."

"What does your boyfriend like to drink?" I asked, hoping to lead her into chatting about last night's incident. "Who is he again?"

"Boyfriend?" Cambria snorted. "Are we still in high school? I don't limit myself to outmoded monikers like that. It represents our societal failure to recognize relationships beyond marriage. And don't get me started on marriage."

"How about bae?" said Dahlia.

Cambria rolled her eyes.

This was the Cam-Cam I remembered. Overcomplicating and overanalyzing everything. I was reminded why we hadn't meshed as teens. She never chilled. "Significant other?"

"Ed Farmer?" mumbled Dahlia.

"Get real," said Cambria.

Hmm, I thought, but said, "Anyway, tell me about your parts in *Pine Hollow*."

"How do you know the title? Did Leonard tell you?" said Dahlia. "It's supposed to be a secret. Sort of. I mean, they leaked it to a few sites so some reporter wouldn't make up a better title and confuse the public when we announced it for real. But for now, they're sticking to 'Ed Farmer's newest sci-fi-fantasy box office hit.'"

I shrugged, preferring to keep Theodore's gossip pipeline to myself. "Speaking of secrets, I heard you're doing another film, Cam-Cam."

She gave me a sideways glance as she sucked down her berry leaf shake.

"A lower-budget production?" I hinted.

Her straw squelched, and she came up for air. "Did Alvin mention an indie last night? I've been waiting to hear about casting."

"No. Lower-budget than an indie?"

"What's lower-budget than an indie?" She tapped her thermos. "Oh wait, like a YouTube production?"

"Maybe." I studied Cambria. Either she was a much better actress than I thought. Or she didn't know about the cottage movie industry that had been in her cottage. "Where were you yesterday? Did you spend any time at the resort?"

"A little. I don't know. Around."

"I hiked Black Pine Mountain yesterday morning," said Dahlia. "It has spectacular views for such a small mountain."

Nodding, I ignored our third wheel and honed in on Cam-Cam. "Around your cabin? Or around somewhere else? Listen, I saw something when I went to your cottage that disturbed me. Do you know what I'm saying? I'd like an explanation of what I saw. I can't shake it."

"I know what you're doing, Maizie." Cambria shoved the thermos in the door caddy and crossed her arms.

"I just want to help you, Cam-Cam. I'm worried."

"You want back in."

Dahlia squealed.

I tensed. "I do not want back in. And I can't work in show biz anyway. I'm on probation."

Cambria waved her hand in the air, indicating the vagaries of an LA probation. "I might be able to get you a small part."

"Like totally," said Dahlia.

"I don't want any part." I scooted to face her. "I really don't. That's not why I'm hanging out with you."

"Then Leonard hired you to watch me."

I sighed and nodded. "You have a rep."

"So true," said Dahlia.

Cambria grinned. "Oh, I know. But so do you. How many times have you been in rehab?"

I chewed a nail. "Real or celebrity rehab?"

"Both."

"One and three."

"And you always bounced back."

"The last one wasn't so much as a bounce as a judge-sanctioned, one-way ticket to Black Pine 'Get out of Jail Free' card."

"I mean when you were still working. It seemed you were able to spin all those incidents in your favor."

"Vicki is good at spin," I conceded. "Left to my own devices, I'd probably be on a *Whatever Happened to This Teen Star*-type show."

"Um, like I don't mean to burst your bubble," said Dahlia. "But you're already on those shows anyway. Unless you relaunch your career and they can edit."

"The difference between then and now is that now I don't care." But that was a disturbing thought. One I hadn't let myself consider. Those shows didn't let you rest on your laurels. More like they let you rest on your failures. Vicki had probably contacted E!, VH1, and Bravo, banking on a higher dollar amount for my fall from grace while my ex-star power was still fresh.

We quieted, contemplating the short burn of stardom. And the singed feeling it caused when your rocket began to fail.

Or at least, that was my reflection when the car stopped before a palatial home on a ridge above the lake. I realized I had let them distract me from the dead-Cambria-in-the-bedroom questions, but a glance out the window further broke that train of thought. Construction equipment lined the half-circle drive.

"This can't be a rental," I said, feeling queasy. "Vicki would not put up with all this construction if she were renting."

"Maybe it was her only choice. It's not like Black Pine is that big. We'd all be in Atlanta if it was closer." Dahlia squealed. "I'm so excited. I love working out."

Of course, she did.

The three story stone home had twin turrets and a four car garage. And a fountain in the front yard.

"Why does she need this much space for a short term stay?" I pulled at the elastic in my pants, my panic turning to bloat. "Is Jerry living with her?"

Cambria's famous lips curled. "Who's Jerry? A new lover? Is he going to be on the show? I heard they're filming *All is Albright* here."

"God, I hope not," I said. "Jerry was my trainer."

Jerry as my stepdad might just put me back in rehab.

EIGHT

#LittleGirlLost #NotFlorida

---

*A*fter a flurry of air kisses and workout fashion compliments, Vicki led us to a ginormous gym with an attached dressing room and cedar sauna.

"That's an interesting fit," said Vicki, eyeballing my Zobha tanks and leggings. "We'll work on that today."

I withheld my sigh. "You're doing work on a rental?"

"You feather your nest no matter how long you stay in it. I've told you that before." Vicki cast Cambria an apologetic look. "We've traded a few zip codes, Maizie and I. Bel Air, Malibu, Hollywood Hills."

"This is a lot more than paint and hanging art. You have construction equipment in the drive." I glanced around at the large open space. "Did this gym come already installed?"

"I tweaked it. Virgin rubber flooring. Great for impacts." Vicki bounced, her platinum ponytail bobbing. She pointed at the walls. "Cork. And reinforced beams for the trapeze equipment."

"Trapeze equipment?" My eyes stole to the ceilings, half-expecting Jerry to parachute off a beam. "Is there a net?"

Vicki snorted. "Nets are for losers."

"You're probably right about that," I said. "A loser would need a net. Virgin rubber isn't going to bounce you out of a broken neck."

"Trapeze is the best for all-muscle toning," said Dahlia. "I tried Circus Fitness in Bel-Air. Awesome for my core."

"Exactly." Vicki's eyes homed in on my middle. "Maybe you want to try it, Maizie?"

"That's okay," I said quickly. "I was doing Tae-Bo. I've moved on to Tai-Chow-Fo."

"I think I've heard of that," said Dahlia. "Martial arts fitness, right? I sometimes train with a friend who does MMA. I think she does that."

Considering I had made it up so Vicki wouldn't make me climb the ladder bolted to the wall, I just nodded. Then realized I'd just created a web where a muscle-bound spider would easily catch me. "Where's Jerry?"

Vicki shrugged. "I'm going to warm up."

"I'll join you. I wanted to talk to you, Vicki," said Dahlia.

"If you must." Vicki marched to the ballet bar, tossing a look back at me.

Keeping an eye out for Jerry, I forced myself to mimic Cambria's warm up which involved muscles I had forgotten to use since moving from California. Panting and sweating, I followed Cambria toward the weights.

"Want me to spot you?" I gasped, happy for an excuse to stand still for a few minutes.

"Sure." She hunkered over a rack of barbell weights, pulled off four, and dropped them in my arms.

I staggered to the weight bench, my arms barely hanging from their sockets, and waited while she fitted them on the bar. "Back to my visit to your cottage yesterday." I glanced around the room to see if Vicki was listening. Which was dumb. Vicki was always listening. I lowered my voice. "I'm not going to say what I saw, but do you know what I saw?"

Cambria reclined on the bench and found her grip on the bar. "No. I wasn't home, remember?"

I moved around to spot her and stared down at her. "You were home. I saw you. On your floor. I looked in your bedroom window. I heard music, and when you didn't answer, I worried you were partying. Alone. I peeked in your window."

Two spots of color flared in her cheeks, but she focused on the bar above her, took a deep breath, and blew out as she lifted. "Count for me," she grunted.

"One. Were you partying? Two. With someone else? Three. Who left you there? Four. But I saw you later. Five. And it didn't look like you had been partying. Six. What did I see? Seven. Because I freaked. Eight. Totally freaked. Nine. Like call-the-police freaked. Ten."

The bar hit the rack with a clatter. Cambria's eyes widened and focused on me. "You called the police?"

We both craned our necks behind us. Vicki had moved from the bar to a rowing machine. Dahlia followed, still chattering. We swiveled back.

"Did you call the cops?" Cambria whispered. "Because that's not cool, Maizie."

"I thought you were dead. Of course, I called the cops."

"God, you're such a narc." Her eyes narrowed. "So what happened?"

"A detective came. We did it on the down-low. Obviously, the resort doesn't want the bad press either. And the detective didn't find anything."

Cambria took another breath, blew it out, and lifted. "Obviously," she panted, "because there was nothing to find. Count."

"One. I still don't get it. Two. I know what I saw. Three. You looked naked and dead. Four. What were you doing? Five. And how did you get cleaned up so fast? Six. And what was with the film equipment? Seven. And where did your partner go? Eight. I won't tell Leonard. Nine. I swear. Ten. I just need to know what happened."

She dropped the bar into my waiting hands. I sucked in a breath and eased the weights onto the stand.

"Your ideas about nudity are prudish and outdated." Cambria sat up, grabbed her towel, and blotted the beads of sweat on her temples. "Are you trying to say the words 'sex tape?' With your notoriety, I'm surprised you don't have one."

"Give her time, dear," said Vicki.

We spun.

Vicki passed a water bottle to Cambria and smiled. "Although I hope you don't, Maizie. Sex tapes are so passé. It's all 'accidental' live videos and taped Snapchats now."

"Really?" Cambria grabbed the proffered water. "Passé?"

"You didn't know?" Vicki's stricken look could have been misconstrued as maternal. Speaking as her daughter, I knew that wasn't possible. It was soliloquy time.

"Sweetheart, don't let that tape get out. With *Pine Hollow* coming up, it'd hurt your relationship with Ed Farmer and the producers."

Theodore must have told Vicki about the movie. Or Vicki had told him. But more importantly, why was Vicki helping Cam-Cam? A friend of mine was no friend to Vicki. Even if Cams and I hadn't been true friends.

"It's a private film," continued Cambria. "But if it did get leaked…"

"Publicity-wise, it would do you well for notoriety because the press would eat up the scandal," said Vicki. "But if what they're saying is true and *Pine Hollow* will be up for awards, it would do more damage than good. I know you've been around as long as Maizie, but this is your breakout role. Stay clean for your first big part and wait until you start to stumble. Then clean again, clean, hot mess, and clean. It's a balance between good and bad publicity. Bad goes further, of course. But it takes longer to get the roles you want that way. I assume your reputation made it difficult to land this role, despite the hype about your craft skills."

"Wow. My agent isn't as foresighted as you," said Dahlia. "Maizie's so lucky."

"Vicki's not my manager any—" I stopped to catch the water bottle Vicki threw before it slammed into my chest.

Vicki stepped around me. "Cambria, honey. Are you looking for a manager?"

"I don't know. I have a great agent. He's managed me well so far."

"Alvin Murphy, right? Young, eager, and passionate. That's good. He got you this role. I'd trust him with that side of your career. And he's with an excellent agency. But your personal life also needs management."

"Wait, a minute." Vicki was going to manage me out of a job. "I'm here to help Cam-Cam."

Vicki's eyebrow arched. "By ratting her out for a little sex tape?"

"I wasn't ratting." Although I'd been hired to rat. "It didn't exactly look like a sex tape. I don't know what I saw. And if that was a sex tape, Cambria, what the Hades are you into?"

"You see what I mean?" Rolling her eyes, Vicki tucked an arm through Cambria's and steered her toward the changing room. Dahlia traipsed behind them. "Just look at how I handled Maizie's career. Every time she lit it on fire, she rebounded."

"I lit it on fire because I didn't want to rebound," I said.

Vicki opened the dressing room door. "Why don't we take a sauna and chat? Dahlia, dear, you could probably use some help, too."

"Totally," said Dahlia.

The door closed behind them.

"Wait, a minute." I charged toward the dressing room door. "You can't steal Cambria from me."

My own words jerked me to a stop.

God, I sounded pathetic. I halted before a mirrored wall, noting the panic paling my face.

Time for a therapy-taught reality check. "Get a grip, Maizie. Is this about Vicki possibly stealing your job? Because you — or Julia Pinkerton you — could convince Leonard to continue with the insurance thing. Vicki will probably use your gig to boost Cam-

Cam's career and possibly denigrate your own, but as long as Nash Security Solutions gets paid for the job and secures a recommendation, that shouldn't matter."

Homing in, I noted the shine to my eyes. Then saw the tremor in my chin and my protruding lower lip. I probed my feelings, à la Renata's coaching. The usual wounded pride, destroyed vanity, and shattered self-confidence remained. I cocked a hip, slanted my eyes in Julia Pinkerton fashion, and took on her voice. "So Vicki becomes Cambria's manager. And possibly Dahlia's. No biggie.

"I mean, she's still your, you know, mother. But as therapist Renata always says, 'You can't choose your parents, only your path in life.' Go out there and live your own life and let Vicki live hers."

I nodded, then altered the nod until it appeared legit. Mirror talks. Who knew they'd be good for more than character development practice? Acting had taught me at least one thing.

"Right." I did a few Tao-Bo punches for luck. Which hurt thanks to Cambria's warmup. I rubbed my arms. "I need ice. And I should probably stop talking to myself. At least, out loud."

Crossing the room, I opened the dressing room door.

Vicki glanced up. She spoke while tucking a towel around her slim figure. "Maizie, did you want to sauna, too? I know how you feel about breaking a sweat. How about a shower instead? This sauna is pathetically small. I might have to build a bigger one in the future."

My stomach rolled at the word 'future,' but I let it go. "No, you go on. I didn't bring a change of clothes."

I turned to Cambria, who had peeled off her outfit and stood with her back to me, nude.

"Maizie, could you hand me a towel?" Cambria glanced over her shoulder and noted my gape. "What? Did I bruise myself?"

I shook my head. "No. No bruise. I just thought you had a birthmark? Shaped like Florida?"

Cambria peered over her shoulder, trying to see down her back. "What? I don't have a birthmark. Is there something on me?"

"There's nothing," said Vicki sharply. "What are you doing, Maizie? Don't make Cambria feel awkward."

I felt my cheeks heat. "Everything's fine. I thought I remembered you having a birthmark shaped like Florida...never mind."

"Come on, Cambria. Don't mind, Maizie. It's been a while since she's worked out. It's probably all that adrenaline rushing to her brain. Or from her brain." Vicki grabbed the handle to the sauna and yanked it open. Cedar scented heat wafted out. "Maizie, we'll meet you on the patio. Have someone fix you something. They don't do fat, fried, or gluten, but you can have fruit. Or a Bloody Mary. Oh wait, you're not allowed those. Just eat the celery."

Dahlia followed Vicki through the doorway. "Catch you in a few, Maizie."

"Yeah, sure." My heart pounded, but I waited until the wooden door swung shut behind them, then ran to find a phone.

The body I saw was not Cambria. Which meant somebody else might have been dead for real.

NINE

#DeadDouble #VillianousVista

---

*I*t seemed Vicki had not adopted Daddy's quaint practice of house phones. After scurrying through rooms searching for one, I pounded back to the locker room to snag Vicki's cell. Luckily, she hadn't changed her passcode — 90210 — and had saved Nash's phone number. When he wouldn't answer, I tried Lamar. He answered, then handed his phone to Nash.

"Why didn't you pick up?" I said.

"I thought Vicki Albright was calling. How was I supposed to know it was you? Why are you using her phone?"

"Never mind that. It's important. The body I saw wasn't Cambria."

"What?"

"I just saw Cambria naked, and she doesn't have a birthmark shaped like Florida on her butt." I waited a beat for Nash to speak. "You better not be thinking about Cambria's butt. Do you get what I'm saying?"

"I get it. I'm trying to process this."

"Someone who looks exactly like Cambria is dead. You need to call Detective Mowry and tell him."

More silence.

"Nash?"

"Still processing." He sighed. "First, we don't even know if whoever you saw was dead. Aren't they actors? Can't they act dead?"

"Her eyes were open."

"For how long before you fell and hit your head?"

"Really? I thought you said hitting my head doesn't cause hallucinations."

"Still doesn't mean she was dead. She might have recovered and left after you took off."

"Someone who looks like Cambria pretended to be dead until I left to call the police?"

"I don't know what to think. Maybe Cambria has a twin."

"We'd know if Cam-Cam had a twin. It would have been news a long time ago."

"I told you this business can get lewd and nasty. I'm not going to list the possibilities of some Hollywood actress having a looka-like appear dead in her bedroom. With movie cameras. All I'm saying is, the girl might not be dead."

"But what if she is?"

"I'll call Mowry. But unless he has evidence other than your testimony, not much can happen. They already canvassed the other cabins. No one was home. No staff was in the area, and house-keeping saw nothing out of the ordinary. You're the only witness. The resort won't let them in the cottages without a warrant."

"Maybe now they can get a warrant."

"Based on a peeping Tom who hit her head and believes she saw someone else because they had a birthmark on their ass? I wouldn't count on it."

"Can't he check for a missing person? Who looks like Cambria?"

"Oh sure. If someone reports Cambria's body double is missing, that'd be perfect. Until then, Mowry's got other cases. And between you and me, he's doubtful you saw anything."

"He thinks I made it up?"

"People do. For attention. You can get arrested for that, by the way." Nash paused. "Not that I think you'd do something like that. Are you still there?"

"I was just thinking. Body double. Maybe that's something we should check into."

"You shouldn't always take me so literally, Miss Albright. I fear my use of sarcasm is lost on you at times."

"No, you were right. We use body doubles all the time. Usually, they don't look that similar, but it could have been the angle. Plus, her hair had fallen over her face." I glanced behind me. The sauna door had rattled but remained closed. "Gotta go. I'll stay on Cam-Cam and see what I can learn."

"Your job is babysitting not looking for a dead body double, Miss Albright."

"You didn't want this job, remember?"

I deleted Lamar's number from Vicki's recent calls and replaced the phone on the chair where I found it. The sauna door opened. Three toweled women exited, pink and glistening.

Vicki dabbed at her temples. "Maizie, are you still in here? If you want to use the sauna, it's free now."

"No, I'm good."

Cambria cocked her head. "Did Leonard say you literally couldn't leave my side? This is going to be awkward."

"I'll speak to Leonard for you." Vicki strode to her phone, picked it up, and began paging through her emails. "Maizie, Cambria isn't going to shoot heroin in front of me. You can wait on the patio."

"I don't shoot heroin," said Cambria.

"Just an expression, dear." Vicki's saber-tooth smile flickered. "I'd say it's none of my business, but that's all changed, hasn't it?"

*T*he patio overlooked a pool with an inset Jacuzzi and waterfall. A low stone wall framed a stunning vista of Black Pine Lake and the Blue Ridge in the horizon. I didn't know you could have a view of anything but the lake and Black Pine Mountain, but of course, Vicki would have the best view in town. I hoped Vicki flipped this rental for one back on the West Coast as quickly as she burned through our California addresses.

Taking my focus off a view that would convince most people never to leave, I downed three glasses of key lime, mint, and parsley infused water and waited for the power trio to appear. Could have done without the parsley, but the detox did refresh my brain. As I saw it, I had a new problem. Several.

A possible dead body. The body wasn't Cambria but looked exactly like Cambria. Not exactly new but a new take on a fresh problem.

Vicki seemed determine to get cozy with my client. There was an algebraic formula for this sort of thing, and it equaled Vicki and me working together. Something I vowed never to do again.

Also, I had nothing to wear to Theodore's party. A new and fresh problem since I've arrived in Black Pine. Nevertheless, completely unoriginal and a bit inappropriate.

I tore apart the parsley garnish considering the unlucky girl's plight. How and why had she been in Cam-Cam's cottage? Was it an overdose like I first assumed of Cambria? If she had been making a "private video" as she said, was the girl a part of it?

My stomach rolled. I choked back parsley, lime, and mint-flavored reflux. Not going to ride that thought.

What if no one was looking for this double? The police wouldn't have any recourse to search for her, other than my testimony. It seemed Nash didn't believe me either. I shoved the water away and grabbed a monogrammed paper napkin to dab my eyes. That poor girl.

If she was dead. Maybe Nash was right, and she wasn't.

But say she was. A dead body was really going to "shit up" Leonard's movie. And I was supposed to stop that from happening. A dead body equaled a huge, expensive problem for the film and everyone related. Also, a major issue for Black Pine Resort. They'd do anything to stop dead-body-in-their-villa-type news from spreading. And the city would also hate it. They'd cajoled the TV and film industry into parking their trailers in Black Pine instead of another Georgia town, like Madison or Senoia. A dead body would cost them a fortune in spin control and hurt their ranking in all those safe and beautiful city lists that enticed location scouts.

Problems were not new to me, Wyatt Nash, or Nash Security Solutions. But the resort, town, and film industry could put us out of business for good. When it came to the blame game, the weakest player always loses. And there was no doubt in my mind, who would get blamed for a dead body screwing up Leonard's big blockbuster release before it even filmed. Not Cambria, even if this was her dead body. Cambria, her agent, and new manager would all have the best attorneys on retainer. Vicki had her lawyer on speed dial.

Come to think of it, maybe leaving these problems to the police — when they finally found evidence other than my memory — wasn't such a good idea. We needed to get a fix on this new, missing body — *Hello Maizie, stop calling her a body* — and figure out what's going on before slipping the news to Leonard Shackleton, Tinseltown, and Black Pine.

That thought, so fresh and new, burned as bright as the neon sign in the Dixie Kreme Donut Shop window. I was still going to have to tell Leonard Shackleton that Cam-Cam had housed a dead body. Ugh.

No more Mr. Nice-to-Cambria-guy. I needed to put the screws to that girl. Hottest celeb of the week or not, it was her villa and her dead doppelganger.

Craptastic.

Vicki, Dahlia, and Cambria sauntered onto the slate patio. I felt another wave of key lime, mint, and parsley-infused nausea. I swallowed hard and stood. "We should bounce. And Cam-Cam, we need a confab. A mucho serious confab."

"They haven't rehydrated. Really, Maizie," said Vicki. "Who

takes a sauna and doesn't hydrate? Do you want to put them in the hospital?"

"I'm fine, but this does look great." Dahlia eased into a chair, scooting back on the plump pillows. "Gorgeous view, Vicki."

"Thank you. The North Georgia Mountains do have some appeal. Of course, nothing like my Hollywood Hills vista. But one must make do." Vicki did the gaze-into-the-distance-for-effect pause. "Maizie, the contract you signed with Leonard? I need to look it over and understand exactly what you are doing for Cambria."

"Why? You don't take care of my contracts anymore. It's between Mr. Shackleton and Nash Security Solutions."

"It's not for you. It's for Cambria." She handed a water to Cambria and eyed my tattered parsley. "Don't gape, Maizie. You know how it pulls the skin to create lip lines."

I snapped my mouth shut, repeated one of Renata's self-actualization mantras, and realized Vicki's interest in Cam-Cam might have a source other than hurting me. "Did they cancel the show?"

Cambria who had been enjoying our parlay from her patio chair slouch raised an eyebrow. "They canceled *All is Albright*? It wasn't in the trades."

"No," said Vicki. "I don't know where that's coming from. The show continues as usual. But now that I'm not representing Maizie, at least at the moment..."

"Anymore," I interrupted. "Ever."

"At the moment," she continued. "I have time to help Cambria. Oh, maybe you, too, Dahlia, dear. And still produce the show. And do my appearances on the show, of course."

Shizzlation. My worst fear confirmed. If Cambria is involved with a dead body, Vicki would be involved with a dead body. "No. You can't do that."

Vicki's simper curled into a sneer. "Really, Maizie. I haven't seen this side of you since you were six."

"It's just not a good idea. At the moment." I scrambled for a better answer. "I'm hired to watch Cambria, so you should wait until I find—I'm done watching her. It's like a conflict of interest. Yes, it's a total conflict. Of interest."

"You don't want Cambria to have professional and personal assistance at this juncture of her career? Right when she's headed for a peak?" said Vicki. "I thought you cared what happens to Cambria."

"No. That's not it. You always twist things."

"I don't understand your issue either, Maizie," said Dahlia. "Vicki was super awesome at helping your career when you screwed it upside-down and backward. Why won't you let her help us?"

"Cam-Cams doesn't need Vicki for that. She has me." The parsley water was doing nothing to cool the heat rushing through my body. "I'm here to make sure she doesn't shit up Leonard's film."

Cambria beautiful lips pursed.

"Jealous much?" said Dahlia.

"Maizie," said Vicki. "I didn't raise you to be rude. Apologize to Cambria."

"OMG." I flapped the Zobha tank. "That's not how I meant it."

"Really? Because you sound like an ungracious brat."

"Vicki. You just can't manage Cambria right now. Stick with Dahlia. No offense, Dahlia." I leaned toward Cambria and muttered, "You know why she can't. Sex romp turned ugly? Ring a bell?"

Cambria rolled her eyes and turned to Vicki. "I want her off the insurance deal, or whatever Leonard used to hire her."

Frigalotious. Or maybe that's exactly why Cambria wanted Vicki to help her. Maybe Cambria thought Vicki wouldn't have any qualms about covering up a dead twinster.

Holy hells balls.

"Contract," I stuttered. "We have a contract. Vicki can't break the contract. The insurance company insisted on it."

"Then I want to be watched by Mr. Nash and not you."

"Oh, hells to the no. Nash is not going to go for that." Did I just say that out loud? I glanced at Vicki who had that mockingly triumphant look. Like when she scored a great ad set for the show during Sweeps Week.

Dammit. I don't know what Vicki wanted from this, but she had somehow gotten it.

"I suggest you back off," said Vicki. "And convince Nash to submit."

"He doesn't do submission."

"Even better," purred Cambria.

"Oh my God." I grabbed my water and swigged, tasted parsley, and spit it back in the glass. I glanced at my bare wrist. Why didn't I wear a watch? "I'm sure it's late. We need to jet. Cambria's got a reading today."

"Oh me, too." Dahlia hopped from the chair and strode toward the door, stretching. "But drop me off at the lake. I'm going to Iron Man swim before I get ready."

Cambria rose and stretched, yawning.

"Do you want me to come to the reading, Cambria?" said Vicki. "I'll just take a minute to shower and throw something on. I could take you."

Cambria took her time, moving away from the table and strolling toward the French doors. "Oh sweetie, no worries. I'll call when I need you."

Sweetie? Dumbfounded, I swiveled my gaze between Cambria's exit and Vicki's frozen half-turn.

"This stays here. And you will apologize," Vicki hissed at me, then marched toward the mixed-stone castle.

What stayed here? Vicki taking Cambria as a client? Or Vicki letting Cambria call her "Sweetie?"

I couldn't tell who was the better actress in this scenario. Cambria pretending she didn't know about the body in her villa. Or Vicki's about-face attitude with Cambria.

Or Dahlia. No one could love exercise that much.

*A*fter dropping Dahlia off for her Iron Man swim — "You should totally try it. I'm rock hard. Do you want to feel my abs?" — Cambria settled back into the leather seat and closed her eyes. I glanced at the driver, wondering if his paycheck included spying for Vicki. Very likely.

"Cam-Cam," I said. "You're in trouble."

She opened one eye, then closed it. "Let me meditate. I've got to rush my prep for the reading as it is."

"Are you going to sign a contract with her?" Oops, that wasn't the question I wanted to ask.

She opened both eyes. The famous lips curled. "I thought you weren't jealous."

"You know that's not it. You can't involve Vicki with your extracurricular bedroom activities."

"Give me a break." Cambria sat up and turned toward me. "But what bothers you more? That she's taking on more clients or that you're not one?"

"She's my mother."

"Which makes it better or worse?"

Honestly, I wasn't sure.

"I think you want back in." Cambria smirked.

"Look, I do not and cannot have any interest in returning to acting. Or any talent-related work."

"You're working for Leonard Shackleton now."

"Yes, but I'm not talent." I ignored her snort and continued. "I know who was in your cottage yesterday. And before this blows up, you better come clean."

She flopped back on the seat and closed her eyes. "It's none of your business."

"What were you doing? Some avant-garde, underground, indie grindhouse thing? Or was it just a hard party that went wrong? How could you jeopardize your career with this? You're on the brink of hugeness. Tell me so I can figure out what to do to help you."

"I'm flattered you think it's art," she mumbled.

"That's like the total opposite of what I'm saying."

"And here's what I'm saying. You're getting paid to watch, not talk. It sounds like you've done enough watching. Now shut up so I can meditate."

"Oh my God. Don't you know you're on a sinking ship?"

"Sink this." She flipped me off and unzipped her bag. "If *Pine Hollow* is sinking, it's going to sink like *Titanic*."

"Exactly."

"The movie, not the ship, idiot. You're one to lecture about jeopardizing careers. Just like when were kids, you're still playing the part, whereas I'm living it." Rolling her eyes, she slipped headphones over her ears, crossed her arms, and refused to speak the rest of the ride.

TEN

#TitanicFail #AssistantToTheAssistant

*C*ambria also refused to let me in the cottage while she showered. I sat in the golf cart and thought about the real *Titanic* and my relationship to impending doom. After a few minutes of panicked shallow breathing, I scurried to the side of the cottage, righted my log, and climbed aboard. Cambria's bedroom looked as before minus the body and camera equipment. Where had the equipment gone? I needed to find out who else had been involved in her private film session.

Cambria exited the bathroom, her hair freshly swept into a purposefully bedraggled bun. She leaned over to grab her Phillip Lim platforms. As I admired her choice in footwear, Cambria's head jerked upright, sighting the window. I ducked and fell off the log.

This time, I tucked and didn't smack my head. I was learning.

I drove Cambria to a waiting Lincoln which drove us to a warehouse redesigned as a studio. She strode past me, middle finger extended, heels smacking the pavement. The studio's door opened, and Leonard Shackleton emerged. He greeted Cambria with a hug and air kiss, then beckoned me to the door.

Sighing, I trudged to the warehouse. "Good morning, Mr. Shackleton."

"Work out with Cambria, did you? She's in fighting form." He eyed my Zobha togs. "You look like Georgia agrees with you. That's fresh to see in a woman these days. Healthy."

Fresh and healthy. I pulled on my tank, wishing I'd remembered to bring a change of clothes to Vicki's. "You should know, Cambria's not cool with my supervision. She stopped talking to me."

"She just told me she wants Mr. Nash to take over your job." Leonard smiled.

"Mr. Nash doesn't—" I caught myself. "Mr. Nash has another case he's working on. I need to continue with Cam-Cam. Despite how she feels. I can handle her."

"I admire your moxie." His eyes ran over my Zobha. "I admire many of your qualities."

An acting background was handy in situations such as this. Like when you wanted to gag and not smile. "So you'll override Cam-Cam's wishes on who gets to babysit?"

"For now. But who can blame Cambria? No adult wants to be thought of as unaccountable," said Leonard. "However, she did this to herself. Why do you think her agent is here? He's sitting on her, too. Alvin Murphy gets a percentage of her percentage. There's not been this kind of nail-biting on a star's delivery since Lohan's return. I hired you because she needs a friend, not a babysitter."

"Cambria's not feeling friendly. She's hiring a new manager. I thought you could tell her to wait on that. I don't want the manager to interfere with…my job."

"No, a manager's good. More eyes on her the better. Cambria's showing she's serious about her career. "

According to what I saw yesterday, she didn't seem that serious about her career. She needed more than a manager to make amends for a dead body double. She needed a jailer.

Oh, boy. I was the jailer. Unless, like, she went to jail for real.

And blew her mongo contract. Would she take Vicki down with her?

"It sounds like Cambria's hoping to use the manager for a PR cleanup," I said.

"Excellent." Leonard beamed. "I hope this is due to your influence."

"Sort of." In the most craptastic of ways, it was my influence that got Vicki involved with Cambria. "But I really think Cambria should wait. There's been an incident already. Before I started yesterday. I want to get it straightened out, but Cambria isn't 'fessing to what happened. Maybe she doesn't know, but I can't be sure. And I can't tell if the situation is serious or not."

The beam darkened. "What do you mean? Be clear."

"I thought I saw Cambria yesterday before dinner. In her cottage. But it wasn't her, just someone who looked like her. It appeared...bad. But I was the only one who saw it. I think. Did you hire a body double for the movie?"

"Shit. Check with casting," said Shackleton. "What did the double do? Do we need a PR cleanup?"

"Um, well, I'm not sure what she did. Or where she went. She looked...unconscious. But then disappeared?"

"Find out," hollered Shackleton. "Why are you still standing here? We've got Cambria covered in rehearsal. Come back when you find that double."

*T*he warehouses had been outfitted with offices, workshops, meeting rooms, and sound stages. Behind the warehouses, production crews hammered and painted, putting the finishing touches on a spaceship and an old-timey still. Golf carts whizzed to and fro. A fixer laden with Starbucks guided me toward the pre-production offices.

I found an assistant to an assistant casting director and put the body double question to the test. Ms. Assistant Assistant, Janet Hillcrest, opened the extensive cast list on her MacBook. The body double hired for Cambria's scenes hadn't left LA. But after seeing her headshot and full body shot, I realized the double wasn't my double. No Florida birthmark. She'd been hired for her tush, not her face.

"Do you do a casting call for lookalikes?" I asked. "I'm trying to track one down."

"Sure. Especially if we need stand-ins for secondary units," said Janet. "There are agencies that specialize in celebrity lookalikes, but they're used more for party photo ops. We need actual actors. Sometimes we'll use impersonators. Most of them are really talented. They spend a lot of time developing their characters. But they only do classic stars or famous movie characters, so I don't pull from those agencies very often. I still have to pour through a lot of head shots, then audition."

"Did Cambria help you at all with the auditions? Meet with any of the doubles?"

"Cambria had final approval, but that was done through her agent." Janet slid her laptop to the side and cocked her head. "You're looking for a specific Cambria double."

I nodded. "Very specific. More of a celebrity lookalike than just a stand-in."

"Which agency?"

"A specific double, but we have no idea who they are."

"Then how do you know them?"

I wasn't going to say I only knew her by her butt birthmark. "Cambria knows her. I think."

"Cambria knows her lookalike but doesn't know her name?" Miss Assistant Assistant gave a thoughtful nod. Knowing someone without knowing someone was normal in our world. "Is she from LA? There are a lot of lookalike agencies out there."

"Possibly? But the lookalike was here in Black Pine."

"That's weird."

"Right?" Even more bizarre, she disappeared. And may be dead.

"Check with the Clone Star Agency. There's one in LA, but they also have an office in Atlanta."

"Awesome."

"Did you ask Cambria's agent? Maybe he hired her?"

"Alvin Murphy? Great idea. You're brilliant." I hugged Janet, breaking Nash's rule number two. But since the rule only applied to Nash, I gave Miss Assistant Assistant an extra squeeze.

Janet squeezed back. I took it as a sign to push my luck. "You don't suppose that while I'm here, we can look up the Clone Star Agency on your laptop?"

"Why not?" Janet clicked through her agency list to the Clone Star website. "This agency has celebrity impersonators and looka-likes. That means some are actors."

We paged through the characters in the Atlanta branch. No Cambria. "She hasn't done a memorable character yet. Maybe after *Pine Hollow*." Janet's eyes sparkled.

I recognized that sparkle. "A lot of people are banking on this movie."

Janet nodded. "Ed Farmer's considered a genius, but not very practical. He wanted to do as much on location as possible. The filming's out here, and the special effects are on the west coast. The CGI is going to cost a fortune. Development took ages. A lot of fighting between the producers and the studio over the budget. Then more fighting during preproduction between the producers, Ed, and the studio's writers. Ed didn't want to give up any creative control. They've already spent a ton just in development."

"But that's normal for a film."

"What's not normal is Ed insisting on Cambria as lead at any cost. He saw her on stage as Lady Macbeth and fell in love."

"Literally?"

"Iconically."

"Wow. I guess he really believes in her."

"Ed says she's a star. It could be a breakout for her, which will, in turn, make the film more popular. Then everyone's happy."

"But she's a risk. She's moving from stage to film via the party-hard highway. Who does that?"

Janet shrugged. "With risk, there's the chance for great reward. As long as she does her job during production, it'll pay off. At least that's what Ed says. Leonard's worried about the release. He needs her to be red carpet worthy. Leonard thinks a lot of about marketing. He's worked a lot of deals with foreign investors and banks to create a bigger budget than the studio investment to give more creative control to Ed."

"So Leonard believes in Ed and Ed believes in Cambria."

"Right." Janet cast her attention back to the website. "Hey, here's you. That's fun, right?"

I peered at the screen. "I guess they don't need my permission to impersonate me?"

"As long as whoever hires her knows she's not actually Maizie Albright."

"It's a little disturbing."

"It says she impersonates you as Julia Pinkerton and you in *All is Albright*."

"But *All is Albright* is a reality show. I'm not a character, I'm me."

"Reality show you." Janet clicked. "Looks like you can't hire her, she's booked."

"Why would I hire myself?"

"Haven't you ever wanted to be in two places at once?"

"A ringer." I thought about the woman in Cambria's room. "One might call it a dead ringer."

Janet squinted at the screen. "I don't think she looks that much like you."

Did Cam-Cam kill the ringer or did someone kill the ringer thinking it was Cambria? Unless the ringer wasn't actually dead, which brings me back to square one. "I'm very confused."

Janet gave me another hug, then pointed me toward the craft service room to "fuel my brain."

I really liked Janet.

ELEVEN

#HipsterHangouts #SketchedOut

*C*ambria's agent, Alvin Murphy, said he'd meet me at the coffee shop, No Sleep Till. A new enterprise that had popped up in a strip mall near the warehouse area used by the studios. I assumed the Beastie Boys reference was for the industry peeps and not Black Pine, who (IMHO) wouldn't get a '80s rap hipster reference.

But maybe Black Pine did. These days, I didn't feel confident in understanding much. I wasn't even sure the Beastie Boys were in the '80s. Late Twentieth Century tends to blend.

I trotted into the cafe. Coffee was truly the Adderall of the beverage world. One sniff and I was buzzing. The shop had a real-faux Brooklyn vibe with the brick and plaster walls, wood floors, and an open rafter ceiling. Of course, this was also the look of Lamar's Dixie Kreme Donuts. Except that plaster was crumbling for real. Still, I felt a nostalgic thrill for my bygone hipster coffee-house days.

Also for my *Sesame Street* cameo, although that was is in Astoria, not Brooklyn.

"How about a nitro cold brew?" The tatted barista leaned on the wooden counter and nodded at the glass display case. "And a donut?"

Hells to the shizzle, their donuts looked good. "What flavor is that?" I pointed at a donut decorated with sprinkles and an iced triple B.

"Bacon, banana, and Bavarian cream."

"Actual bacon sprinkles?" I had to check the tremble in my voice. She nodded and pointed. "And those are maple, licorice, mocha whip. Rosemary, dark chocolate and salted caramel. Lemon, thyme, and green tea glaze. Coffee with Fruity Pebbles topping."

"How about a simple plain glazed? I've already donut imbibed today, but I like to support local businesses."

"Funny, we only have one of those left." She dropped it on a plate. "What else? Espresso, macchiato, or con panna? Or for coffee, we've got cold brew and Chemex."

I felt a twinge in my chest. I'd missed hearing words like "Chemex" and "con panna" in everyday conversation. At Daddy's, we had drip, but Daddy and Carol Lynn called it "coffee." At Lamar's, there was "decaf" or "regular." I held back a sniffle and placed a hand over the lump in my heart.

"Nitro. And make it a pint." I dropped my voice. "With sweetened condensed milk. And a float of half and half," then whispered, "and a double shot of pumpkin spice."

"The Thanksgiving Hangover? Good choice."

I spun around and checked for Vicki. She had a habit of showing up when I was at my weakest. No Vicki. And thankfully, no Jerry. He'd force extra pull-ups for ordering anything that had the words "sweetened" or "pumpkin spice" in the ingredients. However, I did spot Alvin Murphy.

Alvin gave me a quick smile and returned his attention to his phone.

Carrying my donut and coffee to Alvin's table, I noticed several people I knew from the old days. I wormed through the tables saying hello to a makeup artist who helped on the set of *Julia*

Pinkerton, a gaffer from *Kung Fu Kate,* and an assistant from one of my TV movies, *Kid Notorious.* All working on different projects around Black Pine. Amazeballs.

"Hey, Maizie." Alvin set his phone on the table and greeted me with a handshake that ended with a cheek peck. By his grip, I assumed Alvin was serious about last night's Parkour remark. I usually didn't take extreme workout name dropping seriously.

"How are you?" said Alvin. "Still have that asshole Mickey for an agent?"

"Uh, no." I frowned. "But Mickey was really nice."

Alvin gave me a toothy smile and picked up his coffee mug. "Asshole in what he did for your career. I'm surprised Vicki Albright let you keep him on for so long. But then everyone knows Vicki repped you more than Mickey."

This was not how I wanted to start this conversation. I dropped into the barista chair across from Alvin and stirred my coffee. "I don't need representation anymore. That's the only reason I'm not with Mickey."

"Sure," said Alvin. "I heard about your legal drama. How lucky are you that Georgia has such a huge film industry? Although most of the work's down near Atlanta, Black Pine gives some nice incentives on top of the state's tax break."

"Real lucky." I held in a frustrated sigh. "So, so lucky."

"You look good."

I waited for him to say 'healthy,' but it didn't come. I straightened my shoulders, despite the tightness of my Saint Laurent tee. "Thanks."

"How can I help? This is about Cambria, right? I know Leonard hired you."

"Did you hire Cambria a body double?"

He caught my meaning immediately. "Nah, she doesn't really need one out here. I guess Black Pine is too remote for the paparazzi. For now anyway."

"Does she have a friend or acquaintance who's a lookalike?"

"What's this about?"

"I thought I saw someone who looked like Cam-Cam yesterday. It wasn't Cambria."

"Saw someone...doing something I should know about?"

"Possibly." I lowered my voice. "It was in Cambria's cottage. She hinted she was doing an s-e-x tape."

"I think everyone in here can spell." Alvin leaned across the table, waved me closer, and I met him halfway. "Cambria told you that?" he murmured.

I nodded. "Do you know anything about this?"

"I know recently Cambria's batting a thousand when it comes to controlled substances and inappropriate behavior. But she also understands the fine line between what's forgivable in the public eye and what's not. At least, I'm pretty sure she does. She's a smart cookie. She has a lot of good ideas for publicity."

"I'm worried about her. She could blow this chance."

"She better not," said Alvin. "And you better see to it that she doesn't."

"I'm working on it. But I need help. I need names, Alvin."

He pulled away.

I leaned back to nibble on my donut.

Alvin glared at his phone and sipped his coffee, thinking.

"Her boyfriend is here. Actually, I don't know if he's her boyfriend." He rubbed his forehead. "I don't know what she calls him. They're not really public."

"Who is it?" I calmed the excitement in my voice. "Is he staying in the villa with her?"

"No." Alvin coughed. "Stunt guy. Orlando Feelzen."

"Orlando Feelzen?" I rolled his name over my tongue. "For real?"

Alvin shrugged. "You know how it is. Anyway, they hooked up on her last movie. She intro'ed him to casting for this one. Same ol' story."

I knew it well. But without the dead woman in my bedroom.

"Where's Orlando staying if he's not shacking up with Cambria?"

"At the resort. But in the hotel."

"Super." Convenient. I could look for Orlando while I canvassed the other guests. "I'm going to find him and see if I can get his help in getting Cambria to chill." And what he knows about his freaky girlfriend's possibly dead twin.

"Maizie." Alvin gathered my hands in his and gave me the super-serious-agent look. Mickey's favorite. "You know how much is riding on Cambria behaving herself. You're an insider. You know to keep everything on the down-low."

I nodded, wincing at the squeeze in his grip.

"I need your help. Need it, baby."

"Got it." I yanked my hands, but he held fast.

"I know Vicki had her thumb on you pretty tight over the years. And I've got a feeling that's made you want to break free."

I blinked. My meltdown rebellion was that obvious?

"You miss it?" Alvin studied me.

Why would I miss rebelling? I studied Alvin studying me. "Wait, miss what?"

"The life."

I cast an eye at my empty Thanksgiving Hangover glass and the crumbs from my "Kicking it Old School" donut. The cost of hipster food was high, the cost of my weekly lunch budget. (Worth it.) And realized Barney's near or far didn't matter on my weekly clothes budget which was zero-point-zero dollars. "Sometimes."

With a final hand squeeze, he drew away. "I thought so."

"I might miss the lifestyle. But not the attached strings." I dropped my hands in my lap to rub them back to life.

"You miss the money."

How embarrassing.

I shrugged one shoulder. "Money's nice. Especially when you don't have any."

"Vicki cleaned you out. We all figured." Alvin shook his head. "It's a lot easier climbing up than down. I grew up on the South Side of Chicago. I may be white, but it was the hood. Back in the old days, the Murphy's worked for the Capone's. Tough, old neighborhood. Know what I'm saying? I climbed out and couldn't imagine going back. You've had it made for so long, this must be a struggle for you."

"My car was repo'd, and now I ride a dirt bike to work." I sighed. "It's a good thing my probation doesn't allow me on social media because I can't afford a smart phone."

"Do yourself a favor. Do a good job. Keep this issue quiet. Make Cambria happy. Make Leonard happy. There'll be a big reward in it for you, and I know," he tapped the table, "I am certain, your boss will be given some sweet contracts in the future. You'd like that, right?"

Of course, I'd love to win Nash sweet contracts. Personally and professionally.

He smiled at my acknowledgment. "And when your probation runs out if you've changed your mind and want back in…" Alvin stood, smoothed his button-down, and handed me his card. "Let me know. You just call me, and I'll be there for you. You were good, Maizie. Your problem wasn't you. We both know who your problem was."

"Mickey?"

"Mickey didn't have the balls to make a problem, let alone solve one. Mickey had the same problem you did. Vicki Albright."

It's like Alvin had been sitting in on my therapy sessions all these years. But still. "Thanks, Alvin, but I'm living my dream."

Alvin patted me on the shoulder. "Sure you are, kid."

*T*he driver took me from No Sleep to Black Pine Resort. I used the energy from my caffeine and sugar high to create a to-do list while we sped across town. Finding a possible dead woman was at the top of the list. That box remained unchecked. Orlando was sub-listed on that topic. Speaking to resort guests about spotting Cambria's double came third. There was the matter of professional film equipment. Maybe a hobby for Cam-Cam or maybe she rented it? Last on my list was choosing a

Theodore-worthy outfit for his party, but I wrote that in tiny letters so I wouldn't appear shallow.

As I was the only one reading the list, I didn't know who I was kidding. But I really needed to up the hotness factor if Cambria refused my plus one invite.

At the reception desk, I spoke to Cesar, the clerk. Orlando was not in his room. Cesar also couldn't remember the last time he saw Orlando, but the resort was full and busy.

"Maizie Albright, right?" Cesar cut his eyes toward the office and handed me an envelope.

"What's this?"

"It's something to help you." Noting my confused expression, he lowered his voice and spoke through his teeth. "With finding guests? Can you take it before someone sees us?"

"Okay." I slipped the envelope to my side. "Thanks?"

"I'm a fan," he called out. "I'm glad your show is filming in Black Pine. What a treat for us."

As it seemed we were breaking some privacy legalities and as I had no idea why, I didn't correct him about my part in the show. "I appreciate this very much. I can do discreet."

"Your mother said as much," whispered Cesar.

"Say what?" I opened the envelope. A printing of the current guest listing, including room numbers, was inside. "Vicki Albright left this for me? Vicki Albright wanted you to give me this list?"

"Thank her for her generosity," Cesar whispered. "And for understanding why I didn't want to be filmed handing it over."

I chewed my lip. My life often expressed itself with these ethical conundrums. Usually, they're not so conundrum-y. I glanced around the room and lowered my voice. "Did Vicki Albright say anything about Cambria?"

"Oh no, speaking about any particular guest would be in violation of the resort's rules."

"Of course." My brain hurt. "I'm working with Cambria, that's why I brought it up. Um, thanks."

"Anytime."

"By the way, have you seen someone who looks like Cambria but isn't Cambria?"

"I wish." He sighed. "I don't even see Cambria."

"Anybody sketchy asking about her? Giving her trouble?"

He straightened. "We don't do sketchy. Absolutely not. No need to worry, Miss Albright."

"What about a fan? Any fans asking for her? Or lurking about?"

"Like I said, we never speak about guests. Cambria isn't even on the registry."

I glanced at the envelope he had just given me. "But she is staying here."

"I don't know that." He raised his brows.

"Right." No crazy fans stalking Cam-Cam. Which meant she hadn't reached that pinnacle of success, or if she had, Black Pine Resort wouldn't mention it because they didn't do sketchy.

I wandered to the sitting area of the lobby, collapsed on a leather chair, and stared at the envelope. How would Vicki know I needed the resort's guest list? And why would she help me?

Oh, hells. Unless she knew about Cambria's transgression. Which meant, what? That she wanted me to solve the Case of the Missing Body Double? And if I used this list would that mean I was working for Vicki? Because I swore an oath to the universe that I would "live through the last season of *All is Albright*, and when it's all over, I'll never go Vicki again."

But I needed this list.

I smoothed the folded document open in my lap and scanned it.

Cambria was registered as "Diana Prince." I thought she'd be more original.

Orlando Feelzen was registered as himself. Giulio, too, in case the public or paparazzi needed to find him.

Alvin Murphy, Dahlia Pearson, and Ed Farmer had villas near Cambria. Leonard wasn't listed, although he could use an unassuming alias. Perhaps this John Doe in villa eight? I recognized some *All is Albright* crew in the hotel, giving me hope that the

Black Pine location shoot was temporary. Only Vicki had gotten a house.

I double scanned for Jerry.

No Jerry. Unless he was staying with Vicki. My stomach knotted and I tasted curdled pumpkin spice.

I put Jerry out of my head and focused on number three on my list: interviewing guests about body doubles and suspicious activity. I'd start with guests I knew. This early, Giulio was likely at home. Maybe he'd met Orlando. Maybe he also knew his villa neighbors and had seen Cambria with another Cambria.

After scoring a golf cart from Carlos the valet, I pointed the cart toward the villas. Working with the industry while not working "in the industry" could prove itself a sweet deal. If only Nash could understand the benefit. And how much I missed the perks. Like golf carts instead of walking and Escalades with a driver instead of dirt bikes. And muffin baskets.

Speaking of muffin baskets.

I slowed the golf cart and turned back. It took me a minute to find the delivery entrance for the hotel. The huge stone and timber building had a matching false wall hiding the employee area from the cart path that ran alongside the lake. A single drive led to the basement doors and unloading dock. Here were the dumpsters and other unsavory necessities for running a 5-star hotel. Including, as I figured, a patio table and chairs for the resort's employees.

Parking the cart, I waved at the circle sitting around the table, smoking and drinking bottled water and sodas. A man and a woman stood, but the other two remained seated, watching my approach.

"How can I help you?" asked the standing woman. She wore the resort's plaid vest and black slacks like the others. The standing man had a security badge and a tie.

"Just a quick question." I gave them my Teen Award red carpet smile. "The villas are usually cleaned around three, right? But when are the breakfast baskets picked up?"

"Do you need your cottage cleaned at a different time, Miss Albright? Or was there a problem with your basket?"

I shook my head. "No, everything is fine. I'm asking for Cambria. I mean Diana Prince in villa six. Yesterday evening her muffin basket hadn't been picked up. I guess she had a DND on her room yesterday, but did anyone do a turndown service? Do you know who specifically took care of her room yesterday? I'd like to talk to them."

The woman glanced at the man. He grabbed a walkie talkie off the table and ran for the back door, speaking into the walkie while he ran.

"I assure you, there's no issue with the service," I said. "And the muffins are delicious, by the way. Please compliment your baker."

The seated housekeepers glanced at one another. One lifted her cigarette, took a last drag and stubbed it out.

"Nice day." I smiled and bounced on the balls of my feet. "Sorry to interrupt your break."

"Would you like to go inside? Maybe the manager's office?" The woman shifted. "You'll be more comfortable."

"Oh, it's no problem." Then I understood. She and the other housekeepers would be more comfortable. "I'll go sit in my golf cart. You carry on."

Carry on? Where was I? *Downton Abbey*?

Trudging to my cart, I fought off the flush heating my skin that wasn't from the Georgia sun beating on my back. I wasn't following the upstairs/downstairs rules. And I knew the rules. In my past life, I had housekeepers, gardeners, drivers, and pool boys. Although the pool boy was actually a woman named Joyce. Vicki had often harangued me about spending time in the kitchen with the staff. She said they couldn't relax and be themselves if I hung around them. It made me mindful of respecting their space, although Miss Cristina said she didn't mind.

Of course, Vicki also said that Miss Cristina was making me fat, and I might gain an El Salvadorian accent. I didn't think the latter was true, although the former probably was. Miss Cristina made tamales to die for.

In the cart, I studied my list. To give an appearance of staying busy and not interfering with their smoke break, I created a 3.5 check box and wrote: "speak to staff." Checking the box, I felt accomplished. Then I flipped the paper over and began a shoe list for Theodore's party. I had narrowed the list down to a Chloé and a metallic Sergio Rossi with an ankle strap when I remembered a pair of Walter de Silva's I had yet to wear. I looked up and saw the security guard with the walkie.

"Miss Coxon, the manager, wants to see you." He gave an apologetic dip of his head. "Would you mind going back up to the entrance? She'll meet you there."

Craptastic. The same manager who got all uptight over my reporting the dead body. Which would make a person uptight. But I certainly didn't want her all up in my B over the housekeeping service.

"Sure," I said. "Let her know I'll be up in a jiffy. And could you ask her to call Giulio Belloni in villa three to let him know I'll be late? Thanks much."

Granted, the last bit was a power move. But if Miss Coxon had gotten wind of my perhaps illegal room registry list, I'd need some backup. It was time to play Vicki Albright.

Sometimes you had to play the bad guy to get what you really wanted.

TWELVE

#DontMessWithTheB #PowerFail

---

*R*obin Coxon waited for me under the resort's timber and slate portico. I parked the golf cart, gave Carlos an "it's all cool" nod, and greeted Miss Coxon.

"Let's go to your office." I breezed through the doorway with Miss Coxon trailing behind me. "Giulio's waiting for me. I don't want to take up much of your time."

I halted, realizing I didn't know where her office was located. Big mistake. Miss Coxon took the lead, herding me down a short hall behind the reception desk. Vicki would have had the conversation in the foyer where Miss Coxon would have to worry about other guests.

Shizzles, I was bad at power play moves.

We strode into a sitting area, and she halted before a closed door to pull out her keys.

"Miss Coxon," I said, trying to regain my Vicki-inspired character. "I'm in a bit of a hurry. Do you have the information about Cambria's room? Who cleaned it and when?"

She pushed open her door. "Have a seat inside."

"That's all right." I inched my chin higher and folded my arms. "I'm sure you're busy as well. The information?"

"The warrant?"

"Excuse me?"

"I assume you have a warrant. I don't need to give you information about my staff otherwise. And, oh wait, you're not police anyway."

"I'm not here to give your staff any trouble. I'm assisting Leonard Shackleton by helping Cambria." The dropped names hit the floor like a platinum balloon.

"I see." Robin's voice grew frostier. "Then you can relay the issue to me. What do you need to know about the service for villa six?"

"I'd rather talk to the housekeeper myself." I wanted a first-hand account of what she'd seen in the rooms. In case she'd spotted any film equipment. Or blood. Or bodies, for that matter. "The room wasn't serviced at the regular time. I want to know if it was cleaned that night. And if there were any items the housekeeper might have noticed."

"Are the items missing? Are you accusing my housekeeper of theft?"

"No." I dropped my arms. "I don't think so."

"You don't think so? Just why do you need this information? Because you are trying to prove you saw something in Cambria's villa when you were just snooping? And trespassing?"

"I wasn't trespassing. And I was hired to snoop, by the way." That sounded different in my head. "Cambria knew I was coming. Or at least, Leonard Shackleton had sent me to bring her to dinner."

"Wasn't she at the Cove and not dead in her room, like you told the police?" Robin's jaw tightened. "What are you trying to pull?"

"Pull?" Vicki wasn't working. I switched to Julia Pinkerton, a more natural role for me. Placing my hands on my hips, I leaned forward. I could almost feel my old cheer skirt brushing the tops of my thighs. "Listen, Miss Coxon. I don't 'pull.' But I can push. As in push the police to investigate this further. I work for a private investigation office, and we have connections. I know what I saw.

Obviously, it wasn't Cambria, but something's going on in that villa. Something that could cause the resort a lot of problems."

"Are you threatening me?"

"I'm not the threat. The threat comes from the secret in villa six." Whoops, that sounded like an episode of *Kung Fu Kate*. I had switched from teen detective snark to kid spy cornball. "Anyway, I can help you by you helping me. Let's *Jerry Maguire* this problem."

She studied me for a minute. Turned to the phone on her desk. Punched in a number and turned back to face me. "Security, can you escort Maizie Albright from my office? I need her off the premises."

"What?" I tripped out of my forward lean and straightened. "You can't escort me. Giulio's waiting for me."

"And make sure she doesn't return. She'll be trespassing otherwise." Robin hung up and folded her arms.

"You can't kick me off the resort. I have to come to the resort to watch Cambria. It's my job."

"Sorry." She didn't sound very sorry.

"But I'm Maizie Albright."

A knock sounded on the outer door. I glanced over my shoulder. The security guy from the service area, who didn't look so apologetic now. His neck also looked thicker. Which was probably an optical illusion caused by my nerves.

"Sucks to be you," she said and closed the door.

Yes. Yes, it did.

J had hit a new low. I'd never been kicked out of any place that wasn't a club. To be kicked out of a luxury resort, without mind-altering chemicals, was just unheard of. When a girl hits the skids, she needs comfort. To go to a place without judgment. Where selfish indulgence is overlooked. Where everyone knows your name.

I'm speaking, of course, of a salon. And my salon of choice was LA HAIR. However, Tiffany and Rhonda were not my stylists.

Tiffany and Rhonda were my friends. But I also wanted my nails done. It's the comfort food of fashion.

"You're an idiot to get involved," said Tiffany, examining the coat of China Glaze's Boho Blues she'd just applied to my left hand.

"I think it was a good idea," said Rhonda. She spun herself in a salon chair, faced the mirror, and ran her fingers over her long, blonde waves. "Until it turned out bad. Like this weave."

"Which is what makes both of you an idiot." Tiffany shoved my hand into the UV lamp and glanced at Rhonda. "You are not Beyoncé. I told you those extensions would be a pain in the ass. Beyoncé has people to help her with the maintenance. Also, she has the body to go with the length."

"I have the body, girl." Rhonda spun back to face us. "I just don't have the height."

Tiffany snorted. "Excuse me, are we talking about the same Beyoncé?"

True friendship like this, I'd not before experienced. According to Rhonda and Tiffany, friends keep it real. Sometimes painfully so.

"We need the money, and this job is worth a lot of ka-ching and the possibility of an awesome rep for future gigs. How was I to know that Cam-Cam would house a body in her room?" I lowered my voice. The salon was empty, but one of the stylists, Ashley, washed towels in the stock room. "This is on the down-low, by the way."

"Naturally." Tiffany shrugged. "Who doesn't get doing a job for money?"

"I can do down-low like nobody's business," said Rhonda.

"Right." Tiffany rolled her eyes. "Anyway, who are we going to tell?"

"You work in a salon."

Rhonda crossed her fingers and kissed them. "Do you think she's really dead? The lookalike?"

"I really thought so. But where did she go and why? The most obvious: dumping her in the lake. Someone staying or working at the resort. Stashed her somewhere and transported her later that night. Everyone has golf carts."

"Good idea," said Tiffany. "They can drag the lake."

"Nash said it's costly for the police. They can't justify it unless they know someone is really missing."

"Don't forget about what happened to Selena," said Rhonda. "Who's Cambria's fan club president?"

"No idea unless it's her director, Ed Farmer," I said. "But I did ask the resort's desk clerk about stalkers. I don't know about theater fans, but it's possible one might have flown to Georgia to stalk Cambria and killed the double by mistake. Possible but a stretch. And it still doesn't explain why there was a double in her bedroom in the first place. With movie equipment. I'm hoping Cambria's boyfriend might know something about that part."

"Like he did a sex tape with Cambria's double by mistake?" said Tiffany. "If that's what he says, don't believe him. They'll use that excuse every time."

"You need to sneak into that resort is what you need to do," said Rhonda. "Orlando isn't going to help you. Find the house-keeper and talk to her."

"The housekeeper isn't going to talk to her," said Tiffany. "Unless you pay her."

"I don't have any money," I said. "I spent my weekly allowance on a donut and coffee."

"And your nails, right?" Tiffany raised a brow until I nodded. "Okay, if you can't pay her off, then you need to threaten her."

"I'm not going to threaten a housekeeper." I crossed my arms, then uncrossed them. "But you have a point about sneaking onto the resort. I'd love to get a look at Cambria's villa. She wouldn't let me in. And I've got no chance of seeing it with her now."

"You could do a disguise." Rhonda squealed, glanced at the closed stock room door, and placed her hands over her mouth to muffle her words. "I could color your hair and do your makeup. Get some contacts to cover those green eyes. Do a hunchback or something."

"I draw the line at my hair," I said. "But I'd do contacts and a wig. The hunchback is a bit overboard."

"How are you going to get into her room?" said Tiffany.

"Cam-Cam's doing a reading today. She'll keep her bag with the key nearby. If she were filming, I could probably get it from her trailer." I studied the stained ceiling tiles, thinking.

"Do a housekeeper's disguise." Rhonda clapped her hands. "Pretend to clean Cambria's room."

"How am I supposed to get their uniform? They're really strict at the resort."

"I betcha that Giulio could get you a uniform," said Tiffany. "He's still staying there, isn't he?"

"How could Giulio get a uniform?"

"Oh, he can." Rhonda nodded vigorously. "He's got a rep. I've heard."

I slapped my palm against my forehead. "Are you serious?"

Tiffany smirked. "Don't worry, he's telling everyone he's mending his broken heart. That you broke."

"Using me as a…" I choked down my words. "That…"

"I don't think anyone believes the part about the broken heart," said Rhonda. "Don't feel bad. But use it to your advantage."

"Believe me, I will."

J returned to the office on Lucky, which didn't help my feelings of humiliation and inadequacy. Lamar and Nash were not around, and for once I was glad to be alone in the dingy office. I needed time to come up with a plan. A plan that included a way to break the news to Nash that I'd been kicked off the resort without him going ballistic. Also, a solution to that problem would be good.

Why did I think I could play Vicki? I guess there were some characters I just couldn't pull off and "power woman" was one of them. Girl power, yes. Power woman, no. Robin Coxon did a good power woman. Although kicking me off the resort seemed a teensy extreme. It wasn't like I was going to look for dead bodies in all the villas. Just Cambria's.

Speaking of bodies, I called Giulio.

"You're telling Black Pine women I broke your heart to get them to sleep with you? Have you no conscience?"

"Darling, you know I value the subconscious over the conscience. It guides my craft."

"Seriously. Black Pine is not like LA."

"You are right. The women here are wonderful. Not so jaded and bitter."

I bit down hard on my lip and counted to ten. "You're goading me. Listen, I need a favor, and you're going to do this to make up for using me as an unwilling wing man."

"With a private dick case? Then you have to reveal all the dirty little secrets. I am so bored here, Maizie." I could hear his pout. "I want to play cops with you. It's unfair that you have all the fun."

"It's not as much fun as you'd think." I hesitated. "I need to get into Cambria's villa without her knowing. You might be able to help."

"What can I do? Seduce Cambria for you?"

"How does that help? Do you think about anything other than sex?"

"God made me this way, what can I do?"

"I'm looking for evidence in her villa. I can't tell you why. But I'm hoping it's camera equipment. Like the professional stuff."

"I never knew Cambria was a cinematographer. Is it a hobby?"

"Not sure. I thought Cambria was only interested in one side of the camera."

"Spoken like a true diva. And why the interest in Cambria's hobbies?"

It had not gone by my notice that as Giulio's interest piqued, his accent lulled. I needed to be careful. Giulio was a worse gossip than my new friend Theodore.

"You've probably heard Leonard Shackleton hired us to keep an eye on Cambria. She's an insurance risk. I'm just typing up loose threads."

"Darling, you're keeping secrets from your Giulio. Get her key and meet me at my villa. We'll snoop together."

"That's the thing. I'm not allowed on the resort anymore. I'm going to need your help getting to her villa. I was hoping you could get me a housekeeping uniform."

"That's from a *Julia Pinkerton* script."

"It worked great on *Julia Pinkerton*."

"It was a script, darling. I don't think they actually tested for accuracy."

"It'll work. Just see what you can do. But don't seduce any housekeepers. Just steal a uniform, then return it. So it's not really stealing."

"What size?"

"Any size."

"Really, darling? *'Any size?'* What if you burst a seam? Wardrobe malfunctions happen."

I counted to ten using my best yoga breathing to maintain peace. "And be careful. The manager is not impressed with celebrity status."

"Maizie, please lighten up. Your instructions are tiresome."

"I have a lot of rules in my new job." I glanced at the clock on the wall. "I need to check in at the set. I'll call you later to see if you have the uniform."

"I accept my mission. You can reward me later."

By reward, I hope he meant donuts.

*U*pon arriving at the warehouse, I learned Cambria was resting in her trailer. I headed for the crafts room and began loading my plate, hoping to catch a quick meal before doing diva duty.

"We met last night."

I turned and found Ed Farmer behind me. "Yes, we did. Nice to see you again." I fast chewed a mouthful of trail mix and slipped my plate to the side where the mound of food wouldn't be so noticeable. "How did the reading go?"

"We're taking a break." Ed grabbed a plate and stared at the arranged fruit slices. "Leonard hired you to make sure Cambria doesn't get into trouble."

"Yes?"

"Is she in trouble? She seems distracted."

"Um, I'm not exactly sure. I'm checking into that?"

Ed set his plate on the table, pushed his glasses up his nose, then ran a hand through his thick, sandy brown hair. "I know who you are. Let's not bullshit each other. I need Cambria focused on the part and nothing else. She nailed her reading today, but I can tell she's skittish about something. Calm her down."

"Okay. But Leonard wanted me to—"

"I don't care about Leonard. I only care about Cambria right now. She needs to be focused on a good delivery."

"But if she—"

"You're not listening." Ed centered his steely gaze on mine.

I recognized the look. A director's "pay close attention to what I'm saying because you're screwing up my scene" look. Calling on my fear of disappointing directors, I concentrated on Ed.

"Cambria is the racehorse, and you are her goat."

"I'm a what?"

"A stable goat calms thoroughbreds. Look it up."

"I'm a goat." I changed my tone and emphasis. "I'm a goat."

"It's not a line. I'm not giving you direction." He ran his hands through his hair and pulled on the ends. "Not that kind of direction. Just be Cambria's goat and forget this other stuff."

"Do you know about the other stuff?"

"I don't want to know." Ed grabbed his empty plate and stalked away.

Passing Ed, Leonard spotted me, rushed into the room, and closed the door. "Did you find out what the body double did?"

"It's not *Pine Hollow*'s body double. That actress is still in LA.

I'm trying to find who I saw. But Cambria isn't cooperating, the resort won't let me look around, and Ed Farmer wants me to drop the investigation so I can be Cambria's goat."

"What?" Leonard shook his head. "Ed Farmer's interfering? He's a control freak. Pain in the ass. But a brilliant pain in the ass. Do what he wants, the animal whatever, but I need you to find out what happened with the body double."

"Okay." I hated getting mixed directorial notes. A total "trying to please everyone but pleasing no one" Catch-22.

"I need to know this problem isn't going to blow up on us when we're in the middle of production. What did this body double do anyway?"

"I'm still not really sure, Mr. Shackleton. I saw a body on the floor of Cambria's room. I thought the body was Cambria. Turns out she just looks like Cambria." I paused and pushed out the bad news in one breath. "Oh, and the body appeared dead. Which is why I'm worried about it?"

Leonard stared without blinking, rooted to the spot. His ruddy complexion turned white, reddened, then paled again in a matter of seconds. Grabbing my arm, he pulled me from the food table and into a corner of the room. "Are you serious?"

I nodded. "You don't look good. Can I get you a glass of water?"

"No. But good idea." He pulled out a medicine vial, popped the top with his thumb, shook out a pill, and dry swallowed. "Talk."

I explained what happened at Cambria's villa. "And I didn't tell you at dinner because Cambria was obviously alive. I thought she had just been — you know, kinky whatever — and I had been mistaken. Especially since there wasn't a body when I returned with the police. It wasn't until I saw her nude this morning that I realized it wasn't Cambria. No birthmark."

Leonard repeated a litany of curses, then looked at me. "Okay. The police think you just saw an unconscious body. They're not getting involved."

"Right. For now, anyway. If a body shows up, they'll be on it in a heartbeat."

"But a body would have shown up by now, right?"

"I don't really know. I think I learned some statistics about that in my criminal justice classes, but I can't really—"

"I don't want statistics. And I don't want the police." Leonard shoved his hands in his pockets and began to pace. "Find Cambria's boyfriend and ask him what happened."

"Yes. And maybe you could make Cam-Cam talk to me because that would be really helpful."

Leonard spun and retraced his steps. "Cambria. I wonder—"

"And then we'll know what to do, and I can just go back to being a goat." I felt relieved to get this off my chest and have a plan. And a way to force a confession out of Cambria. Which I could report to my mother. And we'd all live happily ever after. Except for the possibly dead woman.

He stopped before me. "Ed Farmer doesn't want you to upset Cambria."

"Yes, but don't you think—"

Leonard placed a finger to my lips. "And I don't want to upset Ed Farmer. Ed is brilliant but fragile. A genius. We can't disturb a genius. Also, he's hard to control, and I choose my battles wisely when it comes to a film of this magnitude. Ed Farmer could make this movie a lot more expensive than it already is. If he has, God forbid, a breakdown or something, it will halt production indefinitely."

"So I should be the goat? Or just keep looking for Cambria's lookalike?" It was hard to get the words out with Leonard's finger mashed against my lips.

"Yes." Leonard pulled off his finger and grabbed my chin. "You've got this."

It was even harder to talk with Leonard gripping my chin. "So you'll talk to Cambria?"

"No." He bent to peck me on the cheek. "I'm glad you understand."

I didn't understand anything. Except I might be a goat.

THIRTEEN

#NoGoat #StripperKicks

---

*G*oat duties proved difficult when your thoroughbred wouldn't let you in her stable. Or trailer as it was. I hammered on Cam-Cam's door. She called me a few names I won't repeat. I told her she didn't mean it.

She told me she did.

I borrowed a folding chair from the makeup trailer's patio set and dragged it back to Cam-Cam's.

"Don't do anything crazy in there," I called. "If I can't be a goat for Mr. Farmer, at least let me do the job for Mr. Shackleton."

No response. I hoped it meant she was sleeping and not inhaling bath salts.

Although come to think of it, I'd not seen Cambria imbibe anything that didn't involve fair trade-cultivated, non-GMO, carb and gluten-free sustenance. Maybe my task as Cam-Cam's handler was as irrelevant as she insisted. Nevertheless, I had a contract, and she had a contract. Also, she had a possible dead body. And now Leonard Shackleton knew about the possible dead body. And had added the body's discovery to my list of babysitting duties.

It's a little hard finding a body when I actually had to babysit.

I hopped out of the deck chair and raced back to makeup.

Borrowed a phone and called LA HAIR. Fifty minutes later, Tiffany and Rhonda, stood in front of the trailer. Slightly agog. Rhonda's cherubic face was tilted toward the tinted trailer window, her mouth open and chocolate brown eyes wide in adoration. Tiffany looked less impressed, but I could spot her interest in the way she squinted past the cigarette clenched between her lips.

Tiff and Rhonda were not part of my former life, so they're still fascinated with celebs. Although maybe not as much now that they knew one. An ex-one. That's how I kept it real for them.

Tiffany's blue-tipped bob swung as she swiveled from the trailer to me. "Cambria's in there right now?"

"I think she's taking a nap. But I'm not really sure since she stopped talking to me." I shrugged. "Hopefully she's not doing anything that screws up publicity or production for the movie. Although she may have done that already."

Rhonda's head had tipped back until her extensions brushed the top of her butt. "Oh, my Lord. I can't believe that's really Cambria's trailer home."

"I can't believe they make trailers like this," said Tiffany. "It's like one of those tiny houses except it's huge."

"She doesn't live there, it's just for chilling on set," I said. "There's a lot of downtime, but you have to be available."

Tiffany gave me a look.

I scrambled to explain. "Cam-Cam will have to arrive at five-ish for makeup and costume, but that takes a while. She'll also be waiting for lighting and sound. They'll do the same scene multiple times — maybe more after the director and producers watch the dailies — but you have to work in breaks for the crew and waiting for the special effects peeps to set up their stuff again, then cameras, lighting, and sound again. The actors have to wait some-where. Some place quiet if they need to learn new lines or work-shop their characters. Or do video conferencing and interviews."

"So they spend a lot of time doing nothing?" Tiffany squinted, revealing her expertly lined and layered eyeshadow/eyeliner combo. "In a trailer that costs ten times more than my house."

"Maybe also doing business deals for their product lines," I said. "But not everyone gets a trailer like this."

"Just Cambria." Rhonda sighed. "She's been on *TMZ* and E! a lot lately. She's the bad girl of Hollywood. At the moment."

"It does seem to depend on the day," I agreed. "Anyhoo, she's in there. Hopefully sleeping or practicing those lines. And she won't come out until I'm back. Hopefully."

"And they're paying you to make sure she's not in there having an Anna Nicole Smith moment?" said Tiffany.

"I guess you could put it that way."

"So why aren't you in there?"

"Cam-Cam doesn't want me in there."

Tiffany cocked a hip and placed a hand on it for emphasis.

"You're right." I sighed. "I tell myself that I don't care what she thinks about me, but I guess I do. And to be honest, I don't want to go in there. It makes me feel…not good."

"It smells?" said Rhonda.

"Jealous," I whispered.

"You miss this," said Tiffany.

"No, I don't." I chewed my lip. "Yes, I do. It's complicated."

"Oh, baby." Rhonda opened her arms, and I fell into her. "Of course, you miss it. Anyone in their right mind would miss it. You had a fabulous life. Money, power, and fame. Who wouldn't miss that?"

"I don't think she had that much power," said Tiffany. "I think her mother had the power."

"True." I sniffled and gave Rhonda another squeeze. She smelled like white musk, but also of hope. And Downey. "I don't miss that. Plus, I've always wanted to be a private investigator and here I am. Privately investigating Cambria's possibly dead body double."

"So go do your detective thing," said Rhonda. "We'll sit here and make sure Cambria doesn't leave. If she does, we'll follow her. And maybe get an autograph."

"You're the best." I gave her another hug then turned to Tiffany.

Tiffany smelled like OPI and menthol. She didn't need hope because she had grit.

Tiff patted my shoulder and shoved me off. "Go find your body."

*L*ike its name, Black Pine Golf and Yacht Club and Resort took up a lengthy bit of real estate. Stretching along Black Pine Lake, the club anchored one end and the resort the other. In the middle was the Cove. As a restaurant and bar, the Cove was open to the public. Therefore, I figured, I had not been barred from entering that property. I had Giulio meet me there with the housekeeper's uniform that would allow me to sneak into Cam-Cam's villa. When I had popped into Cam-Cam's trailer to announce I had deputized Tiffany and Rhonda, I took her key.

Cambria didn't notice me slipping her purse off the floor and behind the trailer's staircase to grab her card. Only that Tiffany and Rhonda were not Nash. Let me tell you, she had plenty to say about that. I reminded her of her insurance issues and took off.

At the Cove, I found Giulio at the inside bar, drinking a Campari and soda. His casual lean against the bar was convincing and the conspiratorial wink he gave the bartender at my entrance, unnerving.

The bartender, Alex — a.k.a. total asshat who had pimped me out to the paparazzi when I first appeared in Black Pine — spied my look and hoofed it to the other end of the bar to slice limes.

"*Ciao*." Giulio bent to kiss the cheek I offered, but deftly turned his head to plant a firm one on my lips. "What no tongue?"

I ignored his playacting. "Where's the uniform?"

He pointed to the bag on the floor and picked up his Campari. "Can I order you something?"

"I'm good." I had hit the craft table's snack section on my way off the set. Turns out I knew the caterer, Big Jim. I always got along well with craft caterers, another disappointment on Vicki's list. Her diet stuck to biting the hand that literally fed her.

"Thanks for this," I said. "Was it too much trouble? No ravishing of any housekeepers?"

Placing a hand on his heart, Giulio mock winced. "Darling, I didn't go near the staff. I had a better idea."

Giulio's ideas didn't win many awards. I gave him my best suspicious brow raise.

"I'm coming with you. It will be like old times. Julia Pinkerton and associate takes the case." He bowed, then slipped his arm through mine. "A sidekick is good, no?"

I slid off his arm. "You were never on *Julia Pinkerton*. Besides, you couldn't pull off a housekeeping act. You don't know which end of the broom to push."

"I could say the same to you." He snorted. "You forget, I also have a villa. My disguise is myself."

"No."

"Oh yes." He winked. "I get you into the resort as my guest."

I opened the bag. "What is this?" I pulled out a pair of seven-inch heels. Blue glitter platform with a clear plastic slide strap. "What the hells, Giulio. Housekeepers don't wear stripper kicks."

He grinned. "There is also a wig."

"It's pink."

"I know." He waggled his eyebrows.

I flapped a tube of black nylon and spandex at him. "This isn't even going to cover one thigh."

"I had to guess your size, but it's stretchy."

"It's not a uniform."

"In a sense, it is. Don't worry, darling, you're going to look fabulous."

"As a hooker?"

"*Passeggiatrice*? I'd never. You are...what do you call it?" Giulio snapped his fingers. "An escort."

"I feel so much better." I squished the bag shut. "You're lucky I'm in a hurry."

"That does not make me feel lucky. But I take what I can get. I'm so bored."

Ten minutes later I stashed my clothes and teetered into the bar, feeling like a sausage on stilts. The black lycra covered me from mid-thigh to upper chest but squeezed all my parts toward my neck. If I looked down, my chin hit my girls. I wanted to kill Giulio, but with the wig and heels, it certainly transformed me. I was unrecognizable. Nobody would see me past my boobs.

Alex did a double take, then shot toward our end. Forgetting the flip top was closed, he slammed into the bar, bounced off, opened the door, and fell out. Grabbing my arm, he hustled me out of the bar, through the foyer, and onto the parking lot.

"You can't work here. We have a dress code. Leave some business cards for my guests, and I can hand them out if they inquire. Where's your car?" Avoiding my bulging chest-ages, he craned his neck, searching for my invisible vehicle.

"Watch it, buster." I'd worked on a voice while I dressed in the bathroom. *Mighty Aphrodite* meets Jade from *The Hangover*. Alex had no idea who I really was. And it felt great to pull one over on him.

Giulio strolled out the door and tapped the bartender on the shoulder. "She's with me."

Alex swung around, red-faced. "I'm sorry, Mr. Belloni. It's just that we have a dress code—"

"Say no more." Giulio slipped a bill into Alex's vest pocket and patted his chest. "Call my golf cart. We go to the villas."

*W*e parked at Giulio's villa — number three — and hoofed it toward number six. Hoofing it in seven-inch platforms is an oxymoron, by the way. Ten steps in and we stopped so I could barefoot it to villa six. The guest registry list told us villas seven, eight, and five were Agent Alvin Murphy's, John Doe's, and Ed Farmer's. Number four had been Vicki's, but I didn't recognize the name of the current guest.

Except for the buzzing lawn mower on the fifth green, all was quiet. Giulio took my hand, claiming it would look more "realistic." Which led to an argument about whether johns would hold hands with hookers.

In the midst of our argument, the lawn mower cut off. A door banged behind us, muffling voices. Giulio pulled me against a tree and flattened his body over mine.

"I should look like I am overcome by passion for you," he whispered in my ear. "In case this person is watching."

"Then I'm going to look like I'm holding out for more money since doing me against a tree is extra. Get off." I pushed on his chest. "I'm not worried about guests. The costume is to get past the staff. You do this, and someone's going to report us for public indecency. That'll get us both hauled away. To jail."

"That would be a shame. Because I am really enjoying this rendezvous."

"It's not a rendezvous. Don't make me sorry I involved you. I'm about to send you back to your villa."

We tried the tiny kitchen entrance on number six. "We've got to go in through the front with this key," I said. "You go in and unlock this door for me. An escort may visit your villa, but I'm going to stick out on Cam-Cam's porch."

"I don't know about that," said Giulio. "There's much innuendo about Cambria's appetites."

"She must be playing some kind of PR game. I don't understand what happened. When I knew her, she was very serious about her craft and her studies. We were kids, of course. But I've not seen her touch anything that qualifies as toxic. People included. Unless you count Vicki."

"Vicki?" Giulio sucked in his breath. "What is Vicki doing with Cambria?"

"She wants to manage her."

Giulio swore in Italian. "I've asked her to do the same, but no. She does not want me. And this season, I'm barely on. She's using the new hires but keeps me here in Black Pine when I could be in LA, doing other jobs while I wait. I've had it with your *madre*, Maizie."

"You're preaching to the choir. Except I've had it with her for the last twenty-five years. Now scoot."

A minute later, he unlocked the door, and I stepped inside.

"Darling, you put the platforms back on. *Grazie amore mio*." He sighed. "I cannot help myself. They are vulgar, but—"

"Let's shelve your shoe fetish." I patted his cheek. "And to be clear, I put them on so I wouldn't leave footprints. Dirt path. Bare feet. You know?"

"What are we looking for?"

"Anything film related. I saw professional camera equipment. Lights, the whole shebang. Cam-Cam's always got her phone with her, but she might have a laptop or a tablet here. Of course, it's probably password protected."

"I am excited," whispered Giulio. "I'm finally doing a *Julia Pinkerton* scene."

"Go be excited while you search."

I scanned the kitchen. The fridge revealed power shakes, water, and a stash of Snickers in the freezer. Likely, the only illegal substance in the house.

Moving from the galley kitchen, I entered the living area. Roomy and comfy with a pile rug, wood floors, and Craftsman-styled leather furniture. "I could totally live here," I said.

"The villas are very comfortable," Giulio answered from the bedroom. "Vicki suggested I buy a home, but why? I am a man of few needs. Most of my needs are served in the villa and at the Cove. You and those platforms could complete me."

"Also, I guess the show comps your hotel stay?" I paused in my search of the bookcase. "Buy a home? How long does Vicki plan to film *All is Albright* here? When I didn't sign for this season, I thought she'd fly everyone back. Did you say she hired more actors?"

No answer.

I entered the bedroom, looking for Giulio and my unanswered questions. For a beat, I stared at the floor where I'd seen the looka-like. I'd dreaded this moment, unsure of how it'd make me feel.

Cocking my head, I tried to picture the body in its fallen position. Then tried to imagine what happened. Flopped to my stomach to check under the bed. Found nothing. I crawled to the spot on the floor and laid like the body. Got the willies and jumped to my feet. Then fell several times, trying to mimic her splay.

The fourth time, I figured she had fallen off the bed, also remembering the slide of the duvet. That's when I noticed there was no Giulio and called for him

He popped his head from a door next to the bathroom. "She has the new Fontana Milano 1915."

"OMG. That's a two thousand dollar purse." I followed him to the little walk-in closet and checked out the small, brown leather satchel in Giulio's hand. "I miss Barney's so much."

Giulio hugged me. "You are so brave, my darling."

I ran a finger across the gold-stamped logo. "God, I'm jealous she has this. What is wrong with me?"

"Let me comfort you, my Maizie." His hand ran over my hip and up my side.

I batted it away. "Nice try. Did you look for anything besides designer items?"

"No camera equipment." He unzipped the top of the bag and rooted around, pulling out a small card and a lipstick. He handed me the card, pulled the top off the lipstick, and smelled it. "*Buon profumo.*"

I glanced at Giulio. "Don't do that. It's bad enough we're going through her stuff."

"I like the color." Giulio paused from testing the lipstick on his wrist and looked at the card I examined. "Is it important?"

I sucked in a breath. "The card's from the couture shop in Palm Beach. Someone wrote, 'You'll always be my favorite Lady M.' I bet Ed Farmer bought this for Cams."

Giulio turned toward a Givenchy hobo bag. "It's not so difficult finding the clues. I could easily do this role."

"This is a better clue for tabloid news, than for me." I gripped

Giulio's hand. The lipstick hung in the air between us. "Did you hear that? Was that a door?"

Giulio's eyes widened. He opened the closet door. "Get in."

"No." I spun in a circle, searching for a better hiding spot. "I can't do closets."

"Darling, I know well your closet-stra-phobia. Close-tro-phobia?" Giulio grabbed my hand, yanking me inside. "There is no time."

He inched the door shut. "Who do you think it is? Cambria? Housekeeping? This is thrilling."

"No, it's not," I whispered, cringing as I bumped into a garment bag. "In real life, it's called breaking and entering, and it's illegal. Stop talking. We'll use up all the oxygen."

I bit down hard on my lip to stop my talking, then placed my free hand over Giulio's mouth.

In the living room, someone paced.

Giulio's rapid breaths struck my hand, chugging like a steam train as I strained to hear. Every hair on my body stood on end.

"I'm on probation." I couldn't breathe in the vinyl tube. My pulse felt erratic. "I'm so going to jail for this."

Footsteps moved from the living room to the bedroom, growing muffled as they passed from wood to carpet.

My bladder tightened, and my stomach loosened. I drew my hand off Giulio's mouth to place it on my chest. The rise and fall quickened. I pulled on the Lycra, trying to draw air into my lungs.

Giulio placed an arm around my waist and drew me closer. I clutched his hand and the Lycra in the other.

The closet door swung open. I shrieked. The lipstick shot out of Giulio's hand and landed on the floor in front of a pair of dusty brown boots.

FOURTEEN

#WhereForeArtThouOrlando
#ClimbOfShame

"What in the Sam Hill are you doing with Giulio in Cambria's closet?" said Nash.

I shoved Giulio off and exited the closet, inhaling oxygen. This was not good. First, I was supposed to be watching Cam-Cam. Second, Nash didn't know I'd been kicked off the resort, so explaining my costume might be difficult. Third, I did not want Nash to think I was consorting with Giulio. In the closet of the woman I was supposed to be watching. He knew I hated closets. It'd seem extra suspicious.

Panting, I babbled, pointing at the places I had seen film equipment. Then I demonstrated the body's positioning by throwing myself on the floor. Which was not flattering in an extreme bandage dress.

Nash's fierce glare did not help matters.

Nor did Giulio, who applauded the scene and asked for an encore. Then drew attention to the lipstick that had somehow become smudged on his neck. He made a show of wiping it off.

"That is not my lipstick—" I stopped my next round of explanation as Nash's hand, which had been tucked tightly under his arms, rose in the air.

"I don't want to know. What are you doing here?"

"Snooping," said Giulio. "Isn't her costume fantastic?"

"You're dressed like that at a resort like this? You're going to get arrested."

"Why should they care if I have the escort?" said Giulio. "The guests will look the other way."

"No, they won't. They'll report you. This is Georgia, not Hollyweird."

"I wish you'd stop calling it that," I said.

"It's unprofessional," said Nash.

I stared at my plastic glitter platforms, then tilted my chin up. "Wait a minute. Why are you here?"

Nash cut his eyes toward Giulio.

"You believe me, and you're checking for evidence of the body, too." I grinned. "But how did you get in?"

"I have an in with maintenance."

"That would have been nice to know before I had to dress like this."

Nash rolled his eyes. "Did you find anything?"

"Only evidence of Ed Farmer's admiration." I waved the tiny gift card.

"Has she said anything more today?"

"No. I left her with Tiffany and Rhonda." At the widening of Nash's eyes, I sped up my words. "She wasn't planning on leaving her trailer, and I trust Tiff and Rhonda to follow her if she does. Leonard wanted me on this. I told him about the body. I was hoping he would talk to Cam-Cam, but I don't think he will. Ed wants her calm and focused on the movie, not on whatever happened here. Leonard doesn't want to upset Ed. But Leonard wants me to figure out what's going on."

Giulio whistled. "You did not tell me any of this. You do Leonard Shackleton's dirty work for him. I thought we are doing Cambria's dirty work. This is much more intriguing. And you did not mention a body."

I spun around to face him. "You need to keep your mouth shut. If this gets out, I'll tell Leonard you were helping me."

"Baby." Giulio ran his hands up my arms. "I'd never give you up."

"Stop it," I hissed.

"Both of you stop it." Nash had knelt on the floor. "Y'all drive me nuts."

My heart flopped. "I already checked under the bed."

He sniffed the carpet, then turned to look at me. "I'm checking for evidence of your body."

"It's not really my body..."

"This is, once again, exciting," said Giulio.

"You are welcome to leave, Mr. Belloni," said Nash. "Miss Albright, turn off the lights and draw the shades as best you can. I need it dark as possible."

After a spirited golf clap, Giulio darted to close the bathroom door. Nash rummaged in a utility case he had left in the corner and pulled out a flashlight. I hit the lights and drew the curtains. The room grayed to twilight. A purplish-blue beam shone on the floor.

"I feel like I'm experiencing CSI as the cop and not the victim this time," said Giulio. "Do you look for blood stains?"

"UV can't detect blood. You need to spray it with luminol or something like that," I said. "But other fluids will show up. If we find a big pee stain, we might have evidence of a body."

The light shone on my face. I squinted, and the light dropped to the ground. "Miss Albright, I'm impressed with your crime scene investigation knowledge."

"I keep telling you the criminal justice professors did teach us some useful things at Long Beach. But I need you to train me as well."

The UV light made a circle eight on the floor.

"You are too cute," said Giulio. "But I want to see the body stain."

The light highlighted a multitude of marks. Most I tried not to think about. But the large one on the floor told us something had been there. Realizing the proximity to my previous flops on the floor, I wanted nothing more than to peel off the tube, dash into the bathroom, and shower.

"It's still not proof she was dead. Only there's a large stain. Someone could have had a drunken accident. Or it could even be some type of cleaner. Housekeeping's been in since and probably soaked it with something." Nash switched the light back on. "I can pass this on to Mowry, but he can't use it for a warrant. We need something else."

"We need to find Orlando Feelzen."

Giulio burst out laughing.

"Seriously, that's the name of Cam-Cam's alleged boyfriend." I made air quotes. "He does stunts."

"You haven't talked to Feelzen yet?" said Nash.

"He wasn't in his room, and they haven't seen him today."

Nash checked his watch, then handed me the key card. "I'm supposed to be back at Cambria's in a minute. If he's still not around, check his room. See if he's got the tape. Maybe it'll show what really happened."

"Tiff and Rhonda are watching Cam-Cam. You didn't want to go near her."

"I got a call, explaining that you've been bumped and I'm on duty. She's ready to leave the set." The weight of his look caused me to shiver. "I also had a call from the resort, letting me know my employee had been forcibly removed and wasn't allowed back."

"About that…"

"Which is why you're disguised as a stripper. Makes total sense."

"Escort," said Giulio.

"I don't know what service you're using, but your 'escort' looks like a low rent stripper," said Nash.

"Hey," I said. "No way could I strip in this dress. I'm going to have to cut it off as it is."

"Do not worry," said Giulio. "I have already thought about how to get it off of you."

"Miss Albright," Nash said quietly. "Let me summarize this mess. You've taken a case I didn't want. You've gotten yourself ejected from the client's current premises, and rejected by the client herself."

"Technically, Leonard Shackleton is the client and Cam-Cam is just—"

"You are zero for three, Miss Albright. And you wonder why I'm not training you in the field? You're lucky you can do the books or I wouldn't have use for you at all. Find out what the boyfriend knows."

Nash picked up his bag and stalked from the room. A moment later, we heard the front door bang shut.

Giulio winced. "I think you're making another career disaster. Is that the right phrase in English?"

I sighed. "I really need to find Orlando."

*I*t was one thing to sneak through the villa area wearing a pink wig, sausage casing, and stripper shoes. It was another to sneak into the hotel where Robin Coxon and her goons patrolled.

Or as some may call them, resort management.

We hurried to Giulio's cottage and called Orlando's room. No answer. I borrowed a coat — Burberry, if nothing else Giulio had style — to wear over the Lycra tube, completing my look as a strip-o-gram. It also made me sweat like the church-going-two-dollar-whore whom I resembled. Giulio grabbed a flat cap, aviator glasses, and flipped the collar up on his Polo.

"It is my American businessman who rents a stripper look."

I shook my head but followed him onto the golf cart to return to the hotel.

"I've heard *Pine Hollow* is a very expensive movie." Giulio glanced at me. "If you don't find this body, it can be disastrous."

"How did you know the title?"

"Everyone knows the title." Giulio shrugged. "They should drop Cambria."

I remembered the card and Dahlia's earlier innuendo. "Ed Farmer may be emotionally invested."

"Maybe they should get another director."

"Leonard's emotionally invested in Ed. Besides, it's probably Ed's script." I bit down on my lip, tasting Urban Decay's "Frenemy." A day of ironies, it seemed. "If what I saw was real, Cam-Cam's going to screw it up. Man, I hope I can find Orlando and clear this up."

"Anyway, I think Cambria will be outshone by Dahlia Pearson."

"Dahlia's part is smaller. You don't believe Cam-Cam can carry the picture?"

Giulio gave another Italian shrug. "Cambria's beautiful and talented, yes. But she lacks something."

"What are you talking about? She was the smartest, most ambitious kid I ever met. Cam-Cam worked harder than me on *Julia Pinkerton*, and she was only a supporting role."

"And how long was she on the show?"

"One season."

"Yet she worked harder than you. It is my point. You and Ed Farmer see the talent and drive. But on the screen, the producers see something else. She doesn't have the...*un certo non-so-che*, you know? She's an A-list actor but not a star." Giulio turned the golf cart from the woods onto the main path. "Even without the weight, Cambria is still the chubby friend. It is an unfortunate reality. She should do theater, not movies. Or go for the humor roles."

"I can't believe you said that. Retract the claws, Shallow Man. I hate that about the industry. Everyone is so 'love yourself as you are' unless you're bigger than a size zero." I squirmed in my bandage dress. "At least Ed Farmer saw beyond body image. Cam-Cam has crazy talent."

"You have never been a size zero," said Giulio. "And you're all the more delicious for it."

"Yeah, right. It's not like we never tried to exercise off the double-Ds for better roles." My thoughts drifted back to Cambria and our child actor days. "I don't get it. Cam-Cam's got a great agent, a chance for a breakthrough role, and she almost blows it by making a home porno? And not even that. It'd been hard for me to believe all those tabloid rumors about her heavy-duty partying. I mean, I saw her in the clubs, but she and I are different creatures."

"You are the more likely hot mess?"

"It's too bad Cam-Cam and I didn't go to the same rehab programs. I'd be able to understand her a little better. Like why she doesn't want me to help her."

"Maybe she doesn't like you." He turned to catch my eye. "Darling, don't look dejected. Everyone can't like you. But I like you. Very much."

"Not as much as you like yourself."

His sigh was more Latin than his lineage. "You wound me yet again. We are nearly there. I will park in the rear and try to sneak you in without much notice. But we need to play the part, so you don't get caught. Scoot close to me and put your hands in the appropriate places."

"When you came up with this costume, did you consider that late afternoon is an odd time for a man to invite an escort dressed like a stripper to his room?"

"We are in Black Pine, Georgia, darling. What do I know about escort etiquette here?" He draped his arm around my shoulders and pulled me into his side.

"And you don't have a room in the hotel."

"Maybe I booked one for the day because I don't want you stealing my Gucci accessories."

I looked up at him. "You've really thought about this, haven't you?"

Giulio slanted a look that dropped from my eyes to my bosom. "I've thought about many things."

I shoved him. "Get over yourself."

"It is unfair. You only have eyes for the private dick. You have the habit of falling for your costar. Like for me, at one time."

I ignored the last bit. Giulio was hired by Vicki for me to fall for him. (Because, ratings.) And stupidly, I did anyway. For a minute. I was the kind of idiot who fell for their costars. "What are you talking about? Mr. Nash is my boss. We just work together. You heard him. He doesn't even like me."

"Boss-director. What is the difference? I see the way you look at him."

"What?" I forced a laugh, then stopped. "Really? Do you think he notices? Oh, my God, I was an actress. How could I be so obvious? Anyway, I'm sure I'll get over it. I always do."

"You always do," echoed Giulio with the perfect twinge of sadness and defeat.

I almost clapped.

We parked behind the hotel. A couple in matching Arnold Palmer pinks half-halted climbing out of their cart to watch us.

"Great costume party," I half-shouted to Giulio. "We'll just change in your room."

We scurried from the carts to the back portico. Using Nash's key, we jerked open the door and slid inside.

"You go first to make sure it's clear for me. I don't want to be caught by the staff. Ms. Coxon could call my probation officer." I shoved him toward the second set of doors.

He turned to give me an appreciative grin. "I am excited again." A second later, he motioned me through, and we slipped into the stairwell.

"Orlando's room is 516." I took off the platforms and started up the stairs.

"I will take the elevator and wait for you. It's better, yes? I can make sure the hallway is clear before you enter." Giulio's head bobbed as he backed out of the stairwell door.

"Thanks a lot."

By floor two, my thighs squeaked inside the Lycra furnace. I took off the coat. On floor four, I pulled off the wig. With the sweat, I figured my ginger hair had darkened enough to qualify as a disguise. By floor five, the dress had become so restrictive, I had to push it up my thighs to give my legs enough room to clear the step. Placing a hand against the stairwell door, I hung my head and panted. The door swung open, knocking me against the stairwell wall. I slid to the floor.

"Stay there," whispered Giulio. "Bell boy."

I didn't really have a choice. My thighs had glued together.

Below me, I heard a door open and slam shut. It sounded several floors down, but I panicked. Pushing my hands and back against the wall, I slid up. Hiked the skirt the rest of the way up and tied the coat around my waist. At least I could move. Moving to the stair, I peered over the railing, but couldn't see anyone. However, I could hear voices.

I crossed to the stairwell door and cracked it. Giulio was lounging against it.

"Not yet," he whispered. "A guest is checking in. They have many suitcases on a trolley."

"Someone's in the stairwell," I whispered. "Where's Orlando's room? Can we make a run for it?"

"It is down the hall, past the trolley." Giulio glanced into the stairwell. "What have you done to my Burberry?"

"I got hot and uncomfortable. Your dress sucks."

"Take off the dress and wear the coat. You will make creases. The Burberry is not a towel."

"Oh my God, stop worrying about your coat. I'm not going to strip in the stairwell. There's someone in here. We've got to get into Orlando's room."

"Bell boy." He shut the door.

Below me, the voices grew louder, the conversation cutting in and out. "—then we'll—out—" said a woman excitedly.

I tiptoed to the railing, peered over, but still couldn't see anything.

"And—gun?" said a man.

Gun? I hung over the edge, caught a bit of movement, and pulled myself back. Rushing to the door, I cracked it. "Giulio?"

No Giulio. Craptastic.

Below me, the conversation quieted. Footsteps pattered on the stairs. I shrank against the wall, cracking the door wider. "Giulio," I whispered.

The voices erupted in a scream. A door banged, cutting off the scream.

"What the H?" I ran to the railing. "Hello? Are you okay?"

No answer.

I skidded down three steps before I remembered I couldn't get caught in the resort. I hung over the rail. "Hello?"

The fifth-floor door opened. "Maizie?" said Giulio. "Come now."

I looked down, then up.

"Hurry. They are in the room, but the bell boy will leave in a moment."

Bounding up the stairs, I slipped out past Giulio. "Something weird is going on in the stairwell."

"A fashion emergency, I know." He grabbed my arm, and we jogged down the hall.

At room 516, I noted the Do Not Disturb sign on the door and knocked. No answer. We scanned our card, slipped inside, then peered into the hall. The bell boy emerged from room 511, grabbed the trolley with one hand, and sauntered to the elevators.

"That was close," said Giulio. "My heart is beating like the bird. I love this detective work. And I can see your panties."

I tightened the coat around my waist. "We'll be quick. You start looking for film stuff in the room. I'm going in the bathroom to fix my dress. I'll poke around for clues in there, too."

"Do investigators actually say clues?"

"I have no idea."

Giulio strode into the bedroom. I opened the door at my elbow.

"His bathroom is disgusting and smells. Why didn't he want housekeeping in here?" I left the door open. I untied the Burberry, letting it drop to the floor, and rolled the tube over my hips and up my waist. I gave up trying to peel it over my chest, leaving the twisted fabric as an ultra-thick bandeau. I closed my eyes for a moment, enjoying the cool air on my torso and legs. Taking a deep breath, I inhaled the awful scent, then bent to retrieve the trench coat.

As I rose, I caught my reflection in the mirror, something I'd been trying to avoid. But there I was, Maizie Albright as the ex-star. I once had a taut workout body, glowing skin, and styled hair from my weekly spa date. I dressed in the trendiest fashion that Barney's and Rodeo had to offer. Now, I displayed the paunch of carb weakness, runny mascara, sweat dampened hair, and a bandeau of stripper Lycra around my boobs. I quickly buttoned the Burberry around my shame and snagged a tissue to fix my mascara.

"OMG, I just saw myself," I called to Giulio. "How bored are you to hit on this?"

"Yes, well, today is not your best look. I'll admit that."

While I pined for a way out of my mess in LA, I never thought I'd look like this. Nor did I think I'd be stuck doing someone's accounting, not able to afford a phone or a car, or even a new outfit for a Black Pine party. I thought I'd be driving around town in my old (new) Jag convertible, outfitted with the latest tech while I scoped out cheating spouses and looked for missing children.

And how did I think I'd ever have a shot with Nash? I looked like a psycho and worse, I was a failure at field work.

"OMG, I'm the delusional has-been actress," I thought. "Is this my Norma Desmond or Baby Jane?"

I pinched my thumb to stop the tears and blotted the mascara beneath my eyes. Sniffed and inhaled the putrid stench again. "What in the helabama smells like that?"

I eyed the closed shower curtain behind me.

OMG, I knew what smelled like that.

Clutching the tissue, I turned, sagging against the counter. "Giulio, we've got to get out of here."

"I have not finished looking through his suitcase. He has an interesting collection of film stills…"

"Stop looking," I hissed. "And maybe wipe off everything you've touched? Quickly."

"I can barely understand you when your voice gets high and squeaky."

"Giulio." I tried to swallow the vomit of revulsion working its way up my throat. "Just hurry."

"Take this." He appeared in the doorway, holding a can of film, and eyed his trench coat. "The creases, not good. But the Burberry with only the shoes? Very sexy. Except for your face. You're so pale and blotchy."

"Put the film down." I pointed at the shower curtain. "We're going to pull that back and find Orlando."

"What are you saying? Is this one of your games where I must guess the movie? *Psycho*? No, that was just women in the shower, yes? Wait. *The Shining*. No, that's also a woman. I'm not good with the old movies, like you."

"I'm saying," I slowly enunciated in a whisper so I wouldn't vomit. "That there is a dead body in the tub. For real."

Giulio's eyes widened. "The smell. Like old fruit and garbage?"

I nodded. "You look."

Giulio dropped the film can and backed out of the room. "You are right. I need to wipe off my fingerprints." He darted around the door.

"Don't leave me in here." I cringed against the sink. "I can't move."

"Come." His head appeared in the doorway, then disappeared. "We have to look."

"No, we go."

Grabbing my elbow, he jerked me from the sink. I grabbed the shower curtain as he yanked me toward the door. The outer, cloth curtain stretched from the rod. Giulio stepped into the vestibule, dragging me with him.

"Maizie, we go."

I gripped the curtain, wrenching the cloth. We watched, horrified, as the plastic under-curtain dragged along the metal rod, then began to rip away from the hanging loops. The rotting fruit smell grew sharper and more pungent.

"What are you doing?" Giulio released my elbow, threw a hand over his face, and flung open the hall door. "Hurry."

The curtain sagged halfway open. I could see the top of a head slumped in the tub. The head was bald, bearded, and wore glasses. I tiptoed into the bathroom. Orlando also had a beer gut. Surprising for a stunt man.

"I don't think this is Orlando."

FIFTEEN

#DopplegangerDilemna #ShesASuspect

"*M*aizie," hissed Giulio from the hallway. "Let's go."

"Oh my God," I said. "There's a dead body in Orlando's bathtub."

"Come on."

"I found another dead body. Why does this keep happening? What's wrong with me?"

"You are hysterical, and we need to go." Giulio strode back into the room, picked me up, and staggered into the hallway. "I don't do dead lift. You have to walk."

"But—"

Giulio gripped me by my shoulders. "Listen to me. You are on probation. You cannot be here."

I stared into the molten chocolate eyes — which, quite frankly, made me feel even more pukish — and tried to center my unraveling brain. "You're right. Let me get that film first."

"You cannot take the murder evidence. Even I know this." Giulio grabbed my hand and dragged me toward the elevator bank. "We are going."

I dug in my heels and pointed toward the stairs. "We can't go to the lobby. I can't be seen."

"You are so difficult, Maizie." Giulio followed me through the door and down the stairs, cursing in Italian.

"Who was in that tub?" I said. "He didn't look like a stuntman."

"I don't want to know. I'm glad I didn't see it."

"I have to call the police. But I was in that room illegally. With Nash's key. Oh my God, oh my God, oh my…"

"Stop it." We hit the fourth-floor landing, and Giulio yanked on my arm, whirling me around. "You must pull yourself together."

"You're right. Get a grip, Maizie." I pinched my thumb skin and took a cleansing *ujjayi* breath. "Think. What would Julia Pinkerton do?"

"I have no idea." Giulio's eyes swept to the ceiling. "I never saw the show."

"You've been lying to me all this time—" I checked myself. "Whatever. I was talking to myself, anyway. I need to focus."

I did a Sunrise Salutation, centering my breathing on past scripts and not current dead people.

"We did not bring a yoga mat," said Giulio. "And we need to get out of this building. Would you hurry?"

I rose from my bent position with a final exhale. "In 'Breaker, Breaker' Julia Pinkerton and her friend, Mabel, snuck out to go to a concert."

"Maizie…"

"On the way to the concert, they stopped at a truck stop. Mabel flirts with a hot young trucker — played by John Cashington — while Julia pumps gas. Mabel's not had a lot of success with boys, so it's a big deal to her." I felt myself calming and released another deep breath. "In an earlier episode, Julia had infiltrated a drug ring. When she goes inside to pay for the gas, Julia sees the king-pin. She can't blow her cover. The drug lord thinks Julia's a dealer, her friend has no idea she's a teenage detective. She'd been trying to find the kingpin for three episodes, only knowing him by a description of a very specific tattoo."

"Why would a drug lord be in a truck stop? Surely he has people to get him the Slim Jim."

"The point is, Julia Pinkerton has a dilemma. Follow the bad guys and abandon her friend? Not only is that not cool, but could be dangerous. Plus, their families don't know they're out. Grab Mabel and leave the bad guy she'd been trying to track? Who knows when she'd find him again. Call the police? They don't have any evidence the kingpin is connected. There's nothing to arrest him on, and it would drive him further underground. Julia had been working on making the connections between the kingpin and his henchmen."

"What did Julia Pinkerton do?"

"She had to convince her friend to leave the trucker and go to the concert. She left the kingpin for another episode."

"So, no police."

"Wait here." I bounded up the stairs to the fifth-floor hall. A minute later, I returned. "I grabbed this." I held up the Do Not Disturb sign, then tossed it on the ground. "Housekeeping will find him, and his death will be reported. I feel horrible. It's going to give someone a terrible shock. I wish I had money to leave them a big tip."

"It gave me a terrible shock. I don't like playing detective as much as I thought."

"It can be upsetting."

"Too much stress."

I nodded.

"I am guessing who played that friend, Mabel," said Giulio.

"Right. Cam-Cam. I didn't even think of that." I tapped my chin. "That's sort of a small world-ish, right? A little ironic?"

"They had a happy ending?"

"Actually, even though Julia Pinkerton chose to go to the concert with Mabel instead of following the kingpin, at the concert, the kingpin kidnapped Mabel because he saw Julia and followed her. It was a cliffhanger ending."

"I see."

"It took two more episodes to get Mabel back, and another three before Julia busted the kingpin. By then, there was plenty of evidence against him. Like kidnapping. And, unfortunately, murder."

"I think I will leave you here." Giulio dipped to double kiss my cheeks, then darted out the fourth-floor exit. "Good luck."

At least I could count on Giulio's consistency. Every Giulio for himself.

I continued down the stairs. Other than my erratic heartbeat, weak knees (maybe due more to the stripper shoes than the corpse), and the churning bile in my stomach, I felt much calmer. All seemed quiet below, which gave me hope that I could sneak out unspotted. Thinking about room 516 gave me the shakes. I focused on a plan to get out of the building and back to the Cove to change. From there, I'd have to break the news to Nash that Orlando was not only missing, but he also had a body count. Unless he was the pudgiest stuntman I've ever met.

The police could now get involved, giving me a feeling of relief. Cam-Cam had totally "shit up" Leonard's movie. No way could the producers keep "murdered man found in bathtub of Cambria's boyfriend's hotel room" out of the news. The odds of Cambria keeping this role certainly seemed against her.

The odds of us keeping the job were even worse. But better than the odds for missing body number one and murdered body number two.

I stopped on the second-floor landing to pant and let my mind stroll over the thought of Cambria losing her job. Could someone be setting Cam-Cam up? Maybe even framing her?

"Duh, Maizie," I muttered. "People don't commit murder to ruin someone's career and reputation. There are easier ways to do that."

Easing down the last flight of the stairs, I mulled over murder motives and stopped before the first-floor door. Easing open the door, I set my eyeball to the crack and peered out into the hallway. The back exit looked clear. I might be caught on camera wearing a pink wig, trench coat, and stripper shoes but there was no way around that. Hopefully, time of death would work in my favor, and there'd be no reason to care about the strip-o-gram entering and exiting at four in the afternoon.

I opened the door a few inches wider to check the end of the hallway opening onto the lobby. Did a double take. Blinked. Popped my head through the door to get a better look. But the scene didn't change. The woman leaning in the lobby doorway and texting on her phone wore a Saint Laurent "Love" t-shirt and Nili Lotan jeans. The same outfit I had stashed in the Cove bathroom.

And she looked exactly like me.

*M*y brain felt too full, so I operated on survival mode. Ducking my head, I exited the building, then fast-walked to the Cove. In the Cove, I found my stashed clothes. Mini Me hadn't stolen them — not that she was mini, she was (unfortunately) full-sized Maizie Albright — and with the choice of wearing the same outfit as my doppelganger or a Lycra tube top and trench coat, I redressed in the t-shirt and jeans.

I needed Nash. His counsel. His advice. His broad shoulders and light blue eyes. Just looking at him would calm me. We would figure this out together and solve the mystery of "Why does Maizie Albright keep finding dead bodies and have a twin who wears her Black Pine attire and not the stylish prêt-à-porter I had been previously (sort-of) known for?"

Not that it bothered me that Mini Me chose my post-Hollywood wardrobe.

Although it did. A little. Okay, I'm shallow like that.

I hopped on Lucky, zipped across the parking lot, and stopped at a Silverado pickup. A pickup that looked exactly like Nash's, even down to the rust stains on the bumper (actually only guessing on the rust stains) and the Georgia Carry sticker in the back window (that I knew for sure). Except Nash was on the set. Wasn't he? I glanced around, but no Nash came bounding out behind the tennis courts. I hadn't memorized his license plates because I always looked for the extra large, hot hardbody when identifying his truck.

Now would be a good time to have a phone. Again, #notwinning on the phone front.

I peeked in the window. Empty folders lay on the bench seat. A Starbucks cup and a coconut water bottle rested in the cup holders.

Starbucks and coconut water. This was not Nash's pickup.

*H*aving stopped at the craft table for much needed, therapeutic noshing, I climbed up the short but steep steps into Cam-Cam's trailer. Unlike her cottage, no key needed.

And, thank the heavens, no body littered the floor. I didn't think I could handle more than one a day.

The galley kitchen was sleek, stainless, and high tech. Ironic and unnecessary for someone who had to keep herself caveman fit. A long leather couch and soft leather chairs faced a giant TV screen on the opposite wall. Not that my *Julia Pinkerton* trailer hadn't been nicely outfitted. Vicki made sure of it. But the bells and whistles on Cambria's trailer appeared more luxuriously obnoxious.

If luxuriously obnoxious was a thing.

Along with the range of other emotions I held, the green-eyed monster also seemed to have gripped my heart.

"I'm living my dream," I muttered. "My teenage dream." My mantra was better fit for a Katy Perry lyric. Nevertheless, now that I couldn't afford a therapist, I needed these reminders. And with the day I was having, I needed all the self-therapy I could get.

"I should probably search this trailer," I mumbled. But my heart wasn't in it. "Later." I set my food service plate on the small coffee table, sank onto the supple couch, and closed my eyes. Then shot to my feet as the trailer door opened. Cam-Cam climbed the steps. With Nash. He looked glower-y, formidable, and in no way happy to see me.

Again.

"We need to chat," I said to Nash. "I found something. Something big. And I don't mean in size. But that, too."

"What are you doing here?" Cambria sauntered to the couch and collapsed on the spot I had just vacated. "Wyatt is taking over your job."

"Ed Farmer wants me to be your goat." Frustration and dead bodies lent a reediness to my voice. "And I need to talk to Mr. Nash."

"I don't need a goat. I just need a body to reassure the insurance company that I'm on the job. I don't want your body." Cambria turned toward Nash and pouted her lips. "I want his."

I rubbed my forehead. There were too many bodies in my recent conversations.

"Wyatt? You want to take care of this?" Cambria turned her face toward Nash, fluttering her eyelashes. A forced coquettishness which seemed at odds with her talent, making me wonder why she felt it necessary to play that part. It would have no effect on Nash. Cam-Cam wasn't stupid, she should have figured that out by now.

Ignoring Cambria, Nash gave me the "what now" look.

I returned the one that said, "I found a dead guy in a bathtub." Or, hopefully, one that conveyed a similar type of urgency.

"Excuse us a minute." He turned and exited the trailer.

I left my plate and followed him across the parking lot to a picnic table beneath a tree. On the other side of the parking lot, the props crew tested a small rocket. A multitude of people milled about, although no one gave us a second glance.

"Did Cambria tell you anything about what was going on in her cottage?" I asked.

He shook his head. "When I arrived, they had her trying on clothes in an RV. I spent the entire time sitting on a lawn chair. There was a piece of Astroturf surrounded by a plastic white picket fence like this is some kind of trailer park."

"It makes it homey. You do a lot of waiting at hair, makeup, and wardrobe. And if you need special effect makeup, forget it. That stuff takes forever. They like to make your wait pleasant."

He shook his head, signifying his feelings about beautifying work places. "I talked to your friends. Cambria didn't tell them anything either. Did you find Orlando or evidence of a movie?"

A power saw roared into life. I used the background noise to blurt out my tale of room 516. The saw cut off, leaving me yelling, "And he was way too hefty to be a stunt guy."

Nash's eyes widened then narrowed. "In all my years doing private investigations, I've only found one dead body. And that was a heart attack victim when I entered a home to put in a security system."

"I know." I clutched my throat, blinking back tears. "I think there's something wrong with me. They never covered this in therapy."

"It's this Hollywood business that's come to town. The bigger the bankroll, the bigger the crime." He waved at the set. "I knew this was hinky from minute one. And now we're going to get involved in a murder investigation. But at least it'll give the police justification for a warrant to investigate what you originally saw. Maybe to search the entire damn resort. Unless the judge is a stickler about privacy."

"You think the killer is staying in the hotel or villas?"

"I don't know what to think. We don't even have a motive. Maybe that film you found will have something on it." Nash paced before the table, kicking clods of dirt. "Any idea for the cause of death?"

"I didn't see any gunshot or stab wounds. Blood on his t-shirt, but it wasn't drenched." I shuddered. "I didn't get a chance to look closely. Just like with the fake Cambria, I knew he was dead. The fact that he was in a bathtub, fully clothed, and not surprised to see me tipped me off."

I swung my legs and considered the thoughts that had previously ping-ponged inside my skull. "Someone looked like Cambria, and now someone looks like me. What if Cam-Cam really doesn't know what's going on? What if she's being set up? Or what if whoever killed her double, really planned on killing Cam-Cam?"

Nash circled back to me and stopped. "So you're saying, Cambria's twin did a home video with Cambria's boyfriend, and Cambria had no idea that someone who looked exactly like her was in her cottage and later murdered because the killer thought it was Cambria? There is no way in hell that kind of coincidence could have happened."

"Maybe that's why they got rid of the body? They realized it wasn't really Cam-Cam."

"More likely, they hid the body after they saw you studying the crime scene through the window and wanted to hide the evidence."

I did not want to think about that. But there it was. "Oh my God. So they hired a fake me? Because they're going to kill me and Mini Me will take my place? Surely she can't mimic me that well? It's like *Stepford Wives* all over again."

Nash planted his hands on his hips. "I'm going to ignore that and chalk it up to spitballing. I need to call Mowry and tell him about your body."

"Please stop calling them that." I took a deep breath. "And please don't tell Mowry I found him. I don't want to involve my probation officer. That's a lot of red tape, and possible jail time I'd like to avoid. And Giulio doesn't want to be involved either."

"Not sure I can do that, but let me tip off security at the resort first. They'll call it in. Black Pine PD will send Mowry since he was involved earlier." Nash stroked his chin. "No idea who it was?"

I shook my head. "But we should Google Orlando just to be sure. Maybe they needed a heavy-set stunt man. I'm sure he'll be the prime suspect. I want to know what he looks like. Why didn't I Google him earlier? What's Cam-Cam doing with a murdering stuntman?"

We both turned to gaze at the rows of trailers.

"She needs to talk," said Nash. "Enough of this 'I'm a star' bullshit."

"It's a half-hearted act anyway. She either needs to try harder or not at all."

He rubbed his scar. "Give a thought as to why you have a double and why she's allowed on the resort even if you're not."

I sucked in my breath. "Shiz. That's got to be Vicki." No, she was focused on Cambria. Theodore? I'd been giving him fashion reports every time we talked. But now that Nash stopped looking like I disgusted him, I didn't want to explain Theodore and *The Maltese Falcon* shop. I'd take care of Theodore myself.

But what was Theodore doing? Playing detective in the fake office? With a fake detective who looked like me?

Nash rocked back on his heels. "My mind immediately went to Vicki instead of *Stepford Wives*, but that's just me."

"I need to see a person about a thing." I hopped off the table.

"Before you go wail on Vicki, let's get Cambria to talk." He placed his hands on my shoulders. "Get your head in the game. You let Cambria and Vicki and all these other jokers shake you up every time. You don't need their approval. You're no longer an actress. Or whatever you call what you were."

"I was—" I stopped. "Okay. You're right. Renata, my therapist used to say..." I could tell he didn't care what Renata said. But both Nash and Renata were right. "It's time to stop feeling bad about my life and start living it."

"You don't do a pity party, I'll give you that." He squeezed my shoulders. "Cambria has no choice but to talk. We're going to spell it out for her. She'll know she's in trouble. We can use that."

"Right." My skin felt tingly. Which might have been from excitement. Or from Nash's giant man-paws resting on my shoulders.

"Anything else we can use? Did you see anything in that hotel room?"

"Other than the film can, no. And that might be nothing, although you usually don't see real film in this digital age. Giulio also found a bunch of movie stills in a suitcase. But I got distracted by the dead guy, and then we took off."

"The police will confiscate everything." Nash rubbed my shoulders. "It wouldn't surprise me if they bring Cambria in for questioning. We'll use that, too."

"Oh no," I said. "Poor Cam-Cam."

"She's a suspect, Maizie. Don't forget, she could have killed these people."

"Right. Except I don't think she did. Cam-Cam's a lot of things, but I don't think she's a killer. When I knew her, she was very focused on her career."

"That's what the folks say about the neighbor kid when they find out he's a serial killer." He studied my face. "Sorry. You okay, kid?"

I nodded. Searching my eyes, he gave my shoulders another squeeze. The moment stretched without awkwardness, a real feat for me. Afraid it would end, I held my breath.

Even with eyes the color of melted glacier water, his hands certainly warmed my shoulders.

In fact, my skin felt scorched. Trickles of liquid fire raced down my back and spread, simmering and fizzing, like molten lava ready to erupt.

"Are you okay?" My voice sounded breathless, and I gasped, hoping to cool off the mounting pressure.

His hands slid down my back to my waist and rested there, but he seemed unaware. His eyes hadn't left mine. I could see the concern that had been masked earlier by his annoyance.

"You've had it rough, Maizie. I keep forgetting I haven't seen what you've seen. Then that Baloney character abandoned you at a crime scene." His eyebrows quirked and knitted together. "I'm sorry I've been hard on you. You've been doing your best."

"It's Belloni, not Baloney."

"Not in my book." His lips pursed, softening the rigid lines of his face. "I can't believe he just left you there. I always thought he was an ass, but that really takes the cake. After dressing you up like a two dollar— Well, it took all my strength not to knock his teeth out."

"It's fine. I didn't want to get recognized on the resort, and I'm used to wearing costumes. On *Julia Pinkerton*—okay, rule number one. But Giulio is a product of his environment, just like me."

"Not like you. Not like you at all." His jaw hardened. "I keep telling you, you're not like them."

But wasn't I? "You don't really know them."

"But I know you."

Holy shizzolis. My heart hammered and I feared a case of oncoming flop sweat. "It's my fault that we're in this predicament."

"I agreed to it, didn't I? I was just ticked about the situation."

I did a quick reflective check. I was awake. This was not a dream. And Nash was not only acting nice (while setting fire to all my lady parts), he also wasn't rebuffing my advances. Or were they his advances? "Who are you?"

He chuckled. "I just feel bad I left you with Baloney. Twice I've failed you."

"Come again?"

"Instead of going together, I sent you to Cambria's alone and you saw...an alleged corpse—"

"Alleged?"

"We still haven't found the victim yet. And I left you with Baloney, and you found another—"

"About to be unalleged corpse."

"I don't think that's a word. Anyway, this is on me. And I'm trying to tell you I'm sorry. You're right. I haven't been training you like I should because I don't want you around..."

"Oh."

"Okay, I like having you around. Maybe too much. It just takes some getting used to is all."

"*Oh.*"

"Dammit."

Oh. My. God.

I tried my best to cut off my thoughts, but there they were, zipping around my head like surfers at Malibu, fighting for spots on a big curl. Nash admitted his feelings for me. Sort of. If "dammit" counted as feelings. He was gazing at me and dragging me closer — by now, I think he realized where his hands had landed because they were running all over my back — and as God is my witness, he was going to kiss me.

Finally.

Finally!

I pressed myself against him, thankful that I had taken time for a sink bath and makeover in the Cove's bathroom. My lips parted and I breathed in his very male scent of Acqua di Selva and frustration-induced sweat. Tipping my head back, my ponytail tickled my shoulders.

This was our moment. In the parking lot of the *Pine Hollow* set. But who cared? It's a story we'd share with our children. Daddy and I had our first kiss after Mommy found her second corpse.

Wait, why were my thoughts going there? Startled, I opened my eyes.

Nash looked like I felt when Carol Lynn served baked potato casserole. That no-holds-barred "I'm going to devour you no matter what the cost" look.

I shivered and took a deep breath, mashing my breasts against his chest. He uttered a low, soft growl. Dipped his head.

The volcano erupted. Every nerve in my body sang "Hallelujah."

(The Andy Grammar version).

"Maizie."

I closed my eyes and pretended I hadn't heard Leonard Shackleton's bark. Grasping Nash's — bulging! — biceps, I drew him closer. And Nash wasn't backing off. I'd hungered for this moment since I first saw him (half-naked) in his office and begged him to mentor me (after he'd finished dressing).

His lips fell against mine, but now they weren't mashing mine into oblivion or attempting any kind of tongue play. They were mumbling curses — new ones, but mostly interesting mashups of old standbys — and his hands had slid back to my shoulders. For a long second, he rested his forehead against mine.

"Dammittohell," he muttered and paused. "I'm sorry. It's no good."

"What in the hell are you doing? We need you now. Why aren't you with Cambria?" Leonard Shackleton's voice grew angrier.

I wanted to scream, "Shut up, Leonard. What's not good? What. Is. No. Good? Me? The non-kiss? Leonard Shackleton?"

Nash wrenched his face away, then his body. "Is there a problem?" he said to Leonard. His voice had fallen a few octaves, and he spun me before him to face Leonard. One hand rested on the back of my neck, and the other awkwardly patted my shoulder.

"Yes, for one, someone's supposed to be with Cambria. Two, she hit her emergency button. Three, an ambulance is about to arrive. What the hell have you two been doing?"

At Leonard's number two, Nash had taken off, jogging toward the trailer.

I was left searching for a reason for number one.

SIXTEEN

#SheisNOTaASuspect
#OopsSheDidItAgain

"What? Why? When?" I scrambled, trying to make sense in an oxygen-deprived brain. "It's only been like a minute since we left."

"It only takes a minute to overdose, Maizie. I thought you knew these things."

"Overdose? On what? I checked her trailer and her villa. There's nothing more than Snickers bars—" Cambria was going to kill me for ratting that out. "Nothing she shouldn't have. It's all protein shakes, oxygen water, and juice infusions."

Leonard's eyes glittered. "Then it was on her."

Oh, God. He was right. I didn't search Cambria. She could have almost anything on — or in — her body.

"I'm so sorry," I said. "We stepped out for a minute to conference. About her other problem. The dead body double problem."

"Didn't look like a conference to me." He strode forward, his voice booming. Around us, the set crew stopped in their tracks to watch us. Somewhere above us, a rocket exploded. "It looked like two horny teenagers getting it on in a parking lot."

He was right. How utterly mortifying. "There's something important you need to know, Leonard. It's about an issue of alleged victims. Actually, there are two victims now, and only one is alleged. I found another—"

"I don't care about that now. I only care about pumping Cambria's stomach and not letting any of this leak to the press." Leonard ran a finger inside his collar. "I called our lawyers and PR. God, what a disaster. Ed's going to lose his mind."

"I'm really sorry. But I don't think you understand the seriousness of the situation. What I'm trying to tell you—"

"What a disappointment." He glowered. "I don't know what I was thinking trusting something this big to you. I thought at least your boss could handle this, but he's one potato in this poky town. What could I expect? I should have let the insurance company handle this."

Evidently, the mention of victims wasn't making an impression on Leonard. Maybe I should return to calling them bodies. "We should probably get to the hospital. We'll talk more after we get the news on Cam-Cam."

"Huh?" Leonard blinked. "Yes, right, Cambria. You can ride with me."

"That's okay. I'll catch a ride with Mr. Nash."

"Like I trust you with him." Leonard crossed his arms and barked a short laugh. "I think we're going to let him stay with Cambria. That's what she prefers anyway. You'll stick with me."

Oh, great.

*O*n Leonard's hired Escalade, Ed Farmer joined us. And Dahlia Pearson. She was "so concerned." I scrambled to get the seat in the back, which Dahlia insisted on taking. Then I scrambled for shotgun, but Ed had already taken the passenger seat. I was stuck sitting next to Leonard.

Of course.

Agent Alvin rode in the ambulance, disappointing Ed who had hoped to stick with his star.

Nash took his truck alone, disappointing me.

While Ed fretted about Cambria, Dahlia Googled overdoses and treated us to anecdotal Reddit comments about near-death experiences.

"Dahlia, I don't think that's helping," I said. Ed Farmer's foot hammered the Escalade floor. The entire SUV shook with his nervous energy. "Maybe look up local treatment plans instead. But keep them to yourself. Silent reading."

"Do they even have those in Georgia? Like licensed therapists?"

"I'm pretty sure the state of Georgia licenses their doctors, Dahlia."

"What about an acupuncturist? I had a friend who totally treated her addictions with acupuncture and goji berries." She looked up from her phone. "Of course, she had a strong will to beat the addiction."

Ed's foot hammering crescendoed. The Escalade revved to match his impatience.

I turned in my seat. "Dahlia, sweetie, your director is going to have an aneurysm if you don't stop."

"He's kind of obsessed with Cambria," she whispered.

"I noticed," I whispered back.

"Have you seen his office? He storyboards with full sketches of her," she murmured. "Everyone else is a stick figure except for Cambria. She's not even illustrated. It's like a mini portrait in each scene. She looks like one of those Renaissance pictures."

Stalker much? I looked over my shoulder at Ed, who now argued with the driver about his speed. Or lack thereof.

"He's brilliant. That's how he works. Hitchcockian." Leonard looked up from his phone to leer at me. "We all have our infatuations."

Oh, God. I turned to look out the window. How long did it take to get to a hospital in Black Pine?

"So, what's with you and Wyatt Nash?" said Leonard.

"Nothing." I wish I knew.

"You two seem more than friendly."

I chewed my lip.

"Is it an open relationship?"

"Relationship? He's free to hire more staff if that's what you mean." I turned to face Dahlia. "So find anything about those acupuncturists? Forget the silent reading. Just give us the entire list."

*W*e converged on Black Pine Hospital's ER like a troop prepared for battle. I scanned for Nash. Dahlia looked for the gift shop. Ed attacked the front desk, demanding information about Cambria, while Leonard tried to keep him from using her name. The sweet ER nurse patiently explained the rules, pointed toward the waiting room, then suggested Ed might need to see a doctor because "his color" didn't look good. Did he have a blood pressure problem?

Considering Ed's color alternated between white and fuchsia, I thought he needed something stronger than a blood pressure check. Maybe a lobotomy.

Ed wandered away to pace the waiting room.

"The patient needs a private room ASAP," Leonard told the ER receptionist. "Why don't you get someone in admin down here? My PR gal will be here in a minute, and she'll need to go over certain procedures and waivers we need signed. While you're at it, I need you to strike Cambria's name from your records. Just put in Jane Doe or something."

"I can't do that," said the nurse. "We already have her name on her wrist band, and it's tied to the records."

"Just swap it out. Get her a new band." Seeing me, Leonard waved me over. "Maizie, we can use your name, right? Just put Maizie Albright on the record."

I gasped. "You can't do that. It'll mess with my health records."

Leonard lowered his voice. "Maizie, we can't have Cambria's name getting out that she OD'ed. Surely, you'd take one for the team? Haven't you OD'ed before?"

"No. And big no." I backed from the desk. "I can't take an OD for the team. It's wrong, and you'll put my probation in jeopardy." The nurse's brow wrinkled. "This isn't an OD. She's being treated for poison ingestion."

"Same difference," said Leonard. "If Maizie isn't going to help, just use Jane Doe. The media will get wise, but it'll put them off, and we can disclaim anything they say."

"Wait a minute," I said, retracing my steps. "Cambria was poisoned?"

"Take the volume down a notch. And don't use her name. Jane Doe was poisoned." Leonard blinked. "What do you mean, poisoned?"

"Just like it sounds. She ingested a poisonous substance," said the nurse. "You'll have to speak to her doctor. If she gives you permission. You know, there is such a thing as privacy laws."

"Something you should well remember," said Leonard. "You'll be hearing from my lawyers."

I tugged on Leonard's sleeve. "Mr. Shackleton, leave the nurse alone. She's just doing her job. Let's wait with the others."

He pulled me into a hard hug. "I don't know what I'd do without you, Maizie."

"Mr. Shackleton." I pushed against his back. "You're squashing me."

He pulled back. "You really soothe me. Nobody can do that. Unless it's prescribed."

Craptastic, I was Leonard's goat now.

"Maizie Albright to the administration desk." Leonard and I searched the ceiling at the sound of my name over the intercom. Extricating myself from Leonard, I approached the nurse again. "I think I was just paged. I'm Maizie Albright."

She nodded. "You're needed. Go wait for your escort by the big 'No Admittance' door."

"What about me?" said Leonard. "I'm Leonard Shackleton."

"I didn't hear a Leonard Shackleton, only a Maizie Albright."

The nurse waved a guard over. "I suggest you sit in the waiting room like I told you the first time."

"I'll report back as soon as I know something," I said.

I left him to complain to the guard and found my escort at a glass sliding door. He led me down various corridors until we reached an examining room. Nash stood in front of the door, his arms folded, his expression grim.

"Did she die?" I clutched my throat. "The nurse said she was poisoned."

He shook his head. "She'll be alright. She can barely speak, but before she was knocked out I got a few words. Something tasted funny, but she didn't take much. Drank some water, it started burning, and she called for help. They're running a tox screen to figure out what it was."

I peered through the window in the door. "Poor Cam-Cam."

Nash leaned near me. "You know what this means? You were right. That double may have died because someone thought she was Cambria."

SEVENTEEN

#VideoKilledThePornStar #Hitchcocking

*I*t took several hours, but the hospital moved Cambria to a private room, and our crew moved with her. By then, her blood work had come back and had identified the various chemicals she'd ingested and vomited.

"She's lucky," said the doctor. "It could have killed her."

Nash had been tapping on his phone. "Ammonia, ethanol, and isopropyl alcohol. This says those are the ingredients for window cleaner."

"Sounds about right," said the doctor.

"I had a friend who tried to snort Comet," said Dahlia. She stood behind Ed Farmer. Ed had taken the bedside vigil chair to watch over Cambria while she slept. "He was that desperate. Just like Cambria. He lost his nose and had to have it rebuilt."

"Not helping," I muttered and glanced at Ed. He didn't show any signs of hearing Dahlia, let alone aware of anyone else in the room besides Cambria.

Nash folded his arms and stared at Leonard. "Do we need all these people?"

Besides our original party, we'd been joined by a PR consultant, a media specialist, and an aromatherapist. While the other two attacked their phone and tablets, the aromatherapist wielded essential oils in various spots around Cambria's bed.

"Where's Alvin?" said Leonard to me. "He was just here."

"He's seeing about programs for Cam's recovery," said Dahlia, rubbing Ed's shoulders. "At least I told him he should since we don't want poor Cambria to relapse."

I glanced at Nash, but he was frowning at the aromatherapist.

"This will soothe and help her to heal," said the aromatherapist, a twenty-something-year-old flower child reincarnation, down to her long braids held in place with a Peruvian headband. Lavender and lemongrass wafted from her twig wand as she dropped oil on my wrist.

She flicked the wand toward Leonard. Without looking at her, he held out a wrist.

Nash gave her a hard look, and she scurried away. Jerking a thumb toward the door, he addressed the room. "Cambria is trying to sleep. You want her to get better, y'all need to get out. Now."

His voice was as large and as commanding as his person. PR, media, aromatherapy, and Dahlia scuttled from the room. The doctor already bought and paid for, strode out with them. Nash shut the door, and Ed glanced up from his chair.

"Mr. Shackleton, Mr. Farmer, Miss Albright." He motioned us inside the bathroom. "Let's convene. We shouldn't have the following discussion in front of Cambria. Or in the hall, where we could be overheard."

Ed and Leonard followed Nash inside.

I stood outside the door, eyeing the tiny room crammed with people.

"Miss Albright, stand next to me," said Nash. "You'll be fine. This isn't a closet. Just for a minute, so we can talk privately."

Taking a deep breath, I slid through the door. We crowded toe-to-toe between the toilet, sink, and standing shower. With a final glance at Cambria's sleeping form, Nash pulled the door shut. Feeling the tiny room shrink, I thought positive affirmations, imagined wide open spaces and sniffed my wrist. When that didn't work, I leaned into Nash and took a quick, unobtrusive inhale of his cologne and felt calmer.

"We need to come to an understanding," Nash whispered. "There's been two deaths and what looks like an attempt on Cambria's life. We need to notify the police about this. They're already investigating the other two."

"What do you mean?" Ed's voice rose. "What are you talking about? Leonard, what's he talking about?"

Leonard made shushing noises. "Ed, everything's fine. Something happened with a body double, nothing to do with us. Not our body double even. Maizie saw it, but she's on it. No worries. A case of mistaken identity."

"Not really mistaken when we're not sure who it is or where she went," I pointed out. "And she was in Cambria's villa, so there's that."

"Today Miss Albright found another body," said Nash. "In Cambria's boyfriend's hotel room."

"What?" Ed's limbs jerked, and he banged into the sink. "What is it with you and bodies?"

"I know, right?" I muttered.

Nash squeezed my elbow.

"Ed, it's just one of those peripheral things," said Leonard. "It's going to be a PR nightmare if it gets out. Cambria made a bad choice in lovers, he's involved in some kind of crime, and it followed her here. Maizie experienced the same back in LA. It happens."

I opened my mouth to protest his last statement, but Nash held up a finger. "Listen, we don't know if this is peripheral. It looks connected, which is why I'm calling the police. I know a police detective, we brought him in at the beginning..."

"He didn't believe me. Don't worry, it didn't get reported at the time," I said.

Nash cut me a look. "But now it's imperative to contact the police about Cambria. They're already involved. The vic in the hotel room is being examined by an ME as we speak."

"Oh my God. Who was it?" Ed massaged his face. "This vic in the hotel room?"

"We don't know. But we do know that Cambria's been poisoned. We have a responsibility to her as a victim to see that this crime is reported."

"We have a responsibility to her as a victim to see that she's protected. Which is your job. One in which you failed," said Leonard. "Ed, do you know where I found him when Cambria was almost dying in her trailer?"

Ed's spasmodic jerking renewed.

"Mauling Miss Albright. While Cambria lay dying, this man was screwing around with his subordinate."

Nash's scar whitened with the hardening of his jaw.

I gulped air and felt my knees weaken. The room darkened as the walls contracted. Nash placed a hand on the small of my back, and my breathing almost returned to normal.

Almost.

"I'll tell you what we're going to do," said Leonard. "Mr. Nash is on guard duty. You will not leave Cambria's side until we get to the bottom of this. Miss Albright will investigate these allegedly-related deaths. We don't actually know if Cambria was deliberately poisoned or if Cambria got the shakes and needed a quick fix. It's not like that's never been done before."

He turned to face me, taking my hand. "I take back what I said earlier, Maizie. You've done a great job of making sure Cambria didn't have any consumable substances. Next time, make sure all things toxic aren't in her reach."

I focused on deep breathing and not on feeling patronized.

"Is there a reason you don't believe your subordinate wasn't deliberately poisoned?" Nash ground out the words. "Are you covering up something?"

"What would I be covering up?" Leonard shouted. "Just what are you accusing me of?"

Ed moaned.

"Ed, I'm sorry for shouting, why don't you go sit with

Cambria?" Leonard shifted to let Ed pass. The door opened, and lavender lemongrass-scented air poured into our tiny tomb-like room.

"Mr. Shackleton." I patted his arm. "Calm down. Mr. Nash is just telling you this is very serious. When Cambria wakes up, we can get more information."

Leonard leaned into me. "You're right. Thank you, Maizie. You need to make Mr. Nash understand what we're up against. Legally."

"Obstruction of justice," said Nash. "Possibly aiding and abetting."

"My God, man," said Leonard. "Any lawyer worth his salt can have those charges removed. The Black Pine Keystone Cops can focus on that murder victim. But telling them about Cambria at this point? Do you know what the insurance company will do if they find out she drank cleaner? How much money we'll lose?"

"The price of her safety?" said Nash.

"That's what you're for, if you did your job," said Leonard. "The studio will lose millions. And thousands of jobs. This affects a multitude."

"You get another actress."

"I'd lose the director and the funding." Leonard placed his hands on his hips, inadvertently knocking me against the toilet. "Don't pretend to know anything about this industry. We have a contract, too. One I doubt you can afford to break. Like I said before, Maizie's going to figure out what trouble Cambria is in. And you and your thick neck are going to act as her bodyguard."

"I'm going to figure it out?" I squeezed my hands together.

Leonard patted my shoulder, then exited the bathroom. "You'll do great. Look what you've done so far."

So far I've found bodies, not answers. Also, Leonard's expectations, like most producers, were unrealistic and vague.

*N*ash and I were finally alone. In a teeny hospital bathroom that smelled of antiseptic and lavender dregs. My world could not get stranger.

Wait. Yes. Yes, it could. Never mind that, universe.

He took a deep breath and placed his hands on his hips, giving me a long, steady look. "It's hinky."

I'd been expecting this line. It was his go-to. "The murders, yes. Leonard wishing to protect the ingénue from the police, not so much. That's standard."

"You think she drank window cleaner?"

"Nope and I don't think Leonard believes that either. I think she was mixed up in something…"

"But."

"But it's un-Cam-Cam-like. Seriously, I can't believe she's gone down this sort of rabbit hole."

"She's surrounded by weirdos. Who knows how they've influenced her. Look at what happened to you. You're not like them, but I can't tell you how many times I bought beer at the TruBuy and saw your face staring back at me on one of those magazines. I'd look at you and think, 'That's Boomer Spayberry's daughter?'"

I shifted my gaze to his boots and pinched my thumb.

"Sorry. Just trying to make a point and damn, I'm doing it again. Don't cry."

"I'm not crying." I looked up. "You're right. Are you really going to play bodyguard?"

"I don't see that I have a choice." He massaged his neck. "Dammit, how did I get myself into this mess? I hate being under the thumb of some asshole."

"Uh, yeah. That's kind of my fault?" Thumbs were my wheelhouse. "And Leonard's sort of…taken to me. I think. It's hard to tell, but he's acting a little…"

Nash's eyes darted back to mine. "Possessive? Like the director and Cambria?"

"Yeah, it's creepy. But Hitchcock results, you know."

"I don't know. The whole business looks incestuous from my point of view."

"Ew. It's more like workplace romance. Close proximity and intense work between strong personalities and beautiful people. That happens everywhere, like..." I bit my tongue to stop the words, leaving me with the metallic tang of humiliation.

"About that." Nash folded his arms. "We can't do this. Earlier, in the parking lot. That was my fault. The guilt of what I was doing to you hit me and you were there, looking...anyway, we can't do this. Obviously. Look what happened."

"Right." I let out an unconvincing laugh, the mark of a bad actress. "So totally right."

He visibly winced. Oh, my God.

"You stay here and I'll just go investigate this crime." What was I doing with my arms? Did I just do the hayseed elbow scoop? I needed to get out of this tiny room. Now.

Nash squeezed out a small smile. "How about you start with the scene of the last crime? Someone could have gone in the trailer while we were at the hospital. Your bike is in the back of my truck." He handed me Cambria's key. "Poke around and see if you can figure out what might have poisoned her. I couldn't look with all the people crowding in after her collapse."

I nodded, closing my hand over her key. "Then what?"

He dug into his back pocket and pulled out a flip phone. "This is a burner. I keep some handy. I should have given you a phone a long time ago, but it's not fancy, and there's no money for a smart phone. Plus, you were being so stubborn about no phones—"

"Okay, okay." I snatched the phone.

"Call me and report in. I'm going to see if Mowry knows anything about the guy in the bathtub. Maybe they'll have an I.D. We'll go from there."

"Right."

"And Maizie," he paused. "Miss Albright. Keep your eye out for this guy." He held out his smart phone. A head shot appeared next to a mug shot. Young, muscled, good looking. Vacant eyes. A sexy, albeit lifeless grin. The mug shot's grin was malicious and sneer-ing. "That's Orlando Feelzen aka Mark Fellson. He's got a record. Misdemeanor possession."

"I can't believe Cam-Cam would date someone like that," I gasped.

"A convict?"

"No, that's not such a big deal." I caught his shocked look. "At least possession. Not in Hollywood. But the guy looks…not bright. Surprising for a stunt man, they're usually intelligent. I can't see Cams going for that. I mean, maybe you just need to get to know him?"

Nash sighed. "I hope you don't get to know him. In fact, if you see him, call me immediately, and I'll contact 9-1-1. Don't try to interact with him. Orlando Feelzen's suspect number one."

EIGHTEEN

#Feel(notso)Zen #RearTrailerWindow

I returned to the studio, waved through by security. The actors and most of the crew had returned to their hotel rooms, although inside the warehouse, some still burned midnight oil. Normal for preproduction crunch time, but with today's shock, the schedules would need to be adjusted. Options discussed. If Cam-Cam didn't recover her voice quickly, the schedules would become a ticking time bomb sitting on top of a pile of money.

Lights showed through the cracks around the conference room doors, their shades pulled tight. In the green room, the craft table had been emptied but for a coffee maker and double box of Dixie Kremes. I took a donut (out of respect for Lamar) and slipped out. Two doors down, the lights were also on in Ed Farmer and Leonard Shackleton's offices, no surprise there. Leonard had dragged Ed back to the studio to strategize their money, marketing, and production issues. I wondered how committed Leonard was to Cambria now that the threat of her implosion seemed an actuality.

The door to Ed's office stood slightly open, but all was quiet inside. I gave the door a gentle shove and saw the storyboards Dahlia Pearson had mentioned. Insiders raved on Ed's sketching abilities, and that much was true. Cards lined the wall, some with bits of dialogue or scene notes, some still empty, others with full action drawings of Cambria. All beautifully rendered. And slightly creepy in light of his obsession with his leading lady.

At the end of the hall, I pushed through the heavy door that led to the parking lot. Safety lights shone on the rows of dark trailers. I picked my way through the lot, counting off rows now that the murky gloom obscured my previous landmarks.

Cam-Cam's trailer loomed bigger and blacker than I remembered. Climbing the stairs, I noted the knocking of my heart and knees. Before unlocking the door, I took deep *ujjayi* breaths, practiced three Tae Bo kicks, and focused on a chi re-center. Shoved my hand into my pocket and pulled out the phone.

It'd been a while. Several months. I'd left my iPhone in California with my debt and crushed dreams. The little flip was cute. I'd had one like it when I was seven. Vicki had gotten it for me during a trip to Tokyo for the Hello Kitty, Hello Toothpaste commercial. At the time, everyone I knew had Blackberry pagers or Nokias, so the flip phone had been totally rad. Until I learned I could only use it for work-related calls and texts so we could write it off. My friends had to call the house phone. Not that I had that many friends. I was too busy shooting toothpaste commercials in places like Tokyo.

I stroked the hard, black plastic, flipped it, and paged through the directory of numbers. Nash and the office. That was it. I plugged in Daddy's number, Lamar, and LA HAIR. And felt better. The phone chirped in my hand. I squinted at the number on the screen, broke in goosebumps, and gave the caller a tentative hello.

"Maizie," said Vicki. "Where are you? I've been trying to find you all day. I need to know where you are."

"Um, how did you get this number?"

"Really, Maizie. Can't you just answer my questions for once?"

"Why?" I realized my heart's knocking had quieted, but the donut and my stomach were doing an uncomfortable tango.

"That would be another question, not an answer. Did your tutor skip that section of grammar?" Vicki offered one of her patented sighs and quickened her tempo. "Are you at the resort? Cambria's not here. And Giulio's missing, too. Are the three of you somewhere else?"

Where was Giulio? "No, I'm alone. Did you try calling him?"

"Brilliant idea. Of course, I called. Look, are you at the resort? You're not at your father's, and this call was forwarded."

I exhaled. The call had been forwarded from the office, meaning Nash still needed me to do the receptionist thing. Vicki didn't have ESP like I'd long suspected. Or at least she hadn't used it in this case. "No and no. I'm working."

She hung up.

I stared at the phone again, my thoughts pitching to and fro. Vicki didn't make sense on a good day, but Giulio was missing. I called Nash.

After reassuring him I was okay, he let out a long breath. "What'd you find?"

"Nothing yet. I haven't gone in."

"Miss Albright, don't make me regret giving you the burner."

"Vicki called me."

"I'm sorry. Anything else?"

"Giulio is missing. He was with me in the hotel, you know."

"Oh, I know. He took off and left you after seeing a murdered corpse. Quite a guy you had there."

"I didn't really have him... Anyway, I don't know where he went when he exited the stairwell. And he's missing. You don't think the killer, I mean, perpetrator got him?"

"No. Shit. Just a minute." My phone beeped while Nash apparently looked at a different screen on his phone. "Let me check on this. Don't worry about Giulio. I'm sure he's fine. Go in the trailer and look for evidence of poison."

He hung up before I could ask about Cam-Cam. I hoped Giulio had met a lady friend with entertaining footwear and wasn't holed up in a bathtub with Orlando.

With a shaky hand, I inserted the key and pushed the door open. "Hello?" I called, feeling foolish.

Low lights had been left on, but I flicked on the overheads anyway. Opening my backpack, I pulled out a pair of latex gloves then began a slow circle of the main room. Bits of plastic and paper — medical detritus that had been protecting the EMT's instruments — littered the floor and couch. One of the club chairs had been shoved into the back hallway. There was a nasty looking wet towel tossed in one corner.

Poor Cam-Cam.

I looked under the sink and spotted the cleaners, but these were untouched, judging by a light layer of dust. In the fridge, I sniffed bottles of smoothies, protein shakes, and water. All but one were still sealed. Likewise, the bananas and other fruit hadn't been bitten, and her chia seed packs weren't opened. I replaced the sealed bottles carefully. Slipping the open bottle of water into a paper sack, I stuck it in my backpack.

In the freezer, I found another bag of mini-Snickers. I pulled a sample, tossed them in another paper sack, and into my backpack. After surveying the rest of the room, I grabbed the edge of the club chair and tugged it back toward the living area. Then paused in the tiny hall. To my immediate right was the guest bath, at the end, the master bedroom. That left one more room. I swung the door open.

"You have a media room?" Jealousy churned inside my gut.

I repeated one of Renata's count-your-blessing mantras and forced myself to be happy for the young actress. Who was now lying in a hospital bed. Possibly due to her own poor choices. Not judging. "Very nice, Cam-Cam. This room will be great for watching the dailies. And hosting game night."

I used to love game night with the crew. But maybe that wasn't a Cambria thing.

Circling the room, I opened built-in mahogany cupboards that covered one wall. No cleaners, no drink, no food. I poked around on her MacBook — password: WonderWoman. She needed a security lesson — but didn't find any personal video collections. Mainly script notes, a Pinterest scrapbook related to the movie, and spreadsheets. *Pine Hollow*'s schedules, marketing, cast and crew listings, and wardrobe and prop suggestions.

"Very organized for a party girl," I muttered. "Good to see you haven't changed in that respect, Cam-Cam."

I left the media room for the guest bath. Other than ibuprofen and Pepto Bismol, she didn't keep any guest meds on hand. Both sealed. I breathed a sigh of relief that I hadn't found a stash of coke or a bag of weed. But then, I wouldn't think she'd be that hospitable to keep them in a bathroom cabinet. Although I knew a few actors and one musician who did. They were always trying so hard to make friends.

The cleaners under the sink had been used. I bagged her toilet cleaner and the Scrubbing Bubbles, then hesitated with her mouth rinse. In therapy, I'd heard patients talk about bottoming out with Listerine, but could you poison someone with Scope?

A door creaked. I froze, bent over my backpack. Scope in one hand, paper bag in the other. I set the Scope and bag on the floor and rose. Tiptoed toward the open bathroom door. Leaving me totally exposed to anyone in the bedroom. If that was the door I heard.

The bedroom door looked slightly open.

Oh no.

Every hair on my body stood at attention. I flipped open my darling phone. Thumb texted Nash, "n trlr bthrm. smn n bdrm!!!!" Kissed the phone and shoved it back in my jeans pocket. Said a light and love affirmation. Then a prayer Remi had taught me from her Sunday School class. Took a deep *ujjayi* breath. (Too deep. Fell back against the sink.) Recovered with two Tae Bo punches. I crept out of the bathroom.

In the living room, I hesitated, listening. No creaking. No footsteps. No nothing. It could have been a case of the willies, I told myself. Orlando Feelzen was on the loose. People were dead. It was late, dark, and slightly spooky in this ridiculously luxurious trailer. But it wasn't like it had a basement where hockey-masked Jason would be lurking with a steak knife.

Or did Jason have an axe?

Either way, was I a private investigator investigating this very private and important case or not? A woman in a hospital bed counted on me. As well as her creepster bosses.

Get a grip, Maizie.

I placed a hand on the half wall, stopping myself from taking the steps to the front door, and turned back. And heard a door snick shut.

My thighs clenched and the donut mixture sped toward my throat.

Like an uncaged animal, Orlando Feelzen charged from the hallway. Looking around, he spotted me.

Every organ in my body somersaulted. My shaking hands rose in the air, and I began to babble. I hardly knew what I said. Something about prisons and Cam-Cam and "please don't kill me."

Orlando shrieked back, his words even less intelligible.

I pivoted to the side, feeling the half-wall at my back. My *Kung Fu Kate* training kicked in, forcing my body into a low, wide stance with my fists clenched.

"You don't want to do this," I recited a *Kate* line for emphasis. And for courage. "I've got the law on one side and my posse on the other. Meet."

My arm snapped up. "Attack."

The second elbow jutted sharply. "And Defend. My posse is gonna kick your fanny from here to doomsday."

He rushed toward me.

Why did I pick that line?

I screamed something in Chinese and adjusted my pose. His foot flew out, catching my knee, and an elbow knocked my arm to the side. I tucked into the fall, hit a step, and felt his boot slam into my side. Orlando pounded down the stairs and out the door. I continued my roll down the stairs, landing at the bottom. The door swung back and smacked my back.

Dazed, I did a quick inventory of bodily harm. Not bad. Pulled myself to my feet. Fixed my ponytail. And ran out the door, dialing Nash.

"What'd you find?"

"Orlando Feelzen. In Cam-Cam's trailer. But he took off."

"Shit. Okay, don't do anything. Where is he now and where are you?"

"Somewhere in the trailer lot."

"Both of you?"

"Yeah, it turns out I've got good *Kung Fu Kate* muscle memory. But Orlando knows taekwondo. I think. Maybe karate. It's hard to tell when he's just trying to kick and punch his way out the door."

After a long beat, Nash took a breath. "I can hear you panting. Tell me you're not looking for him."

"Good point about the panting. I need to start jogging again. Why did I let myself go? I hate it when Jerry's right. I also need to find a kung fu sensei in Black Pine. It's really handy to know."

"Miss Albright." Nash's voice cut through my babble. "Go back to the trailer, lock the door, and wait for the police."

I slowed my pace to a fast walk. "He's going to get away."

"Let him." He hung up.

The phone chirped. Peering around wardrobe's trailer, I pressed answer.

"Call me back when you're in the trailer." The phone went dead.

My adrenaline high dropped several degrees. I crept back toward Cam-Cam's, shining the light from the phone's face under trailers as I walked. Satisfied that Orlando wasn't hiding nearby, I reentered the trailer.

Quietly. Carefully.

My backpack lay on the floor of the bathroom. Reality crashed as I scooped the bagged mouth rinse into the backpack. Holy Frig, I'd chased Orlando, fugitive and a known suspect in two murders and one attempted murder. What was I thinking? No wonder Nash had sounded irritated.

He got irritated when he worried about me. Really irritated.

Kind of sweet. And a turn on.

I forced my brain toward a more practical analysis. All those years of kung fu had paid off. I'd defended myself on pure acting training. I lifted my shirt, peeled back my waist clincher, and saw the trace of a bruise. Self-satisfaction deadened the pain. *Julia Pinkerton* and *Kung Fu Kate* had served me well tonight. I'd actually learned real snooping and martial arts skills from TV characters.

And all those parent review sites had said my shows weren't educational.

Maybe I didn't need as much training as I thought. Common sense and character development classes would see me through.

Pulling out the phone, I thumb-skimmed my tiny directory to Nash's number. And hesitated. Better yet, I'd call the girls and tell them about my mad detecting skills. Then call Daddy and tell him how much I loved my new job now that I was out in the field and not behind a desk. He enjoyed hearing stories about the payoff of hard work. Both mentally and financially. Or I'd call Lamar. He'd want to know how I'd done tonight. Unlike Nash, he'd congratulate me.

I might have a phone problem.

Or a pride problem. As my mind wandered over the events, I realized I'd done nothing much other than collected some bottles of cleaner and not gotten myself killed.

Also, it was late. Really late. Normal people were sleeping.

With that thought, I turned my attention back to the collection of evidence. The bedroom and master bath awaited. At the door, I hesitated, knowing it had once hidden Orlando Feelzen. Cambria must have given him a key to the trailer. Had she been housing a criminal?

Aiding and abetting, Cam-Cam? With a side of accessory.

What had happened to that girl? I shook my head and set myself to the task of rooting around in her drawers, closet, and bathroom cabinets. Nada. My stomach growled, the donut's energy used up in the Orlando standoff, and I considered returning to the craft table on my way out. I bagged more mouth rinse (did she have a fear of halitosis or what?) and hair product. My stomach growled again, and I recognized the scent of food now that I wasn't sniffing shampoo.

In the bathroom trash, I found Craft's cardboard plate and their delicious foody remains. Cam had loaded up, which surprised me. She even went for my favorite pie. There was an obvious giant-size bite in the piece. A huge no-no for someone who needed to look like she subsisted on squirrel and dandelions, yet could fight aliens bare-handed.

Wait a minute.

I sucked in my breath, recognizing the mix of jelly beans, Milano cookies, trail mix, and an unwrapped pastrami sandwich in the bottom of the can.

This wasn't Cam's food. This was my plate, one I had filled earlier before the disastrous parking lot kiss. I hadn't gotten a chance to eat anything. Cam-Cam had snuck a bite of my food. I lifted the trash can and sniffed the chocolate peanut butter pie.

I dug out my phone and pressed Nash's number.

"Where've you been?" he growled. "I've been waiting."

"I think I found the poisoned food," I gulped. "It was mine. I think I was meant to be poisoned."

NINETEEN

#SixDegreesofHitchcock
#ChocolatePeanutButterDie

---

*W*hen it comes to direction, actors are sometimes conflicted on how best to accomplish a scene. The director's approach may go against her own instincts. Or the director herself might be conflicted.

For example, I was told by Nash, "Get out of there." Then, "No, wait, I'll get security." Then, "No, I'll come. Dammit. Let me get someone to stay with Cambria. Don't move."

"You can't leave Cam-Cam," I said. "We have orders. Leonard threatened us legally and financially if we didn't do exactly as he said."

"I don't care what that sumbitch said," said Nash. "I'm coming to get you. Feelzen's still at large."

"We don't know for sure the poison was meant for me. Let's talk this through. I got the food and arrived at the trailer alone. I set the food on the coffee table and I remember wanting to eat it, but I was tired after finding the dead guy in the bath—"

"Take some notes on this and get back to me. I need to make some calls. I know a real bodyguard. Wait for me in the trailer."

"No, no. Just a minute. Then you and Cam-Cam came in, and I needed to tell you about the bathtub victim. We went to the parking lot and... You know what happened there. And then Leonard showed up. That means Cams took the bite from my pie while we were having a moment—"

"Let me get to the point. No one could have administered the cleaner to your food after you received the plate. Unless it was during the few minutes we were 'having a moment,' which seems unlikely. Where'd you get the food?" He paused. "By the way, I don't like the phrase 'having a moment.'"

"You don't? I'm not sure what else to call it."

"Focus, Miss Albright."

"Right. Craft service. They have a buffet of snacks set up if you miss the meal times. I'd sort of..." I rushed through the next part, "gotten in the habit of filling a plate when I arrived on the set. Or leaving the set. Old habit. Actually, not so old, since I wasn't allowed to—"

"Anyone could have been poisoned?" His breath hissed. "This is a lot more serious. Someone's targeting the entire movie?"

"Yeah, no. The chef had chocolate peanut butter pie especially for me. He's an old friend of the family. Big Jim. Caters DeerNose events. This morning, I saw it on the menu. I asked him to save me some."

"Please don't tell me he put your name on the pie."

"Not a whole pie. I'm not that bad. Just a piece." My face heated. "He wrote my name in chocolate on the plate. With this adorbs drawing of little dancing peanuts. I love Big Jim. He's über talented."

"Do you know how long the dancing peanuts sat there?"

"Not exactly. "

"Anyone on the set could have seen it, then doused it in chemicals found in any cleaning closet. Including Orlando Feelzen. Who left a dead vic in his room to stay in Cambria's trailer." He cursed. Colorfully. "Wait there. As in, do not move." He hung up. I stared at my phone, wishing I could have a conversation with someone who ended with "goodbye."

Someone on the set wanted to kill me? Suddenly the trailer

seemed full of noises. Real or imaginary, I wasn't sure. Holding the trash can, I crept into the living room and peered through the window into the dark parking lot. I didn't feel safe in the trailer. Orlando had a key. The more I thought about Orlando, his key, and his alleged ability to murder, the more the walls of the trailer seemed to shrink. My earlier bout of *Kung Fu Kate* adrenaline had sapped my energy. I no longer felt confident in my abilities in anything.

I mean, holy frig, I could have eaten chocolate peanut butter pie with a side of window cleaner. Knowing me, I would have popped half the slice in my mouth and swallowed before registering that it even tasted like chemicals. Maybe even finished the whole thing. And Big Jim had left me a mongo piece, like a quarter of a pie.

That was just pitiful. Jerry was right about carbs being the death of me.

My chest hurt, and I clutched the trash can against it. I needed out of the trailer. It felt stuffy and reeked of near death and Orlando's cheap cologne. I would run for the warehouse where people were still meeting. Then I'd join security and wait for Nash. Or better yet, get on Lucky and drive home so Nash could stay with Cam-Cam.

Although how to carry a trash can on a dirt bike was a real puzzle.

I took a deep breath, skipped the Tae Bo stuff so I wouldn't dump the can, and slipped out the front door. The quicker I got away from the trailer, the better. In the dark, every shadow seemed to move. Every sound was amplified. Footsteps rang somewhere in the distance. A golf cart whirred. Clutching the garbage in one arm, I edged along the trailer, shining my phone light beneath the trailer and into dark crevices.

At the edge of Cam-Cam's trailer, I was sure I could hear someone strolling the parking lot. Hopefully, a security guard, but I wasn't taking the risk. I ran for the studio building. My feet slapped the pavement, and the can smacked my torso. The metal

door loomed ahead, a security light shining above it like a beacon.
I slammed to a halt before the door, jostled the can and phone, and
grabbed the big handle.

Jerked. Knocked. Beat on the metal.

Okay. I'd been locked out. Security didn't know I was in the
trailer lot. And I skipped the sign-in on purpose. I'd just have to
cross back through the dark (and scary) lot full of trailers, then the
grassy field surrounding the big parking area, and see if the tall
metal fence had a gate in the back. I mean, it'd have to have a gate,
right? This was once a warehouse with tall garage doors for
unloading trucks. Although the gate was probably locked. Just like
this door. Lots of expensive equipment and accoutrements around
here. Best to keep things locked tight.

Friginometrous.

I sank against the warehouse door and squinted into the
gloomy trailer lot. Chain link fences had been a specialty in the
Julia Pinkerton: Teen Detective repertoire. Particularly in city scenes.
She could scale a chain link lickety-split. But I didn't remember
Julia ever carrying a garbage can up a fence. Even a short, non-
kitchen trash variety.

Nothing to do but go back to the trailer and wait for Nash's
rescue. Which would be princess sexy except it was self-defeating.
Self-defeat was not sexy. And if I was trapped in the lot, so was
Orlando.

Fear was also not sexy.

"Nice target you're making under this light, Maizie." Julia
Pinkerton's snark whispered in my thoughts. "Haul ass back to the
trailer. And maybe take a different route in case you're being
followed, braniac?"

Fear did weird things to me. But if it took a *Three Faces of Eve*
moment to motivate me, so be it.

I tip-toe ran toward the trailers. Took a right at the second row.
Jostling the can, I found my phone, ready to shine its light beneath
the trailer and expose any hidden monsters.

And found one.

I had little memory of making it back to the trailer. But after locking the door and almost vomiting into the trash can (remembering at the last minute why I couldn't), I leaned against the door and thanked my lucky stars I'd made it. Stumbling up the stairs, I deposited the trash can on the floor, shoved the EMT mess aside, and sank onto the couch. I stared at the ceiling for a long minute, willing the last few days to disappear from my mind. When they didn't, I dug out my phone and kissed it. Flipped it open and cursed it.

The charge was almost out.

Quickly, I pressed Nash's hot button. "I'm in the trailer."

"You're finally listening to me. Good. My buddy will be here in a minute."

"Not totally. I made a run for it. And was locked out of the studio building. And ran back."

"Miss Albright—"

"And found Orlando Feelzen."

"Shit. Did he see you?"

"No."

"You'll be alright, hon. Just stay calm."

"I'm calm. Super calm. Like, so calm I can't analyze my emotions because I have none. I think that's called shock." I took a deep breath. "We have a situation."

"Just hang on. I'll call security to get you out of there. And we'll get police backup. I don't care what Shackleton says."

"I don't trust security. I don't trust anyone here. I don't even know if I trust the police at this point." I gulped, pinched my thumb skin, and a tear leaked out. "I did it again."

"Did what?"

"Orlando Feelzen is dead."

"What?"

"I think I'm cursed." I stared up at the ceiling and counted mahogany panels. "Orlando was here, and now he's dead. But this time I know how he died."

"Maizie..."

"He was stabbed."

"Oh, Maizie. Hon." Nash's voice cut away and he called out to someone in the distance. His comforting baritone returned. "Stay where you are. I'm leaving now."

"Someone's out there. I'm stuck in this trailer and someone's out there. I feel like Jimmy Stewart in *Rear Window*. Just waiting for them to find me. That's three victims, Nash. Four if you count Cam-Cam and that one was meant for me." My voice warbled and slid into a whisper. "I take it back about *Rear Window*. I'm that teenager in every slasher flick who's just found her horny boyfriend dead in the closet. Except I'm not Jamie Lee Curtis. I'm her dumb friend who tries to hide in the basement."

"You're not stupid, and you're not stuck. I'm coming to get you. You hear me?" His hurried footsteps rang through the tinny phone line. A door clattered. "Just hold on."

"Oh my God," I said. "I need the princess rescue. I'm pathetic."

"You're not pathetic."

"I am." I leaned over, feeling the blood rush to my brain. "I thought I could do investigative work. I wanted the excitement of field work, to get out from behind that desk. I forced your hand and took a chance on a client. And look where it's gotten me. I'm being hunted like a stuck pig. Like literally. I'm stuck here because of a piece of pie. And you have to unstuck me. If I were any kind of investigator, I'd rescue myself."

"You listen to me, Maizie. I keep telling you, this is not normal investigative work. It's not your fault that our client has gotten involved in this kind of criminal activity. From here on out, if we ever take a client like this again — which I sincerely hope not — I'm vetting the crap out of them before I agree to a contract."

I sniffed and sat up. Nash said "we" and "our."

"And you're not a pig. You're an intelligent, beautiful woman. Who lacks confidence. And common sense. Sometimes. But I'm going chalk that up to your upbringing. Look how you defended yourself against Feelzen."

"Poor Orlando. I think he was scared of me. And now he's dead."

"Let's get back on track. You should—"

I pressed the phone against my ear, straining to hear him. "Should what? Hello?" I pulled the phone away. Dead.

Holy Frig. I was in a teen slasher plot. Had I pulled a *Cabin in the Woods* trigger, accidentally starting the slaying process? Knowing me, the trigger had been a donut. I squeezed my eyes shut and tried to remember where this had started.

With Cambria's villa. Seeing the body double who disappeared shortly after I saw it. Orlando was dead. Guy in Orlando's room, also dead. Hells, I had forgotten to ask Nash about him. But anyway, he was related to Orlando and Orlando was related to Cambria. And I had seen a dead Cambria. Therefore…

This was some unholy word problem.

Therefore, whoever had killed Cam-Cam's twin had seen me spotting her. There was the trigger. We, the hunted, were all six degrees of separation from Cam-Cam. More like a Will Smith one degree. I was *The Man Who Knew Too Much*.

That's two Hitchcocks. Very foreboding for me. Except Jimmy Stewart always made it out alive. This wasn't *Psycho*, the deaths were related, and not to his (or her) mother. If we could figure out the motive, we'd catch him.

I breathed out a long sigh, stood, and did three Tae Bo side kicks. Then fell into a crouch at the sound of a key scraping the front door lock.

TWENTY

#HotAndHeavy #JasonsKnife

Halloween lessons learned, I only wished this trailer had a basement for hiding. Whoever was at the door was not Wyatt Nash, and I was not sticking around to see who it was. Staying in my half-crouch, I ran into the bedroom and examined my hiding choices. Bed. Closet. Bathroom.

Under the bed was certain doom in all horror movies. The bathroom was bigger than a closet and would give me a fighting chance. Also, hiding in a closet was a good way to bring about hyperventilation and fainting, leaving me unable to defend myself. I slipped into the bathroom, leaving the door cracked to make my hiding not-so-obvious, and listened. The snick of the front door shutting told me someone was intent on keeping their entrance private.

The perp crept up the stairs and into Cam-Cam's living room. And seemed to be waiting. For me to come out?

They knew I was in here.

I was going to die.

No. In the mirror, my eyelids narrowed, and my mouth drew into a tight sneer. Julia Pinkerton's green eyes stared back at me, and in my brain, she whispered in fierce, unrealistic but brave teen speak. "You may be cornered, but bitch, we fight back. You battle until Nash arrives. This is no princess rescue. This is you surviving. Make it happen."

"The posse is ready," whispered Kung Fu Kate.

I switched back to Julia, who was more resourceful than kung fu quips. With the stealth of a teenager opening the liquor cabinet, I opened Cambria's bathroom vanity and retrieved items I'd already explored in my earlier poison hunt. Hairspray, a lighter, Band Aids, and a metal nail file. Cam-Cam was low on weapons. I bandaged the nail file to my inner left wrist, set the hairspray in easy reach on the counter, and palmed the lighter. Then shoved a bunch of Band Aids in my pockets.

Just in case I needed them later.

Shifting to the balls of my feet in a slight crouch, I readied to spring forward with my homemade torch. Julia Pinkerton had done this in Season Three, Episode Five, "Death's Got My Six." Or was that Episode Seven? Facing down an arsonist with an ironic twist (or a clichéd twist as one writer had argued), Julia gave him a taste of her version of medicine. He'd doused her in gasoline and held the lit flame in one hand while he taunted her. She grabbed a can of hairspray from her purse and shot a chemical spray at the flame. Which miraculously didn't burn her. And backflipped out of the room before he could get to her.

I could no longer do backflips, but I could shoot him (or her) with fire and use the surprise as a getaway. Anyway, that was the plan.

Listening for footsteps, I realized I'd heard a faint rustling that had just stopped. Holding my breath, my pulse pounded beneath my nail file shiv. Goosebumps pebbled my skin. A hollow, dull thud proceeded the footsteps, but they were retreating. The feet pattered down the stairs. The door clicked. And the trailer became tomb-like once more.

Were they gone? Or tricking me? My heart now thudded at the base of my neck. I shifted my feet, bouncing lightly. Flicked the lighter in preparation. Glanced in the dark mirror and made out

Julia's pissy countenance. Put the lighter out. Grabbed the hairspray and snuck around the bathroom door. Placed the hairspray on the dresser and moved toward the bedroom door. Flattened to the wall and listened. Hard.

Nothing.

I edged closer to peer out the crack but could only see the hall's opposite wall. Flipping around, I put my eye to the crack. No movement. No sound.

They were either über patient — like the lion waiting for the gazelle to resume grazing — or they'd left. I didn't want to be the gazelle, but — like the girl with the dead, horny boyfriend — I needed to check the basement. I understood the horror girlfriend now. You could only stand this sort of suspense for so long. Were they going to kill you or not? Bravery included a certain amount of stupidity, but also a willingness to be in control of one's destiny.

I picked up my hairspray and readied my lighter, preparing for my destiny. Slipping through the bedroom, I snuck down the hall and peered into the living room. Empty. Just to be safe, I released a pent-up screech — like something once heard on *Braveheart* — and leaped into the living room. I raced around the room, screaming, my lighter flaming and my index finger trembling above the hairspray button, itching to press and torch the terrorist.

The door flung open. I spun toward the stairs, shooting a flame toward the front door.

"Maizie," shouted Nash. "Hold your fire."

*A*fter examining dead Orlando, Nash escorted me to his truck. I could barely walk with the adrenaline rush I'd spent in almost torching him. He loaded my bike in the back. At the security gate, the guard waved us through the front gates. Nash pulled through, hopped from the truck, and entered the guard booth. A few minutes later, he returned.

"Did you tell him about Orlando?" I asked.

"I asked to see the logs."

"I'm leaving a lot of bodies for people to find."

"You want to tell that to your probation officer?" He checked my quick head shake. "Mowry wants to call your probation officer anyway. He's worried about you. And he should be, considering someone wants you to eat Windex."

"Her." I sighed. "My probation officer is a her. She already doesn't like my job and doesn't care about my dreams. But I can't keep leaving dead bodies around for some poor security guard to stumble upon. I should have stayed and faced the music."

"We don't know if whoever killed Orlando is still there. Which puts you in danger." Nash rubbed the spot between his eyebrows. "I'm taking you home. I'll tell Mowry I found Orlando. I'd feel better if you stayed at the cabin."

"Forever?"

He rolled his eyes. "I know that's not going to work."

"You're protecting me."

Nash flashed me a venomous look. "Somebody's got to. I swear you don't have a lick of self-preservation."

As we sped toward the other end of town, Nash's clenched jaw eased and I gave conversation another try.

"How's Cam-Cam? Did she wake up?"

Nash shook his head. "Hell, I've been staring at her, willing her to wake up. Not that she can talk. The doctor said her throat is burned by the chemicals. I'm struggling to feel sympathy for her. She holds the key to this mess. My buddy will keep an eye on her tonight."

"What about Giulio?"

"I've got less sympathy for him." He cut his eyes toward me. "Sorry. Resort hasn't seen him. Not much we can do there."

"I hope he's okay."

"Yes," Nash said stiffly.

I changed the subject. "They returned to the trailer to get the evidence. And I stupidly left the trash can at the top of the stairs, super easy for them to find. They killed Orlando, and they took the garbage but didn't look for me. They didn't search the trailer at all. Why?"

Nash pursed his lips. "Presumably, they found what they wanted but didn't know you were there. I think they planned to get rid of the evidence in the trailer when no one would see them. But we don't know if they knew Orlando was hiding in the trailer or if they just got lucky."

"Anybody stand out in the security logs?"

"That booth records license plates, and all these California people rent their vehicles. That's going to take some time to research. We might be quicker than the police, except Black Pine PD will confiscate the security video footage. And they'll see you and that damn bike."

"Don't get mad at Lucky." I examined Nash's grim look. "I'll be brought in for questioning, but we're working for Leonard. Hopefully that will be enough to satisfy them and my probation officer. Leonard's not going to be happy about this at all."

"Imagine how Orlando feels."

I shuddered. "And what about the other guy? Did you get any info from Detective Mowry? What about the film?"

"Don't know. And no ID on the vic. Mowry doesn't think he's local, but he could be from Atlanta. He looked vaguely familiar to the resort staff, but they couldn't place him. If he's not local, he must have been staying somewhere in Black Pine. They're checking with the other hotels. Unless he was staying with Orlando without the resort's knowledge." Nash paused. "Mowry sent me a picture of the crime scene. What you didn't see was the considerable dent in the back of his head."

"Oh." I crossed my arms and shivered. "A dent."

"Mowry thinks the perp opened the hotel door for this guy. The victim walked in, and the aggressor walloped him on the back of the head, drug him into the bathroom, and rolled him into the tub. Wiped up the mess. He left the towels in the hall and resort staff picked them up. They weren't bloody enough to raise an eyebrow. The police did bag the room's iron. There was a hair on it."

"Orlando looked strong."

"Yeah, but I don't think Orlando gave himself a fatal contusion." He glanced at me. "Orlando was also caught by surprise. Not stabbed. The blood you saw on his neck came from the back of his head."

"You rolled him over?"

"Didn't touch him, of course. It was hard to see him under the trailer, too. I just knew what to look for after hearing about the other victim. Now I wonder if the same happened to the woman you saw. You said she was facing you, right?"

"Yes." I thought about those blank eyes, staring at me. Between the eyes, her nudity, and the birthmark on her hip, I hadn't noticed if the back of her head had been flattened. "Her hair had fallen forward. I guess the back of her head could have had a....dent."

We'd reached the Spayberry gates, half-hidden by the forest surrounding Daddy's cabin. Nash leaned out his window to tap in the security code. Sliding back in, he glanced at me. "Hey, you okay?"

I stared at him. "I don't know."

He placed a hand on my arm and turned his attention back to the opening gates. The drive was long and dark. I heard the yips of the Jack Russell pack and saw the house lights glowing in the distance. His hand felt solid and comforting, but my focus was on the flattened heads. And wondering if that particular lack of observance on my part was good or bad. Also wondering why the perp decided I'd get a chemical dessert instead of a wallop to the back of my head.

I fingered the back of my skull, my head suddenly throbbing. Exhaustion or sympathy pains. Or both.

Security lights flared on in the drive as we pulled before the palatial cabin. Nash jerked the truck into park, lifted his hand from my arm, and half-turned in his seat. "I'm not going to let anything happen to you."

"I'm not locking myself in my room."

"I know." He pulled in a deep breath. "But I want you to carry a firearm. I don't care what kind. Boomer probably has enough to spare, and it won't take much to convince him to give you one. Has he trained you?"

My chin jerked up. "I know how to use a gun. Every summer visit was spent out in the woods doing target practice with Daddy. I also did firearms training on the set with Detective Earl King and in the Kids Police Academy. And I was on the Long Beach rifle team. It was one of the reasons I got the role as Julia Pinkerton."

Nash's brows climbed, and he pursed his lips into a long whistle. "Miss Albright, I'm impressed. Next time Lamar and I head to the gun range, we'll take you along. Maybe we could place a friendly wager on your accuracy." A dimple winked on the cheek opposite his scar.

"I've collected an arsenal in birthday gifts starting with a Daisy and ending with a Browning last year. Daddy even bought me a .38 Special for my sixteenth birthday. A pink Smith & Wesson." I rolled my eyes. At the age of four, one parent had given me my first rifle. The other my first Armani.

I'd wanted a Sally Secrets. I had to buy her myself with my first paycheck.

Nash looked impressed again. His eyes had rounded, and the dimple appeared where he'd sucked in his cheek. "My piece is also a .38 Special. Not pink, though. I like its weight. Imagine, that. We have matching Smith & Wesson's."

"I'm not carrying a gun."

The smile disappeared. "Why the hell not?" he growled. "Somebody wants to put you out of commission, probably because you keep walking in on their killing spree. Granted your judo-whatever provides an element of surprise, but I don't believe for one minute you're going to karate chop this bastard into submission."

"It's kung fu, not karate."

"Either way, I want you protected with a weapon that's not your hands."

"It's not going to help me any if this guy — or woman — is clobbering victims from behind. You want me to pull a gun on anyone standing behind me? It's a good way for me to accidentally shoot someone. I've done that, remember? Or I could get shot. If they're strong enough to drag that guy into a bathtub and Orlando under a trailer, they're strong enough to take a gun from me."

"Then I'm telling Leonard we're leaving Cambria with my buddy and I'm going to be your bodyguard."

My heart beat a little faster as I envisioned a Kevin Costner/Whitney Houston situation, but then Julia began snarking about rescuing princesses. "Leonard will pay the bodyguard and sue us for breach of contract."

"I don't care."

"That's stupid. You almost lost your business earlier this summer. You've worked too hard to try to rebuild it again." I tried one of Renata's goal-focused explanations. "This is my responsibility. I did this to your business. I'm going to fix this. I'll be more careful. But first thing in the morning. Because it's been a long day what with all the deaths. And attempted deaths."

He stared up at the ceiling. "I didn't want a partner. I like being alone. Even with Jolene, she left me alone to do her own thing."

I didn't like the mention of Jolene Sweeney let alone a comparison to her. I also didn't like the thought of losing my job in the face of losing my life. "I know my way around a studio lot. I'll find a way to poke around the set without alerting any of our suspects. And I promise not to eat anything…with my name on it."

His eyes narrowed.

"I need to talk to Big Jim. He's known me most of my life. If the police find out about the poisoning, Big Jim's reputation could be ruined. It would also break his heart. I've got to speak with him first so we can figure out how the pie was poisoned." I crossed my arms and tilted my head, my ponytail brushing my shoulder. "I'm sensible, and you know it."

He laughed. "Miss Albright, you're a stubborn thing when you want to be. There's a fire in your gut I rarely see, but when I do…" He whistled. "Look out."

I smiled.

"And you don't look like you're going to lose your lunch anymore."

The dented heads. I'd almost forgotten.

He stretched an arm across the back of the seat. "I'd like to see that arsenal. Do you have your own cabinet?"

I nodded. "In the study. We all have one. Well, Daddy's got six. They line the room. Very tasteful. He had them made from lumber on his land. Oak. Super solid." I sighed. "Although, if it were me, I think bookcases would have been prettier. Like the library in *Beauty and the Beast*? With the matching spines and marbled paper? Better yet, a wall of oak wardrobes. But that's Daddy. He likes paperbacks and artillery."

While I'd been talking, Nash had slid closer. His fingers played with the ends of my ponytail.

I shivered. In a good way.

"Sorry." He withdrew his fingers but left his arm stretched out. "You're an interesting woman, Miss Albright. You surprise me."

"Because I like clothes more than firearms?" I smiled, easing back against the seat to give him more access to my ponytail. And other parts.

"No. That you have guns at all. But considering your father's been on the cover of every hunting magazine, I guess I shouldn't be surprised. I bet he's been photographed as much as you. Never thought about that."

"True," I said. "Vicki was a model once, too, you know."

"Oh, I know. Jolene used to go on about her all the time. They were in the same beauty pageants." His lip curled and the arm bent, to prop his head.

The back of my neck felt cool. And lonely. "I guess I'd better go in. It's late. The dogs are out, and they'll wake everyone." The Jack Russells' barks had amplified as they circled the truck, waiting for the occupants to exit. But more importantly, I was reminding Nash of his ex-wife again and that wasn't pleasant for anyone. Particularly me.

"You didn't do those beauty pageants, did you?"

I turned from the door and found him staring at me. "Not really. A few toddler ones, I think. There wasn't any point to it when I got older. I had plenty of contracts."

"Is it hard on a person?"

"What?"

"Being beautiful? The expectations, I guess."

"I don't know." But I did. "It wasn't enough for me. I mean, I wasn't that sort of beautiful. Not that I think I'm beautiful. Or was beautiful. It was useful in my jobs to look appealing. But expectations are— Renata said…"

He leaned toward me and cupped my cheek. "You are. Beautiful."

OMG. My body trembled. Starting at my shoulders and racing to my toes. I curled them inside my Golden Goose sneakers.

His hand slipped from my cheek to cradle the back of my head. "I keep thinking about you finding these victims, and it doesn't seem right. You're too beautiful for this sort of work."

"I don't think—" His hand lightly rubbed my scalp and I had to stop myself from purring.

"But then there's something else there. Grit? I don't know. I can't figure you."

Vicki's feminist spirit would have been offended, but I scooted closer. "I'm serious about real training, Nash."

"I don't like worrying about you." His other hand stole to my cheek and stroked. "Damn, your skin is soft."

"Nash, I want this. Very badly." My ambiguity was purposeful. I lowered my voice. "You know I can do this. With or without a gun."

"Partners have each other's backs. This isn't right." He spoke drowsily as he caressed my cheek. "Lord, I want to kiss you."

"Just do it," I whispered. To myself.

He drew closer. "It's a major problem. You're distracting."

"No more yoga outfits, I promise."

"It's not that. Well, it's also that." His lips landed in my hair.

"Why do you smell so good? When you're not there, the office reeks."

"The office smells like donuts."

"You smell better than donuts."

I closed my eyes. I don't think a more romantic line had been mentioned in the history of romantic lines.

"We can't do this. I've told you, it's no good," he said, but his fingers continued to stroke my cheek. "You want to partner with me, but you're distracting with your looks, good smell, soft skin, and funny stories. I want you. That's no good in a partner."

Wait, this didn't sound romantic. I tilted my head back to look at him.

"Maizie, can I kiss you?"

I nodded. I liked it better when he didn't talk. But I had a horrible suspicion. Those thoughts fled as his lips landed on mine. Soft, supple, and strong. I melded myself against him, and he dipped my head back, snuggling it into his palm. His mouth moved against mine and fulfilled every fantasy I ever had about this moment. The fragrance of his bergamot aftershave and that other scent that was all his own acted like a drug, intoxicating me. His soft stubble scraped against my skin, but I didn't care. I pressed closer. His tongue teased my lips then dipped inside to deepen the kiss.

My thoughts spun out of control. I clung to his shoulders, bent backward against his strong arms.

He paused, almost panting. "I'm sorry. But Lord, you taste good."

I pulled him against me. His head bent and angled, his lips catching the corner of my mouth, then slid along my jaw to my neck. The kisses left my skin hot and cool, tingling with anticipation.

At my throat, he stopped and drew back. "You should quit. I'll talk Boomer into hiring you at DeerNose. You could work in security."

"No." I drew his face to mine and kissed him, bruising my lips against his.

He drew me into his lap, running his hands to my waist and up to my rib cage, where I hoped he didn't feel the edge of my Miracle Suit waist clincher. "You're luscious. Lord Almighty, He knew how to make a woman when he made you."

I didn't care if he felt the edge of my Miracle Suit. I guided his hand higher and moaned into his ear.

We were going from zero to one-twenty in point two seconds. It felt like a dam cracking. A lit match tossed into a Southern California forest.

No, that volcano, churning with bubbling magma and threatening to blow. Except less violent and way sexier. So deliciously right. And maybe a little wrong.

I returned to concentrate on the sensation of his lips, hands, and extremely robust body pressed against mine. One hand gripped his shoulder and the other kneaded the back of his neck. His tongue plunged, and I gasped.

He pulled back to stare into my eyes. Cool blue warmed and fuzzy with desire.

"I'm going to have to fire you," he muttered and dropped to my neck again, nipping and nuzzling my skin.

Wait, what?

TWENTY-ONE

#FathersDaughter #HideAndSeek

I froze beneath him, trying to analyze the seriousness of his claim without the oxygen needed for my brain to analyze anything. He'd found that spot on my neck that drained my head of blood.

In a non-vampiric sort of way.

A thump on the window caused us both to jerk away. A thump made by the butt of a rifle.

Daddy. With a Winchester. Or Remington. Despite my gun closet, I still couldn't tell them apart.

Scooting away from Nash, I adjusted my clothing and rolled down the window. "You're about ten years too late for this role."

"Maizie Marlin Spayberry, what are you doing in my drive-way? Where is the sense God gave you?"

I hated to think where that sense went in the last ten minutes.

Nash leaned around me. "I apologize, sir. I have no excuses. Won't happen again."

I whirled around to flash Nash a look. "We have plenty of excuses," I muttered. "First off, we're not sixteen."

"Wyatt Nash, you'll hear from me in the morning," said Daddy. "You, of all people, should know better than to let your willy override your better judgment. With my daughter. You're just lucky I recognized the Silverado."

"Yes, sir."

A different kind of heat licked my neck and flushed my cheeks. "Daddy," I gasped. "I'm twenty-five."

"And living in my house because of the same lack of sense that led you back here from California. Although that lack of sense was a blessing." He paused, probably confused as I was. The gun butt pointed toward the cabin. "Get out of that truck and get inside. I've been waiting to have words with you anyway."

Words. Words with Daddy were never good. I wanted more words with Nash. Like was he serious about firing me or was that some weird turn-on? If so, not judging. That's an easier fetish to digest than others.

I turned toward Nash, but he was already slipping out of the truck. I scooted across the seat, out the door, and followed him to the back of the truck. Small terriers bounced around me, then dashed to the porch at Daddy's whistle.

"Nash," I said. "Wyatt. I'm sorry about Daddy. He never got the chance to chase away my dates in high school. He's just making up for lost time."

Ignoring me, he unfastened the bungee cords he'd used to secure Lucky. Bungee cords, I realized, he now left in the bed for the securing of Lucky. He'd taken to toting my dirt bike. Maybe more than he'd taken to me.

"You need some help there, son?" called Daddy from the porch.

"I've got it, sir." Grabbing Lucky, he pulled her to the end of the bed, lifted her, and placed her between us. Way too symbolically for my liking.

"Take care, Miss Albright. And by that, I want you carrying that Smith & Wesson." He dipped his head, refusing to look at me. "I apologize for tonight."

"You don't need to apologize—" I was cut off by the slam of the truck bed. "Maybe we got carried away, but you know this was inevitable. Directors would give their right arm for the kind of sexual tension that's been building between us."

"My life is not scripted. Good night, Miss Albright."

"That's not what I meant."

"I know what you meant." Nash leveled me with an icy blue gaze. "But we agreed. This is no way to conduct business. You've got a choice. It's me or the job. Either way, I'm good with your decision."

"I didn't agree to that, and I'm not good with either. It's not fair. You know I need to work for you. Not only to have a job but also to get the two-year training for a PI license. But you mean more to me than a job."

He ran his hands up my arms and rested them on my shoulders. "And that's why we can't fool around. I will do better by you in the future. This is my fault. Boomer was right. I wasn't thinking with my head or acting as a gentleman."

"It's not your fault."

Nash shook his head and strode to his open door.

"Night, son." Boomer saluted him from the porch, the rifle cradled in his arm.

I watched the truck roar from the drive, sending the dogs into a barking frenzy, and marched to the porch. "And here I thought I had only one parent who'd undermine me."

"You'll get over it." He turned to open the front door, then punched in the security number. "This place is as good as Fort Knox thanks to Wyatt Nash."

"I've done some upgrades."

"And I thank you for it. Listen, young lady. It's no secret that Wyatt Nash has been put through the wringer by a woman. Jolene Sweeney. That's his ex."

"I know who she is, Daddy."

"Well, then I'd expect you to act smarter. I know a little about the entanglements of beautiful women." He stroked his long beard, musing on prior entanglements, while I pretended I hadn't heard those words. Because, *ew*. Even if he was talking about Vicki. Which I preferred never to think about.

"It doesn't matter anyway." I followed him through the foyer and into the living room. "Thanks to you, Wyatt said he wasn't interested in dating if we're going to work together."

"Smart man. You don't shit where you eat."

"Daddy!"

"It's an expression." He slammed a hand against the swinging kitchen door and held it open for me. Set the rifle on the kitchen table and poured two cups of coffee. "Sit."

I didn't like it, but I sat.

"If you haven't caught on, I'm het up." He sat across from me but still managed to tower over me.

"Oh my God, it's not like I'm fourteen and you caught me with the pool boy."

"Lord Almighty, Maizie, that better not be a real story. I could kill your mother for many things, but if I find out—"

"It's also an expression." Sort of.

"Anyway, that's not why I wanted to talk to you. Do I need to remind you of the provisions of your probation agreement?"

"No. Why?" Craptastic. Had my probation officer already learned that I'd taken up the discovery of bodies? "Am I in trouble?"

"You're gonna be if you don't stop this filming business." Boomer peered at me down the length of his nose. "That California judge said you're no longer to be involved in the entertainment industry. I know that after all those years it must be a hard thing to give up, but Maizie, it's for your own good. TV turned you into a downright idiot, getting into all those scrapes with drug dealers and whatnot."

I ignored his dig about my troubled ex-fiancé. "Daddy, I'm working for Leonard Shackleton, but I'm not involved in the movie itself. In fact, now it's more of a criminal investigation. It's pretty exciting. Although, I shouldn't be excited about murder — so morbid — but I'm investigating. Nash is acting as a bodyguard to

Cam-Cam. I think you'd be proud of me. Bonafide detective work." I bounced in my seat. Until I saw his look.

"Don't lie to me, girl. You're letting them film you. I saw you myself at that new office on Palmetto."

"What?"

"I'm about ready to tan your hide, Maizie Marlin Spayberry. You're sneaking around behind my back. And Wyatt Nash's back. And even worse, the judge's back. To do what? Feed your vanity?" At my look of confusion, he halted his tirade. "Baby girl, is your mother drugging you or something? That woman has stooped pretty low in her life, but I didn't think she'd do anything like that."

"I have no idea what you're talking about. I wasn't anywhere near Palmetto Street today." I counted off bodies as a means of location checking. "Mostly the resort, the set, and the hospital. Maybe I was at the office, but only for a minute. I'm exhausted. It's been a super long, super rough day and night. Daddy, I keep finding corpses."

It was his turn to look confused. "Like that movie with Bruce Willis?"

"Not ghosts. Actual bodies. Murder victims. The criminal investigation I just told you about is a murder case."

"Well, who was getting filmed on Palmetto Street? Because she sure as hell looked like you."

"That's a good question." Vicki had stooped pretty low in her life, but she might have hit rock bottom on this one. I pushed away from the table and circled it to place my arms around Daddy's neck. "Thank you for trying to protect me."

He kissed me on the cheek. "That's what fathers are for."

"Daddy, I mean this in the sweetest way. But you need to lay off my love life."

"Then don't do it in my driveway."

*D*addy wasn't the only one waiting up for me. When I crossed the five thousand square-foot cabin to my bedroom, I found my sister in my bed. Remi flipped on the bedside light at my entry.

"Took you long enough," she said.

"What are you doing up? You're six. You need your sleep."

She rolled her eyes. "That's all they want from me. Sleep and eat. What am I? A hippo?"

"Do hippos need a lot of sleep?"

"I don't know. They're just so cute." She wrapped her arms around her knees. "Did Daddy talk to y'all?"

"He had words for me." I winked. "Then I had words with him."

She slapped her face. "You can't get sassy with him, girl. Don't you know nothing? You got sent to your room."

"I sent myself." I yawned and lowered myself next to her. "I'm exhausted."

"Where you been?"

"I was looking for someone."

"Did you find them?"

"Eventually. But first I found someone else, then someone almost found me, then they found the guy I was looking for, then I found him. And he was in bad shape. It was terrible."

"Sounds like hide and seek. You never play that with me."

"Okay," I yawned. "Some other time."

"I like Sardines better."

"You're a weird kid."

"We need more people for Sardines." She sighed. "It's lonely when you're gone."

"I'm sorry." I snuggled her against me. "My job is keeping me busy right now. Although Nash would be happier if I stayed and played hide and seek with you."

"You should." Remi combed through my hair and wound a

strand around her finger. "Maybe he could play, too. Then we could do Sardines."

"He doesn't want to play with me anymore. And I'm sad." I flopped on my back. "This sucks, Remisita. Really sucks. I haven't felt like this since… Maybe never."

"You shouldn't talk like that."

"You're right. Renata would tell me that I'm seeking fulfillment from another person instead of directing my energies into achieving my life's purpose. And that's becoming a licensed private investigator. I think. But what if Nash is my life's purpose? I'm confused."

"I mean you're not supposed to say 'sucks.' I don't know about the rest. But you can still play hide and seek."

I bolted upright. "You're right. And I can do both at the same time. Without a gun." I scrambled for the burner, plugged it in, and pressed the LA HAIR number. "I need to make an early appointment."

"I'd never play hide and seek with a gun." Remi leaned toward the floor and began pulling stuffed animals into the bed. "That's just asking for somebody to get hurt."

"Exactly, Remi."

I left the message, entered the bathroom, and returned to find my entire bed filled with one six-year-old and six-hundred stuffed animals. I left her to find another bed.

I had an early appointment at LA HAIR, but first I needed confirmation (again) that Vicki was ruining my life (again). Luckily, Theodore was an early riser. He said sunrise was his best light. After visiting him and LA HAIR, I could get on with my life. As in finding out if someone really wanted to end it.

Theodore's Neoclassical Revival — the exact words he used to describe his house — was found in old Black Pine, a few blocks from the old downtown. Which meant a few blocks from the Dixie Kreme donut shop. And Nash.

Although he never confirmed the fact, I knew Nash lived in that office while he sought to reclaim his business and everything he lost in his divorce from Jolene Sweeney.

My poor, sweet Nash.

Of course, wasn't this more evidence that we couldn't have a relationship? Neither of us had a real home. Or money. We were no better than teenagers with a truck and a dirt bike between us.

Oh my God, my life was pathetic.

I was (maybe) in love with a man who (maybe) had nothing to his name besides part ownership in a dirty, old private investigation office. It was so tragically romantic. Like *La Bohème*. Except without the singing. Or tuberculosis.

Although Nash and I had more dead bodies.

I parked Lucky on the street before Theodore's stately home, pulled off my helmet, and pinched my thumb to stop a string of broken heart tears. Climbing the porch stairs, I took in the sea grass love seat and chairs. A steaming teapot sat on a coffee table. I rang the trilling bell, and a moment later Theodore made his entrance. In a Japanese robe with long sleeves and a giant crane on the back. A ginger cat wound through his legs, then shot off the porch after a bird.

"Morning, darlin'," he squealed and deposited air kisses over my cheeks. "Let's sit on the porch and have a cup of matcha. It's wonderful for digestion and full of vitamins."

My appetite sank. Didn't anyone drink coffee anymore?

I sounded like Lamar.

He moved toward the loveseat, the sash trailing after him. Embroidered slippers peeked below the robe. Patting the seat next to him, he motioned me over and began spooning green powder into two mugs.

I sat beside him but turned to face him. "What's going on between you and Vicki and someone who looks exactly like me?"

He eyed me, then poured steaming water into the mugs. "Do you want to whisk or shall I?"

"You." I crossed my arms. "Theodore. Sweetie. I've been seen around town. And it's not me. Vicki's going to get me in trouble with my probation officer with this stunt."

"You know Vicki better than me, why don't you talk to her?"

"That's exactly why I'm talking to you. I can't talk to Vicki. Come on, I know you know about it. You know everything that's going on in town."

Sighing, Theodore set the dripping bamboo whisk on a tiny china plate. "All right. But quid pro quo, Clarice."

"Deal. I haven't forgotten about your party tonight." I picked up the scalding mug and set it down again.

"You promised already."

"I keep my promises. Although I don't think Cambria can make it."

"I heard she's in the hospital."

Theodore really did know everything that went on in Black Pine. "Yes, throat issues."

"Hmm." He cocked his head, studying me. "Back to that in a minute. Vicki. Your sweet mother—"

I snorted, and he laughed.

"Couldn't help it. Anyway, you have to feel a little sorry for her. She's under contract to fulfill another season of *All is Albright*."

"I don't feel sorry for her. She entered those negotiations without asking me whether I'd do another season."

"Hop off that high horse for just a minute, honey. Whatever the backstory, she's still under obligation to produce the show. And she is. Without you, as per your wishes." He giggled. "However, she hasn't exactly told the network that you're not in it."

I gasped. "How does she think she's going to get away with that?"

"According to Vicki, there's still footage from last year and a lead-in to your new career in Black Pine. She found someone that resembles you…"

"I've seen her. She more than resembles me."

"The B-roll is the actress acting as a detective. But the main story is the adjustment to life in Black Pine for the rest of the cast. By the way, have you seen the new Nash?"

"What do you mean the new Nash?"

"Total hottie that Vicki hired to play PI in your cameos."

"They're not my cameos. Oh, my God. Nash will kill her." I sucked in a breath. "What does he look like?"

Theodore reached into the pocket of his robe and pulled out his phone. He had a not-so-small album of the Nash Hottie.

"Wowsers." I took the phone from him to examine the pictures more carefully. And to enlarge parts of his physique for better inspection.

"I know, right?" said Theodore. "He'll be at the party."

I darted him a look. "Really?" Hang on. I was (maybe) in love with my boss. That was enough for me. But still… I took another look. "Name?"

Theodore smiled. "I know what you're thinking, girl. You wish."

I handed him back his phone. "Back to my original point. I know you've been reporting my wardrobe to Vicki. She has my Barney's personal shopper on speed dial. It'd be easy to dress Not-So-Mini Me to match. But it's causing a lot of problems. She has to stop filming the fake me."

"Lana Miles." He smirked. "Not-so-mini? Feeling insecure, sweetie?"

"The hallmark of an actor is insecurity, Theodore," I snapped. "Vicki has to stop filming this Lana Miles. Daddy just ripped me a new one, thinking I had strayed back to the dark side."

"Poor Boomer." Theodore laughed. "Alright, Clarice. Your turn. Why's Cambria in the hospital? And I can't believe it's her throat. She couldn't have stripped her vocal chords. She's not a singer. I know for a fact they haven't even started shooting yet. She had a meltdown, didn't she?"

"It is her throat." I held up my fingers. "Scout's honor. Although there's been some weird stuff going on related to Cambria or the movie."

He leaned forward. "Do tell."

"Are you going to tell Vicki to stop trying to clone me?"

His fingers flew before my face and snapped. "Done."

That was too easy. But telling Vicki and Vicki following Theodore's advice were two different things. Jesus could reappear on earth just to tell Vicki to stop filming my body double, and she'd say, "I'll take it under advisement" then ask him about the mansions in heaven. "What's the view like? And how exclusive is that neighborhood really?"

Ah well, Theodore was my gossip dealer. I needed to keep him happy if I needed him for a later fix. "You didn't get this from me, but I heard there was a murder on the set last night."

Theodore held a hand before his open mouth. "Girl. I haven't heard anything on the police scanner. Who was murdered? Someone important?"

"Everyone's important, *sweetie*."

"Retract the claws." He rolled his eyes. "You know what I mean, Miss Priss. I want details."

I picked up the steaming mug and set it back on the table. "You didn't hear anything on the police scanner? A 10-54 or a 187? Possible dead body and homicide? Nothing like that?"

"Nada. A patrol unit was sent to the set late last night, though…"

"And?"

"And nothing. They had nothing to report."

"What the frig."

"I'll look into it." He waved a hand, and his long sleeve dipped into the mug of green tea. "Dammit."

"For a tea stain on silk, sponge it in lukewarm water, then rub glycerin into it. Leave it for half an hour, then rinse with warm water."

"You're a wonder." His brows arched. "Smarter than your ta-tas make you look."

"I had a great wardrobe tech once who was a genius for stain removal." I shrugged. "Also, who doesn't love silk?"

"You may be mad at me, but we get each other. There are so few people in Black Pine who really appreciate fashion."

"True that."

The cat, back from her bird hunt, hopped onto the love seat between us and attacked the cane with her claws. Theodore swatted at her and received a scratch for his efforts.

I rose from the love seat, then leaned over to hug him. "Be careful with Vicki, though. She's got claws, and she bites."

"So do I. That's your problem, sweetie. You need bigger teeth." He brandished his gleaming veneers.

"I have no interest in becoming a shark. See you at the party." I turned to glance over my shoulder. "How many plus ones am I allowed?"

"Looking at your figure, I'd say you need at least three." He winked and blew me a kiss. "Be fabulous."

I was determined to live up to that expectation. But not in the way Theodore expected.

TWENTY-TWO

#MaizieMakeover #InPartnersWeTrust

I didn't know which bothered me more, knowing Vicki was using a stand-in for me or knowing Theodore helped her to do it. But Vicki would have to wait. At least now I knew one of Theodore's secrets: a police scanner. I trusted he would have picked up a murder call-in. How hard was it for security to find a body when I'd stumbled upon Orlando in the dark?

As much as his rejection stung, I needed to call Nash or go to the office. The office had donuts and coffee. Donuts always helped in the face of humiliation. Plus Nash needed to know I meant business. Both his and ours.

I carried my loot from the first-floor shop up to the office, where I found Lamar. He didn't want a donut but took a Dixie Kreme cup of coffee. In a Styrofoam cup.

So retro.

"My intel tells me the police didn't find Orlando," I said.

"We were just discussing that." Lamar sipped his coffee. "No body, but they called in forensics anyway. Your anonymous tip was enough for probable cause."

"But…"

"But BPPD can't get a warrant to search the entire set. Probable cause only allowed for the trailer lot. No body and not enough evidence to search inside the trailers."

"It's the studio. They have good lawyers."

"And a lot of money wrapped up in our town," said Lamar. "I'm going to find out who was on the set last night. And I need to talk to Big Jim about that pie."

The door to Nash's inner sanctum banged open, and he strode out. "I just finished talking to Mowry. They I.D.'d the bathtub guy. Billy Goodwin. A videographer."

"What type?" I handed him a coffee and a donut.

"Does it matter?" He handed me back the donut and sipped his coffee. "He's not employed by the movie people. They checked that out."

"You don't think it's odd that a videographer was in Cambria's villa, making what looks like an illicit movie with Cambria's looka-like and then died?"

"I find all of this more than odd. It's—"

"I know what you think about the movie business. But most people don't hire a professional to shoot a private video unless they plan on an audience seeing it." I studied my mostly eaten donut. "Except weddings. And bar mitzvahs. Bat mitzvahs. Quinceañeras. Okay, maybe it wasn't an illicit video but some funky rite of passage? No, that's just disgusting. Maybe they were in a cult, and it was a snuff film? An exclusive gang membership?"

Nash rolled his eyes.

"Right, that's a little out there even for Hollywood. But you never know." I popped the last bite of donut in my mouth and spoke with it tucked in my cheek. "I'll keep it in mind while I'm investigating Cambria's poisoner today."

"The poisoning was meant for you," growled Nash.

"Potato po-tah-toe, when it comes to who was poisoned." Noticing the hard set to Nash's jaw, I scrambled to clarify. "Leonard will want some results today. If someone tried to kill me, at least we should get paid for it."

"Where's your .38 Special?" demanded Nash.

"At home. I have a plan."

He stalked toward the couch and stood over me. "We didn't discuss another plan."

"There's a lot of things we didn't discuss last night." I expertly arched a brow, JP-style, then rose to stand beneath him. "But the word partner was tossed around. And partners need to trust each other."

His nostrils flared. His jaw twitched. The icy blue eyes narrowed.

The donut did that weird stomach dance, but I held my ground.

"I stick to my word, Miss Albright," he murmured. "Do you want to keep your job?"

"Are you going to trust me?"

His eyes ran down my Helmut Lang halter-neck tank and back to my face. From the corner of my eyes, I saw his hands clench.

"Cambria better talk today." He spun away from me and reached for a gym bag. "Lamar. Keep an ear out. I'll be at the hospital."

"Will do," said Lamar. He watched Nash stalk from the room, then turned to me. "I hope you do have a plan. You get yourself killed, and that boy will lose his damn mind."

J had a plan. Because I was me, my plan involved makeup, hair, and wardrobe. But you know what you know, right? At least Giulio wasn't in charge this time.

Giulio, who was still not answering his phone. I'd texted him throughout the night, unable to sleep with worry.

The girls were waiting for my pre-office hour appointment. I would call it the perks of celebrity, but that wouldn't cut it with Tiffany. She'd only come in early for a friend, and that was even better.

"Are you sure you want to do this?" asked Rhonda. She glanced at Tiffany who hummed and as she mixed chemicals in a plastic bowl.

"It's either this or a gun. I don't want to use a gun."

"You need to find some middle ground in your life. Dr. Phil says choosing extremes is not crushing it; it's crushing you." Rhonda tapped a finger against her lip. "Or maybe that was Dr. Oz. Wendy Williams? I can't remember."

"Me? I'd take the gun any day." Tiffany grinned and waved a paint brush. "But this is going to be fun."

I squirmed in my chair. "Remember, I still have to look fabulous. Theodore's party is tonight. You're coming with me, right?"

"A Black Pine party. I've never done a downtown party." Rhonda fingered her long tresses. "I think I need a change, too, Tiff."

"One subject at a time." Tiffany cackled.

I swiveled to study Tiffany. "You're licensed for hair, right? You know what you're doing? Because my hair has been through the Hollywood ringer with chemicals, heat, and products. I don't have natural body or thickness. It's all an illusion."

"It's not that much of an illusion," said Rhonda. "But we know hair. Right, Tiff?"

I sighed. Ted Gibson, they were not. But it wasn't like I could afford Ted Gibson anymore. I'd already seen the brown contacts and outfit they'd picked out for me. I wasn't just getting a disguise; I was getting uglified. "Now that we've figured out that someone is trying to kill me—"

"Girl." Rhonda's hands flew to her mouth. "That's bad juju. Don't say it out loud."

"Voldemort isn't trying to kill her," said Tiffany. "It's the reality of the situation."

"You just don't have the issue with violence that I do, Tiff," said Rhonda. "There are things you don't say to the universe. Like cancer. Or tax audit. Hammer toes. It's bad juju. Everyone knows that."

"Anyhoo," I said. "We're pretty sure it's because I saw the dead

Cam-Cam who is not Cambria. I need to figure out who the woman is. I can't stop thinking about her family and friends and how much they must miss her."

We took a moment to let that sink in. During the moment, Tiffany tossed a cape and towel over my shoulders and began pinning my hair into sections. I said a silent prayer for the dead lookalike and another for my hair.

"Cambria's got to know if her twin was in her hotel room." Tiffany wielded her loaded paint brush, then slapped it against my scalp. "The police will get it out of her. Or your boss. He's scarier than the police."

"Except Cam-Cam can't talk when she's under sedation. Her doctor is being paid by Leonard Shackleton to keep her sedated."

Tiffany snorted. "Rich people."

"Famous people," corrected Rhonda.

"Nash thinks that's hinky, but Leonard is playing CYA for the film. Probably because Leonard doesn't trust Cambria either." I cringed as color trickled down my forehead. "I'm pretty sure the double must have been hired by Cambria. How else could she get in Cam-Cam's room?"

"Maybe the boyfriend had a key?" said Rhonda, dabbing at the color with a towel. "He was staying at the resort, too."

"Orlando had a record," I said. "Maybe he hired someone to look like Cambria and did...whatever they were doing...in her room so no one would know it wasn't Cambria."

"I'm confused," said Rhonda. "Why would that be a thing?"

"Orlando wanted a video of him and fake Cambria doing the dirty?" said Tiffany. "Or a video of him killing fake Cambria? And hired a professional camera dude to get one? That's..."

"You're right. It doesn't make sense." I crossed my arms over the cape, then slid them back under as Tiffany began attacking my neckline. "At least we know the bathtub guy is the filmographer Billy Goodwin. I looked him up. He makes private videos. They're...eclectic."

"Disgusting eclectic or disturbing eclectic?" said Tiffany.

"Eclectic-eclectic," I said. "His stock for sale are mostly nature videos, although he's freelance and open to anything. He's done commercial shoots, weddings, and theater work. He's old school. Shoots with a Super-16. An Arriflex. It uses actual film. 16 millimeters. Probably what Giulio found in Orlando's room. Everything's digital now. That makes it even weirder."

"You'd think he'd shoot something kinky?" asked Tiffany.

"No idea. But I'm sure nature videos don't pay the bills."

Rhonda pursed her lips. "You said Cambria is super serious. Super serious doesn't usually go with super freaky."

"I guess she's changed," said Tiffany.

"Or she's a good actress," I said. "And Cambria is an outstanding actress."

TWENTY-THREE

#Closetraphobia #CrocodileSmile

*F*ortunately for me, a change of appearance meant nothing to studio security (Mike) as long as I had the appropriate badge. The actors and crew were going through various stages of altering appearance, either on purpose or through time-crunch neglect. The appropriateness of my badge — private security answerable to Leonard Shackleton — allowed me to check the security footage. The video showed most people related to Cambria had been on the set the previous night: Ed Farmer, Leonard Shackleton, Dahlia Pearson, Alvin Murphy, Cambria's publicist, Holly. My nemesis, Robin Coxon. And almost twenty other people, not counting those who had checked in earlier in the day and never left, which was close to fifty more.

Not helpful.

Although Robin Coxon belonged to the resort and not the set. List that on things that make you go hmmm.

Mike wasn't impressed by — nor understanding of — Shackleton's "private security." He also wasn't impressed by my new makeover. He'd been a *Julia Pinkerton* fan and was still a "redhead fan." Mike was forty-ish. So, *ew*.

No security cameras had been watching the trailers, just the equipment rooms, parking lot, major entrances, and main building exits.

Also, not helpful.

The previous night, the perp must have moved Orlando's body. A body would be hard to hide.

I looked at Security Mike. "I heard the police couldn't search the trailers."

"The studio doesn't want the disruption as there wasn't enough evidence that anything untoward had happened." Mike liked to emphasize three syllable words by slowing his speech to hit all the syllables.

"I heard two people saw a man under a trailer. A dead stunt man. That's pretty *untoward*."

Mike shrugged, causing a greater chasm between his tie and belt.

"The police looked in the spot and didn't find anyone," said Mike. "I have my doubts that the anonymous caller saw anything. It's a prank. I mean, how could they get on set?"

"Maybe the anonymous caller was a crew member who didn't want to get involved? Maybe the perpetrator of the death moved the body."

"I think we would have seen someone hauling a body off the lot. There wasn't even evidence of an alleged body. The police had a forensic guy out there early this morning. If they found something, we would have heard." Mike hauled up his pants, straightened his tie, and gave me the "gotcha" eyeball.

"Black Pine police is not *CSI*. They have to take samples to a lab and that takes time. This also means the alleged perp allegedly cleaned up the crime scene." Just like in Cambria's villa and with Billy Goodwin in the hotel room, I thought. Maybe they were coshing victims with a 20-gallon jug of bleach.

"Alleged crime scene," said Mike, interrupting my *CSI* thoughts.

Remembering Renata's advice on patience, I took a deep breath and counted to twenty while imagining Mike as a "victim of his own mentality." It wasn't Mike's fault that his morning had been inundated with the police and Leonard Shackleton's private security specialist. "Who was on duty last night?"

"Fraser. He didn't find anything on patrol."

I also hadn't seen Fraser on my patrol. I didn't have a lot of faith in Fraser. I had a feeling Fraser had been snoozing on a golf cart while my bleach jug killer had snuck off with Orlando's body. "Can I look inside the alleged trailer beneath which the alleged victim was allegedly found?"

"The police couldn't get a warrant to see inside anything."

"I'm not the police. I work for Leonard Shackleton."

The name drop got me a groan. "You'll have to ask Dahlia Pearson. It was her trailer."

I picked up my jaw, left the security building, turned toward a secluded corner, and called Nash. "Orlando was under Dahlia's trailer."

"Who's Dahlia again?"

"Cambria's costar. You met her at the dinner and again at the hospital. She loves unnecessary helping, does the Iron Man for fun, and can deadlift three times her body weight."

"She looks one hundred pounds soaking wet."

"One hundred pounds of solid muscle. She checked in at the set last night."

"Interesting."

I tapped a quick soft shoe shuffle. I loved it when Nash said things like "interesting" instead of things like "Are you kidding me?"

"And Giulio thinks she'll steal the show from Cambria. Dahlia has more potential star power but less experience."

"Giulio?" He spat the name out like it had soured.

"He's still missing."

"Sorry. I had my contact at the resort check his room." Nash sighed. "It looks like Giulio didn't sleep at his villa last night. But they couldn't tell if anything was missing, not knowing what was there before."

"Oh." I pinched my thumb and continued with a cheerier tone than I meant. "Robin Coxon of Black Pine Resort was here last night, too. Along with everyone else related to this case except for those dead or who look like Cambria."

"Interesting."

That didn't have the same inflection as the Dahlia Pearson interesting. "I think Robin wants to kill me. I'm moving her up my suspect list."

"Figuratively wanting to kill you is different from actually planning a homicide."

"I could give the resort bad publicity by proving someone had been murdered in one of her villas. Thereby unseating Robin's position of power."

"That's a weak motive."

"Still a motive."

"Everyone went back to the set after the hospital?" Nash paused. I imagined him pacing the hospital room. "Why would they do that and not go back to their hotel rooms?"

"Cambria's hospitalization would cause a major schedule adjustment. Work that wouldn't wait. Leonard and Ed would also need to hash out an appropriate news release with Cambria's agent and publicist."

"What about Dahlia?"

"No clue. There'd be no reason to invite her to those meetings."

"Better check into that," said Nash. "Damn it, I hate being stuck in this hospital room. Cambria is still sedated. I need her to talk."

"I have a feeling Leonard wants her unconscious for that reason. If he decides to cut her loose from the role, then it will change."

"This is a cutthroat business."

"Movie making is financially risky. The production company will budget about a hundred million in publicity for this movie. Leonard won't want to use the money spinning a star's connection to three murders. He'd rather put it in TV ads."

"Good God." Nash took a deep breath. "I don't like this, Miss

Albright."

"I know."

"It's not safe for you to be investigating. The money is not worth it to me."

"Nash, I know Jolene is using red tape to keep Lamar from buying her out. She wants to see Nash Security Solutions fail." Because Jolene's a vindictive, petty bitch. But speaking it aloud might make me look equally vindictive and petty, so I kept that part to myself. "We need Leonard's business. Not just for the cash flow, but also to show future clients we can handle anything."

"Can *we* handle anything?"

I closed my eyes. The word "we" rung like a bell in the chapel of my heart. But a bell pounding your chamber walls could also be painful. *We* was not the same as *us*.

"We can handle this. You watch Cambria and if she wakes at all, get her to talk. As for me, I'm on a strict diet. I'm avoiding any "eat me, drink me" signs. And I'm in disguise—"

"Please don't tell me you're on that bike, riding around in stripper shoes."

"No way." I wrinkled my nose at Rhonda's Grandma's blouse and slacks hiding my distinctive figure. "Giulio would not approve."

Nash waited for a respectful beat before continuing. "By the way, Vicki is looking for you. I found her at the hospital, trying to get into Cambria's room before visiting hours."

"Fracktastic." I crept to the corner of the security building and peered out, sniffing the air for Chanel No. 5.

"Miss Albright, please be safe. Watch out for Dahlia Pearson and the others, just in case. They had opportunity even without a good motive."

"I need to get inside Dahlia's trailer."

"That doesn't sound like being careful."

"Don't worry. I'll wait until she's off-set. I'll visit Robin Coxon first." And hung up before I could hear his groan.

*R*obin Coxon had visited the studio after hours and as any good investigator would say, "wha's up with that?" She also had issues with me finding dead people on her resort. I get it. But overreact much, Robin?

I strolled into the big stone and timber building and through reception. My disguise got me past Carlos the valet and Cesar at reception. Not even a second glance. How depressing. Depressing I had grown vain enough to mind. Renata would have had a field day with that reality check.

At Robin's office, I didn't knock. I walked in for this performance.

Robin's head jerked up from her computer screen. "Hello? Can I help you?"

"Yes, Robin," I said. "You can tell me why you were on the *Pine Hollow* set last night. Because people seem to die when you're around."

"What?" Robin cocked her head, squinted, then reached for her phone. "Maizie Albright? I—"

"I know what you're going to say." I was reprising my Vicki "nerves of steel" role. This time I was too emotionally exhausted from losing friends and finding corpses to dial it back. "I'd like to point out some facts. Fact one: I saw an unconscious, possibly dead, now missing woman in one of your villas. Fact two: A murdered man was found in one of your hotel rooms. Fact three: you were on the set of *Pine Hollow* the night another man was murdered. What do you have to say for yourself?"

She stared at me.

I returned the stare. With a raised eyebrow for effect.

During that window of time, a tiny thought emerged, grew, and blossomed into a monstrous idea. No one knew I was at the resort. Robin had the opportunity. And she was tall. Probably strong. She'd know where to find the iron in Orlando's hotel room, that's for sure. If Robin Coxon had killed all those people, was this a smart idea to accuse her of murder?

God, I needed real investigative training in the worst way. Telling me to "be careful" wasn't instructive enough.

Losing my Vicki verve, I began to back toward the door. "So you just think about that, Robin."

Robin pushed out of her chair. "You slanderous little whore."

"I'm telling you the facts," I said, using Julia Pinkerton's snarky comeback voice. For courage. "And speaking of slander? I've always been a serial monogamist. I just have very bad luck with men."

What was I even saying? As I spoke, I'd been mentally rehearsing *Kung Fu Kate* kickboxing steps. Robin was tall, but she wore heels. If I could get her off balance, I'd have a better chance of running before she cracked me in the back of the head.

Or I could just get out of there. Like now. "Good day, Robin."

"You just waltz in here to accuse me of murder and leave?" Robin turned toward a keypad on the wall and typed in a number. "I don't think so."

Behind me the door vibrated, resounding with a metallic *chong*.

Oh, my God, I was locked in with Robin.

"Where's Giulio?" I said. "What have you done with him? He was innocent."

"So you're the one who notified the police that he was gone? What is it with you and the police? It's bad enough we had a man die in the hotel. Now I'm getting questioned about Cambria's and Giulio's villas."

"What about Giulio's villa? I thought they didn't find anything?"

"What are you talking about? The police don't have a legal right to go into his villa. At least yet."

"Yet? What do you mean by yet?"

She ignored me and tapped on her phone.

"Robin, what happened to Giulio?"

Had she locked Giulio in here? The room was normal-sized, yet that heavy bolt-in-the-lock *chong* had given me a *Star Wars* trash-compactor vibe. I jerked. A thrumming sounded from the air duct above me. Noisy air conditioner or was she going to squeeze the oxygen out of the room?

I ran a finger under my collar, then wiped the orange makeup on my jeans. *Get a hold of yourself, Maizie. You're a professional. Your disguise is melting, but Nash said you had grit. You can do this.*

I flipped open my phone and hovered my finger over Nash's name. Just in case. Not because I needed a rescue.

"Maybe you'd like to tell the police what happened to Giulio again?" I said, waving my phone.

Her attention snapped back to me. "You're such a pain in the ass. The police questioned me already. I told them I don't ask where my guests go, as long as they pay their bill. The *All is Albright* show is holding his villa. He's not checked out. He's not officially missing, you idiot."

"Officially? That's just a handy word. Like allegedly. What were you doing at the studio last night?"

"Paying my respects," said Robin. "I heard that Cambria had taken ill. I wanted to offer the resort as a place of recuperation as soon as she could be released. We have an in-house nurse and can put equipment in the villas."

"Oh." I paused. "How did you hear Cambria had taken ill?"

"It's my business to learn these things. I care about my guests."

"Vicki Albright told you. Is she paying you or are you paying her?"

"Millennials. You lack respect and common courtesy." Robin stepped forward and peered down her nose at me. "Why do you want to know my whereabouts last night?"

"That's my business. To know things." Oddly, Robin's defensiveness gave me courage. "You're working with Vicki Albright."

She tilted her chin. "Vicki Albright has been a guest and has arranged for the resort to host many of the *All is Albright* celebrities and staff. What of it?"

"Do you know she's my ex-manager and ex-producer? I saw someone who looked exactly like and dressed exactly like me in the main resort building. I know Vicki has a stand-in imitating me for the show. Tell me the real reason I'm not allowed on the resort property."

"Ask Vicki yourself." Sneering, Robin snatched her cell phone from the desk, scrolled with her thumb, and tapped the speaker button.

"What is it Robin?" said Vicki.

"Maizie Albright is here. Making accusations—"

"I want a word with you, young lady."

"Vicki," I said. "People have died. I have a job to do."

"I believe drama should be left to the working actors. Like Cambria. Except, oh yes, she's in the hospital. Thanks for letting me know. Oh wait, you didn't." She hung up.

Robin strode to the pad on the wall. "Get off the resort." Behind me the lock *chonged*.

"Did you know Vicki arranged for my double to get a listing of all your guests and their room numbers?"

Robin whirled around. "That's not policy."

"Vicki doesn't care about policy. She pays to get around policy. Just like she paid you to make sure I wasn't around to blow her filming schedule. Couldn't have the real Maizie appear with the Maizie lookalike." And I thought once again about Cambria's body double. "That poor woman. You really need to have them drag the lake before some golfer finds a floater. If you really care about your guests."

I shot out of the office before I could hear Robin's angry reply.

*R*obin Coxon might want to kill me, but I agreed with Nash. There wasn't a strong enough motive for her to kill two actors and a filmographer. In fact, leaving a body at the resort was more of a hindrance than a help, regarding resort management power. I crossed her off my list. Although a crazed Cambria fanatic was still in play — after all, the soundtrack from *Selena* now looped in my mental playlist — I'd focus on the *Pine Hollow* circle. All of them — including Leonard as John Doe in villa eight — had rooms at the resort. They could have stashed the double and dropped her in the lake later that night.

I wondered if they had wrapped her in those satin bed sheets. What a super sad ending to a life.

At the studio gate, the production assistant checked me in, then told me Dahlia Pearson had left for her workout. She was probably running a marathon or climbing a mountain, but I decided to peek in her trailer before talking to craft service.

Nick in Key Control had told me a key wasn't needed for her trailer. I'd flashed my badge and a lot of Leonard Shackleton name dropping on Nick. Apparently, if one were to murder a stunt man, this would be a handy trailer from which to do it. Either for Dahlia or anyone who knew she didn't like to carry a key because she "had no trust issues."

Air-quotes by Nick.

I knocked, but all was quiet on the Dahlia front. I considered her strength, determination, and unrequited jealousy of Cambria. Knocking Cambria off the movie was a motive, although that particular blend of crazy-plus-envy was more a Golden Age of Hollywood thing when shock treatment went hand-in-hand with Oscar trophies. It made more sense for Dahlia to expose Cambria as a diva slut than kill her. Dahlia probably feared the video would ruin the movie's rep with bad publicity. Or that Cambria's video would make Cam-Cam a bigger star.

To kill all involved with the video? Major Looney Tunesville. And wouldn't Dahlia have figured out the lookalike wasn't Cambria during her murderous rampage? Or is that what set off the rampage?

Now I was more confused.

Dahlia's trailer wasn't as beautifully appointed as Cam-Cam's, but still lovely. I felt the accompanying wave of lifestyle envy. Just like in my former life, I was still hiding from Vicki, except now I was poor and hiding from Vicki.

Dahlia's trailer smelled like pot and heavy-duty cleaner with a hint of lemon verbena. The bleach smell grew stronger as I crept toward the bathroom. I slowly pushed the door open, sniffing carefully, and stepped inside. Yanking back the shower curtain, I glanced into the empty tub, then checked beneath the sink. No cleaners although the bathroom did smell recently disinfected.

Turning the corner down the short hall, I entered the master bedroom and checked the adjoining bathroom. I found Dahlia's bong and her copious pot stash, but no bodies and no cleaners.

Palming the burner phone, I thumb dialed and sat on Dahlia's bed. "Nash. Dahlia doesn't have any Scrubbing Bubbles in her trailer."

"You know this why?"

"She's not here. It's cool." My gaze roamed the room and stopped on the closet door. "Her guest bath smells like it's been scoured, but there's not even a bottle of bleach in sight."

"A cleaning service could have been there recently."

"I'll check." Standing to the side of the closet, I reached for the handle, swung the door open, and jumped back. "No bodies in the closet."

"With your luck…"

"Yeah, I was surprised, too." Shuddering, I closed the closet door.

And heard the echo of a door shutting.

I sucked in a deep breath.

"What is it?"

Covering the phone's receiver, I crept toward the bedroom door to peer out in the hall. A shadow fell across the living area's floor. Quietly, I drew the door shut but stopped it from closing completely. I placed an eyeball to the crack, couldn't see enough to make a difference, then glanced around the bedroom. Closet, bathroom, bed.

Closet was the most logical choice. Craptastic.

Inside my palm, Nash's voice vibrated.

Squeezing my eyes shut, I opened the closet door and stepped inside. My heart hammered, my pits sweated, and my stomach churned. I brought the phone to my ear. "I'm in the closet."

"You hate closets."

"Dahlia came home," I whispered.

"I told you—" He broke off with a litany of curses. "Listen, let me—"

"No. Stay with Cambria. She could be in danger. But more importantly, when she wakes, you need to be there to question her. When she's still sleepy and drugged out. Before she thinks about why she shouldn't talk."

I clapped the phone shut, shoved it in my back pocket, and opened my eyes. Plastic bagged outfits crowded the closet. My stomach cramped and windpipe burned as I imagined the swell of garment bags closing around me. I shut my eyes and took deep breaths.

A door thudded. Footsteps pattered into the bedroom. A *thwack* caused me to jump, rattling the hangers. I held my breath and edged back. The bags slithered and whispered. Thin plastic caught at my hair and clothes, sticking and tangling. I batted at the plastic, recoiling at their rustle and cling.

My fingers and toes felt like ice. My neck and chest damp. Hives broke out in a swath of nerve-induced perspiration. Feathery plastic threatened to swaddle me. My lungs battled for air. Each breath sucked plastic closer, slipping over my skin and clinging to the hairs. Goosebumps broke on my scalp. It took all my willpower not to rip the bags off their hangers.

Death by wardrobe smothering. Seemed symbolic.

I inhaled, held air for a ten count, and exhaled. The bags fluttered. I inhaled again, detected a pungent aroma, and exhaled more slowly. Felt calmer. Then prayed I wouldn't be stuck in this nightmarish closet for however long it took Dahlia to get baked.

The wall of the closet thrummed. Water rushed through pipes. My shoulders eased away from my neck.

Someone belted an Adelle classic.

I pushed at the dry cleaner bags, moved to the front of the closet, and cracked the door. The bathroom door stood open. Adelle tunes grew louder. The shower droned. I crept from the closet. The bags followed. Beating back the bags, I shut the closet door and spotted a pile of items on the bed. Glanced at the bathroom again and slipped to the bed.

A binder with "script notes" written on the cover had been tossed next to Dahlia's purse. The Fendi pouch lay open, its contents threatening to spill on the bed quilt. I pawed through the items and found a single key card for the studio.

This was not a trailer key. Dahlia didn't believe in keys anyway, and Dahlia didn't need a key to get into the warehouse building. Why would an actress need a studio key card? There was always a door guard on duty. Props, maintenance, rigs, and other set crew might have key cards to their respective storage rooms and offices, but actors wouldn't need them.

With a squeak of the pipes, the shower ended.

I scooted out of the room, key card still in hand. Flying down the steps and through the front door, I halted. A golf cart screeched to a stop, blocking my path.

"Maizie," said Vicki.

I glanced behind me, shoved the key card into my pocket, and edged away from Dahlia's front door.

"I know what you're doing." Vicki settled her DITA sunglasses on top of her head, careful not to mess her platinum style, and planted fists on her tiny hips. "This has got to stop. I'm beside myself."

"I'm sorry?"

"I've been worried sick. Sick. Honestly. I thought I was going to —" Her eyes squeezed shut and forehead threatened to pucker. Botox did its job, but I knew the sign of stress. "Why are you doing this?"

"Oh my God. I forgot you saw Nash. He told you?" I'd almost been victim number four. Or was it three? Poor Vicki. One tended to forget she was also my mother.

Her eyes still shut, she gave a sharp nod.

"I'm totally okay. And I'm being care—"

Her eyes flew open. "And now this. What have you done? How could you?"

"Done?"

"To your hair. And…" She waved at my outfit. "Are those," she gasped, "Birkenstock sandals?"

I glanced at my feet. We hadn't taken the time to take the color off my toes. Deborah Lippman's "Stargasm" pink glinted in the sunlight.

"And polyester? What is going on with your hair? It's flying straight up into the air. Did you get the opposite of a keratin treatment?"

"I think that's static electricity."

She tried to snort but choked instead. "I mean. Really."

"It's okay, mom—Vicki. I'm fine."

"She's fine," she said to the heavens.

Patting my static-y hair, my eyes teared. I knew Vicki loved me in her own way, but I'd never seen her this distraught. "I'm sorry. I didn't mean to upset you like this."

The sea glass green eyes lowered from the sky to center on the pair that no longer matched her shade. "You should have thought about how upset I'd be. I had to learn about this from a *local*. Then find *Mr. Nash* in the hospital room?" She spat out both descriptions with equal distaste. By local, I assumed she meant Theodore and felt even sorrier for him. "They wouldn't even let me in."

"Wait. You're talking about Cambria?"

"Of course. Who else would I be talking about?"

I clasped a hand to my heart, unable to respond.

"Cambria's the one in the hospital," continued Vicki. "She's the one who was poisoned. I know you're jealous of Cambria, but this is low. You should have contacted me. As her manager, Cambria needed me. Both at the hospital and at the meetings that I know must have been going on last night."

Behind us, the door creaked. Dahlia had heard the shouting. I thought of the key and the body that had been recently under her trailer. Goosebumps broke on the back of my neck.

"I've got to go." I rounded the corner of the trailer before Dahlia could spot my physical alteration. There'd be no point to a disguise if my one of my suspects saw me. I'd be forced to start carrying the pink gun.

"Hey Ms. Albright," said Dahlia. "What's going on?"

"I'm speaking of poor Cambria's poisoning."

"I guess you could say sniffing drain cleaner is a kind of poison."

I plastered myself to the side of the trailer to listen.

"Dahlia, dear," said Vicki. "It wasn't Cambria's nose that was ripped up. It was her throat and stomach."

"I guess I see your point," said Dahlia. "Who were you talking to?"

"Never mind that."

"I hope Maizie's not in trouble again. She's not been helping Cambria at all, from what I understand," said Dahlia. "That's why Mr. Nash is Cambria's sitter and not Maizie."

"Really?" Vicki's voice lowered.

I closed my eyes to concentrate on her words.

"How does Mr. Shackleton feel about that?"

"Ed Farmer isn't happy about it. And if Ed isn't happy, Leonard won't be either," called Dahlia. "The truth hurts, but one must keep it real." Dahlia's uptalk tone dropped to serious, then slid toward menacing. "Maizie should lay her landmines elsewhere if she knows what's good for her."

WTH, Dahlia. And what did that mean?

"Come inside, Vicki. I want to talk you about something."

"I could use a water," said Vicki. "Bottled. No gas. French spring, if you have any."

"Don't go in there, Vicki," I muttered. Dahlia's trailer smelled like heavy duty cleaner with no cleaner in sight. Plus, there was the issue with the missing dead body beneath it. No good motive, but that was no reason to put Vicki in jeopardy.

I rounded the corner of the trailer, but Vicki had already gone inside.

TWENTY-FOUR

#KeytoEdsHeart
#DoubleStuffedIndemnity

*A*fter standing with my ear pressed to Dahlia's door longer than good judgment warranted, I decided veiled threats toward me didn't mean Vicki was in any danger. After all, Vicki had voted Maizie off the island. She'd chosen Team Cambria and Team Dahlia. That seemed safe enough. For Vicki, anyway. I trudged back to the warehouse, repeating one of Renata's self-actualizing mantras, then stopped to examine the key card.

The key could lead to wherever Dahlia stashed her bodies. Or something completely innocent. Like a storage room where she stashed her props and costumes.

Although she had a trailer for that. I'd seen her plastic-bagged costumes. I'd almost inhaled them.

Either way, I wanted to find the door that went with the card. While I walked, I tried calling Giulio again, then called Nash to explain I hadn't died from garment bag asphyxiation.

"Leonard Shackleton, Dahlia, and Cambria's agent have been here," said Nash. "Also, Ed Farmer, who's still here."

I could hear muffled words in the background.

"What he'd say?"

"Something about you failing at goats? I don't know." Nash lowered his voice. "The guy is nutty if you ask me."

"That's well known. Genius nutty."

"I was thinking more like fruitcake nutty. He's holding Cambria's hand and reading lines from a script. He said he didn't want her to miss rehearsal. She's still unconscious."

"That's sweet." I thought back to the fully drawn storyboards and Dahlia's veiled references to Ed Farmer's Cambria obsession. "Also a little stalker-y."

"That's what I'm here for." Nash sighed. "Stay in contact."

At Key Control, Nick scanned the card. I gave him a little white "Leonard Shackleton gave me this key, but I can't remember what it's for" lie. Nick was much more obliging (and gullible) than Security Mike. We learned Dahlia's key card worked on Ed Farmer's door.

That's what I call a big "aha" moment. I mean, why would Dahlia have a key to her director's office? Did she steal it? Was Dahlia a thief and a murderer?

I scurried through the busy building, avoiding eye contact and carrying a clipboard I borrowed from Nick. Clipboards made one appear official. Also, helpful for hiding one's face. With a quick "all clear" look-see, I flashed the card against the scanner and entered Ed's office. Shut his shades and left the light off. The storyboards caught my eye once more. Cambria in all her sketched-out glory. Creepapaloozaville. Particularly in the dim light. Dahlia's supporting character was barely a rough sketch. More like a fleshed-out stick figure.

That would bug me, too, Dahlia. But enough to kill Cambria's double? I turned to take in the rest of the room.

The scattered papers on the conference table didn't tell me much, other than the schedules were still a mess of highlighting, underlining, and red arrows. Using the light from my burner phone, I found a copy of the press release.

"The producers of Ed Farmer's newest blockbuster regret to inform the public that their current star, Cambria, was hospitalized for a throat ailment. At this time, production will not be delayed, and they expect Cambria to make a rapid recovery."

I wondered how long it took them to craft those two sentences. I also wondered if Dahlia had seen the press release and if the word "current" had jumped out at her as it had done for me.

Circling the room, I stopped behind Ed's desk. Sketches littered the top of the desk, many of Cambria. One of Dahlia.

I picked up the Dahlia sketch and shined the phone's light on it. It looked like a head shot except she seemed to be leering at him. Maybe he had sketched her badly. Or it was the lighting. I flipped it over. "Phyllis Dietrichson."

Wait. What? Wasn't that the Phyllis from *Double Indemnity*? Barbara Stanwyck had played the scheming, murdering seductress. Barbara had been nominated for an Oscar, yet lost to Ingrid Bergman for *Gaslight*.

Was Ed planning on remaking *Double Indemnity*? But wasn't that *The Postman Always Rings Twice*? Or did he mean something else? Like a pointing finger-type hunch?

I slipped the sketch under the blank sheet on my clipboard and moved on to his desk drawers. Found no interesting Suspect X notes, smoking guns, or 20-gallon jugs of bleach. No bodies, cameras, or cleaners in the credenza, either. His official film notes were not there, but neither was his laptop. I remembered the tiny notebook Ed used for sketching during that first dinner, but that wasn't included in the detritus of loose paper and photos shoved into the top drawer.

Order reigned in the file cabinet. The director had to take off his creative beret and replace it with a business man's fedora. I flipped through folders of mostly legal or invoice variety. The actor's head-shots from casting had only their character's names handwritten on them. Nothing interesting. But a file with the name Cambria Johnson caught my notice. I scanned the papers, barely registering the content through the legalese until my tired eyes stopped on a receipt attached to a copy of her artist liability insurance.

An insurance contract would be standard stuff for a notorious actor, even if her notoriety had been recent. Cambria wasn't a big star yet, so her antics made her risky. The producer's investors would have demanded it. However, the insurance bond had been backed by Ed Farmer with her agent underwriting a percentage.

The director was beholden to Cambria for completing this movie to the tune of twenty million.

Holy hells balls. Leonard had said "chunky liability coverage." I guessed chunky was the new fat. Why did Ed lay down that amount of money for an actress who'd gone from TV to stage to tabloid headline news? Cambria's Lady Macbeth must have been epic.

Voices from the hall seeped into the room. I shoved the paperwork back into the file cabinet and slid to the door. Splitting the door's shade, I peered into the hallway. A group of arguing executives strode into Leonard's Shackleton's office. A moment later, Alvin Murphy and Cambria's PR rep, Holly, hurried in. I cracked the door, spotted Leonard Shackleton ambling down the hall, and closed the door. Waited a full minute and squinted through the shade. He stood in the doorway to his office. Staring at Ed Farmer's door.

Shizzles. My fingers dropped the shade, and I held my breath, waiting another minute. My clipboard hand shook. Peeking from the bottom of the louvers, I saw Leonard's door shut. I could hear the din of voices inside.

As they say in Hollywood, time to make a break for it.

*H*alfway down the hall, I realized I'd forgotten the key card in Ed Farmer's office. I halted, but there was nothing I could do except hope that Dahlia (would get caught) thought she'd left it there. Behind me, the production meeting voices grew louder. I turned and spotted Leonard's open door. Clamping the clipboard to my chest, I spun toward the doorway on my right. Conference room. I stepped through, closed the door.

And found Detective Mowry.

"Maizie Albright? I almost didn't recognize you." He caught himself before his nose wrinkled. "That's a...different look."

My chuckle sounded both forced and fake. "What're you doing in here?"

"Waiting to speak to Mr. Leonard. We had an anonymous tip last night." He placed his hands on his hips. "Another disappearing body."

"Aha."

"You wouldn't know anything about that?"

"I certainly did not leave an anonymous tip." That had been Nash. "Speaking of bodies, I heard about the one at the resort. Did you find any interesting evidence? Maybe, I don't know, some film? Nash told me you said he was a videographer."

"Why would you think there was film?" His warm brown eyes studied me. "And not video?"

Doh, Maizie.

"Wild guess?" I gave him my *Maxim* smile, then adjusted. The police would find *Maxim* smiles suspicious. "Nash told me his name. I looked Billy Goodwin up and saw he works with real film. That's unusual these days. Remember, I saw film equipment in Cambria's villa that night. I'm just wondering if his death is related."

"Wonder all you want." He smiled pleasantly. "And why are you here?"

"We're still working for Leonard Shackleton. I was on my way to visit craft service and took a wrong turn. Do you know Big Jim?"

"Makes an awesome BBQ." Mowry smiled. "He sponsors our annual department picnic. Didn't realize he was doing catering for the movie people. Big Jim's a friend of Boomer's, right? I forget you have roots here."

"He and Daddy go way back. Football, I think." I pressed my clipboard against my chest. "I was just going to ask him...about his pies."

"Have you tried his chocolate peanut butter pie?"

I felt my eyes widen and quickly smoothed over my surprise. "I believe so."

"You'd remember. It's one of his signature desserts." He sighed. "I love that salty sweet combo. Rich and creamy. Tastes exactly like—"

"A Reese's Peanut Butter Cup," I broke in, then recovered. "Or at least that's what it sounds like. The way you're describing it…"

Mowry grinned. "Yes, ma'am. I'd kill for some. Maybe I'll go with y'all and see if he has any hidden in the back. Convince him to let you have a piece. I bet you'd love it."

"Great." Craptastic. I couldn't have Mowry join me for a pie poison discussion. "But aren't you waiting to talk to Leonard?"

"Right." Mowry cleared his throat. "Another time?"

"Later." I shot him a JP finger gun and hustled out.

$\mathcal{M}$y head ducked, I hurried through the dining room, avoiding eye contact with the various crew members, and shot through the kitchen door. Rushing past the long row of stainless steel counters, I found the kitchen manager's office door open, and Big Jim inside. We exchanged a chorus of "how's your daddy," "that's some hairdo," and "did you try my okra scramble this morning, these movie people like their vegetables."

Smoothing my hair, I noted the considerable number of staff walking to and fro. "Can we shut the door? I'm hoping to speak to you privately."

"Bless you hon', but I need to keep an eye on my people. This room is just too teeny to close that door. I can barely breathe in here as it is." Big Jim didn't necessarily sit in his office chair as encompassed it. Both in size and demeanor. "What's this about?

I scooted closer and lowered my voice. "Yesterday's chocolate peanut butter pie. Any complaints about it?"

"Complaints?" Massaging the folds beneath his chin, he tilted his head to study me. "You mean because of the fat content?"

I didn't want to tell him what I meant. "So everybody liked the pie?"

"Let's see." He pivoted toward the desk and tapped on his computer. "I made six pies plus the lil' one for y'all. Yours disappeared, no surprise there." He chuckled.

I bit my lip.

"Used Georgia peanuts because these movie people like to eat local. I don't know what they think they're going to eat in the winter unless it's greens and cabbage." He pointed at the spreadsheet on his screen. "Looks like we had one pie left over. You want to take it home?"

I brightened before reality sank in. "Thanks but I can't. I'm riding a dirt bike these days, Big Jim."

"Now that's a shame. I bet Remi'd like a taste."

"Detective Mowry's around. He's a big fan."

"Is he here? That boy loves my food about as much as y'all. Good man, Mowry." Big Jim stared over my shoulder. "Are you a prep chef or a cafeteria worker? You know better than to leave a dirty station. Haul your ass over to clean up that mess."

Watching the cook, he nodded then focused back on me. "Excuse me for that, hon'. Now why are you asking about complaints? How was that lil' one yesterday? Lord love you, Maizie, I've never seen such passion over chocolate and peanut butter. Made me a happy man to make your favorite."

The declaration felt like a punch in the gut in light of what had happened.

"I never got the chance to try it," I spoke slowly and toed a circle with a Birkenstock. "Someone else beat me to it."

"What do you mean?" He pushed out of his chair, crowding our space. "I put your name on that plate in chocolate. I ask you, what kind of a person takes another person's chocolate peanut butter pie?"

"Cambria. She's the star of the show."

"Well, I never."

"I'm so sorry Big Jim, but the thing is, Cambria got really sick after eating it."

"She couldn't handle the fat content." He folded his meaty arms. "Serves her right for stealing your pie."

"No." I took a deep breath and rushed through my words. "Now don't tell Daddy. But someone added a heavy dose of cleaner to her pie. And I think the cleaner was meant for me."

He gaped. "Dear Lord, why on earth?"

"I think I saw something I shouldn't have seen. Don't say anything to Mowry yet. I don't want people to think poorly of you. I need to know who had access to the pie so I can clear this up before word gets out."

"Lord, they may be lazy sumbitches, but I'd swear on my life by my kitchen staff. Not knowing when you'd show in the dining hall, I just set the pie on that table in there myself." He took a deep breath, and his lip trembled. "Anyone could have tampered with it after the fact, so to speak."

"That's what Nash and I thought. It's not your fault." I took his hand and patted. Big Jim was a sensitive man. I'd seen him bawl over a smoked pig at a DeerNose charity cookout. His love for feeding people was only exceeded by his love for feeding the needy. And the pulled pork was that good. "Where do you keep the cleaning solution? Any in the dining room?"

"Of course not, but we have plenty back here. My staff should have noticed someone messing around in the cleaning closet, though. I supposed there's some stored in the nearby bathroom." He swept a hand at his eyes.

"Bathroom. Got it." I patted his other hand, then hugged him.

"My sweet Lord, to think I'd been a party to poisoning. " Taking a deep breath, his neck swelled, his face reddened, and his voice grew hot. "If you find out who did this, you tell me, girl. I have words for this…this reprobate."

Hugging him, I mentally berated myself for putting Big Jim through this anguish. Then berated myself for berating myself because investigators should be tougher. Feelings would get hurt when you were trying to find a murderer. But still, poor Big Jim.

"For mercy's sake." Stepping away from our hug, he addressed someone behind me. "Where you taking that garbage? Do you not have the sense the good Lord gave you? We've got our own bin in the back. You're going the wrong way. You can't march those through the mess hall."

"That bin needs to be picked up, Chef," said the worker. "It stinks to high heaven. Must be full."

I glanced behind me. A young man gripped two full bags in one hand and balanced two more over his shoulder.

"What are you talking about?" said Big Jim. "The trucks came yesterday morning."

"Hells," I muttered and turned to Big Jim. "I bet I know what's making that stink. Put Mike in security on it. Tell him it's an alleged smell. Better have him page Detective Mowry. And save the detective that extra pie."

TWENTY-FIVE

#FatalCamtraction #SleepingPsycho

I checked the dining room's bathroom for cleaner —
Toilet. Countertops. Bleach. Window. Drain. Mildew. A
smorgasbord of cleaning chemicals. No problem poisoning a pie
from the bathroom. — and rushed to get off campus before the
police arrived. In the parking lot, I remembered Vicki. And Dahlia.
And Dahlia's weird threat. And Ed's loony sketch of Dahlia with
the *Double Indemnity* mention.

How could I forget my mother? Being in charge of an investigation was exhausting. And made my brain hurt. I tapped her
number into my phone. Voice mail. She had turned off her ringer.
Figured.

Or Dahlia had done something to her. It wasn't like this killer
was patiently biding their time to off the victims. These were
immediate murders. The perp must be crazy desperate to remove
all evidence to the original crime. Including people.

I rubbed my neck. I was part of that chain of evidence. My
stomach rolled. I thought of Cambria in the hospital. Nash
guarding her instead of guarding me…

Stop it, I thought. You're no Whitney Houston.

Vicki could handle herself, couldn't she? I stared at Lucky, longing to get away. I had a plethora of suspects and a handful of vague motives. A woman was still missing and presumed dead. The police investigated the other two deaths. But to make Leonard happy, I needed to get to the bottom of the mysterious body in villa six (wasn't that a Nancy Drew?) to clear Cambria's name (which seemed impossible) and more importantly, his precious blockbuster (Good luck with that Leonard).

And figure out who was trying to kill me before they actually did it.

Shizzles, what if Dahlia was a real-life Phyllis Dietrichson? Vicki could hold her own in any meeting, pitch session, contract negotiation, and red carpet moment. But could she defend herself against a skull cracking killer?

A siren wailed in the distance. The police. I needed to get away before I was trapped. Detective Mowry would want to question me (been there, done that, takes forever) and they'd call in my probation officer. Who'd call Judge Ellis. Who might ship me back to a California jail to stand trial for being the fiancé to an idiot (Girlfriend Before the Fact) when according to my probationary requirements, I was supposed to stay far, far away from anything movie related.

The siren grew louder.

Vicki was super fit. She still did weighted pilates, and that wasn't even a thing anymore. If Dahlia tried anything, Vicki could…

What was I thinking? I had to save my mother.

I spun back toward the studio entrance, held out my pass, ducked my head into my clipboard, and ran through the halls toward the backlot door. No one paid any attention. On set, clipboard rushing was de rigueur. In the backlot, golf carts zipped past me as I sprinted for Dahlia's trailer. Didn't bother knocking, but quietly opened her door and listened for voices.

No voices.

Craptastic. Where were Vicki and Dahlia? I felt panic rise from my stomach to burn my throat. I crept up the stairs and peered around the half wall. No one in the living room. Bedrooms and bathrooms were also empty.

What had Dahlia done with my mother?

I called Nash. "Dahlia has my mother. What do I do?"

"What do you mean she has your mother?"

"Dahlia invited Vicki into her trailer, and I just let her go because I didn't want Dahlia to see me." I sniffled. "Oh God, it's all my fault. Again. And I've got to question more people and the police are here—"

"Stay calm. Investigators keep a cool head."

"Okay." I took a deep breath.

"You're conclusion jumping again. It's probably innocent. They went to lunch or something."

I looked at Dahlia's wall clock. One of those cats with the twitching tail and creepy eyes. Was that ironic or psychotic? "It's not lunch time. It's barely past breakfast."

"Shopping maybe." His voice sounded far away.

"Vicki has people for that. What are you doing?"

"Texting Vicki. When I get a ping, I'll let you know where she is." His voice slowed to a soothing crawl. "I know you're worried. Dahlia wouldn't do anything to Vicki. Why would she? Don't run yourself in circles, Maizie. Stick to your list. Who's next?"

"Ed Farmer. Make sure he doesn't leave." I chewed my lip. "Nash, if they're really missing, it's my fault."

"You're not the one doing this, Maizie. You've got a big job to do. But I know you can do it."

I peered out Dahlia's door, then huddled back inside as a golf cart zoomed past. At the all clear, I clasped my clipboard to my chest and jogged to the studio building. Inside the door, a policeman checked badges and asked questions. I spun around and exited.

Frigalicous. Now, what do I do? Climb the fence? Like that wouldn't attract attention.

I re-entered the building. Stood in line and held out my badge. Officer Holcomb squinted at the picture and looked at me. "Is this you?"

"Makeover."

"You're orange."

"Self-tanner." I waved my clipboard, shrugged, and gave him Nash's favorite descriptor. "You know, movie people."

"Hang on." He studied my name, the picture, then cocked his head. "That name. Didn't I just hear it?"

"In the kitchen?" Big Jim and Security Mike had blown my cover and reported me as the finder of Orlando to Detective Mowry. Off to the police station I go.

"Kitchen? Are you a cook?" As I shook my head, he snapped his fingers. "Wait, you were on that TV show…Pinky-something."

"*Julia Pinkerton: Teen Detective.*"

"That's it." He smiled. "What happened to you? You're like a behind-the-scenes worker now?"

"Yes. Behind-the-scenes. Exactly." I guessed Officer Holcomb was not a fan of entertainment news. And I wasn't going to give him a summary of my *E! True Hollywood Story.* "I have an appointment off the set. Can I go?"

"Hang on." He reached for his walkie and reported my name and request.

I waited for the "hold her for questioning" command. Dahlia's sketch hid beneath my clipboard paper. Would they look at my clipboard and ask where I'd gotten the drawing? Could I be charged with theft? Burglary? Sweat dampened my neck.

"You can leave. Be sure to officially sign out at the front and leave your number."

"Thanks." I held out my hand for my badge.

Still holding my ID, he studied me again. "Most people ask why the police are here. You're not curious?"

Shizzles. "I, uh, heard about it from a crew member. Someone found—" I snapped my mouth shut. Catching myself, I wrinkled my nose and lowered my voice. "They said someone in craft service was hurt."

"Not exactly." He smiled and handed back my card. "You shouldn't believe gossip."

"So what did happen?"

"Can't say. I'd look for an office memo later."

I thanked him and rushed through the building. My stomach spasmed with each step, shooting stress-induced heartburn into my chest and throat.

Wow that was close. If I'd said, "found a body in the dumpster," he would have stopped me for sure.

Although, maybe I should have told him about Vicki and Dahlia. My conscience set off another stomach convulsion and I clutched my chest. Jerry was wrong about diet killing me. More like work-related stress. Or desperate-killer-related stress.

I swiped at the sweat beading on the back of my neck and wiped my hand on Rhonda's grandma's slacks, leaving a black mark. I rubbed at the streak and smeared it. That's what I got for choosing a wash-out rinse. Maybe I should've taken one for the team and done permanent color.

Grabbing my helmet, I straddled Lucky, then lurched forward. My phone buzzed from my back pocket. With a shaky hand, I pulled it out and jammed it under my helmet, hoping the caller was Vicki. Or Giulio. Or Nash.

Zero for three.

"Maizie, it's Leonard. The police have arrived on set. I just learned security discovered a body in the kitchen garbage."

"Um, yeah. The victim is Orlando Feelzen, Cambria's alleged boyfriend, who was involved in the alleged personal video at her villa. I accidentally found him last night when I was…Running from him. I found Orlando in Cambria's trailer and kind of… Scared him away. Which sort of…Got him killed."

"You did what?"

"It was a confusing situation? Also, a very scary situation?"

"I don't understand." Before I could explain, Leonard cleared his throat. "Nevertheless, I specifically said no police."

"Sorry, Mr. Shackleton, but if a body is found, the police have to be involved." To calm myself, I switched to a tone similar to the one Officer Holcomb had used with me. Cop cool. Very soothing.

"It's on the set," Leonard cried. "There's no way to disconnect that crime from our film."

"I think the cat left that particular bag a while ago, Mr. Shackleton."

"The press will hound us," moaned Leonard. "I'm going to blow the marketing budget on spin alone. God, what a nightmare. I just met with the other producers about the schedule changes. This movie is already giving me an ulcer."

I could relate. Maybe my symptoms weren't heartburn. "Listen, we now know Orlando Feelzen didn't kill the filmographer or the body double. I did learn that my pie was poisoned. Cambria took a big bite. Whoever killed Orlando and the rest was more interested in killing me than killing Cambria. That's good, right?"

Leonard made a choking sound.

"I spoke with Big Jim of Big Jim's Catering. He put the pie out himself. I trust him. I believe our perp saw my name on the pie plate as an opportunity to stop my investigation. Probably took it to the bathroom, used the window cleaner and brought it back. With all the comings and goings in the craft service room, nobody would have noticed."

"Our craft service dining room?" he moaned. "Can it get worse?"

"Well, Cambria could have died — or me for that matter — so there's a silver lining." I didn't wait for Leonard to respond. "By the way, does Ed Farmer have plans to do a *Double Indemnity* remake with Dahlia?"

"Not that I know of. What does that have to do with anything?"

"Maybe nothing." Probably better to ask Ed Farmer than panic

Leonard any more. "Nash is guarding Cambria. Your star is safe. See, we're fulfilling all your expectations. I'm going to check on Cam-Cam at the hospital now. We need her to talk, Mr. Shackleton."

"The doctor believes sedation will allow her throat to heal faster. She shouldn't try to talk at all."

"Some would believe you want the doctor to sedate her so she can't explain what happened. Because it would incriminate your star." This I stated in my head. Julia Pinkerton would have asserted it aloud. I still needed to get paid for this job.

To Leonard, I said, "We could give Cambria a whiteboard or paper and a pen. She doesn't have to literally talk."

"I'm firm on this."

Leonard, you're moving up on my suspect list. "I'll talk to you later."

"I want to meet in person. Later. Tonight. At your office. I'm busy with meetings and now, the police. But we need to convo about all this, Maizie. In person."

My stomach did another flip. I pounded my chest and forced out a choked response. "I sort of have this party tonight?" Oh, my God. Why did I say that? "You know, I'm just super busy with this investigation. I wouldn't go to the party, except I promised. A quick appearance—"

"Party? The Theodore Malthus event?"

"You know Theodore?" I took a calming breath. "Of course, you do." Shizzles, Theodore. You are too good at concealing your cards.

"I'd forgotten about the party. It's exclusive, so should be safe."

"Okay then—"

"Only a few photographers were invited from the media. Not local. Atlanta, I believe. The AP and entertainment news could pick something up. Our PR team and camera crew will be there, too, of course. I hadn't planned on going, but was sending the actors and Ed."

"Right, publicity for the movie." I bounced on the bike seat, eager to get through my list so I'd have time to focus on panicking. "So talk to you later?"

"We should carry on. For appearances, at the very least. We're not down yet, Maizie. If the news is bad, it'll be big. But big news is still big news." He paused. "I'll pick you up at eight."

"Wait. What? You mean the party? But I planned to bring my girlfriends."

"No girlfriends, Maizie. You're still working, remember? We'll go together and use it as an opportunity."

"Opportunity for what?"

"Observing potential suspects? I don't know. You're the expert on investigations. I'll pick you up at home?"

"The office," I said quickly. And hoped my fake office was still there.

*A*t the hospital, my heart warmed to see Nash. Until I spotted the rise in his upper lip upon seeing me.

"How is this better than carrying a weapon?" he whispered. "You look like Halloween. All orange and black and brown. Even your eyes."

"But I don't look like Maizie Albright."

"That's true." He scowled. "What'd Robin say?"

"Not much. She went to the studio to finagle more money for the resort by offering convalescence for Cambria. Which she called 'paying her respects.' And then told me I didn't have any respect..." I rolled my eyes. "Haters be hating. Anyway, I found out the real reason I was kicked off the set. Vicki's filming *All is Albright* there and didn't want me to know."

This time Nash rolled his eyes. "You hear from Vicki or Giulio?"

I shook my head.

He patted my shoulder.

"Did you know the police rescued Orlando from the kitchen garbage?"

He nodded. "Talked to Mowry."

"Whoever is doing this must be strong."

We simultaneously glanced at Ed. Sitting next to Cambria's bed, he sketched in his small notebook. He was wiry, not paunchy like some directors I knew. And fairly young for an established director. Still, he was no Dwayne Johnson. He wasn't even a Nash. Could Ed bash people's heads in and haul them around to later fling in lakes, bathtubs, and dumpsters?

"Mr. Farmer," I called. "Do you work out?"

Startled, he looked up. "Of course."

I glanced at Nash. He waved a hand for me to continue. I strolled to Cambria's bed and stood across from Ed's chair. A gentle beep emitted from the equipment. Cam-Cam appeared peaceful. Her generous lips relaxed into a serene smile. Like Snow White waiting for Prince Charming. Or was that Sleeping Beauty? I guess it depended on which fairy tale Ed preferred.

"Someone did her hair and makeup?" I said. "And dressed her?"

"I did," said Ed, gazing at Cambria. "Actually the nurse did. I just supplied the necessary items."

"Yeah, that's…" I wanted to say nice, but I just couldn't do it. My nerves were frazzled. "Really weird, Mr. Farmer. And considering all that's happened, you're giving off a Hitchcock vibe. Hitchcock movie, not the director."

Nash had moved to the opposite corner of the room. He remained silent, but I could feel his mental note taking.

"I suppose it looks that way to you."

"Yep."

"It's all about perspective," said Ed. "That's the key. You just see this from the wrong viewpoint."

"How about from Cambria's perspective, when she wakes up and finds herself dressed in a white nightgown with you reading scene notes to her?"

"She'll know I care about her."

"Cam-Cam might see that a little differently," I muttered. "So you're setting a scene. The director concerned for his ingénue. Or the director concerned that his investment might flake on his project? I know about the bond you paid for Cambria's insurance policy. And the amount you'll owe if she's fired."

Behind us, Nash stirred.

"That's not what this is about. Thinking about insurance when Cambria's lying here is tactless." Running a hand through his thick hair, he peered up at me from over the frame of his glasses. "You're the one who neglected your job. Not Cambria."

"This is about failing Cambria?" I took a deep breath. "I know what she ate. And I know it was not meant for her. We stepped away for a minute..."

"Spare me your excuses. You didn't do your job from the beginning."

"Cambria's also not innocent in this situation," I said. "She could have told us what happened in her villa, but she refused to talk."

"None of us are innocent." Ed pulled off his glasses and rested his forehead in his hand.

"Were you punishing me for interfering? With poisoned pie?" I said. "Is that another role you're playing? Judge and executioner?"

"I don't play roles, I create them," he said.

"What are you guilty of?" growled Nash.

Ed's head rocked against his hand. "Nothing that has to do with this."

I looked at Nash. He fluttered his fingers to me to continue, but I didn't seem to be getting anywhere. I pulled the clipboard from my backpack. "What about Dahlia Pearson? Is she innocent?"

He shoved his glasses back on. "I'm sorry?"

"Dahlia the actress is different from the real Dahlia, isn't she?" I held out his sketch. "Phyllis Dietrichson? Is this how you think of her? Is that why you didn't want her in the lead of *Pine Hollow*?"

"Where did you find that?"

"Do you think Dahlia's like Phyllis? Scheming? Capable of planning a murder?"

"Of course not." He slid back in his chair and folded his arms.

"You're talking about my supporting actress. I would never think that about her."

"Oh my God, Mr. Farmer, please tell me the truth." I'd kept calm, but I felt the panic rise. "I left my mother with Dahlia."

"Your mother?"

"Vicki Albright." I felt Nash behind me. He didn't touch me, didn't make a sound, but his presence bolstered me. "I can't get in contact with Vicki. I can't find her."

Ed shook his head.

"Mr. Farmer, you're acting suspiciously. Don't you get that? Two people connected to Cambria have been found dead. Another is missing, and that's not counting Giulio Belloni and Vicki Albright. You want to tell me or do you want to tell the police?"

"Tell the police what?"

"What you know about Cambria's misdeeds? And about Dahlia's? Do you think she's Phyllis Dietrichson or not?"

Ed stared at Cambria. His shoulders trembled, and he turned to face the wall. "She is. But not in that way."

"In what way?" Nash moved to stand beside me. "Be clear."

"We're sleeping together, okay? Dahlia and I." He turned back, his face wet with tears. "I'm sorry Cambria. I just— I'm weak. I'm Walter Neff to her Phyllis. I don't feel about Dahlia the way I do Cambria, but I couldn't help myself. She's just that good."

"Who is Walter Neff?" Nash glanced at me. "What in the hell is he talking about? I can't follow this guy. He talks in circles."

"Walter Neff's the insurance salesman in *Double Indemnity.* Phyllis seduced him to help her get a big insurance policy on her husband and murder him."

"What the hell?" Nash turned to me. "You said he had an insurance policy on Cambria. How does Dahlia benefit?"

I shook my head. "That can't be it. It's not a life policy. The policy is backing her finishing the movie. If Cambia died, he'd lose twenty million."

"Twenty million? What the hell," said Nash.

Ed had gathered Cambria's hand between his. "I'd never hurt

Cambria. Her brilliance has been overlooked for too long. I wanted this movie to push her into the limelight."

"She's been in the limelight lately, Mr. Farmer. Her tabloid fame is worse than mine."

"Exactly. They don't know the real Cambria. Few of us do. That's why I need to adjust the public's perspective with her role in *Pine Hollow*. As a director, I determine how the audience understands a scene. I can control how they feel about a character or an event. Cambria knew I could do this for her."

Nash touched my arm and jerked his head toward the door. He held the door open as we stood in the hall where we could watch Ed without him listening.

"I don't get this guy," said Nash. "All this perspective business. Do you understand what he's talking about?"

"I think so. He sees Cambria's potential as a serious actress, the Cam-Cam I knew as a kid. But Cambria was working against that with this whole party girl act."

"Are you sure it's an act?"

"You've seen her villa and trailer. The most unhealthy thing in it is fun-size Snicker bars." I licked my lips. "Which is probably why she went for my chocolate peanut butter pie. Although Big Jim's pie is more like a Reese's Peanut Butter Cup."

"Let's stick to the point, Miss Albright." Nash tapped his watch. "What's with all this Dahlia business? He's obsessed with one and sleeping with the other? Did he incriminate Dahlia or not? I don't get your movie references."

"I'm not sure." I tapped my lip. "Dahlia seduced him like Phyllis Dietrichson did Walter Neff. He couldn't help himself. I guess that's why Dahlia had a key to his office. Maybe for trysts? Or she swiped it so she could help herself to...film notes?"

"Trysts seem more likely." Nash paced between the door and the opposite wall. "We still don't have a solid motive. What about the insurance angle?"

"If Cambria can't do the movie, the loser would be Ed Farmer.

He paid for her insurance bond." I folded my arms over the clipboard and paced the opposite route Nash had taken.

Five steps, turn, five steps, turn. Surprisingly therapeutic. I glanced into the room, then at Nash as we passed.

"Leonard and the other producers paid their own completion bond to the distributors, guaranteeing the entire movie will be done on time and within budget. Hence his super stress," I said. "If Cambria breaks Ed's bond, Leonard will break Ed's, and the investors could break Leonard's. The movie wouldn't get made unless a bigger studio took it over. Leonard would lose his share of the investment and Ed would lose all his creative control."

"So they're all sunk if this actress does something stupid."

"Maybe that's Dahlia's angle. Maybe she hired the filmographer, Orlando, and the double to make Cam-Cam look bad? Then seduced the director to drop his star and put her in the lead?"

"That's not a murder motive."

"True. Plus, Cam-Cam hinted she knew about the filmmaking." Meeting Nash between the door and the wall, I touched his arm, and he halted his steps. "I think if Ed discovered Cam-Cam's home video, he'd do anything to stop it from getting out. He'd want to protect Cambria's reputation, so Leonard doesn't fire her."

"Or lose money on her bond. Twenty million." Nash whistled. "Anything to stop Cambria from 'shitting up' the movie."

"Leonard wants Ed Farmer to direct. Ed wants Cambria to star. But if it comes down to it, Leonard will replace Cambria. He's the producer."

"That's a solid motive." Nash glanced into the hospital room. "I'm calling Mowry. He needs to haul in Ed Farmer for questioning."

"What about Dahlia?"

Nash shrugged. "She was trying to climb the ladder the old fashioned way."

I punched his arm.

He smiled, rubbing the spot. "Nice right hook. Look, Dahlia might attempt for Cambria's role by sleeping with the director and making Cambria look bad, but it's not a strong enough motive for killing three people. Money is."

"I still don't like it."

"But he's the one acting like a psycho." Nash jerked a thumb at the man sketching sleeping Cambria.

"Yep. Hitchcock."

TWENTY-SIX

#PartyLikeIts1984 #ThreeTimesTheLadies

*a*t LA HAIR, I slumped in a salon chair and broke the news about Ed Farmer.

"Shocking," said Rhonda. "He's so famous."

"Hell, they're all famous, Rhon," said Tiffany. "Doesn't keep them from being psychopaths. Fame probably gives them a leg up."

"You think y'all were screwed up to begin with or was it the fame that did it to you?" asked Rhonda.

I mused over my rehab stories. "I'm not qualified to answer that. And I have more bad news."

"Lord almighty," said Rhonda. "If it's about Beyoncé, I do not want to know."

"It's more like local news." I explained Leonard's adamant request to take me to Theodore's party unaccompanied.

"Damn," said Tiffany.

"So uncool," I said. "This job has been stressful enough without his ambiguous sexual harassment."

"Sue him," said Tiffany.

"Too ambiguous," I said. "Believe me, I've been in enough unambiguous situations to know."

"It's okay, Maizie," said Rhonda. "We understand."

"It's not okay," I said. "Leonard thinks this is a date. He's our client, but this is not a date. I'm still not entirely convinced Ed Farmer killed those people even with the money angle. My mother and Giulio are still missing. All my suspects are going to be at this party. I need to go. Leonard's my client, so I guess I'm going with him."

"What about your boss?" said Rhonda.

"Nash's overseeing Cambria's move to the resort. Robin Coxon arranged it." I rolled my eyes. "Our client is still paying us for guard duty. I think Leonard's hoping a crazy fan is going to pop out of the woodwork, try to kill Cambria, and resolve the mess."

"Killing his star resolves the mess?"

"Trying to kill her. Which Nash would prevent. And if he doesn't, Leonard will sue us. Nash is guarding Cambria while I'm stuck trying to find out who's killing off Cambria's villa party."

"Are the police convinced Ed Farmer did it?" asked Tiffany. "Because that might be a real party pooper, you know what I'm saying? Isn't this Ed Farmer's big movie?"

"I don't know if Leonard knows yet. Last I heard, Ed's at the station for questioning. The police are probably checking all his alibis. He's been in proximity to each murder."

"Who would have thought?" said Tiffany. "Maybe he learned his murdering skills from his action movies."

Rhonda shuddered. "Back to the party. What are you wearing? I was going to wear my Aunt Carmen's cruise ship dress. She'll be glad to know I can't wear it 'cause she worried about lending it to me."

"I never decided on an ensemble." I sighed. "At this point, I don't even care."

Tiffany cocked her head. "You don't care?"

I shrugged.

"Rhon, you hear that? Maizie doesn't care about what she's wearing. Since when don't she care what she's wearing?"

Rhonda spun my chair to face her. "You told T. Malthus, Esquire, you'd look fabulous for his party."

"I know. But he's just as bad as everyone else. Vicki. Dahlia. Leonard. Cambria. Friggin' Robin. They don't seem to give a shizzle that people have died. How can Theodore have a party when three people were murdered, and Cambria's in the hospital? How can I go to a party and look fabulous knowing this? It's in poor taste. And totally gruesome."

"Girl." Rhonda placed her hands on my armrests and bent close to eyeball me. "You're not looking fabulous for them. You're doing it for the woman you found. You're going to the party to eyeball those suspects. And you'll look hot for the street cred. We'll do you up again."

"You're right." I straightened. "I owe it to that woman. We still know nothing about her other than her birthmark and a resemblance to a deviant actress."

Rhonda rubbed her hands together, dashed to the receptionist desk, and returned with a plastic crate. "What look are you going for tonight? Could you mention 'makeup by Rhonda of LA HAIR' when they ask what you're wearing?"

"It's not a red carpet, but okay."

Rhonda stacked makeup boxes before the salon mirror, then pulled out bottles.

"Um, Rhon?" I said. "Orange is not a good color for me. I need to lose the tan."

"And your hair." Tiffany plugged in a fat curling iron and cracked open a new case of bobby pins. "We need to change your hair. Maybe an updo. Unless you want extensions."

I bit my lip. "I think no extensions. And maybe a rinse out? Matte black makes me look like a ghost in those Japanese horror movies."

"How about turquoise for your hair?" said Tiffany. "And I still have those lavender contacts. That's a nice combo."

"Hard to blend when you're turquoise." I leaned over the counter to take out the brown contacts.

"Sapphire blue?"

"Girls, I need to look like Maizie Albright for this role."

"I guess if Ed Farmer's arrested, you don't need to hide anymore," said Rhonda.

"Actually, I've learned disguised skulking gives me heartburn. I'd rather talk to people, and a disguise doesn't do me any good for that. Besides, I'm going with Leonard. I'd have to tell him it's me."

Tiffany held up a bottle. "We'll switch you back to ginger and give you a deep conditioning treatment."

"Let's make this happen." I popped her JP's finger gun, walked to the row of sinks, and plopped into a chair.

Humming, Rhonda fanned her makeup brushes on a towel. Tiffany started toward me, her arms full of towels. Watching them, I sniffled.

"You don't mind doing this? I feel like I'm taking advantage of your salon abilities," I said. "I'm standing you up. You've always wanted to go to a Black Pine party."

"That was Rhonda," said Tiffany. "I don't care if it's a Black Pine party. I just like the free booze and food."

"Of course we don't mind," said Rhonda. "You'll take us another time. Girl, we're going to make you look so good, the party invites will not stop. It'll be like this." Hands in the air and hips swinging, she danced in a circle, then dabbed for effect. "Booty all up in the house. Twenty-four seven. Three sixty-five. The invites will be rolling in."

"It better not be like that," said Tiffany. "Or we're never going to a party."

I clasped my hands to my heart, my eyes brimming with tears. "You better call your Aunt Carmen for that dress, Rhonda. Screw Leonard. I'm taking both of you on our date. He's getting three times the lady. "

*a*t the Dixie Kreme Donut Shop building, I parked Lucky, changed in the Nash Security Solutions bathroom (which smelled like bergamot and lost opportunity), and walked to my fake office. The girls met me there. Rhonda wore optimism and spangles. Tiffany wore fishnet and a pluming vape. I wore L'Agence's star sequin dress and a gold anklet. The anklet was my nod to *Double Indemnity*. I wasn't going to *Maltese Falcon* for Leonard, but the stars were meant as a reminder that I had once been one.

I was no longer in awe of these *Pine Hollow* people. Familiarity breeds contempt. So does questionable morality and murder.

After the usual girl chat about clothing choices, we gazed at the brick building where Sam Spade might have had an office if he had been Southern and an ex-celebrity.

"Are we going inside?" said Tiffany.

"No key," I said. "Anyway, Vicki's using it as an *All is Albright* prop. That's why Theodore had it ready so quickly. It's not real."

Plus, I still hadn't told Nash about it. Which I planned to do as soon I got the nerve. So, never.

"Your dream is real," said Rhonda. "In two years, you can buy it from T. Malthus, Esquire. And hire us as your assistants."

"I can't compete with Nash Security Solutions. That'd be ungrateful after he trained me." I paused. "Actually Nash hasn't trained me. But he's got two years. Unfortunately, now that I know how much a private investigator makes, I won't be able to hire anyone."

"Reality bites," said Tiffany. "You ready to go back to Looney Land? Maybe this time your mother won't keep all your money."

"La-la Land. And no. That reality bites, too. I may miss the perks, but spending time with these people has made me remember what I hated about my old career. Better real reality than fake reality."

"Did you forget about all the death?" said Rhonda. "Because I would choose fake acting over murder any day."

We contemplated the dark building, reality, and murder. Then turned toward the street as a vehicle approached. Leonard's Escalade.

"I thought he'd have a limo," said Rhonda.

The back door opened and Leonard leaned out. "What's this? I said no girlfriends."

"It's either them, or I'll call Mr. Nash and switch jobs with him. He can take you to the party. It's just business, right?" I jerked my thumb toward the office. Rhonda stuck a hand on a spangled hip and Tiffany drew heavily on her vape.

"Right," said Leonard. "Get in."

*T*heodore's garden covered the three pillars of Southern party decor: fairy lights, Mason jars, and flamingos. A tiny feathered flamingo rode on the lapel of his robin's egg blue Haspel. Frosted glass flamingos bobbed in his tiered fountain. Concrete flamingos — tastefully made from pale pink crushed shells — decorated the tables and lighted the steps on his veranda.

Theodore gave me a double-cheeked kiss. "I forgive you for wearing black sequins to a garden party. Let's call it ironic. But you do look stunning, honey."

"I like the flamingos," I said. "You outdid yourself."

"Not really. I wanted elephants but held back in case we had to cancel." His voice dropped to a whisper. "All these murders."

"Of course." My tone dried.

"And you brought plus three, sweetie. I didn't mean it literally." He smiled graciously at Rhonda and Tiffany, rubbernecking the Black Pine A-listers who'd surrounded the bar. "More irony."

He gave Leonard a double-clasped hand shake. "Mr. Shackleton. It's an honor and a delight."

Taking his hand from Theodore's, Leonard placed it on the small of my back. "Do you know if my publicity gal got the list of media outlets invited? She has some sound bites prepared."

Theodore waved his hand, and a young, Haspel-suited man

appeared. He also had a flamingo pin but wore his seersucker in pale gray. "Take Mr. Shackleton to the prepared green room."

"Maizie?" Leonard's thumb stroked my spine.

With a discreet sidestep, I said, "I need to speak to Theodore," and gave him my Julia Pinkerton finger gun salute. "Still on the clock, you know. Your clock."

Gray seersucker whisked Leonard away. Theodore tucked my arm through his. "Let's stroll."

"My friends…"

Another seersucker suited youth appeared with a tray of food and drinks. He bobbed a bow and presented the tray to Rhonda and Tiffany.

"We're good," said Tiffany, scooping up a fistful of cheese straws. She grabbed a glass of pink liquid. "Go do your thing."

"Keep an eye out for Dahlia Pearson," I said. "And save me a cheese straw."

"Hello, sweet thing." Rhonda took the tray from the young man's hand and slipped her free arm around his elbow. "You're going to give us a tour. Inside and out."

Theodore nodded to the young man and led me down the winding garden path. "I thought you'd gone brunette."

"Did you get that insider info from Robin Coxon or Vicki?" I snapped, then gusted a long sigh. "Theodore, do you know where Vicki is? She's not answering her phone. Giulio has disappeared, too."

"Oh my dear, you know your mother. She's probably up to something."

"I'm not sure about that. I'm worried. I may have gotten her in trouble."

"Hold that thought." Theodore pressed a hand to my arm, nodding toward a small cluster of movie people.

We waxed pleasantries and moved on. Strolling around a rose garden, we nodded at guests and arrived at a pergola covered in a flowering vine thick enough to act as drapery. Small Mason jars filled with winking lights hung from the overhead beams.

"We'll have some privacy in here."

I peeked around the vine and saw most guests still crowded the bar or sat on the veranda. Tiffany and Rhonda had disappeared inside the house.

"Your momma will turn up. Giulio on the other hand, I don't know," continued Theodore. "Word is he's about to get cut from *All is Albright*. He hasn't been showing up to the location shoots. Even when you're benched, you still need to go to the game. Bad boy."

"That might not be his fault." I bit my lip and turned to face Theodore. "I'm worried something awful has happened to him. He was helping me and might have gotten caught by whoever killed the man they found in the resort."

Theodore bowed his head. "That's terrible. I heard the man they found made movies. Professionally."

"Yes, his name was Billy Goodwin from Atlanta."

"Did the police catch the person who killed him and the stuntman yet?"

"I'm not sure." I studied him. "Theodore, what do you know?"

With a quick glance past the pergola, Theodore grasped my hands and turned me to face him. "You know I'm Black Pine's premier lifestyle designer. That comes naturally with my heritage."

"Heritage?"

"My name. Malthuses have been around forever." He shrugged. "It's a Southern thing, honey. Anyway, I also function for Black Pine in another capacity. I told you earlier, I'm a resourcer. I resource people, things, events, locations. I just know how to get things."

"Okay?"

"For example, Vicki Albright contacted me to find an actress who resembled you. And Nash. Although she didn't really care if the actor looked like Nash. He just had to look like 'walking sex.' Her words, not mine."

I pulled my hands from his. "I already figured that out. You checked Clone Star and found Mini Me—"

"Lana Miles. You met her. She worked as your secretary in your fabulous office for half a minute."

I opened and closed my mouth.

"Before your panties get too bunched, let me get to my point. Miss Cambria contacted me, too."

I grabbed Theodore's hands and gripped them. "I needed to know this three days ago. Talk."

"Cambria wanted someone who looked like her, too. Except this actress, for a hefty paycheck, had to be willing to perform before a camera, if you get my euphemism."

At my angry nod, he continued. "Couldn't use a reputable place like Clone Star. I went with Craig's List."

"Who is she? Do you know what happened to her?"

"Stella Craven. I think that's her," he coughed, "stage name. We colored her hair and used contacts, but her facial structure is similar."

I dropped Theodore's hands, feeling like I needed a long, hot, sanitizing shower. "What happened to Stella?"

"I'm concerned." He studied the overhead Mason jars. "And ashamed. And feeling horribly guilty. Cambria offered me a handsome price for resourcing. I had nothing to do with the actual job. Stella and the filmographer were paid well, too. Still, that's no excuse."

"You hired Billy Goodwin?"

"He was harder to find, oddly enough. Cambria wanted someone who used actual film. She said the video had to be high quality and artistic. She was afraid someone who filmed digitally would go 'too blue.'"

"Oh my God. Cambria was always such a nerd." My stomach knotted. "She overthinks everything. She can't even pull off home porn without making it a production. God, what a diva."

Theodore pinched the bridge of his nose. A tear rolled down his cheek. "I didn't realize that Stella might be in trouble until I heard about Billy Goodwin. And I just found out about him today."

"We need to go to the police with this. It connects the murders to the missing girl. They haven't really been able to act without any information. Maybe they can get a court order to make the doctor wake Cambria and get her to confess to murder."

"Murder? Why would Cambria murder Stella? She'd paid her up front. Cambria didn't want anything to do with the actual film session. She just set it up."

"What about Orlando Feelzen?"

"She brought him from California. I know nothing about him except entertainment news." He grabbed my hand. "Am I an accomplice to murder? Maizie, you have to believe that I had no idea Stella was missing. I knew the job was sordid, but I didn't presume it dangerous."

"I'm not a lawyer, Theodore. But I don't care if the woman was willing, you should have told Cambria no. I don't know what Cambria was planning on doing with that video, but whatever it was, it was wrong."

"Tell Cambria no?" Theodore placed a hand on his chest. "She's a movie star."

"In my experience, that's not going to let Cambria off the hook. Your party can continue without you." I took his arm. "I assume Detective Mowry wasn't invited. If you don't want the police here, we need to go to the station. I need to call Nash, too."

"I was afraid of that." Theodore sighed. "Let me have a moment with my staff. They'll keep the party rolling. If I can't be here, at least it'll photograph well."

TWENTY-SEVEN

#TheLadyorTheTigress
#BlindedByTheSight

I left Theodore to search for his people, and I went in search of mine. I strode up the veranda stairs and combed the crowd for Tiffany and Rhonda. Unable to get through the back door, I rounded the wraparound porch and entered the house through the side entrance. In the kitchen, the catering crew arranged party trays. A waiter pointed me to the front of the house. More people crowded the spacious living room. In a paneled library, I found Leonard.

"Maizie, there you are." Leonard strode across the thick oriental rug. "We still need to talk. Let's go somewhere more private."

"I'm sorry, but I'm on my way to the police station. There's been a development in the case."

"Does it have to do with Ed? You should have told me he's there." Leonard folded his arms. "We need to talk. Now."

"What about Ed?" squeaked Dahlia. She peeked over the edge of a wingback chair then rose to meet us. A strapless maxi dress made a beautiful show of her sinewy arms and muscular back.

"I thought you'd be here."

"Of course." She shrugged. "What's going on with Ed? You didn't tell me anything, Leonard."

"Ed didn't call you, Dahlia?" I felt a surge of Julia Pinkerton teenage cynicism. "I thought you'd be one of his two calls."

"What? Alvin, did you know anything about Ed?" called Dahlia. "Isn't he with Cambria? How's she doing?"

Glancing behind me, I saw Cambria's agent stroll into the room, a stunning woman on his arm. He smiled apologetically at the woman, led her to the hall, and returned. "Hello, Dahlia. Leonard. Maizie? I just checked. Cambria's about the same. They moved her to her villa. Sleeping peacefully."

Of course she is, I thought. That's what good drugs do to a person.

"Dahlia," I said. "I've been trying to reach you all day. Do you know where my mother is?"

"I don't always check my messages. Have you tried to call her?"

"Duh," I said, matching Dahlia's tone. "You were the last person to see her."

"I'm sure that can't be right. Unless she never left my trailer."

I narrowed my eyes. "What does that mean?"

"Leonard?" said Alvin. "Anything going on that I should know?"

"Not now, Murphy," said Leonard. "Maizie, find us an empty room. We need a one-on-one. I think there's a room upstairs."

I grabbed Dahlia's arm. "We're going to use it first."

She wrenched her arm from my grip. "What do you think you're doing?"

"You need to tell me about Vicki."

"Get over yourself." Dahlia stalked from the room.

I followed, calling her name.

Dahlia slipped past a group standing shoulder-to-shoulder within the tight hallway. I elbowed my way inside. Pushing through, I stepped into an empty space. The hallway brightened, darkened, then filled with burning, dancing eclipses. I slapped a hand over my eyes. The crowd behind me booed.

Squinting through my fingers, I made out a professional photographer. He waved a hand. Someone circled an arm around my shoulders, drew me back, and clamped me in place. The flash ignited my retinas once again.

"Great smile, Miss Albright," called the photographer.

Muscle memory.

I stumbled forward, blind and blinking.

More people crammed the living area. I bumbled through, tossed around in the mosh pit of a party. "How is this exclusive? Is this even code?" I called. "Anyone seen Dahlia? Or Theodore? Two women in cruise ship dresses?"

Laughter erupted. At the far end, chords swelled from the piano, and a jazz quartet began playing. I opened the front door, looked out on the front porch. On the sea grass love seat, a couple made out. Three people sat on the front rails, smoking. No Dahlia. No Theodore. No Rhonda and Tiffany.

Closing the front doors, I fought my way back through the living room, down the jammed hall, and into the kitchen. The smell of garlic and herbs heated the space. I bumped into a waiter and knocked over a tray. Apologizing, I helped him pick up the fallen food — tiny ham and pimento biscuits. Such a sad waste — and asked about Dahlia. Shoving a dropped sandwich in my mouth (five-second rule), I muscled through to the back veranda. Took a quick turn around the enclosed garden (for the air, if nothing else) and returned to the living area.

"Dahlia?" I called.

"Maizie?"

I turned toward the voice in the crowd. "Rhonda?"

A minute later, a man was shoved aside. My friends appeared bearing empty glasses.

"Where you been?" said Tiffany.

"Trying to find Dahlia. I think she knows where Vicki is. But I can't find Dahlia."

"This way." Rhonda dropped their empty glasses on a Chippendale table.

Tiffany picked up a small concrete flamingo and shoved it in her purse. "I think they're party favors. He's got plenty anyway."

Entering a smaller hall, we passed a queuing line.

"Bathroom," said Rhonda. "Been like that all night."

We traipsed into the kitchen and up the backstairs.

"Shortcut," said Tiffany.

"We had the tour. We know where we're going." Rhonda's spangles glimmered with each step. "I got a phone number from one of those cute waiters."

"Great," I said. "I hope you're having a good time. Because this is one of the worst parties I've ever attended."

"You just have a lot going on," said Rhonda. "You can't cut loose, and it makes you edgy."

"Murders do that to me."

At the top of the stairs, we stopped before another door. Tiffany knocked. "It's another guest bathroom. This one has a chandelier and a couch. Everyone waits in line downstairs, and there's this one up here. The waiter told us."

"Jeremy," sighed Rhonda.

"Jeremy told us," said Tiffany. "Anyway, Mr. Theodore locked the bedrooms. Smart man. Dahlia must have gone in here."

"Thanks. You want to help me corner her?"

"Alright."

I watched Tiffany crack her knuckles. "We're not going to jump her."

"Unless she tries to get away."

"Lord have mercy," said Rhonda. "Tiffany you can't jump peoples at a party like this. I'll block the bathroom door. But if she comes at me, I'm leaving. I don't want anyone messing with my Beyoncé hair. And if anything happens to this dress, Aunt Carmen will kill me."

"Nobody is doing anything," I said. "We're just talking. Then tell the police what Dahlia says."

"I'm out. I ain't talking to any cops." Tiffany turned from the bathroom door and sped down the hall.

I fisted my hands on my hips, then let out a sigh. "You go, too, Rhonda. I don't want to chance your dress. Do me a favor and text

Mr. Nash. Tell him Theodore knows the mystery woman. Her name is Stella Craven. And if you see Theodore, make him wait for me."

"Okay, baby." Rhonda charged down the hall. "Wait, Tiff."

I banged on the door again. "Dahlia, let me in." I rattled the doorknob. It turned in my hand. Pushing the door, I entered a marble and oak bath. Sinks and a glass shower lined one side of the generous space. A velvet chaise lounge rested below the glass chandelier. On the far end, a pair of matching oak doors remained closed. Built-in closets flanked a large, mirrored vanity where a delicate stool lay on its side.

"Dahlia?" I righted the stool. Then acknowledged the oddness of its fallen state.

Downstairs, the din grew. A heavy bass thrummed through the floor. A lit candle scented the space with orange spice. The flame flickered. I glanced over my shoulder at the closed hall door, then at the facing twin doors. They stood like sentinels.

The lady or the tiger.

Taking a deep breath, I grasped the knob of the door on the right. Toilet and bidet. Shut the door. I gripped the left-hand knob. Closet.

A big, dark closet. Found the light on the wall.

Then wished I hadn't.

TWENTY-EIGHT

#HereLiesLana #Flamingoed

$\mathcal{M}$y shriek bounced off the marble tiled walls. I backed away from the closet. I yanked open the hall door, realized I was still screaming, and clamped a hand over my mouth. Downstairs, the music had stopped and the crowd hushed. I locked the bathroom door, pulled it shut, and flattened myself against the wall. Dizzy, I sank to the floor and laid my head on my knees. Closing my eyes, I saw Stella Craven lying on the floor of Cam-Cam's bedroom. Then saw myself on the floor of Theodore's closet. But it wasn't me on the floor of Theodore's guest closet. Rather Lana Miles. With her head bashed in.

I opened my eyes. A thunderous racket reverberated on the front staircase.

The party was coming to me.

Crab-like, I scuttled around the corner, hopped to my feet, and ran. Stumbling down the backstairs, I caught myself from falling and spotted half the kitchen staff watching me.

"Where's Theodore?" I called. "Call the police. 9-1-1. There's a woman in the upstairs bathroom closet. She's badly hurt."

A cook wiped her hands on a towel. "I'm a volunteer EMT. What's wrong?"

I pinched my thumb. "She's fallen. An injury to the back of the head. It looks bad. I left her... I locked the door to the bathroom so..." I couldn't say, "so the crowd wouldn't mess with a crime scene."

"So she didn't get trampled in the crowd," I continued. "Oh, my God. Why did I even leave her?"

I knew why. Because someone had thought Lana was me. I'd freaked out.

Oh, my God. How could I flake at a time like this?

Another cook rummaged in the kitchen desk. "Theodore keeps his keys here." He tossed a ring to the EMT volunteer. "I'll go with you."

I grabbed the arm of a seersuckered waiter. "Jeremy? Find Theodore. Tell him what happened."

Halfway up the stairs, the EMT stopped. "There's a million people in the hallway."

The other cook glanced at me. "You coming?"

"She's shaking." Wiping his hands on a towel, the dishwasher approached me. "Maybe you should sit down. Do you want a glass of water?"

Shaking my head, I staggered to the back door. "Fresh air."

The veranda crowd had dispersed, but small clusters of people milled around the garden. Evidently they hadn't heard the screaming and subsequent stampede. Staying in shadows of the house, I gazed out beyond the fairy lighted railings and searched for recognizable faces. Rounding the corner of the porch, I ran into one.

Shizzles, it was not my night.

A tall, auburn-haired beauty spoke into a phone. She wore a flowing white sundress that made her look like a Grecian goddess. Nash's ex-goddess.

Craptastic.

She narrowed her eyes and said to her phone, "Call you back."

"Just passing through, Jolene." I pivoted to get around her.

She blocked my pass. "What are you doing here?"

"I was invited by Theodore? "

Landing a hand on her hip, Jolene slanted me a look. "Is Wyatt here?"

"God, no." I whooshed out a breath. "I came with Leonard Shackleton. And Tiffany and Rhonda. And I need to get back to the party? Because there's an emergency?"

"I know what you're doing." She pursed her lips.

"I know. I uptalk when I get nervous." I stammered. "It's not you. It's the emergency. And I need to get back to work?"

"Work." Jolene barked a sharp laugh. "Enjoy your work. I doubt it lasts much longer."

She shoved past me. "Amazing how Theodore's parties get lamer as this town becomes more famous."

"He calls it irony." My comeback was half-hearted. Dead body double flashbacks kept me from focusing on Jolene's cryptic digs. I sank onto a decorative stool. With a trembling hand, I pulled my phone from my small bag.

"Nash."

"I got the text from Rhonda. What's the story?"

"Later. I found another body." My words tripped over my tongue fighting their way through the story. "Maybe she's not dead? Lana Miles. Oh God, but she looked like the others. Except she also looked like me. Now I'm worried about Theodore. Someone might have overheard us talking. I hope not. I hope they were just trying to kill me like before. God, they have horrible luck with that. Good for me but...Oh God, it's horrible. Poor Lana. I'd blame Vicki, but she might be dead, too." I moaned.

"Slow down."

"My double. Lana Miles. Hired by Vicki to act like Maizie Albright for the show's B-roll. Someone hit her on the back of the head and hid her in a closet. Probably with a cement flamingo. There's just so many of them. Theodore stocked his party with murder weapons and didn't even know it."

Nash swore. Then swore again. "I'm coming."

I stared at the porch rafters. The ceiling had been painted sky blue. I focused on the blue and took a deep breath. "I was looking for Dahlia when I found Lana."

"Black Pine police?"

"One of the cooks called 9-1-1."

"Are the police there now?"

"Not yet."

"Wait for the police. Whoever did this is going to figure out it wasn't you pretty quick." Nash took a deep breath. "Dammit. No. Too risky. Maizie, get out of that house. Find a neighbor to take you in until the police gets there."

"A neighbor?" I rubbed my temple. "What about Ed Farmer? Is he still with the police?"

"I don't know." The curses he used made me blush. "Should I get someone to stay with Cambria? Dammit. Where's Tiffany and Rhonda?"

"Somewhere inside. We came with Leonard."

"Stay away from Leonard. Avoid everyone at the party." He paused. "Malthus. That's a Black Pine name. Does he live in the old district? That's not far from downtown. Can you get to the office and lock yourself in?"

"Um." I looked at my feet. T-strap sandals again. Would I ever learn? "I'll try."

$\mathcal{F}$rom the corner of the house, I group texted Rhonda and Tiffany. "Get out. Get out. Get out."

Then typed, "DON'T RIDE WITH LEONARD. Uber? Xoxo Sorry. xoxo."

Around the corner, a cacophony of voices grew. My cue to get the hells out.

I dashed down the veranda steps and into the garden. Surely Theodore had a back gate. Most of these old Black Pine streets had alleys. Ornamental trees, bushes, and statues hid the garden walls. The sunset we had enjoyed from the pergola had long passed. Unless an area was wrapped in Christmas lights, I couldn't see worth a darn. Theodore and his family had done a good job making a person forget they were trapped.

Not trapped, secluded.

I stepped off the path and into a flower bed to walk along the hidden wall. A shed loomed behind a vine-covered colonnade. An old wooden gate was set into the fence.

Behind me, a swell of voices had grown. I squinted into the dark. People lined the veranda and some began to spill out into the yard. I grasped the handle and pushed on the gate. The wooden door creaked, moved a few inches, and stuck.

Someone called my name. Someone not Tiffany and Rhonda.

I held my breath and slipped a leg through the gate. Wiggled and pushed. Shoved my shoulder through.

"Please don't let the killer find me stuck in this door," I said to the inky sky. "It'd really be hard for them to miss me here."

Using my butt cheek, I heaved my weight against the old door. It groaned. Loudly.

"Is someone back there?" called a man. A flashlight beam swooped to and fro, lighting up the pergola.

Sucking in my stomach, I squirmed through the crack. Felt my sequins scratch against splintered wood. My heels slid in the gravel. Panting, I left the gate open and squinted into the alley. Lights gleamed behind me. On the other side of the street, the houses were dark. The neighbors were probably at Theodore's party. In the distance, I could see a streetlight.

I ran for the streetlight. My flushed skin felt clammy, and my insides had knotted again. I thought back to poor Lana Miles, lying on Theodore's closet floor.

What if leaving her for dead hadn't caused her to die?

That thought — one I had fought off until now — brought me to a halt. I leaned against a fence and gagged. "Please forgive me, Lana. And Stella Craven. Billy Goodwin. Orlando Feelzen."

I bent over and lost the ham and pimento. "I am the worst private investigator. The worst." Sagging against the fence, I found a tissue and a mint in my gold handbag and made a mental tally of people I knew at the party. Individuals who wanted to literally kill me. People who would benefit from the death of Stella Craven, since she was corpse numero uno.

Leonard. He stood to lose the most. Of course, murder wasn't even good for bad publicity.

Dahlia. She'd escaped from my "where's Vicki" interrogation.

Anyone working for Cambria would lose serious moola if Cambria lost her role in *Pine Hollow*. Most of Cambria's entourage had been there. Minus Vicki. Alvin Murphy was there with a date. I couldn't see Cam-Cam's spindly publicity assistant, Holly, whacking Billy Goodwin with a hotel iron.

Could Ed Farmer have snuck into the party? It was possible the police didn't have enough to hold him.

What about Theodore? Maybe he didn't want to go to the police that badly? What did he gain? His reputation?

Sirens wailed. A patrol car roared past the alley. Flashing patrol lights bounced around the sky.

Shuddering, I turned back toward Theodore's house. I couldn't run away from this. My mother and Giulio were still missing. Another woman might be dead because someone thought she was me. I couldn't put another person in danger. I also didn't want to hang out with the police. But with the attack on Lana Miles, I couldn't deny my involvement to Mowry. If it got me in trouble with my probation and landed me back in California, so be it.

Hopefully that wouldn't happen. Because I needed to flush out the killer before they got to Cambria.

J snuck through the garden and onto the veranda. Announced my presence and learned, "the movie people are inside." In the kitchen, a policewoman spoke to the caterers. The living room had been cleared. I found Leonard and Dahlia in the library "green room."

"You're okay? Where've you been?" Leonard rushed forward and pulled me into his arms.

"I'm not dead," I said, pushing away.

"I can see that." He folded his arms. "Somebody's hurt upstairs. They told us we can't leave. I knew this party was a bad idea."

Internally, I rolled my eyes. Externally, I said, "Dahlia, you're not getting away this time. I've got contacts on the police force. Why did you take off?"

"You bore me. I didn't want to talk." She shrugged. "Sorry, but I have to keep it real."

"Dahlia, where's Vicki?" I shouted.

"I don't know." She folded her ropey arms. "She turned me down. I hope you're happy."

"She? Vicki? What, wait?"

"You child stars and your mommy issues." She rolled her eyes. "Vicki said she decided not to manage anyone outside her show."

"And then what happened?"

"I left? Because there was no reason to stay?"

Shiztastic. What happened to Vicki? Maybe the killer returned to the scene of the crime and found Vicki. And that same person could still be here. I turned to Leonard. "Where's Ed?"

"Oh God, Ed." Leonard shook his head. "Last I heard he was being questioned by the police. Why is this happening to me?"

"Happening to you? You haven't been murdered." I saw his face and apologized. "You're in shock. Okay, that's understandable."

"Maizie Albright?"

Detective Mowry stood in the doorway to the library.

"Funny how we keep meeting." My voice shook.

"Not funny." Mowry beckoned. "Mr. Shackleton, we need this room."

"It's about time. They wouldn't let me leave." Leonard strode forward a step and took my hand. "I'll give you a ride home, Maizie. Dahlia, you too."

Dahlia scooted toward the door.

Mowry blocked her exit. "We need statements. You'll find an officer in the hallway to take each of yours."

"Maizie?" said Leonard. "A little help here?"

"I can't help you make a witness statement," I said. "But if you need to make any kind of confession, I'll sit with you. I'll even hold your hand through it. You know what they say, confession is good for the soul."

"You'll go alone," said Mowry. "I'll talk to Maizie here."

"She works for me," said Leonard.

"And I work for the city of Black Pine. This woman needs to make her own statement," said Mowry. "If you really need someone to hold your hand, I'm sure we can find a substitute. I know several excellent policewomen."

Grumbling, Leonard stalked into the hall. Dahlia followed.

Mowry closed the door. "Let's hear it. Everything."

I spilled. Everything.

"Remind me to take you fishing," said Mowry. "I wonder if you have the same luck with fish that you do with finding victims."

"I'm sorry we did our reporting anonymously, but my probation officer isn't very understanding."

Mowry thumbed his lip.

"Why Cambria wanted a professional video of this nature, I don't know. But I do know someone found out and decided to stop them. And me."

"That sounds like a *Kung Fu Kate* plot."

I gasped. "The *Kung Fu Kate* audience was intended for preteen girls. I'm appalled you'd think that."

"Not the dirty movie part. The stopping 'them and me' part."

"It sounded better in my head. Why do you know *Kung Fu Kate*?"

"I have a six-year-old daughter."

"Oh."

"You're surprised?"

"I didn't see a ring... I mean, you seem kind of young," I stammered. "It seems weird because I have a six-year-old sister. I hope *Kung Fu Kate* isn't too violent for your daughter. Remi's not allowed to watch anything but *Sesame Street*. Although she said Elmo gets on her last nerve."

"Divorced." Mowry placed a hand on his hip. "And thanks for your concern."

I studied my garden-stained T-straps and hoped I hadn't insulted his parenting skills. Parents tended to feel touchy about TV content.

"I'm worried about you. Judging by the victim's injury, she had her back to them, like the others. I'm not ruling out it's because she looks a little like you, but we'll have to investigate."

"You don't see the resemblance?"

Mowry's cheeks grew rosy. "I don't like to draw conclusions until I have all the facts."

"What about Vicki and Giulio? Any news?"

"Nash did have me look into it. I don't believe it's related."

"Are you sure? I last saw Vicki with Dahlia. And Giulio disappeared after we found Billy Goodwin." I saw his look. "I know, I'm sorry. As soon as we saw Billy, we got out of there. We reported it."

"I know. Anonymously. You also trampled over a crime scene."

"But is it really trampling when you don't know it's a crime scene?" I gave him my sincere *Teen Vogue* smile. "You can see why I'm worried about Giulio. And Vicki? I don't trust Dahlia, and I couldn't reach either of them all day. Dahlia says she doesn't know, but Vicki is not answering her phone, and no one's seen her."

I placed a hand on his arm. "Some don't know this, but Vicki's my mother."

His stance relaxed, the stern cop face replaced by a softer, more understanding look. "I did look into their disappearance. On the day you found the body, Giulio took a cab to Black Pine airport. Vicki was also seen at the airport. Took a private plane to Atlanta. Flight details are Homeland Security jurisdiction, and that's a whole lot of red tape. I'm not investigating further. I really don't think it has anything to do with this case. They're not suspects."

"They're peripherally related?"

He shook his head. "Can I send you home in a car? I'd take you myself, but kind of busy here."

"I'll find a ride," I said brightly.

"I don't work that way." Mowry smiled. "Good try, though."

Hells, I thought. I didn't come back to this house of horrors just to get sent home with a cop babysitter. "Maybe I should check on Leonard?"

"Look, I'd say I appreciate what you're trying to do, but I don't appreciate it at all. You're going home in a squad car. And stay there until we figure this mess out."

"How long's that going to take?"

"As long as we need."

Yeah, that's not going to work for me, I thought. "How about a ride to my office instead? Nash is meeting me there."

Mowry folded his arms and studied me. "Fine. I trust Nash."

Lucky was also at the office, and if I got there before Nash, I'd meet him at the resort. I needed words with the other person related to this private movie. After all, Cambria had won Ed Farmer's heart as the scheming, conniving, and manipulative Lady Macbeth. Phyllis Dietrichson had nothing on the Lady.

Lady Macbeth's guilt drove her to sleepwalk, whereas Cambria slept soundly. Too soundly.

I had a feeling someone directed that act behind the scenes.

TWENTY-NINE

#FakingIt #StarryNight

I hadn't planned on Nash waiting outside the Dixie
Kreme building. He loomed large and formidable on the
sidewalk. The cop driving me didn't exit his car. Seeing Nash, he
said, "Looks like you're safe," and took off.

I cowered on the edge of the sidewalk.

Nash didn't move. "Where's your .38?"

"It's too heavy to carry in a purse?" The Row's gold bag
hanging across my shoulder caught the Dixie Kreme security light
and sparkled, drawing attention to my idiocy. "It was a party. I
couldn't strap on a shoulder holster over this dress. That'd be
gauche. And forget a garter holster. It'd ruin the lines of
this dress—"

His eyes rounded, his jaw squared, and he marched forward
until he stood above me, nostrils flaring.

I stopped talking.

"I'd like to say I'm happy you got here safely," he growled. "In a
squad car, no less. But I'm not happy. Not happy at all."

"I kind of have to go?" I said. Quietly. More to myself than
to Nash.

"You 'kind of' have to stop doing this to me." Nash spun to pace the sidewalk. "I can't deal with this. I left an unconscious woman in her hotel room because of you. And then I stood on this sidewalk, not knowing if I should head out on foot to find your dead body. You could have been anywhere between here and Magnolia Circle."

"I should have called? Except I was being questioned by Detective Mowry?"

"Stop talking like that."

"You're making me nervous."

"I'm making you nervous?" He spun back to me, grabbed me by the shoulders, and lifted me to my toes. "I've had about ten anxiety attacks in the last ten minutes."

I placed my hands on his shoulders to steady myself. "I'm sorry? Really, really sorry? But I need to get to Cambria. She's the last link in that chain now that the perp thinks I'm dead."

Nash triple blinked, and his jaw tightened. "You're killing me, kid."

His lips fell on mine. Hard and bruising. Devouring. The hands slipped from my shoulders to slide over my back. His breath stuttered, the lips softened, and he crushed my body against his.

Angry kissing, I thought. This would be totally hot except for Cambria.

Gently, I slid my lips from his and found a spot on his chest to lay my cheek. His heart thudded, and I closed my eyes, committing the beat to memory. The arms tightened around me.

"I have to go," I said. "Cambria."

"She doesn't deserve you dying for her."

"And I don't deserve you." I tipped my head back, gave him a shove, and smiled. "Partner."

He stepped away. "Right. Partner."

I should have been glad to ride in Nash's truck and not on Lucky. I was more interested in quizzing him on hospital details than enjoying a drive that wouldn't flash my short-skirted thighs to all of Black Pine. "Did you ride in the ambulance with Cambria to the villa?"

"No."

"Did you see them hook her up to all that equipment?"

"No."

"Cambria is an excellent actress. We assumed the doctor was still giving her drugs, but this move might have been arranged to give her more privacy. In *Julia Pinkerton*, Season Seven, they left her in a hospital coma as a cliffhanger for Season Eight and... What's wrong with you?"

He kept his eyes on the windshield, cranked the wheel, and burnt rubber on the turn into the resort. "Nothing. She could be faking the coma. Obviously, I can't tell when women are faking."

I didn't want to know what sort of faking he was talking about. "We'll simply check her IVs. They really wouldn't stick her if she was acting. Or would they? Cambria was a huge fan of Method."

"There's a nurse. I didn't leave Cambria completely alone. Although I'm going to feel real bad if that nurse is hurt."

"If the nurse is hurt, I'm going to lose my mind," I said and moaned. "Do you know how many people have died because of me?"

He skidded the truck to a stop and turned toward me. "This is not your fault. Don't say that."

"Thank you." I stretched a hand toward him and stopped when I saw his flinch. I shoved that to a part of my brain I currently didn't need to use. "Are we going to hijack a golf cart?"

He shook his head, put the truck in gear, and bumped the truck onto the golf cart path. "Robin Coxon isn't going to like this, but I'm in too big of a hurry to care."

*N*ash parked the truck at the edge of the glen where the path turned, leading to the villas. "We'll walk from here. I don't want to alert anybody."

"Right." I wished I had worn sneakers with the L'Agence.

"Take this. And I don't want to hear 'no.'" He laid a Smith & Wesson revolver on my lap. Black not pink. "You know how to use it, right?"

"Yes, but—"

"I'm not asking to you be Dirty Harry." He grabbed my hand. "You grew up around firearms. Your life is in danger. You're really going to put anti-gun ethics over your life?"

"No, but—"

"Kid, if it comes down to protecting you or Cambria…just don't make me do it." He dropped my hand. "Please take the weapon and defend yourself. Why are you being so difficult?"

"The last time I held a gun…" I pointed to his foot. "Accidents happen. I don't trust myself."

"Oh." He blew out a breath. "Well, the odds are in my favor it won't happen again. Please do this for me."

I picked up the gun. "What about you?"

"I've got these." He pointed to a massive bicep. "And I don't want to hear one of your karate lines."

"Kung fu. But okay." I emptied my handbag and tucked the gun inside.

"It's not going to do any good in there," said Nash. "Put your phone back in your purse and carry the .38."

"You're still limping from the last time I held a gun. I don't have a pocket or belt." I slung the chain strap around my neck and drew an arm through. "Either the phone or the gun stays in the truck."

"Lord Almighty, you're stubborn. When we get to Cambria's place, you check on the nurse. I'll do recon. I want to check the surrounding cottages."

We slid out of the truck and walked the wooded path in silence. I noted Giulio's dark villa and the low lights in five and seven, Ed Farmer and Alvin Murphy's, cottages. Dahlia's villa was further along the path, but I could see a faint light shining through a back window in number eight, John Doe. AKA Leonard Shackleton's.

Singing frogs near the lake covered the sound of our steady

footfall. No sound or movement in the cottages. A perfect setting for a Jason Bourne-type thriller. Or another horror movie.

In villa six, the curtains were drawn. A golf cart rested in the parking space. Placing a finger to his lips, Nash motioned me forward. He slipped into the woods to the left, skirting the bedroom wall. I took a deep breath, patted the lump of metal in my purse, and tiptoed onto the porch. No muffin basket and no way to see in the windows. Using the key Nash had given me, I opened the door.

The nurse snoozed in a leather mission chair. I gently shook her awake and flashed my Nash Security Solutions business card.

"We're here to relieve you. You can go home now."

She led me into Cambria's bedroom. Sleeping Beauty still lay tranquilly. A bleeping heart monitor sat on the bedside table, and an IV bag hung above her bed.

If this is fake, props to the prop department. I jiggled the bag and tapped the heart monitor.

"Don't do that," said the nurse. "I'll be back early in the morning to check on her. But rest is best. They want her throat and stomach lining tissue to recover."

"Of course," I said. "I'm sure everything will be just fine. But if one of these happens to come unplugged, what would happen?"

"Why would they come unplugged?" said the nurse.

"I'm just wondering if they're connected to some alarm…" Or if they were connected at all.

"Just don't touch anything. Let her sleep."

I followed the nurse to the door and watched her leave on the golf cart. I retraced my steps to stand over Cambria's bed.

"Cam-Cam, you got yourself into a big ol' mess, didn't you? You never could do anything simply. On the *JP* set, I remember the director telling you to 'just have fun with the character.' You gave him sixteen versions of 'having fun.' Dude, if you wanted to release a sex video for the publicity, it only takes an iPhone and one click on Youtube. Why do you have to make everything such a production?"

The monitor beeped. Cambria's eyelids fluttered, but her face remained relaxed. In acting classes, we're taught to move our eyes behind the lids to fake sleeping. I wondered if yanking her plugs and rolling her out of bed would wake her. But if she were really drugged to recover from the poisoning, I'd hate to have that on my conscience.

"Except I already have all these dead people on my conscience. Do you? You should. You've jeopardized your career and the careers of everyone on *Pine Hollow*. Millions of dollars at stake. No wonder you're playing possum."

I lifted her hand. She had a monitor wrapped around one finger. I dropped the hand. It flopped back to the bed. The monitor bleeped.

Maybe she was still drugged.

"This role isn't fitting for you, Cam-Cam. You like a strong female lead, not the damsel in distress. Who are you protecting? Or hiding from?"

I watched her lidded eyes roam, then turned away. Skirting the area where I'd seen Stella's body, I chose a tight path between the bed and window and tried Nash's favorite thinking method.

"Ed Farmer loses his film and his bond if you're kicked off the movie. Leonard's publicity budget will take a hit if your dirty movie's found out. And he might lose his director and the funding if the investors want to retaliate. Dahlia, on the other hand, benefits by your bad publicity. Unless it tanks the movie."

Before making my turn, I pulled back the curtain and squinted into the dark, searching for Nash. No Nash.

"Then there are your people. They have a lot to lose by your screw up. Weren't you getting net and gross points? They don't usually make those contracts for upcoming stars. Your agent must be good. Alvin impressed Vicki, and that's hard to do." I dropped the curtain and faced the bed. "Where did Vicki go? And Giulio? Why would they fly out without telling me? Were they scared?"

The front door opened and shut.

"I'm in here, Nash," I called.

"How is she?" said Ed Farmer.

Whipping around, I teetered in my heels. My hand caught the purse swinging in a lopsided arc. I popped the clasp but left the strap hanging around my shoulder. My right hand gripped the gun inside the purse. I pushed open the bedroom door with my left. Taking a deep breath, I assumed a Julia Pinkerton mental attitude. What my director liked to call "tough girl in a tight spot."

Much better than "scared woman afraid to shoot the wrong person."

Striding forward, I met Ed in the living area and closed the bedroom door behind me. "What are you doing here, Mr. Farmer?"

"Checking on Cambria, of course."

"How did you get a key to her villa?" I moved to the window, pulled back the curtain, and peered out. Classic "cabin in the woods showdown" stance. It had an *LA Confidential* climax vibe.

"The door wasn't locked."

"Like hell," I said.

"Really," said Ed. "You want me to show you?"

Ed wasn't following the bad guy role well, but I wasn't switching characters just yet. "Mr. Farmer, what happened at the police station?"

"It's a mix-up. We straightened it out."

"Likely story." With my hand in my purse and my sight fixed on Ed, I moved to the door. Keeping my back to the wall, I fumbled for the door and pulled it open.

Someone had taped over the bolt.

"Craptastic." I picked at the tape and ripped a nail. "Oh, come on."

Someone was determined to have access to Cambria. Like Ed Farmer?

Resuming Julia's headspace, I closed the door. "What did you tell the police?"

"I had to explain my whereabouts at specific times over the last few days. I called my assistant to help with that. Understandable though. These deaths... I'm sure they're checking everybody's alibis. It's interesting, isn't it?"

"Interesting? It's horrible."

"Not the deaths. The police procedure." He pulled a sketch book from his pocket and flipped through it. "Let's see. First I rode in the back of the patrol car, then I had my pockets emptied and searched. I was fingerprinted. Oh yes, and I sat in a holding cell for a short time. Great for research. I imagined myself the hardened ex-con, accused of a crime I didn't commit. How would I prove my innocence?"

I groaned. He was working on his next script.

"Mr. Farmer, what did you tell them about Cambria? And Dahlia?"

"I admitted my dalliance with Dahlia." He adjusted his glasses. "I promised to rewrite some of her scenes. And give her a bigger role in my next feature."

"That's what Dahlia wanted? More lines? Not the lead in *Pine Hollow*?"

"God, no. Dahlia knew she had a better chance for a supporting actress nomination. Best actress is much more competitive. Dahlia's got some great physical endurance scenes in *Pine Hollow*." He frowned. "She slept with me to get me to rewrite the comedy bits. No more of that. I learned my lesson."

"Would Dahlia do anything to protect the film?" My voice rose in excitement, and I coughed, deepening it back to tough girl. "Like murder?"

"Murder? Dahlia won't kill a spider. She runs a rescue shelter for hedgehogs and exotic mice. But she had no issues seducing me." He stared at the floor. "Maybe I encouraged her? I'm weak. How could I do this to Cambria?"

"I'm sure the guilt is eating you up, but I'm more concerned with motives for murder." His obsession was getting on my last nerve. I found it easy to turn up Julia Pinkerton's high school snark. "It's not like Cambria's been that loyal to you. You must know what she's done."

"Cambria's certainly devoted herself to the character."

"Her character?" Keeping half-turned toward Ed, I returned to the window and peered out into the dark, searching for Nash. Shouldn't he be back by now?

I glanced back at Ed. "I actually don't know anything about her character. Except she lives on a mountain and is super buff."

"Ellie May's a prostitute. At least at the beginning of the movie. White trash. But when aliens invade, she uses strength of character and her mountain knowledge to lead a group of hillbillies to defend their land. That was my pitch."

"A hooker?"

Ed Farmer nodded.

"Just how was Cam-Cam devoted to the character?"

"Cambria hired an exotic dancer to give her lessons in the art of seduction. She held a big party at a club to showcase the dancer's talent. All for the cause of destigmatizing prostitution. That was a media feeding frenzy. Misinterpreted, of course. I told Leonard we could bring those media clips back to work in our favor after the release. It'd redeem poor Cambria and draw more attention to the film."

"She wants to legalize prostitution? It objectifies women."

"Cambria thinks it shouldn't. She feels if it's legal, prostitutes could break the chains of enslavement to pimps." He shrugged. "Cambria was actually the one who came up with the idea of using the media clips later. She's very savvy."

My fingers slid from the .38, and my purse bounced hard against my hip. I didn't need the gun. Ed Farmer wasn't believably playing the villain. And gripping a gun in my purse made my hand cramp. "What kinds of scenes does Cambria have in this movie? Of the adult variety?"

Ed raked his sandy brown mop. "She has several romantic scenes. One that will give us rating trouble if we're not careful. As a prostitute, those scenes are hot. We have a body double lined up for certain shots. Cambria's very modest."

"She's too modest to do a love scene but wants everyone to

support prostitution?" I sighed. "Any plans to use leaked videos of the love scenes for publicity?"

"Oh no, that'd be lewd. Playing a prostitute is totally different. They're sympathetic. A classic vulnerable character."

"Have you met a real hooker?"

"We didn't actually have any in advisory roles." He moved to the bedroom door. "Can I see Cambria now? I need to check on her."

I ran to block him. "Ed, go home. Get to your villa and lock the door. If anyone wants in, pretend you're asleep."

"Can you explain the rationale for this behavior?"

"Someone you know has been killing Cambria's study buddies. That's my rationale. I have an idea who it could be, but I could be wrong, so I don't want to say. I need you to hide from everyone connected to *Pine Hollow* to be safe."

"You have a hunch." Behind his glasses, his eyes grew large.

"I don't like that word. It makes me sound like I'm back on *Julia Pinkerton*."

"I don't care." He grabbed my shoulder and jerked me away from the door. "Cambria. I'm coming."

I lunged after him. With the flat hand of my hand, I slammed the door. He flung an arm out, hitting the side of my neck. I crashed against the wall. My purse fell to the floor.

Ed darted for the door and bolted through. "Sorry," he called. "So sorry." The lock on the bedroom door clicked.

"What in the freakistan was that?" I rubbed my neck and stared at the door. "Ed, what are you doing?"

Behind me, the floorboard creaked. "Nash?"

I half-turned. An object loomed in my vision. Before I could identify it, an intense pain shot into my shoulder, rocketed through my neck, down my arm, and reverberated along my spine. I screamed. My knees buckled. My head thunked the floor. Bright spots speckled the darkness.

Like the stars on my L'Agence, I thought and blacked out.

THIRTY

#NoChipmunks #NotaNashInSight

I woke up with the worst hangover in my life. An awful combo of grogginess, dull pain, and dizziness. Reality darted in like a piercing arrow. "Holy hellsbah." I was alive. I'd take the hangover. But I wasn't sure if Ed Farmer, Cambria, or Nash lived to say the same.

I stifled a sob.

Fighting through my despair, stupefaction, and weird pain in my neck, I realized my right arm lay beneath me, numb. I rolled off my arm and sat up. I still couldn't feel my arm. I shook my head, trying to clear the fog. My curled legs stretched and my heels hit a barrier. A wall.

Hang on. Dark. Enclosed space.

For shizzle's sake, I was in another closet.

With no arm.

I shot to my feet, slammed into a bar, and fell to the ground in a litter of clothing. Tentatively touched the space where my arm had been. Still there. I continued to pat. No feeling.

OMG. How can my left hand touch skin and muscle and still not make a sensation in my arm? It was there, wasn't it? Was this a phantom limb thing?

"Happy thoughts, Maizie. Breathe. Breathe. Breathe…Okay, too much breathing."

Dizzy, I sank my head between my knees. I couldn't turn my head.

"But you have a head. Happy, happy thoughts. Let's get out of the closet. And find some ibuprofen."

Someone moaned. How big was this closet? Wait, the moan was faint. Like it came through the wall.

I placed my left hand on the door, slid it up to the knob, and turned. A slice of light fell on the closet floor. I hungrily scooted toward it. The air rushed in cool and fresh. I saw a bed and heard beeping. Cambria's closet.

Was Cambria in the bed? Ed? I pushed on the door, slid forward. No Ed. Debris littered the floor. Scrunched wet newspapers. Ziplock bags. Pill bottles. And Dahlia's bong?

I scooted back inside the closet. Obviously, pain had made me delirious. My poor brain had recreated some long forgotten party from my youth to compensate for my dead arm. Was my subconscious telling me to crawl out and smoke a bowl to numb my mind to the horrors of the previous week? Or to deaden the emotional pain?

Was I that emotionally connected to Nash, that I could subconsciously know he was dead?

Tears streamed. I couldn't pinch my thumb with one hand to stop them. I swallowed hard and wiped my nose with a fallen dress. Nash had been scared for me. That was why he had kissed me on the sidewalk. And had given me a gun. Although the kiss resonated more.

Lamar had warned me, and I had gotten Nash killed.

Beyond the closet, the moaning continued.

I choked on a sob, held my shoulder with my good hand, and pushed to my feet using my elbow. Letting the arm dangle, I found the light switch and ripped a Dries Van Noten scarf off a hanger. Using my teeth and the working arm, I managed a sling. Then remembered my other accessory. Where was my purse?

Frantically, I tossed fallen clothes, seeking my gold chain bag. No purse.

I couldn't even do the simplest things right. How hard was it to keep a gun clutched in your hand?

Although I might have shot Ed.

Or the person who attacked me. That would have been helpful.

I pushed the closet door and stepped into Cambria's room. No sleeping beauty. The moaning continued. In the bathroom, I found Ed Farmer. His face was bruised and bleeding, his clothing torn. Someone had beat the crap out of him. Kneeling next to him, I used my left hand to feel his pulse. Beating steadily. "Ed?"

No response other than a low moan.

I rinsed a washcloth and wiped his face. A bruise darkened his eye and blood had dried beneath his nose. I slid a towel beneath his head and found a handful of pills that had rolled under his chin.

Taking a deep breath, I reentered the bedroom. The room stank of chemicals. Ran to the bedside and found the emergency call button. Pressed it. Was it working? Pressed it again. Phone? Cambria had a phone. I pawed through her bedside table. No phone.

Glancing around the room, I tried to make sense of the drugs and Ed and no Cambria. Maybe I was on drugs, too. Maybe this whole week had been some weird trip. I was back in California having taken something without asking because a friend had said it would make me feel good.

If Nash wasn't real, I had an awesome imagination.

"Nash," I said. Then quieted. The bedroom door was closed. I didn't know who was on the other side. I stole to the door and laid my ear on the wood. Cracked the door. Saw a pair of bare feet dangling from the couch.

And smelled more funky fumes.

"No." I pulled the door wide and rushed out.

Cambria lay on the couch. More drug paraphernalia had been

scattered on the floor. A smashed iPhone. Razors. Spoons. More wet newspapers. The fireplace had been piled with logs and newspapers, but a trail of logs led from the hearth to the Oriental rug. On the coffee table, a pile of broken lighters had been tossed on top of a pile of newspaper. I touched the newspaper. Soaked. My fingers smelled like lighter fluid. A rolled joint lay next to the newspaper.

"They're going to set fire to the villa. The police will think it was some wild party gone wrong."

I dropped to Cambria's side and slapped her face. "Cam-Cam, wake up. You're in trouble."

She moaned and blinked, her words drowned in rough coughing.

"Come with me. You need to get outside."

I slipped my free arm beneath her shoulder, and a fireball of pain rocketed through me. I couldn't lift her. She flopped back to the couch.

The tears started again. I slapped my cheek to stop them. Another shot of pain reverberated in my neck and sharpened in my right shoulder. I tripped over piles of newspaper and found my purse under the couch.

The fifteen hundred dollar purse had been splashed with lighter fluid. But Nash's .38 Special was still zipped inside. I grabbed the purse and lurched into the kitchen. Open and spilled alcohol bottles littered the sink and floor. The tiny microwave was open and a metal bowl sat inside.

Snatching the bowl from the microwave, I threw it in the sink, and unlocked the back door. Where was Nash? With one hand, I unzipped my purse and pulled out the revolver. I stumbled out the door, unsure where to look. The other villas were dark now. How late was it? Were Leonard and Dahlia asleep or dead? Where was Alvin Murphy? Boxing and Parkour-loving, hip-to-be-cool, let's-all-get-rich Alvin?

Leonard loved Ed Farmer the way a rich patron loved his artist.

Leonard might lose funding for his film, but the film industry was built on hope as much as dashed dreams. Every great producer had failures, and Leonard Shackleton had enough hits to ensure future investments. After all, China and Russia were still ripe for the picking. Leonard might not care about a wayward actress, but he'd never risk the life of his favorite director.

An agent gone temporarily insane by the thought of losing his job and big money on a risky actress? That made more sense. Agents were notoriously high-strung creatures — as was everyone else in Hollywood — their lives depended on the whims of flighty creative types. Agenting was a game of herding fanciful, self-absorbed cats. How many times had Mickey's eyes filled with pain when I explained my dumb reasons for blowing off an audition?

More importantly, Alvin had also put money down on Cambria's insurance bond.

Plus Alvin could schlep bodies, bang heads, and KO Ed Farmer easy-peasy-lemon-squeezy. Didn't he do some kind of boxing?

Treading lightly, I circled the villa, stopping before I reached the porch. I made my way around the other side. No Nash. I couldn't see a damn thing in these crazy dark woods. How was I going to find him?

Should I leave him and get help? I chewed a thumbnail and paced the surrounding woods behind the villa. Stopping by the pile of logs where I had found my original spy stool, I spotted a pair of boots. I ran to Nash's fallen body. A broken piece of wood lay nearby. He lay face down, the back of his head wet with blood. I felt for his pulse. His neck was too thick.

"Nash, please wake up." I leaned over him.

Not risking moving his head or neck, I flopped my bad arm to the side and flattened myself on the ground. Wiggled closer and snuggled my face near his. Felt his breath on my cheek. I sighed in relief then kissed him on his temple.

An eye opened. Then fluttered closed. He moaned.

It was enough for now. I pushed off the ground with my good arm. Patted Nash's pockets. No phone.

I had to find Alvin before he set fire to the villa. If he planned on burning the cottage to the ground with everyone inside, he still needed to lug Nash's muscle-bound body inside.

Alvin was strong, but he'd need help for that. All that dead weight.

Don't think that.

I raced toward Alvin's villa. Next door, close enough to keep an eye on Cambria. He'd probably heard the same pounding music I did that fateful night. Knowing Cambria had been on an intense workout, he'd gone to check it out. And found someone who looked exactly like Cambria cavorting for a camera. She was nude. Recreating Cambria's love scene? Alvin had probably gone ballistic. And something happened. They argued? Or Alvin had simply knocked her down in anger. Billy and Orlando had escaped. Probably passed me on their golf carts.

Alvin had heard me come to Cambria's door, had seen me looking in the bedroom window, then met me at Leonard's big dinner. Where I questioned Cambria about playing dead in her villa.

Idiot.

Alvin knew he had to get rid of me before I figured out what had happened. He sat across from me at No Sleep, sipping coffee and asking if I wanted back in the business.

If I had said yes, would this have turned out differently?

I climbed Alvin's porch. His door stood open. A plastic jug of lighter fluid had been tossed in a corner. A loud beeping broke the silence. I whirled around. Red lights flashed from the golf cart pad, the beeping cut off, and the lights disappeared. The whirring motor accelerated. Alvin was using the golf cart to haul Nash's body to the villa. He had probably done the same with Orlando in the backlot and with poor Stella on that first night.

Taking the porch stairs two at a time, I tripped, righted, and ran toward the wood pile. My arm sling banged against my ribs with each step. It felt like some random object was knocking my side.

I tried not to think about the loss of my dominant arm and

focused on keeping the grip on Nash's Smith & Wesson. With the hand that had never previously held a gun.

THIRTY-ONE

#SouthPaw #HoldOnLoosely

---

*S*potting the golf cart lights ahead, I stopped near a tree. The headlamps cast a glow on the woodpile and Nash's still form. The golf cart jerked to a stop, inches from Nash.

I shoved the gun's grip against my hip and pushed the release latch. The cylinder flipped out. Wiggling my fingers through the opening, I shimmied my palm toward the grip. Raised the .38 to eye level and checked for rounds. Flipped the cylinder back. Experimentally shoved it into my right hand.

Like trying to get a dead fish to hold a gun.

I whimpered. I had no plan. I didn't know if I could aim with my left hand. I didn't want to accidentally shoot Nash. I didn't really want to shoot Alvin.

Okay, maybe I did. A little.

"Stop." I stepped from the tree and yelled, "The police are on their way."

The golf cart lights illuminated Alvin who hunkered over Nash. He looked up. Too dark to judge his reaction. He cupped a hand above his eyes and squinted into the dark. "Who's there?"

"Maizie." I backed against the tree for support, but my target felt too far for safety.

"Maizie? How? I fed you Vicodin. You should be out like…"

"Like Ed Farmer and Cambria?" Vicodin. No wonder I felt like I was skimming above reality. "I think it's working pretty well for me right now." I giggled. Then stopped.

This wasn't funny at all. Was that shock?

No time for shock, Maizie.

"Christ." Alvin stared into the tree tops. "Why does this keep happening to me?"

I ran for the next tree. Closer. But not close enough to trust my aim. If I could coax Alvin to me, he might rush me. Knock me down and out. But that'd be close enough to shoot him. Before the "out" part. Hopefully.

God, I did not want to shoot a person. I didn't even like shooting deer, and I was a Spayberry. They lived off venison most of the year.

Focus, Maizie.

Ignoring me, Alvin bent over Nash and slid his hands beneath Nash's shoulders. Grunting, he jerked Nash up and hauled him toward the golf cart.

I jogged forward on my heels and balanced the .38 against my dead arm. "I have a gun."

"Classic." His nervous laugh was much better than mine. "She can't be poisoned, felled, or drugged and pulls guns out of thin air. Maizie, you're a marvel. Wish I had signed you myself."

"Put him down. Gently."

Alvin propped Nash against the cart and strolled a few steps away. He held up his hands and studied me. "Do you know how to use that handgun? Your arm looked pretty messed up last time I saw you."

He was probably right. The revolver felt backward in my left hand. "You should trust my aim, Alvin. I was born in Black Pine. I've been loading buckshot since I was four. Why do you think I've mostly gotten action roles?"

"Right." Sighing, Alvin bent to sit on his haunches. He placed a hand on an upright log for balance and regarded me. "You know, I don't think you'll do it. Babe, you may have been born here, but I know where you grew up. On studio lots. You don't have it in you to shoot me. If I had that gun, I would have already used it. And why doesn't this guy have a gun? I looked but no gun."

"I have it."

"Aha. Not yours." Popping up, he swung the piece of wood and rested it on his shoulder. "Maizie, do you remember I'm from Chicago? We know baseball. As kids, we used sticks, brooms, whatever was handy."

I adjusted my stance. My mind felt fogged, and I focused on keeping Nash out of the .38's range.

He took a practice swing, then pointed the log toward me. "Drop that gun, or I'll cave his head in. What's one more smashed head at this point, am I right?" He gripped the wood with both hands and swung it high.

"No, stop," I screamed.

"Drop the gun. You fire, I'm coming for you. I'll risk your aim." The wood sped toward Nash's skull.

The revolver thunked on the ground.

"Good girl." The wood smashed into the golf cart behind Nash. His head flopped to his chest.

I shrieked.

"Now kick the gun toward me and walk forward."

My big toe thudded against the gun, and I hopped in agony. The revolver scooted a foot across the hard-packed ground and stopped in a pile of pine straw. I walked forward, kicked again, but used the side of my foot. A flurry of pine straw rained on my toes. The .38 slid across the ground and landed ten feet from the golf cart.

Alvin raised the log. "No improvising, Maizie. Follow my directions, or your boss gets whacked in the head. I didn't use a log this size the first time I got him. He went down like a rag doll with a stick."

"I understand." I hobbled forward and kicked. The gun zipped across the bare earth. It disappeared into the golf cart's shadow, stopping with a soft thud. "It's on the other side of the cart."

"Get over here."

Reaching the golf cart, I dropped next to Nash. He sat slumped against the golf cart, shoulders bowed and chin resting on his chest. I laid my hand on the back of his sticky neck. Through the tight, thick cords, I felt a tremble. I slid my hand around to his face and felt the short pants blowing from his nose. "Nash?"

He didn't move.

The log slammed into the cart. I screamed, falling back.

Alvin grabbed my arm, yanking me to my feet. "This would've been a lot easier if you had just stayed in that closet. How are we going to do this?" He glanced down at Nash and squinted past the golf cart. "Gun would be easier but harder to get."

My stomach cramped and my thoughts flailed. I snatched at an idea. "What about the film?"

His grip tightened. "What film?"

"Giulio—I mean, I was the one who discovered Billy Goodwin in the tub and tipped off the police. But before I saw Billy, I found a film can and took it. Billy was shooting Stella and Orlando with the Arriflex when you found them, right? You didn't get the camera. His website said he uses an Arriflex."

"I took the camera from the hotel room." He shook me. "What film are you talking about?"

"It's not digital. The Arriflex uses real film. 16 millimeter. Or sometimes 35—" My teeth rattled. "It's famous for that. You should know. You're in the industry."

"I'm not a film geek. I'm an agent." Alvin's smile flashed like a switchblade. "Thanks for the lesson, but I could care less. Now, what's your poison? Bad reference, sorry. You're hard to poison. Gun or bat? Bullet or whack?"

"You don't understand." My words stuttered. "I have the film and it shows you attacking Stella."

He threw me against the golf cart. My bad shoulder slammed into the windshield, rocking the cart. Nash swayed but stayed upright.

"Godammit," Alvin shouted. "This has been one long nightmare. Where is this film?"

I racked my brain for appropriate Julia Pinkerton scripts. "At the office. In a safe." Julia Pinkerton's safe had thumb, voice, and a retina scan. A little overboard. "It has a thumb print scanner. I'll take you."

Hopefully, between now and arriving at the nonexistent safe, I'd think of something better. Particularly since Detective Mowry had the film canister that might not even have evidence of a crime.

"Too bad I don't have a hacksaw." Alvin grinned. "Joke. No time."

My stomach clenched and I tucked my thumb inside my fist. "I'll give you the film, just let everybody go."

"Can't do that. Get in the golf cart. I'll take care of you later."

"What about Nash? And Ed and Cambria?"

"Casualties of the situation. I'll use the gun. I hate to be obvious, but it's more accurate. Then I'll have you light up the cabin and we'll bounce. You could be helpful in getting me out of town. You ever play the part of hostage on that show?" He brandished the log and shoved me toward the cart.

"Please don't hurt them. I'll help you get out of the country. You don't have to kill anybody." I stumbled forward and grabbed the cart's seat with my left hand. Stepping inside, I half-turned to watch Alvin.

He straightened his arm, pointed the log forward, then swung it toward my head. "Hand on the wheel."

Scooting forward on the seat, I gripped the wheel.

"The gun?"

"Near the rear passenger wheel, I think."

"Keep that hand on the wheel, Maizie. If I see you move, here's what's going to happen."

From the corner of my eye, I saw the log swing. I yelped at the booming bash of metal and wood. The frame bent, the golf cart shook, and the roof tilted. My heart pounding, I craned my neck but couldn't see Nash. I choked out a cry.

"Hand on the wheel, Maizie." Letting the log dangle from his hand, Alvin backed up, watching me.

From my periphery, I saw Alvin take a step, then disappear. The grounded thudded, and Alvin yelped.

No time to check on Nash, I thought. Get that gun before Alvin does.

I dove off the cart to the far side and landed on my knees, catching myself with my good hand. Crawling forward, I felt along the ground for the gun. Patted near the back tire. Had the cart moved? Where was it?

On the other side of the cart, the sounds of a heavy scuffle continued. Grunts, thumps, and smacks. I had faith in Nash, dented head or not, he had Alvin beat in size.

But Alvin was agile and strong. And didn't have a dented head.

I flopped on my stomach and reached under the cart. My fingers touched metal. Drawing back, I gripped the gun in my left hand and pressed my back against the golf cart. The cart rocked. I pushed to my feet. Teetering in my heels, I rounded the cart, pulled in my elbow, and squeezed it against my waist.

Two bodies writhed on the ground, grappling. The coppery tang of blood and musty stench of old leaves hung in the air. This was no orchestrated movie fight, more like a UFC battle. Their movement caused shadows to dance, making it difficult to see. One had a leg hooked around the other. Alvin appeared to get an arm lock on Nash. Nash churned, flipping back and forth. He stretched out an elbow to slam a fist into Alvin's back.

Alvin arched his back but then tightened his arm beneath Nash's head. Nash's chin jerked up, and he gulped air.

"Nash." I couldn't shoot. I couldn't tell where one man ended and the other began.

My hand began to tremble. I pressed my elbow harder into my side. Used my thumb to flip the safety. Leaned against the cart to steady myself. The lights of the cart shook.

My quaking shook the cart. Get a grip, Maizie.

Alvin was on top of Nash, pinning him down with one shoulder, yanking the headlock higher on Nash's neck. Nash pounded Alvin's back and sides. He was too tall. Too big. His legs began to kick and flail beneath Alvin.

How could he be too big? Why wasn't he winning this fight?

I hesitated, then squeezed my arm tightly against my hip, locked my elbow, and pulled the trigger. The bullet smacked into the wood pile. Bark and sawdust exploded. A log splintered and cracked. An avalanche of logs rolled from the pile.

Alvin fell flat against Nash. He glanced over his shoulder and sat up.

Nash jerked upward. Pulled back his elbow. The fist slammed into the side of Alvin's head. Alvin swung sideways but stayed upright. His return was slow, but he tracked Nash's fist and pulled back his own.

I ran forward, squeezing my elbow against my side. I balanced the gun on top of my dead forearm and aimed it at Alvin. "It's done. Nash, get out from under there."

"You won't do it," said Alvin. His smile dripped blood. He wiped his face on his shoulder.

Nash slithered out backward from beneath Alvin. Panting, he drew his body into a crouch and waited.

I gritted my teeth, shifted my body a few degrees, and pulled the trigger.

Alvin fell to the side, balled up, then flipped on to his back. He held his hands up. "Close, but I ain't dead yet." He laughed.

I readjusted my stance. "I missed on purpose. I'm aware I have three shots left."

Nash grunted. "Let me have the .38, hon'."

"No," I said. "I can handle it."

"Maizie, you're hurt."

"So are you."

"Kid, look at him. You got it done. I'm not complaining. Now take a break." Nash stood, towering over Alvin. He pressed a boot heel into the corner of Alvin's shoulder and motioned with his hand. "Let me have it."

"Are you going to kill him?"

Nash glanced up and met my eyes. "Not if I can help it. But I'm afraid you will."

I backed toward Nash slowly, fixing the barrel on Alvin.

Nash snaked an arm out and guided me to his side.

"It's okay." His arm wrapped around my waist and he placed his hand over my grip. "You handled this real well. Nice shootin', Tex."

I felt his finger flip the safety and I let him slide the revolver from my grip. Relieved of the gun, my hand trembled then shook.

Nash tightened his arm around me. "And you're shooting southpaw. Boomer'd be impressed." He switched the Smith & Wesson to his right hand. "You're a mess again. That sling doesn't match your dress. And your stars are falling off. Too bad. That was a good lookin' dress."

My remaining sequins hung by threads. The gold stars looked more like stardust. "That's the problem with stars. We tend to fall."

"You mean implode." Alvin laughed. "Tell me about it."

"Shut up," said Nash and ground his heel.

Alvin howled in pain.

Nash trailed his left hand along my back. "This arm is worrying me." His hand glided against my right shoulder.

My knees buckled and the blood rushed from my brain.

Nash's hand slipped to my left hip, and he pressed me against his side. "That bad? Did he do this to you?"

"I can't feel my arm. I think it may be dead," I whispered. "But he fed me Vicodin, so I'm not really sure?"

Nash pulled in a deep breath and snuggled me against him. "I've got you."

"Christ," said Alvin. "Kill me now."

"Mr. Murphy, if you have put my partner out of commission, you better believe I'm going to kill you." Holding me with his left, Nash straightened his right arm and flipped the switch on the safety. "You better start praying the police arrive real soon."

THIRTY-TWO

#Lunchable
#Takes2ToMakeaThingGoWrong

J woke in the hospital. The antiseptic smell and sound of the blipping heart monitor startled me. I squeezed my eyes shut, afraid to find myself back in a closet. But I remembered the police arriving. An ambulance had followed. Several ambulances. Nash had shaken off the EMT who wanted to examine his head. He'd climbed in the ambulance next to my gurney. And then I was given more Vicodin. Or maybe Percocet.

Something wonderful like that, because the rest had blurred into a beautiful sleep.

Opening my eyes, I smiled at Nash. His blackened eye had a tiny, butterfly bandage on the lid. His nose was red. And his scar stood out whiter than usual. He looked a mess but in a sexy, badass way that took most actors hours in makeup.

I probably just looked a mess. My new sling was white, cotton with no label. "Vicki and Giulio?"

"They're not back in town yet. But safe. I saw them on the cover of some tabloid at the TruBuy."

I sank back against the pillows.

"The Spayberry's have been here," he said. "They left you something."

The swinging bedside tray held a wrapped plate. Across the room, baskets of fruit, bouquets of roses, and other arrangements lined the long windowsill. Sunlight slanted across the end of the next bed, but a curtain hid the occupant.

He shook his head and pointed to a camo gym bag. "Clothes. They'll be back to pick you up. Remi wanted to see the baby floor."

"Great," I said but feared I'd leave the hospital outfitted in DeerNose.

"I brought you something, too."

"I hoped this was from you." I peeked under the wrapper and squealed. A fried green tomato, pimento cheese BLT. With a side of sweet potato fries.

As lunches went, this would be in my top five. Maybe number one.

"I didn't bring the lunch. I should've." He blew a sigh from his nose and pointed at a balloon tied to a stuffed animal sitting on the bedside table. "That's from me."

The balloon said, "Congratulations." The animal was unidentifiable. Brown. Four short legs. A long snout.

"It's an armadillo," he said. "I think."

"It's cute?"

"Remi thought so. She named it Steve. She also likes the balloon." Nash snorted. "I'd sleep with one eye open if you want to keep Steve."

"She can't have Steve." I pulled the tray closer. "Is lunch from the girls?"

"No, they're coming in later to do your hair and makeup." Nash moved to unwrap the plate for me. "Lamar brought you a bag of donuts. Assorted."

Hospital life had its rewards. I grinned.

Nash studied me. "I'm glad you're in good spirits. Considering."

"My shoulder's just dislocated. I'll be fine." I studied him. He didn't sound fine. "Are you okay? Concussion?"

"Yeah but it's no big deal." He smoothed a hand over his head.

"Listen, we need to talk."

A knock rattled the door. I flinched and my hand struck my heart.

Nash patted my good shoulder. "It'll take some time."

Detective Mowry stepped inside. Nash dropped his hand, returned to his chair, and folded his arms. "Mowry."

Mowry nodded to Nash. "How are you feeling, Maizie?"

"Hungry," I said. "I guess you need a statement or something."

"That can wait. I hope you like fried green tomatoes." He smiled. "One of my favorites. I thought you'd like it."

Surprised, I murmured a thank you. "How can I help you?"

"Can I sit?" At my nod, he pulled a chair toward my bed. "Nash, some privacy?"

Nash rolled his eyes and strode into the hall.

Feeling more confused, I watched him leave, then turned back to Mowry. "What's going on? Am in trouble, Detective Mowry?"

"Call me, Ian." He shook his head. "You're really something else. I mean, I wish y'all had waited for the police before storming the resort. Robin Coxon's not happy in the least."

"She should be happy Alvin Murphy didn't torch the villa. And there weren't more dead bodies on the site."

Ian laughed. "Very true. Listen, I already read Nash the riot act. I understand you were just going to guard Cambria, not interfere with a police investigation. Although I distinctly told you to wait at home."

"You did. But I was concerned for Cambria."

"We were busy at the Malthus house, and I should have thought about your job for Shackleton. Lana Miles is in the ICU, by the way. They think she'll recover."

"Good." I took a large bite of the Southern BLT so I wouldn't have to talk.

"I'm afraid this may seem inappropriate." He squirmed in his seat. "I really like you, Maizie. I wondered if after you're healed and back on your feet, would you have a real lunch with me?"

I choked. Ian Mowry poured me a glass of water. I took my

time sipping.

His cheeks reddened. "I'm not real good at this. I don't date much."

"Wow." I searched for words. "Lunch?"

"I hope you don't mind, but I asked Nash if you were seeing anyone. He said he didn't think so. Maybe Giulio, but I guess you heard about him?"

I shook my head. I wasn't processing what I was hearing. "Can you bring Nash back in here, please?"

A moment later, Nash tromped through the door. Glowering, formidable, and refusing to make eye contact.

"Ian, can I give you an answer later?"

Mowry smiled. "Not a no. That suits me just fine."

I waited for Mowry to leave, called up Julia Pinkerton for strength, and turned to Nash. "So are you pimping me out to the police department? Is this a way to get us off the hook for interference or something?"

"No." Nash picked up the stuffed animal, rotating it in his hands. "This was stupid. Why did I buy an armadillo?"

"Nash."

"We made a deal. I broke it." He crushed the armadillo to his chest. "It tore me up to see you hurt like that. And I just mauled you anyway."

I picked up the emergency cord. "If I press this will they bring me more drugs?"

"Why? Are you in pain?" He dropped the armadillo at my feet and grabbed the call button. "I'll get the nurse."

"I want drugs so I don't have to think about this." I crossed my arms. "Which is how I ended up in real-not-celebrity rehab. Denial. Thanks a lot. Renata's going to be super disappointed in me."

"Maizie." He rubbed his forehead. "Miss Albright. We made a deal. Partners or you quit. You made it clear, you want to be partners. And I handled it badly."

"I made it clear?"

He dropped to the chair. His eyebrows rucked together, and the polar blue eyes appeared pained. "Listen, I promise to do things right. I'll train you. Two years. We had a deal. I'll stick to my promise. Just, no more murders. Or movie people."

"So that's it?" I swallowed a whimper.

He forced a smile. "Lamar and I'll see you back at the shop as soon as you feel able. Rest. Take your time."

Leaning over, his lips stopped just above my forehead. Jerking upright, he patted me on the head, dropped the armadillo in my lap, and hustled out of the room.

"I guess I got what I wanted, Steve." I sniffled and squeezed the ugly brown animal. "I'm going to be a genuine private investigator. No longer stuck with doing the books. Real lunches."

I'd just eat them with a broken heart.

"Well, that was lame," said a raspy voice from the other side of the curtain. "Way to stand by your man. But it's smart to choose career over a relationship that will obviously fail."

"Cam—" I couldn't call her by the childhood nickname. Our childhood felt too long ago. "How are you not in jail?"

The curtain yanked back. No longer Sleeping Beauty, she sat upright, arms crossed. "I'm recovering from being poisoned. And I didn't kill anybody."

"I didn't mean murder, I meant pornography." I arched an eyebrow, JP-style. "Georgia's much stricter about it than California. You hired a professional cameraman. That makes it hard to claim as private. Of course, you never got the chance to distribute."

"Whatever." She flopped over on her side, her back to me. "I should get credit for hiring a professional. I wanted something curiosity-seekers would find more compelling than repulsive. And I needed it to tell a story. That's what I told Billy anyway."

"And what about Billy? Orlando? And poor Stella? Dead because of you."

"Because of Alvin, not me. So tragic. Anyway, it was all for a good cause."

"Promoting prostitution? Or was the cause for Cambria? A sexy trailer for the movie, not sanctioned by the studios, accidentally released. If the public backlash got too hot, your lawyers would say, 'that's not even Cambria.' Or were you going to pretend it was you since you're this big feminist-whatever? Except you don't even have the cajones to make it yourself."

"You wouldn't understand." Cambria continued to stare at the window, then sat up. "I've been in the business as long as you, almost twenty years. Killing myself for all those little roles. Getting the part of Julia Pinkerton's friend. Which was what? One season before they wrote me off? A season and a half?"

"You had a nice death scene. And you were on the stage."

"No one knows stage actors anymore." She coughed and reached for a water bottle. "It occurred to me, do the young actors who get top billing arrive there just on merits? No. They also have notoriety."

"They also have merits," I said. "And according to Leonard and Ed Farmer, you do, too. Obviously not when it comes to ethics or morals—"

"I know my talent. I could continue doing movies like *Pine Hollow* for years and years. For what? To become Maggie Smith? I want it now. I studied my role models. I've tried the party-whore route, and it's just tawdry. Sure, I made the news. Tabloids and entertainment gossip. Plus, risked jail time. Then I'm stuck with a huge insurance clause in my contract, although it could be worse. Look what happened to you."

I sucked in another breath. "Then why did you hire Vicki?"

"I didn't. I just made her think I was going to do it."

"Oh for shizz's sake—"

"Spare me. That woman had it coming." She rattled a laugh, leading to a coughing fit.

Vicki did. But still.

"When the party girl thing didn't work as I hoped, I did more research and realized I needed to be the victim. The public likes to feel sorry for a celebrity. They eat up that kind of news. Their curiosity is the key to my success. Combined with this film, it'll ensure a box office hit and my name lodged in everyone's brain."

"And you blew it."

"I don't know about that. Here I am, hospitalized after my psycho agent killed three people and tried to kill me and my director. Leonard hasn't fired me. Filming is going to be crazy delayed, but it's the most glorious PR campaign ever made. Leonard can afford to wait for Ed and me to recover." She clasped a hand around her throat. "Oh my God, I could get an Oscar for this."

Sucktastic, I thought. She's probably right.

"Life's so unfair, Steve," I said to the brown lump. "I guess we fight for truth and not justice these days."

I sped up my recovery by target shooting with Daddy. I hid Steve from Remi, who thought it a better game than Sardines. I had lunch with Detective Ian Mowry, which was weird but also nice. I wasn't used to nice. So, I went back to work.

In the Dixie Kreme Donut building, I climbed the donut-scented stairs with a heavy heart. I had a permit in my pocket, and my pink Smith & Wesson holstered on my hip. My burner phone rode in my back pocket. I wore jeans, a t-shirt, my somewhat sensible Golden Goose sneakers. And an Ottotredici scarf as a sling. I wanted to impress my seriousness on Nash. Although I wouldn't tell him the .38 Special wasn't loaded.

From Mowry, I'd learned Alvin's killing spree started when he backhanded Stella Craven during an argument ensuing from his discovery of Cambria's film session. Stella had cracked her head against the leg of the bed. Billy, the filmmaker, and Orlando, acting as Cambria's boyfriend, took one look at Stella and ran. I showed up. Alvin freaked out. And the rest was history.

Except the police were still dragging the lake. They'd found the camera Alvin had tossed. Just not Stella.

"So it's kind of my fault?" I'd said to Ian between gulps of pulled pork. "If I hadn't peeked in the window, Alvin might not have panicked."

"Don't ever say that." He'd leaned over to dab sauce off my

chin. "You had good instincts. You knew something wasn't right. I just wish you'd called me first."

I had called Nash first.

I told Ian, "Next time," but in my mind, I thought, "You big fibber. You'd still call Nash."

This weighed on me as I dragged my sneakers onto the landing, down the hall, and turned the old-timey doorknob of the Nash Security Solutions door.

Inside, Lamar jerked his chair upright and greeted me. I hugged Lamar and pointed at the inner door.

"He's in a meeting. I don't think you want to go in now. Jolene's here."

"What's going on?" I said, glad I hadn't loaded the revolver. It might be tempting to accidentally shoot Jolene.

"She's giving him hell, as usual." Lamar smiled. "Look at you, all dolled up for your first day back. You look like a real PI."

A knock sounded on the glass door. I flinched. The door opened, and I sniffed, detecting something other than fried dough. My stomach danced sideways, and I sneezed. Chanel No. Five.

Vicki breezed in, followed by Giulio.

"*Ciao.*" Giulio rushed forward to pluck a kiss from my lips, then both cheeks. "Darling, you look so down-home dangerous. It's fantastic." He leaned to whisper, "For this office. Don't wear it in public. That cute gun pulls your jeans down. Maybe an ankle strap is better?"

"Maizie," said Vicki. "I've had one hundred and sixty-three texts and messages from you. I thought it best to see you in person. And Lord knows why, but I guessed you'd be here."

"Where have you been? I was worried sick. And I was in the hospital. Almost killed several times. You'd think a mother would want to know that. And you." I turned to Giulio. "What in the hells happened to you?"

"Darling, you are sweet to worry." He placed a hand on his chest. "I returned to my home country. The reason, this ache in my heart. It would not stop. I had to get away."

"To Italy? Heartache? For me?"

"Poor, darling Maizie." He trod across the dusty floor to Vicki's side. Paging through her phone, Vicki gave him the side-eye. Giulio swept her free hand into his and leaning over, he kissed the back of her hand. "My heart ached for this one."

I placed my good hand on the .38. "Excuse me?"

"Giulio took off to Italy because his role had been severely diminished when you quit the show." Vicki yanked her hand from Giulio's and continued her phone perusal. "Viewers love Giulio, so when I finally located him, I flew to Milan to convince him to rejoin the cast. Promises were made. I stayed longer than I intended. I manage Giulio now. After the Cambria disaster, I decided to keep management within the family. Now you know."

"No." I watched as Giulio wrapped an arm around Vicki's waist. "I don't know. Lamar, are you understanding what you're seeing?"

"Not rightly," said Lamar. "But it's better than daytime TV."

"We're getting married," said Giulio. "You must be excited. I'll be your papa, my sweet Maizie."

I clamped a hand over my mouth, wishing I hadn't eaten three homecoming donuts. "That's disgusting."

Vicki's sea glass greens frosted. "I beg your pardon? That better not be an ageist remark."

"He used to date me. I'm your daughter."

She waved a hand. "That was for the show. This is for the show."

"*All is Albright* is a reality show. I didn't know he was hired to date me at the time. I don't think Giulio does now."

He shrugged. "Love is strange, *cara mia*."

"We're going to need security for the wedding," said Vicki. "It'll be shown during Sweeps Week."

"Oh my God." I shook my head. "No way. I don't care what you pay. We're not doing it."

"Who said anything about you doing security?" Vicki's feline grin stretched and curved. "At the wedding, I need you to give me away. Perhaps make a speech at the reception. I haven't decided. Anyway, we're hiring the other half of your business for security. The one with the better office."

"What other half?" Was Nash splitting our office so he wouldn't have to see me? I clutched my stomach. "I think I'm going to be sick."

Vicki strode to the Nash's office door, pounded, and opened it. "Jolene. I'm done here. Let's get the details hammered out. But somewhere cleaner."

Lamar and I exchanged a glance, then stole a look inside the office. Nash stood with his back to the door. Crossed arms, his Guns and Roses t-shirt tight across his shoulders. He stared at the ceiling. I followed the look to the brown water stain. Shaped like Florida. Of course.

Jolene rose from a chair, dropped a folder on Nash's desk, and turned slowly. Her smile matched Vicki's. "Congratulations. I think it's so sweet—"

"Spare me," said Vicki. "I've been gone too long, and I have a million things to do."

Giulio swung Vicki's Fendi bag over his shoulder. "*Ciao*, Maizie. We'll have the family dinner soon, yes?"

Jolene blew a kiss at Nash's back. "Wyatt, I'm sure we'll talk soon." She let her gaze roam over my t-shirt and jeans, then shook her head. "Thank the Lord, I don't do lunch. By the way, I heard your probation officer's interested in your last client. You're welcome." Chuckling, she sauntered out the door.

I crossed my arms over my stomach and stared at Vicki. "You're really doing this? Why?"

"I have to make a living, too, sweetheart." She crossed the room and touched my chin. "I think you forget that your career was mine. We all have to make do. You're doing it like this," she waved at my t-shirt and jeans, "and I'm doing it like that." She fluttered a hand at Giulio.

Giulio strode across the room, gathered Vicki under his arm, and swept her from the office. He was always mindful of a healthy dramatic exit.

I fell onto the couch. "Unbelievable. I guess I should be glad it's not Jerry."

Hearing the door slam, Nash strode out, carrying Jolene's folder. "It's bad."

Lamar studied him. "She's not going to sell?"

"She set up her own damn office. On Palmetto. She plans to compete with us."

I jerked. Theodore's fake office was on Palmetto. Craptastic.

"Compete with you?" said Lamar. "But that's competing with her own business."

"Jolene doesn't give two shits about the business. She's just punishing me." Nash parked his pacing before my spot on the couch and stared down at me. "She claims Leonard Shackleton's already been there. And our name is on a shade. Ours. As in mine and yours."

I let my head thunk against the back of the couch.

"I don't care," he said. "Not really. Just tell me this."

I opened an eye.

"Are you serious about being partners?"

I nodded.

Nash's smile curled and a dimple popped in one cheek. "Miss Albright, I'm going to teach you everything I know. We're going to beat Jolene at her own game. Together we'll break that she-devil. And when the two years is up…"

My heart pattered. I straightened. Half-rose from my seat.

"Watch out, kid." He whistled. "Because I'm selling. And then we're no longer partners. We'll give her something to worry about." The band-aid rose with his eyebrow.

Two years was a long time to go without lunch. But this was my armadillo's father.

I shot him the JP finger gun. "Let's make it happen."

Thank You for Reading 16 Millimeters

Thank you for choosing Maizie Albright's second case.

If you enjoyed 16 MILLIMETERS, would you please leave others know? Leaving a review is a huge help to both readers and authors. Thank you so much! And if you let me know you reviewed -- by email or by social media message -- I'd love to send you a Maizie Albright bookplate or other swag with my thanks.

And do sign up for my newsletter to get updates on new releases, discounts, giveaways, and events. All my newsletter subscribers get a free short story and are entered into subscriber-only giveaways, like receiving a signed advanced copy with each new release! I love my readers!

Just go to my website at www.larissareinhart.com to get in touch with me!

<3!

Larissa

On the Maizie Albright Series

While I was in Japan, Georgia became the number one place to film movies, leaping past California, New York, and Canada. And thanks to Pinewood Studios building their American headquarters a few miles from my home, my hometown has become a mini-Hollywood. I've returned to Peachtree City, Georgia, and now have hipsters in my Kroger and movie stars working out in the local gym (not that I would know on the last one, but my BFF saw Thor doing pushups on her way to Zumba). There's something called Vitality Bowl next to the Kroger. It claims to only make healthy food. And the quaint (old and dirty) BBQ joint I loved has disappeared.

"Georgiawood." This is what partly inspired the Maizie Albright series but with a heroine who's about 180 personality degrees different from my other series' heroine, Cherry Tucker.

In the first book, 15 MINUTES, ex-teen TV and reality star, Maizie Albright, returns home to Black Pine, Georgia, determined to start a new career as a private investigator, modeled after her childhood starring role in *Julie Pinkerton: Teen Detective*. For a license in Georgia, she needs training and there's only one gumshoe in Black Pine: Wyatt Nash of Nash Security Solutions. He's got a hard body, Paul Newman eyes, and no interest in having an ex-actress for an apprentice. Unbeknownst to Maizie, the reality show cast of *All is Albright* and her stage-monster manager also follows her to Georgia.

Maizie's got a big learning curve to overcome — not only in private investigations but also in life as a non-celebrity — but an optimistic disposition, years of therapy, and donuts will help her become the independent thinker her manager always hoped she wouldn't become.

I truly believe with the right attitude and donuts, you can "make it happen" just like Maizie.

xoxo

Larissa

Movies in 16 MILLIMETERS

In references to or literally mentioned.

All About Eve

Beauty and the Beast

Braveheart

Cabin the the Woods

CSI (not a movie and take your pick)

Double Indemnity

Dirty Harry

Downton Abbey (not a movie, but maybe someday…)

Jerry Maguire

La Bohème (technically not a movie…)

L.A. Confidential

Friday the 13th

Gaslight

Harry Potter (any in spirit)

Halloween

Macbeth (not a movie but deserves the mention)

Mighty Aphrodite

Psycho

Reality Bites

Rear Window
Selena
Sesame Street (Also not a movie)
Six Degrees of Separation
Star Wars
The Big Sleep
The Bodyguard
The Bourne Identity
The Hangover
The Maltese Falcon
The Man Who Knew Too Much
The Postman Always Rings Twice
The Shining
The Silence of the Lambs
The Sixth Sense
The Stepford Wives
The Three Faces of Eve
Titanic
Whatever Happened to Baby Jane

About the Author

Larissa is a 2015 Georgia Author of the Year Best Mystery finalist, 2014 finalist for the Silver Falchion and Georgia Author of the Year, 2012 Daphne du Maurier finalist, 2012 The Emily finalist, and 2011 Dixie Kane Memorial winner. Her work also appeared in the 2017 Silver Falchion Reader's Choice winner, *Eight Mystery Writers You Should Be Reading Now.*

Larissa, her family, and Cairn Terrier, Biscuit, have been living in Nagoya, Japan, but once again call Georgia home. See them on **HGTV**'s *House Hunters International* "Living for the Weekend in Nagoya" episode. Visit her website, LarissaReinhart.com, find her chatting on Facebook, Instagram, and Goodreads, and be sure to join her newsletter for a free short story: http://smarturl.it/larissanewsletter.

Also by Larissa Reinhart

PORTRAIT OF A DEAD GUY, A Cherry Tucker Mystery #1

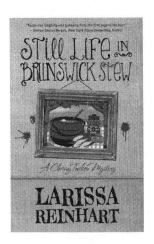

STILL LIFE IN BRUNSWICK STEW, A Cherry Tucker Mystery #2

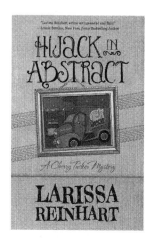

HIJACK IN ABSTRACT, A Cherry Tucker Mystery #3

DEATH IN PERSPECTIVE, A Cherry Tucker Mystery #4

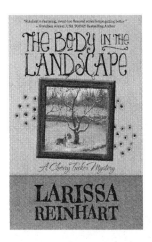

THE BODY IN THE LANDSCAPE, A Cherry Tucker Mystery #5

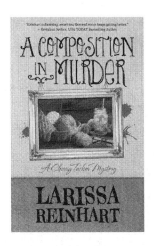

A COMPOSITION IN MURDER, A Cherry Tucker Mystery #6

HEARTACHE MOTEL Three Interconnected Mystery Novellas
(including "Quick Sketch," A Cherry Tucker Mystery prequel)

"The Vigilante Vignette," A Cherry Tucker Mystery Novella
#5.5 (first published in MIDNIGHT MYSTERIES, 9 Cozy Tales)

15 MINUTES, Maizie Albright Star Detective #1

16 MILLIMETERS, Maizie Albright Star Detective #2

THE 12 SLAYS OF CHRISTMAS, a cozy mystery novella box
set (with "A View to A Chill," A Cherry Tucker and Maizie
Albright novella)

The Maizie Albright Star Detective Seires

---

15 MINUTES

10Days
FindTheWoman
GetTheJob
DoNOTFallinLove

"Child star and hilarious hot mess Maizie Albright trades Hollywood for the backwoods of Georgia and pure delight ensues. Maizie's my new favorite escape from reality."

— Gretchen Archer, *USA Today* bestselling author of the *Davis Way Crime Caper* series

15 MINUTES, Maizie Albright Star Detective #1

#WannaBeDetective When ex-teen star Maizie Albright returns to her Southern hometown of Black Pine, Georgia, she hoped to rid herself of Hollywood tabloid and reality show hell for a new career as a private investigator. Instead, Hollyweird follows her home. Maizie's costar crushing, but now for her gumshoe boss. Her stage-monster mother still demands screen time. Her latest rival wants her kicked off the set, preferably back to a California prison.

By entangling herself in a missing person's case, she must reprise her most famous role. The job will demand a performance of a lifetime. But this time, the stakes are real and may prove deadly.

16 MILLIMETERS

BabysitTheStarlet
FindTheBody
AvoidTheKiller
TryNotToFallInLove

Body doubles, dead bodies, and hot bodies abound...Wait, what?

"Fresh from Hollywood get ready to bubble along with Maizie Albright Star Detective. She's # adorbs." — Jena's Books

StillAWannabeDetective In continuing her career-makeover quest as a for-real detective, ex-teen and reality star Maizie Albright has a big learning curve to overcome. A sleuthing background starring in a TV show — *Julia Pinkerton, Teen Detective* — does not cut the real life mustard. It doesn't even buy her lunch, let alone extra condiments. Her chosen mentor, Wyatt Nash of Nash Security Solutions, is not a willing teacher. He'd rather stick Maizie with a safe desk job and handle the security solution-ing himself. But Maizie's got other plans to help Nash. First, win Nash's trust. Second, his heart.

Wait, not his heart. His respect. His hearty respect.

So when a major movie producer needs a babysitter for his hot mess starlet, Maizie eagerly takes the job. But when her starlet appears dead, and then not dead, Maizie's got more than an actress to watch and a missing corpse to find. Body doubles, dead bodies, and hot bodies abound when the big screen, small screen, and silent screams collide. Maizie's on the job, on the skids, and on thin ice, hunting a killer who may be a celebrity stalker. And Maizie just might be the next celebrity who gets snuffed.

Look for Maizie Albright's third book, *NC-17*, in 2018. Maizie Albright also appears with Cherry Tucker in the December 2017 novella, *"A View to A Chill,"* (for a limited time in the Christmas cozy mystery anthology, *THE 12 SLAYS OF CHRISTMAS* and later as a single).

"View of a Chill" first appeared in The 12 Slays of Christmas
(Dec. 2017 anthology)

May your Days Be Cherry and Albright

In this Rashomon-style Christmas mystery, while Cherry Tucker suffers from flu-induced visions of murder, Maizie

Albright's on the hunt for a missing granddaughter whose criminal stockings have long been filled with coal.

When Halo's most notorious artist, Cherry Tucker, thinks she sees a crime through her bedroom window, her feverish claims are ignored by her family. Trapped in bed, influenza is the least of her problems. Deputy Luke Harper can't be found. She can't tell fevered dream from reality. And a very bad Santa knows Cherry's spotted his Christmas killing. It's going to take a Christmas miracle for Cherry to recover.

Meanwhile, ex-celebrity and #WannabeDetective Maizie Albright's determined to help an elderly woman find her missing granddaughter despite her private investigator boss (and not-so-secret crush) Wyatt Nash's claims that the grandmother's annual plea is nothing but a dangerously wild goose chase. This holiday, Maizie's search takes her away from her family and Nash to Halo, Georgia, where a storm threatens her nerves and her quest. When a deviant elf learns Maizie's looking for the granddaughter, they put Maizie on Santa's naughty list. And this Santa gets his holly jollies from murder.

A Sneak Peek of Portrait of a Dead Guy

A Cherry Tucker Mystery #1

In Halo, Georgia, folks know Cherry Tucker as big in mouth, small in stature, and able to sketch a portrait faster than buckshot rips from a ten gauge — but commissions are scarce. So when the well-heeled Branson family wants to memorialize their murdered son in a coffin portrait, Cherry scrambles to win their patronage from her small town rival. As the clock ticks toward the deadline, Cherry faces more trouble than just a controversial subject. Between ex-boyfriends, her flaky family, an illegal gambling ring, and outwitting a killer on a spree, Cherry finds herself painted into a corner she'll be lucky to survive.

* Winner of the Dixie Kane Memorial Award * Nominated for the Daphne du Maurier Award and the Emily Award * A Night Owl Reviews Top Pick

one

In a small town, there is a thin gray line between personal freedom and public ruin. Everyone knows your business without even trying. Folks act polite all the while remembering every stupid thing you've done in your life. Not to mention getting tied to all the dumbass stuff your relations — even those dead or gone — have done. We forgive but don't forget.

I thought the name Cherry Tucker carried some respectability as an artist in my hometown of Halo. I actually chose to live in rural Georgia. I could have sought a loft apartment in Atlanta where people appreciate your talent to paint nudes in classical poses, but I like my town and most of the three thousand or so people that live in it. Even though most of Halo wouldn't know a Picasso from a plate of spaghetti. Still, it's a nice town full of nice people and a lot cheaper to live in than Atlanta.

Halo citizens might buy their living room art from the guy who hawks motel overstock in front of the Winn-Dixie, but they also love personalized mementos. Portraits of their kids and their dogs, architectural photos of their homes and gardens, poster"-size photos of their trips to Daytona and Disney World. God bless them. That's my specialty, portraits. But at this point, I'd paint the side of a barn to make some money. I'm this close from working the night shift at the Waffle House. And if I had to wear one of those starchy, brown uniforms day after day, a little part of my soul would die.

Actually a big part of my soul would die, because I'd shoot myself first.

When I heard the highfalutin Bransons wanted to commission a portrait of Dustin, their recently deceased thug son, I hightailed it to Cooper's Funeral Home. I assumed they hadn't called me for the commission yet because the shock of Dustin's murder rendered them senseless. After all, what kind of crazy called for a portrait of their murdered boy? But then, important members of a small community could get away with little eccentricities. I was in no position to judge. I needed the money.

After Dustin's death made the paper three days ago, there'd been a lot of teeth sucking and head shaking in town, but no surprise at Dustin's untimely demise from questionable circumstances. It was going to be that or the State Pen. Dustin had been a criminal in the making for twenty-seven years.

Not that I'd share my observations with the Bransons. Good customer service is important for starving artists if we want to get over that whole starving thing.

As if to remind me, my stomach responded with a sound similar to a lawnmower hitting a chunk of wood. Luckily, the metallic knocking in the long-suffering Datsun engine of my pickup drowned out the hunger rumblings of my tummy. My poor truck shuddered into Cooper's Funeral Home parking lot in a flurry of flaking yellow paint, jerking and gasping in what sounded like a death rattle. However, I needed her to hang on. After a couple big commissions, hopefully the Datsun could go to the big junkyard in the sky. My little yellow workhorse deserved to rest in peace.

I entered the Victorian monstrosity that is Cooper's, leaving my portfolio case in the truck. I made a quick scan of the lobby and headed toward the first viewing room on the right. A sizable group of Bransons huddled in a corner. Sporadic groupings of flower arrangements sat around the narrow room, though the viewing didn't actually start until tomorrow.

A plump woman in her early fifties, hair colored and high-lighted sunshine blonde, spun around in kitten heel mules and pulled me into her considerable soft chest. Wanda Branson, step-mother to the deceased, was a hugger. As a kid, I spent many a Sunday School smothered in Miss Wanda's loving arms.

"Cherry!" She rocked me into a deeper hug. "What are you doing here? It's so nice to see you. You can't believe how hard these past few days have been for us."

Wanda began sobbing. I continued to rock with her, patting her back while I eased my face out of the ample bosom.

"I'm glad I can help." The turquoise and salmon print silk top muffled my voice. I extricated myself and patted her arm. "It was a shock to hear about Dustin's passing. I remember him from high school."

I remembered him, all right. I remembered hiding from the already notorious Dustin as a freshman and all through high school. Of course, that's water under the bridge now, since he's dead and all.

"It's so sweet of you to come."

"Now Miss Wanda, why don't we find you a place to sit? You tell me exactly what you want, and I'll take notes. How about the lobby? There are some chairs out there. Or outside? It's a beautiful morning and the fresh air might be nice."

"I'm not sure what you mean," said Wanda. "Tell you what I want?"

"For the portrait. Dustin's portrait."

"Is there a problem?" An older gentleman in a golf shirt and khaki slacks eyed me while running a hand through his thinning salt and pepper hair. John Branson, locally known as JB, strode to his wife's side. "You're Cherry Tucker, Ed Ballard's granddaughter, right?"

I nodded, whipping out a business card. He glanced at it and looked me over. I had the feeling JB wasn't expecting this little bitty girl with flyaway blonde hair and cornflower blue eyes. My local customers find my appearance disappointing. I think they expected me to return from art school looking as if I walked out of 1920s' bohemian Paris wearing black, slouchy clothes and a ridiculous beret. I like color and a little bling myself. However, I toned it down for this occasion and chose jeans and a soft orange tee with sequins circling the collar.

"Yes sir," I said, shaking his hand. "I got here as soon as I could. I'm sorry about Dustin."

"Why exactly did you come?" JB spoke calmly but with distaste, as if he held something bitter on his tongue. Probably the idea of me painting his dead son.

"To do the portrait, of course. I figured the sooner I got here, the sooner I could get started. I am pretty fast. You probably heard about my time in high school as a Six Flags Quick Sketch artist. But time is money, the way I look at it.

You'll want your painting sooner than later."

"Cherry, honey, I think there's been some kind of misunderstanding." Wanda looped her arm around JB's elbow. "JB's niece Shawna is doing the painting."

"Shawna Branson?" I would have keeled over if I hadn't been at Cooper's and worried someone might pop me in a coffin. Shawna was a smooth-talking Amazonian poacher who wrestled me for the last piece of cake at a church picnic some fifteen years ago. Although she was three heads taller, my scrappy tenacity and love of sugar helped me win. Shawna marked that day as a challenge to defeat me at every turn. In high school, she stole my leather jacket, slept with my boyfriend, and brown-nosed my teachers. She didn't even go to my school. And now she was after my commission.

"She's driving over from Line Creek today," Wanda said. "You know, she got her degree from Georgia Southern and started a business. She's very busy, but she thinks she can make the time for us."

"I've seen her work," I said. "Lots of hearts, polka dots, and those curlicue letters you monogram on everything."

"Oh yes," said Wanda, showing her fondness for curlicue letters. "She's very talented."

"But ma'am. Can she paint a portrait? I have credentials. I'm a graduate of SCAD, Savannah College of Art and Design. I'm formally trained on mixing color, using light, creating perspective, not to mention the hours spent with live models. I can do curlicue. But don't you want more than curlicue?"

Wanda relaxed her grip on JB's arm. Her eyes wandered to the floral arrangements, considering.

"I have the skill and the eye for portraiture," I continued. "And this is Dustin's final portrait. Don't you want an expert to handle his precious memory?"

"She does have a point, J.B," Wanda conceded.

JB grunted. "The whole idea is damn foolish."

Wanda blushed and fidgeted with JB's sleeve.

"The Victorians used to wear a cameo pin with a lock of their deceased's hair in it," I said, glad to reference my last minute research as I defended her. "It was considered a memorial. When photography became popular, some propped up the dead for one last picture."

"Exactly. Besides, this is a painting not a photograph," said Wanda. "It's been harder as Dustin got older. I wanted to be closer to him. JB did, too, in his way. And then Dustin was taken before his time."

I detected an eye roll from JB. Money wasn't the issue. Propriety needled him. Wanda loved to spend JB's money, and he encouraged her. JB's problem wasn't that Wanda was flashy; she just shopped above her raising. Which can have unfortunate results. Like hiring someone to paint her dead stepson.

"A somber representation of your son could be com- forting," I said. Not that I believed it for a minute.

"Do you need the work, honey?" Wanda asked. "I want to do a memory box. You know, pick up one of those frames at the Crafty Corner for his mementos. You could do that."

"I'll do the memory box," I said. "I've done some flag cases, so a memory box will be no problem. But I really think you should reconsider Shawna for the painting."

"Now lookee here," said JB. "Shawna's my niece."

"Let me get my portfolio," I said. Pictures speak louder than words, and it looked like JB needed more convincing.

I dashed out of the viewing room and took a deep breath to regain some composure. I couldn't let Shawna Branson steal my commission. The Bransons needed this portrait done right. Who knows what kind of paint slaughter Shawna would commit. As far as I was concerned, she could keep her curlicue business as long as she left the real art to me.

My bright yellow pickup glowed like a radiant beacon in the sea of black, silver, and white cars. I opened the driver door with a yank, cursing a patch of rust growing around the lock. Standing on my toes, I reached for the portfolio bag on the passenger side. The stretch tipped me off my toes and splayed me flat across the bench.

"I recognize this truck," a lazy voice floated behind me. "And the view. Doesn't look like much's changed either way in ten years."

I gasped and crawled out.

Luke Harper, Dustin's stepbrother.

I had forgotten that twig on the Branson family tree. More like snapped it from my memory. His lanky stance blocked the open truck door. One hand splayed against my side window. His other wrist lay propped over the top of my door. Within the cage of Luke's arms, we examined each other. Fondness didn't dwell in my eyes. I'm never sure what dwelled in his.

Luke drove me crazy in ways I didn't appreciate. He knew how to push buttons that switched me from tough to soft, smart to dumb. Beautiful men were my kryptonite. Local gossip said my mother had the same problem. My poor sister, Casey, was just as inflicted. We would have been better off inheriting a squinty eye or a duck walk.

"Hello, Luke Harper." I tried not to sound snide. Drawing up to my fullest five foot and a half inches, I cocked a hip in casual belligerence.

"How's it going, Cherry?" A glint of light sparked his smoky eyes, and I expected it corresponded with a certain memory of a nineteen-year-old me wearing a pair of red cowboy boots and not much else. "You hanging out at funeral homes now? Never took you for a necrophiliac."

This time I gave Luke my best what-the-hell redneck glare. Crossing my arms, I took a tiny step forward in the trapped space. He stared at me with a faint smile tugging the corners of his mouth. If I could paint those gorgeous curls and long sideburns — which will never happen, by the way — I would use a rich, raw umber with burnt sienna highlights. For his eyes, I'd mix Prussian blue and a teensy Napthal red. However, he would call his hair "plain old dark brown" and eyes "gray." But, what does he know? Not much about art, I can tell you that.

"I thought you were in Afghanistan or Alabama," I said. "What are you doing back?"

"Discharged. You still mad at me? It's been a while."

"Mad? I barely remember the last time I saw you." I wasn't really lying. My last memory wasn't of seeing him, but seeing the piece of trash in his truck. And by piece of trash, I mean the kind with boobs.

"You were pretty mad at the time. And I know you and your grudges."

"I've got more to do than think about something that happened when I was barely out of high school."

"Are you going to hold my youthful indiscretions against me now?" He smiled. "I'm only in town for a short time. You know I can only take Halo in small doses."

"If you're not sticking around, I can't see how my opinion of you matters. Not like you asked me about your sudden decision to join the Army and clear out of dodge."

"That's what you're mad about?"

Dear God, men are clueless. Why He didn't sharpen them up a bit has to be one of life's greatest mysteries.

"There are a number of things you did. But I'm not about to print you out a list."

"We had some good times, too."

"Which you sabotaged with your idiocy."

"You're one to talk," he mumbled.

I took another step forward, but Luke didn't move. His eyes roamed from my face to my boots. My irritation grew. "Do you mind? I need to get back to Cooper's. I'm working." I shoved him out of the way, dragging my unwieldy portfolio bag behind me.

"Just trying to put my finger on what about you changed."

I clamped my mouth shut as an unwelcome blush crept up the back of my neck.

"I know," he continued. "Your boots are plain old brown. Where're those red cowboy boots?"

I stomped toward the funeral home. "At home with my Backstreet Boys albums. I don't have time to play catch up with you. I've got stuff to do."

"How about playing catch up later, then?" I glanced back to see a glimmer of a smile. "Don't you think it'd be fun to stroll down memory lane? Does everybody still hang out at Red's?" The sunlight played with the auburn highlights in his dark curls and the tips of his long, black eyelashes.

Lord, why does he have to be so good looking? It was incredibly unfair how easily beauty weakened me. Gave suffering for art a whole new meaning.

"It was seven years ago," I said before I could stop myself.

"What?"

"Not ten years," I corrected. "But a lot has happened in seven."

"I bet."

I found Wanda shredding a tissue in the viewing room, watching JB bark orders at the assorted non-nuclear Bransons who then cowed and scurried as if he were the king of Forks County. He owned many businesses that supported most of the Branson clan, including the big Ford dealership, but he had actually inherited the Branson patrilineal power seat. Ironically, the two Bransons who never bowed to JB were his son, Dustin, and stepson, Luke. And that was where the similarities between Dustin and Luke stopped.

Luke and Dustin were never close. Luke loved his mother and put up with Dustin when she remarried. However, Luke got out of Halo as soon as possible. Couldn't blame him, with a cold stepfather and a mother pouring her attention into rehabilitating an emerging sociopath. But poor Wanda had her hands full.

Made me wonder, though. With Dustin out of the picture, was there now more room for Luke? Interesting that Luke left the Army right when his stepbrother got offed.

Hating that ugly thought, I hurried over to Wanda. "I just ran into Luke," I said, giving her shoulder a quick hug. "I'm glad to see he's here to help you through this."

"Yes, it is a blessing. Served his time, you know, and of course, he won't tell me his plans yet. But that's Luke. Doesn't like to worry me."

"Keeps his cards pretty close to his chest, does he?"

"Look at him," Wanda waved at her son. "I've never been able to tell what he's thinking. Just like his father, God bless him. Maybe it was losing his daddy so young. He just keeps everything clammed up inside."

Spotting his mother's wave, Luke wandered into the viewing

room. He had always been a wiry guy, displaying his strength in high school on the wrestling team and fighting behind the Highway 19 Quik Stop with the other boys carrying boulder-size chips on their shoulder. He still seemed dangerous, yet more settled and confident. There was no softness about him. Luke was all hard edges.

"Oh, I don't know," I murmured. "I lost my daddy young, too, but I've always been an open book."

"Well, boys and girls are different," said Wanda.

"Don't I know it." I swung one palm to my hip but waved my other in casual deference to Luke's arrival. "Let's go sit, and you can take a look at my portfolio. While you're looking at my samples, I'll sketch some ideas I have for Dustin."

"What's this?" Luke asked. "Ideas for Dustin?"

"I'm having Dustin's portrait done," Wanda explained. "I'll hang it next to the painting of him as a child. That one's thirty-by-forty. I'd like them to be the same size."

Holy cow, that's a big picture of a dead guy, I thought, but nodded my head as if it was the most reasonable idea in the world.

"That's downright morbid." Although he directed the statement to his mother, the accusation lay at my feet. "I swear you haven't changed Cherry, with all the nutty art stuff."

I felt like telling Luke, this is your mother's crazy notion, not mine. Instead I responded in my most proper aren't-you-an-idiot drawl, "Your momma is just dealing with this horrible tragedy the best she can, God bless her. It's a memorial."

"A memorial for Dustin? You don't know what Dustin was mixed up in, Mom. Death doesn't turn a sinner into a saint. God knows you tried your best. More than his own father."

"Come on, Miss Wanda," I tugged on her arm. Between Luke and Shawna, I was going to lose this commission. "I'll get you a cup of tea and you can look at my paintings. It'll get your mind off things for a minute, anyway. I've got a real cute one of Snug, Terrell Jacob's Coonhound."

Wanda beckoned JB and they conferred for a moment. With a shrug he followed her out of the viewing room.

Luke shoved his hands in his pockets. "You spent all that money on art school to paint pictures of dogs?"

"I spent all that money on art school to become a professional artist," I said. "It's early days yet. For now, I take what I can get."

"Including painting the departed?"

"You ever heard of a still life?" I shot back and stalked out of the viewing room, swinging my portfolio bag behind me.

I followed Wanda and JB into a little room crowded with a table and chairs. Unzipping the large bag, I pulled out a binder of photographs of my college works and a sheaf of plastic-encased photos of my newer stuff. Snug the dog, a horse named Conquering Hero, and a half-dozen kid portraits. I much preferred animals to children as subjects, something you don't learn in school. Getting a four-year-old to sit still is damn near impossible. However, you take a well-trained dog in the right pose, and you've got the perfect model. Snug the Coonhound sat better than most people. We had an easy working relationship, what with Snug's deferential silence.

No need for forced conversation with that subject. Of course with this job, I couldn't expect any conversation either. I could make do with photographs.

But first I needed to get the job.

"I don't know why you're wasting my time looking at pictures," said JB. He tossed the portraits of Snug and Hero on the table.

"This one is just beautiful, Cherry," said Wanda, hold- ing up a Sargent inspired painting. The model wore a sheet draped like a toga, but the effect was tasteful with wonderful folds to show depth and shadow.

"I'm glad you pointed out that one. Don't you love the light on her face? You might not be able to tell, but that's not an oil paint- ing. I had a tight schedule, so I used acrylics. They dry quickly and I didn't have to varnish the painting immediately. Someone mentioned you displaying the portrait at the funeral service? Oils wouldn't dry fast enough to get the painting done without messing up the color."

"I was fixing on making a photo display for the service when I realized we didn't have many of Dustin after he passed a certain age." Wanda's face colored and she cast her eyes away from JB. "I've just been in a tizzy, not knowing what to do with myself and not sleeping. That's when I got the idea for the memory box. Started gathering stuff Dustin left in his old room. Then I remembered the family portraits we had done at our wedding and thought maybe a new painting would be a nice tribute."

"Let her have what she needs," said JB. "A picture's not bringing him back, but if it makes Wanda feel better, she can have it."

"I totally agree, sir," I said. "That's why you should let me have the honor of painting this portrait. You can see what quality I can produce. You don't want a final memorial done by an amateur."

"What about Shawna?" he said, eyeing me. "Although Shawna did set a pretty hefty price for painting my son."

I squirmed, caught between a rock and a rattlesnake. JB would sell out his niece for a cheaper price. But probably wouldn't help me underbid her, either.

"A portrait lasts for generations." I began with my salesman pitch. "My paintings are heirloom quality and will be around long after..." Since the subject was dead, I stopped before my mouth ate my foot. "Anyway, a portrait is priceless."

"Priceless? You talking free?" JB leaned back in his chair.

"Of course a professional artist would base the price on other features. Number of people. Intricacy of the clothing, jewelry and props. Complexity of the background. And of course, the size." I could not get over the size.

"How complex is a coffin?" He steepled his hands under his chin. "And we don't need background details."

"JB, don't be cheap," said Wanda. "Like Cherry said, we're talking heirloom quality."

"Who in the hell wants to inherit a picture of Dustin in a coffin, Wanda?" JB said. "Even if little Dustins start crawling out of the woodwork, and God help us if that happens, I'm sure none of them will want this painting. We can cut some corners, here."

"Coffin portrait?" I said, swallowing hard. My mouth went dry, and I had trouble getting my tongue to form intelligible words. "I thought you'd want me to work from snap-shots or something. Dustin standing in a field, looking off to heaven, that sort of thing."

"Oh no," said Wanda. "That would be phony. Dustin never would have stood in a field unless he was hunting, and I doubt he thought about heaven much." She cast a quick look at her husband. "I want him as he is now. And realistic. None of that abstract stuff."

I gulped. "As he is now." The man was murdered. An abstract would be easier to stomach. Not like anyone would enjoy looking at David's "The Death of Marat" in their TV room. "All right. Uh, do you want me to create a pose, or do you want the whole, um, coffin?"

"Could you paint it like we were looking down at Dustin? Like angels gazing?" Wanda's moist blue eyes stared off into the distance and I shivered.

I grabbed my notebook and made a quick sketch. "Something like this?" I showed her the rough illustration of my idea.

"Oh, it's just perfect," she said, grabbing the sketchbook to shove at JB. "Let's give Cherry a chance, honey. I really want this view. Shawna said she has an allergy to formaldehyde so she couldn't paint Dustin this way."

"Tell you what." JB leaned forward, hands flat on the table. "I'll give you a shot. I want Wanda to be happy after what all she's endured with Dustin. He was my son and I owe her that."

"Yes, sir," I said, although my skin still prickled from the word formaldehyde.

"But," he said, "you got to have the painting done for the funeral. The whole she-bang. Wanda can choose between you and

Shawna, so you better make it good. She likes quality. After the funeral, I'm done. Wanda can hang up his picture and look at it all she wants, but I'm putting this whole blasted deal out of my mind. I'm paying off his creditors right and left, dealing with folks' complaints, and living through the embarrassment of the way he went. Do you know what they are saying about him?"

I knew, but I sure wasn't going to say. Folks thought a bad drug deal or payback from a robbery ring. Or someone just got tired of Dustin's mouth and went postal on him. Hard to say with Dustin. There were so many crimes to choose from.

"I'll work up a contract," I said. "Thank you for this opportunity. I'll get cracking right away and I'll also do the memory box."

"We'll have Cooper set out the body for you then." JB didn't smile but I did see a flash of teeth. "Got to admire your tenacity, Cherry. I hate to say it, but stories I heard about your family made me question your reliability."

A shot of heat worked its way from my toes to my scalp. People always bring up my family's history over the years, but it never got any easier.

"My reputation is important to me. I am judged by my own actions as well as those that surround me. You know how people like to talk."

"Yes, sir."

He looked at me evenly. "I'm glad we agree on this issue. As a businesswoman, you have your own reputation to protect and a lot of history to overcome."

A million comebacks crossed my mind, but none were appropriate for a bereaved father sitting in a funeral home with a large check that could have my name on it. I swallowed my pride and tried not to choke. "I'll bring that contract by tomorrow."

He had better keep his end of the bargain, because after that humiliation, I sure as hell wasn't working for free.

79854631R00221

Made in the USA
Columbia, SC
30 October 2017